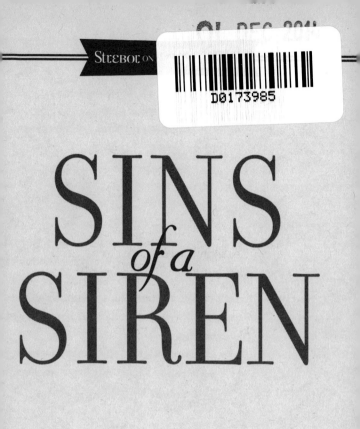

STREBOR ON

SINS
of a
SIREN

ALSO BY CURTIS L. ALCUTT
Fatal Intentions: Sins of a Siren II

Strebor ON THE Streetz

SINS *of a* SIREN

A NOVEL

Curtis L. Alcutt

SBI

STREBOR BOOKS

NEW YORK LONDON TORONTO SYDNEY

SBI

Strebor Books
P.O. Box 6505
Largo, MD 20792
http://www.streborbooks.com

© 2011 by Curtis L. Alcutt

ISBN 978-1-59309-334-1
ISBN 978-1-4516-2876-0 (e-book)
LCCN 2011928050

First Strebor Books trade paperback edition October 2011

Cover design: www.mariondesigns.com
Cover photograph: © Keith Saunders/Keith Saunders Photos

10 9 8 7 6 5 4 3 2 1

Manufactured in the United States of America

For information regarding special discounts for bulk purchases, please contact Simon & Schuster Special Sales at 1-866-506-1949 or business@simonandschuster.com

The Simon & Schuster Speakers Bureau can bring authors to your live event. For more information or to book an event, contact the Simon & Schuster Speakers Bureau at 1-866-248-3049 or visit our website at www.simonspeakers.com.

THIS NOVEL IS DEDICATED TO MY LATE COUSIN,
DENISE "TU-TU" EMERY.
Enjoy your stay in Heaven. The void you left in
our hearts can never be refilled, but the memories
you left us can thankfully be relived.
Rest in Peace, kinfolk…

ACKNOWLEDGMENTS

First let me thank God for choosing me as a vessel to share my tales with the world. Next, I'd like to send a special shout-out to the supporters and friends I've been blessed to have met while patronizing Carol's Books in Sacramento, CA. In no particular order: Rickey T. Boyland, Titus Thomas, Rod Thompson, Delaire Doyle, Fernando Walton, Shon Miller, Jamie Nero, Kimberly Biggs, Doc, Leroy, Lisa Pattee, Kevin Bowan, Nicole Mattox, Deneshia Johnson, Warren Spirling, Veronica Kyle, Bobby Mitchell, Allan, T.A. Scott, Portia Dickens, Simply the Band, Tammy Dillard, and her highness, Sharon Wright. I am truly honored to be in the orbit of such an awesome collection of friends.

My sons, attend unto my wisdom, and bow thine ear to my understanding. The lips of a temptress drip with honey, and her mouth is smoother than oil; but her end is bitter as wormwood, sharp as a two-edged sword. Her feet go down to death; her steps take hold on Hell. Her ways are moveable, that thou canst not know them. Hear me now therefore, O ye children, and depart not from the words of my mouth. Remove thy way far from her, and come not nigh the door of her house.

—Proverbs 5:3-14

One

"Mmmmmm, *Trenda!* Don't stop! *Suck* that mutha-fucka!" Darius yelled as he ejaculated.

Trenda Fuqua, the sultry, short, thick, beige-colored woman wiped cum off her chin, cheek and neck. "I *told* you to tell me before you nut; I damn near got some in my mouth!" She stood, snatched the long blonde wig off her head and threw it in his face. "You *know* I don't drink babies." She then glared at him and thought, *not yours, anyway.*

Darius reeled his dick in and zipped up his pants. "It ain't gonna hurt you to swallow every now and then, baby!" He grinned and rubbed her short, neat, rusty-red afro. "Besides, it'll make your hair grow."

She slapped his hand off her head, picked up her purse and removed her equalizer—a stainless steel Butterfly Knife she called "Baby." In three quick flicks of her wrist, the razor-sharp blade left a two-inch scratch across his tan, flat stomach. "*Bitch!* Are you *crazy?*" He wiped the small beads of blood with his fingertips, looked at it, then glared at her. "I should knock the shit out of you!"

She held the blade inches from his navel. "Next time you put your hands on my head without my permission, I'll show you what your intestines look like."

He smiled as he put on his white T-shirt, bulletproof vest and dark blue uniform shirt. "That's no way to talk to a friend."

She closed up the Butterfly, placed it back in her purse and removed a tube of rose-colored lipstick. "You stopped being a 'friend' once you started shakin' me down for your sick-ass sex fantasies."

He buckled his utility belt and adjusted his pistol as she applied a coat of her lipstick. "From what I hear on the street," he picked up his uniform cap and placed it on his faded haircut, "I'm the only friend you got. I heard last week that one of the 'deliveries' you made to Orlando came up two-hundred-and-fifty-grand short. Now the Island Boys are lookin' for you. And you know those Haitian gang-bangers don't play."

"That's some bullshit. You know goddamned well it was your punk-ass partner, Tyrone, that robbed me." She fixed him with an icy glare as she put away her lipstick. "And I *know* you got half the money."

He walked over and stood in front of her. "You might wanna watch ya mouth." He grinned as he gazed at her bare breasts. "Besides, that's the kinda shit that happens when you're late with my payments."

She picked up the wig, placed it in her purse and glowered at him with her green eyes. "Kiss my ass; don't make me have to turn your dirty ass in…I ain't fuckin' wit' you no more."

He upholstered his Glock, snatched her by the throat and placed the barrel in the cleavage of her thirty-eight D-cup breasts. "Look, you dope-runnin' ho', you got it twisted; I'll tell *you* when it's over. And don't you *ever* threaten to tell anybody, *anything* about me. You got that?"

She thought about what he and his partner did to her connection, Diamond, two years ago and continued to stare him down. Darius grimaced and gripped her throat tighter, cutting off her air supply. Her toes barely touched the floor as the six-and-a-half-foot tall man choked her. *I swear on everythang you gonna pay for this shit*, she thought right before he tossed her on the motel's worn-out carpeted floor.

He stepped over her as she fought to catch her breath. "I'll see you here at the same time next week. Bring the short-haired blonde wig with you."

A rain-filled burst of wind attacked the room as he opened the door and left. She staggered to her feet. *Time to end this bullshit.*

Two

After catching her breath, Trenda walked over to the desk that sat across from the bed. *I got somethin' for you, mutha-fucka.* On the desk, her camcorder sat underneath her black wool jacket. She removed the strip of black electrical tape, which she had used to cover the glowing red recording light. She then replayed her sex session with Darius on the monitor. *Oh yeah, your wife is gonna love this.*

She washed up, put on her black jeans, black boots, and black Baltimore Ravens sweatshirt, packed up the camera and left the Sandman Motel. *I can't believe I let Darius treat me like some kinda ho for this long!* Flipping up the collar of her wool jacket, she walked to her silver Isuzu Rodeo as the rain saturated her hair. *Every Friday night the same shit. I've been his fool and pussy-provider for way too long.*

The years she'd spent hustling dope and people ran through her head as she pulled out of the motel parking lot. A dentist in Philadelphia had purchased the Isuzu she drove after spending a weekend of enjoying her oral skills. A Baltimore Orioles baseball player had furnished her former apartment. She lost it while doing time in the Federal Detention Center in Philadelphia. A high-powered D.C. lawyer she'd whipped her goods on, had helped get, and keep her out of jail. Her list of sexual victims stretched from Boston to Miami. Some called her a prostitute; some called her a whore. Trenda considered herself a twenty-six-year-old entrepreneur; she used what she had to get what she wanted.

"Where you been, heffa?" Piper, Trenda's roommate, asked. They shared a two-bedroom apartment in the Park Charles apartment complex. Piper, a tall, bronze and heavyset student of the University of Maryland, chewed on a fish stick as she stared at her soaking wet roommate.

Damn! She looks just like Queen Latifah with her hair like that. Trenda took the camcorder case off her shoulder, then removed her jacket. "I had a couple of job interviews."

"It's almost nine. You must have had more than a couple of interviews." Piper pointed her half-eaten fish stick at the camcorder bag. She brushed her silk-wrapped, neck-length hair out of her face. Her dark brown eyes scrutinized Trenda. "Did you audition for a job as a photographer?"

Piper, you my girl, but if you don't stop sweatin' me, I'm gonna strangle your ass, Trenda thought as she searched for an alibi. She knew Piper wouldn't stop inquiring about her whereabouts until she received a satisfactory answer. "I was gonna take it to the camera shop over on South Charles but it got late on me. My light has been trippin'."

Piper stuffed the rest of the fish stick in her mouth and swallowed it. "Let me have a look at it. I fixed my mom's camera when it had a similar problem."

Oh shit! If her jealous ass finds out about me and Darius, I will have to kill her. She placed the camcorder on the floor next to the caramel-colored sofa. "That's okay, hon. I called Sony and they told me to ship it to them since it's still under warranty."

Disappointment filled Piper's voice and face as Trenda refused her help. "Oh…okay. I just wanted to help…"

Fuck! I don't wanna deal with her whinin' all damn night. Trenda held her arms out and gave her a well-practiced fake smile. "Come here, baby."

Even though she was a foot taller than Trenda, Piper sometimes acted like a twenty-two-year-old infant. Her wealthy parents contributed to her spoiled behavior. They provided their only child with anything she wanted. They paid for her education, apartment and her new Range Rover. Piper looked into Trenda's green eyes as she accepted her hug. "I missed you today."

"I missed you, too, boo-boo."

Trenda felt Piper's hand slowly inch down her back and rest on her ass. "Mmmm, Trenda," Piper moaned. "I get so wet thinking about you…Mmmm…"

Even though livin' here rent-free for the past year was

cool, I'm definitely not gonna miss havin' to sex her big ass. Plus, it's gettin' harder and harder to hide the fact that I transport large amounts of dope up and down the East Coast. Trenda slowly worked her way around Piper. As she hugged Piper from behind, Trenda let her hand slip down beneath the waistband of Piper's white sweatpants. "Mmmmm, I can feel you drippin'."

Piper tossed her head back and rubbed on her gigantic breast. "Yessssssssss, rub my clit…mmmmmmm."

Trenda stared up at the ceiling as she massaged and fingered Piper's fat, wet pussy. *Thanks to Darius's punk-ass, most of my regular customers don't fuck wit' me no more.* She inserted two fingers deep inside Piper's leaking pussy as she groaned with pleasure. *I've seen his stuck-up wife. Ain't no way he's gonna give up makin' me his sex slave when he has to go home to that cold bitch.*

"Yessssssssss! Yessssssssss! Faster, baby, *faster!*" Piper moaned as Trenda continued to finger-fuck her.

Trenda added a third finger. *It's time for me to get outta Baltimore. Ain't shit here for me but trouble. Hell, I might as well be a ghost to my funny-style family.* She used her thumb to massage Piper's clit as she increased her finger-fucking speed. *And this is definitely the last time I'm gonna make this big bitch nut*, she thought as Piper screamed out in pleasure and saturated Trenda's fingers in warm orgasmic juice.

Three

After sending Piper off to bed satisfied, Trenda went into the bathroom, locked the door and stripped. She then turned on the hot water and added some pear-scented bubble bath. As she waited for the bathtub to fill, she examined her sexy frame in the large mirror mounted to the back of the bathroom door. She grinned at her reflection. Her firm breasts, dark brown suckable nipples, flat washboard stomach, small waist and wide hips had conquered many men *and* women. "Like I always say, 'if you keep ya body tight, you'll keep ya money right.'"

Before entering the tub, Trenda turned off the lights. She loved bathing in complete darkness—if she bathed alone. A merry-go-round of thoughts on how to escape her plight filled her head. A bolt of lightning exploded outside the frosted bathroom window. The following deep bass note of thunder made the shelves in the medicine cabinet rattle. "Wherever I end up goin', it's damn sure gonna have better spring weather than here."

She washed up, dried off, put on her red satin robe and exited the bathroom. As she crossed the living room, she noticed that her camcorder bag was no longer next to the sofa. *What the fuck?* Panic leaked from her pores as she scanned the living room. No sign of the camera bag. Down the hallway, she saw light coming from Piper's room. *Oh shit! I hope that girl didn't—*

Trenda quickly and quietly made her way to Piper's bedroom door. She peeked into the room and saw the camcorder on top of the TV and herself on Piper's TV screen, sucking Darius's dick.

She peeked further into the room and saw Piper standing next to the bed naked and staring at the TV with tears running down her face and dripping from her chin. She also held a long, brass, pointy letter opener in her clenched fist. Trenda attempted to tiptoe to her room. *I gots to get the hell outta here and let that girl cool down!*

Before Trenda could leave, Piper spotted her and paused the tape, freezing Darius in his uniform right before he pushed Trenda to the floor. She glanced at the doorway and into Trenda's eyes. "I *knew* I shouldn't have trusted a ghetto hoochie like you! I let you move in with me and give you my heart and *this* is how you thank me?" Piper yelled, shivering with anger.

"Hold up," Trenda said as she watched Piper take a step toward her. "There's a reason I had to make that tape. Besides, what the hell are you doin' lookin' at my stuff without my permission?"

Piper glared at her. "I called myself surprising you by fixing your camcorder while you were bathing, you ungrateful bitch!"

Although Trenda's affluent family was from Randallstown, Trenda preferred to hang out in the inner city areas of West Baltimore. She, along with her two older brothers, was raised in a very religious home. Her father was the minister of his own church and her mother reinforced his preaching at home as a full-time housewife. The constant pressure of being under her family's moral and religious thumb drove her desire for freedom.

Once she reached the age of seventeen, as her mother tried to beat her with a belt after finding a book of matches in her backpack, Trenda slapped her and ran out of the door in her Catholic school uniform. That was the last time she'd seen or heard from her family. That was nearly ten years ago.

Trenda glanced down at Piper's right hand, which held the letter opener. She looked back into her face. "Why don't you calm down so we can talk this shit out?"

Piper grimaced and wiped the tears off of her face as she quickened her pace around the bed. "Fuck you! I'm not going to listen to *any* of your bullshit lies!"

Trenda had to think and move quickly; Piper was a foot taller and a hundred pounds heavier than she was. "Piper, back up off me," Trenda said as she pulled Piper's bedroom door closed and took a few steps backward, into the hallway.

"Bring your ass here, you fucking cunt!" Piper screamed as she yanked the door open.

Trenda ran into the living room as the door rattled on its hinges after slamming against the bedroom wall. "Owww!" Trenda yelled after banging her shin against the coffee table. She stood behind the sofa as Piper charged down the hallway. She desperately wanted to check her wounded shin, but dared not take her eyes off her angry roommate. "I'm warnin' you, Piper. Leave me the fuck alone!"

Piper kicked the coffee table out of her way, leaned over the sofa and lashed out with the letter opener. She barely missed Trenda's face, but she did leave a deep gash on her right shoulder. "I'm going to cut your fucking eyes out!"

Trenda braved a peek at her shoulder as she ran toward the kitchen. A small, dark stain formed on the shoulder of her red satin robe. The circular kitchen table provided even less of a barrier than did the sofa. *I gotta stop this crazy bitch!*

Piper ran into the kitchen gasping for breath. For a second, the sight of her reminded Trenda of a sweaty, naked and insane female walrus. Aware that she had Trenda trapped, Piper gave her a maniacal grin. "I've got your ass now!"

Trenda frantically sought an escape route, but found none. As Piper lifted the letter opener over her head, Trenda spotted the eighteen-inch-tall peppermill on the table. Piper lunged over the table at her.

In a quick, adrenaline-fueled movement, Trenda grasped the solid walnut peppermill, leaned to her left and clubbed

Piper on the side of her head. As Piper yelped with pain, she managed to drag the letter opener across Trenda's right cheek. *That bitch cut my face!* Trenda bared her teeth against the pain and brained Piper twice more on the back of the head with the peppermill.

Piper's eyes rolled up, revealing the whites, before she collapsed onto the table. Trenda held the peppermill in midair, ready to bash her again, but Piper went limp and rolled off the table, striking her head on the linoleum floor.

Trenda panted as she stared down at the fallen big woman. Piper didn't appear to be breathing. Trenda held the peppermill high as she tapped the side of Piper's head with her toe. She didn't respond. *Oh shit! I gotta get the fuck outta here.* The imagined sound of a jail cell door slamming made Trenda move. Having already spent an unbearable six months in a Philadelphia jail for a parole violation, she had no desire to spend the next twenty-five-years-to-life in the Gray Bar Motel.

She shoved the table out of the way and sprinted to her room. *Where are my goddamned sweats?* She tore off her robe and dug through her dresser drawers. Failing to find a pair of sweats, she removed the damp jeans and sweatshirt she'd worn earlier from the hamper and pulled them over her naked body, before slipping her bare feet back into her soggy black boots.

No matter how fast Trenda tried to move, it felt as if she was running out of time. She snatched open her closet door and grabbed her "Travelin' Bag"—a black-and-white Reebok gym bag, which held two sets of sweats, socks, underwear, tennis shoes, two sets of fake driver's licenses and one thousand dollars in cash. Her hustling lifestyle taught her to be ready to run at anytime, from anywhere.

She sensed the sand in her mental hourglass running out. "Think, don't panic, *think!*" Trenda said as she grabbed her cell phone charger and tossed it in her bag. Next, she picked up her New York Yankees cap and Reebok bag and ran out of the room. "Keys! Where are my fuckin' car keys?"

Trenda spotted them on the floor next to the coffee table that Piper had kicked askew. She slapped the cap on her head and scooped up her keys. Before fleeing the apartment, she went to the kitchen and checked on Piper. *It looks like she moved.* Trenda cautiously got on one knee and examined her.

She then placed her hand by Piper's nose and mouth and felt a weak, warm breath escaping. *At least her crazy-ass ain't dead, but she looks kinda fucked up.* The small flow of blood from Piper's ear was a bit disconcerting.

Trenda got to her feet and went to the wall-mounted yellow telephone. *I don't need a murder on my head.* She picked up the phone and dialed 9-1-1. After hearing the dispatcher answer, she let the phone receiver fall to the floor, knowing they would send a patrol car out to investigate. *Time to get the hell out!* Grabbing her bag, keys and purse she fled the apartment.

Four

"C'mon now, Griff! I know you can give me more than two grand. My car ain't but a year old," Trenda said to the heavy, dark, thick-glasses-wearing man in front of her. He ran a junkyard in Chestertown where— for the right price—he could make unwanted vehicles disappear, no questions asked.

"How you get that cut on ya pretty face?"

She touched her wound and in the light cast by his dim yard lights, found blood on her fingertip. "I ran into Freddy Krueger. Look, I ain't got time to socialize. How much you gonna give me for it?" A dull throbbing pain reminded her of her shoulder injury.

He ran his hand over the hood. "You gotta remember, there ain't a big demand for Isuzu parts around here." He looked from the cut, into her green eyes. "Now, if it was somethin' like a Benz, I could break you off a little mo' change."

She checked her watch as they stood in the light rain, in front of the trailer Griff lived in, which sat in the back of his messy junkyard. Her instincts told her she had to get going. She then focused on him. "I been bringin' you customers for years. Two grand is the best you can do?"

He grinned and stared at her large breasts. "Well, maybe if you spend the night, we can figure out a way for you to earn a few mo' ends."

I wouldn't fuck you wit' somebody else's pussy. She snatched the wad of cash out of his dirty hands and stuffed it in her pocket. "Fuck it, but you gotta drop me off on North Charles Street."

He grinned. "I'll have my man Julio take this piece of shit out back and gut it. I'll put what's left in the car crusher." He pulled a half-smoked cigar out of the pocket of his greasy overalls and fired it up. He was so busy looking at Trenda he didn't notice the tall, skinny crackhead that stood at the entrance to the junkyard watching them. "Tim, didn't I tell you to stop hangin' around here wit' ya beggin' ass?"

The filth-ridden dope addict held up one dirty hand. "C'mon, Griff. I'm just tryin' to get enough change to get some food, or a job." He then looked at sexy Trenda. "How 'bout you, sista? Can you help a brotha out?"

Trenda glared at him. "Hell naw…I ain't got shit for you."

Griff took a couple steps toward the dope fiend and he quickly walked away. A moment later, Griff turned and looked at Trenda. "You ready to go?"

"Yeah…get me the fuck outta here," she said as she removed the blonde wig from her purse and tossed it inside the Isuzu.

After arriving at Piper's apartment, a pair of cops found a semi-conscious Piper and called for an ambulance. One of the cops walked into her bedroom as he searched the apartment for clues as to what had happened. He stopped and stared at the TV screen. "Yo, Robbie, come check this out!"

After entering the bedroom, Robbie's eyes went to the TV. "Fuck me! Joey, is that officer *Kain?*"

Joey broke out in a big grin. "Yup, that's Darius. I bet Captain Kelly would *love* to see this arrogant asshole on film!"

Robbie returned his grin. "Oh yeah! I *knew* he wasn't on the up-and-up. Ridin' around in that new Escalade and always braggin' 'bout all the pussy he was gettin'… he got on my fuckin' nerves." Robbie then unplugged the camcorder from the TV and packed it up. "Time to take his ass down."

Five

T renda had Griff drop her off a mile away from the train station. She then waited until he drove out of sight, then hailed a cab. "Where you goin' tonight, lady?" the young black cab driver asked, as he gazed at her through the Plexiglas shield between them.

She pulled the door closed. "Penn Station." The cabbie's flirtatious stare annoyed her. "Can you turn around and get goin'? I don't wanna miss my train."

The cabbie sensed her hostility and turned around. "A'ight, we'll be there in a minute."

"Oh fuck!" she yelled as she went through the contents of her getaway bag. "I forgot the goddamn camcorder!"

The cabbie looked at her in his rearview mirror. "Somethin' wrong?"

She sat back with her hands over her face. She slowly wiped them down her face and shook her head. *Oh well, I guess I ain't gotta worry about Darius's punk ass no more anyway.*

Ten minutes later, at 11:48 p.m., she handed the cabbie a twenty and hurried inside the Amtrak station. She removed her wet baseball cap, beat it against her leg, then put it back on her head. She then hurried to the only open ticket window. "Helloooooo! Where are you traveling to, ma'am?" the spike-haired, thin moustache-wearing, medium-built, Asian man behind the glass asked. His frilly voice, tongue piercing and thumb rings made one question his manhood.

Confusion filled her face. *Damn, I didn't think about that; where the hell am I goin'?* She then scanned the red digital schedule board over the ticket counter. *I need the next thing smokin' outta here.* Her eyes stopped on a train leaving at 12:07 a.m. "Gimme a ticket for that train goin' to Oakland."

The ticket agent quickly typed on his keyboard, then asked, "Round trip?"

"One way." Trenda checked her watch as the agent continued to type. "How long is the ride?"

"About three days."

"How much?"

"It depends on your accommodations. Would you like a coach seat or roomette?"

She heard the sound of an approaching train. "I dunno... I ain't ever rode a train. Do they have beds?"

The agent gave her a condescending gaze. "You'll want a roomette." He looked at his screen, then back at Trenda. "Are you traveling alone?"

The sound of the train's air brakes announced its arrival. Anxiety filled her voice. "Yeah, yeah, just me."

The agent rolled his eyes from the scratch on her face to his screen. "That fare is $299 plus an additional $286 for the bedroom. Do you still want it?"

She spotted an Amtrak security guard in a transparent, rain-covered poncho talking into his two-way radio as he entered the ticket area from outside. She dug into the pocket of her jeans and removed her bankroll as she stared at the blond-haired guard. "Yeah…I want it."

After purchasing her ticket, she pulled the bill of her cap down low on her forehead and went to board the train. She peeked back over her shoulder and noticed the guard walking toward the ticket agent window. She checked her watch while standing in line to board the train; midnight straight up. *C'mon, y'all…let's go!*

After boarding the train and receiving directions to her roomette, she checked the time and breathed a little easier. *Cool, the train should be leavin' any minute now.* She entered her small roomette, closed and locked the door. She then tossed her bags on one of the reclining seats and collapsed into the other one. She checked her watch. "Damn, it's ten after twelve. Why ain't we movin'?"

A specter of panic paid her a visit. Ignoring her instincts, she went to her window, eased the curtain back a few inches and peeked out. "Oh hell no!"

Outside, about twenty yards from the train, she saw the original security guard along with two additional guards talking to the conductor who had taken her ticket. Trenda quickly pulled her curtains closed. She sat back and tried to slow her breathing and racing pulse.

The plans of the just are legitimate; the designs of the wicked are deceitful. —PROVERBS 12:5

Shut up, Daddy!

Many people in her position may have said a prayer, but after growing up in her household, she refused to seek comfort from the Higher Power. She preferred to get her comfort from cash or good sex.

A sudden jerk of the train shook her out of her sense of impending doom. *Yes! It's about damn time we got goin'!* As the train picked up speed, she worked up the nerve to peek out the window again. To her horror, the security guard looked directly into her eyes as the train pulled past him.

Frozen with fear, she couldn't retreat. Her eyes locked on the guard's blue eyes briefly before the train banked to the left, ending the moment.

Six

Damn, *I gotta pee*, Trenda thought, an hour later, as she waited for the train to leave the D.C. train station. Her fear of running into a security guard kept her locked in her room with a full bladder.

Once the train left the station, she slowly opened her door and looked down the corridor. *Cool, ain't no guards out here.* She then eased her door closed and walked to the restroom, at the end of the car.

After draining herself, she looked into the mirror as she washed her hands. *Shit, I hope this cut don't leave a scar.* She then gently lowered the shoulder of her sweatshirt and inspected her other wound. She winced as she wet a paper towel and cleaned up her cut. Fortunately, it had stopped bleeding, but it looked deep. She nearly lost her balance as the train wobbled over an old bridge. *I sure hope this muthafucka don't hop off the tracks!*

Outside the bathroom, her stomach growled. *I wonder if they got food on this train.* She worked up her nerve, opened the sliding doors between the cars and stepped through. The car was nearly vacant. A few reclined seats held sleeping passengers. In the dimly lit car, a sign on the wall of a dinner plate and utensils pointed toward the next car. She held on to the vacant seats as she tried to get used to the motion of the train.

I didn't know trains had two levels. She followed the signs that pointed to the dining car. After ascending the stairs, she spotted an abandoned counter. Behind the counter was a grill. *Damn! I wish the cook was on duty. I could use a big-ass hamburger right now.*

Her stomach rumbled. Before leaving the car, she noticed a pair of vending machines on the far side of the grill, next to the dining tables. She reached into her pocket for some cash as she walked over to the machines. "Hey, don't put any money into the soda machine. It took my dollar and didn't give me a soda."

She nearly jumped out the window. She failed to see the bald headed, chunky, brown-skinned, smiling, brown-eyed man sitting at one of the dining tables. A laptop computer and open bag of corn chips sat on the table in front of him. "Oh…thanks…" she managed to say as she composed herself.

"I didn't mean to scare you, sorry." He then worked himself out of his seat, adjusting his glasses as he walked over to the vending machines. "Let me treat you to dinner."

Trenda read the sincerity in his face. His smile and precisely trimmed full beard was warm and inviting. "Don't worry 'bout it; I'll take a rain check."

He stepped in front of her and slid a dollar into the

machine. "No way. I wouldn't be able to sleep if I didn't make it up to you."

Trenda tried not to smile, but his was contagious. "I don't usually go to dinner wit' strangers."

He stepped back and offered her his large hand. "Okay, let's fix that. My name's Eli Bockman; but everyone calls me 'Box.'"

Trenda inserted a second dollar into the machine, then shook his hand. *I better use one of my aliases.* "My name's Mya…Mya Collins."

He reminded her of a professor in his round, gold-rimmed glasses, baby-blue dress shirt and tan khaki pants. "Ahhhh, Mya…it fits you. That's a very pretty name."

She turned back to the machine and selected a bag of pretzels and a small package of beef jerky. *He is kinda cute, but I'm way too tired to fight "Big Boy" off right now.* When she turned around to give him one of her patented excuses to stop his advances, she was surprised to see that he'd gone back to his seat.

He picked up a pair of headphones that were plugged into his laptop and placed them on his head. She then opened her pretzels and nibbled on one as she walked over to his table. "Thanks again."

He removed his headphones. "What did you say?"

"I said thanks for dinner."

Like many men before him, he was drawn to her emerald eyes. "You are very welcome, Mya." He went back to his laptop screen.

Something about his gentleness intrigued her. "Why are you workin' on that computer so late?"

He clicked his wireless mouse a few times, then spun the laptop around for her to see. "I'm playing chess."

She covered her mouth and yawned. "Well, have fun; I'll catch you later."

He glanced at her breasts before turning his laptop around. He then gave her a smile. "Meet me here for breakfast. They start serving at six."

She walked away, giving him a perfect look at her nice behind. Without looking back at him she said, "I'll think about it."

Minutes later, she entered her room and locked the door. She placed her snacks on the table and stripped naked. She then inspected her aching body. "Oh shit! Look at this damn bruise on my shin." The scratch on her face was no longer bleeding, but a nagging itch took its place as the wound tried to heal. "I swear I'm gonna go back and kill that bitch if I get a scar from this cut."

She converted both reclining seats into her bed, then sat down and thought about her situation. Too tired to finish her food, she lay back on the bed. The rocking motion of the train and *clickety-clack* of the wheels on the tracks caused her eyelids to slowly close.

Seven

T renda awoke at 1:30 p.m. to the residual aches and pains from her injuries. *I need a long hot bath and a massage.* She then slowly sat up and swung her legs over the edge of her bed. *I'm sure glad they got showers on this train.*

As she sat naked on her bed, she heard a buzzing sound on the floor. "I wonder who the hell is lookin' for me." She picked up her purse and removed her vibrating cell phone. "*Goooooddamn!* I got sixteen missed calls."

After seeing that half of her missed calls were from Piper's parents, Trenda's thoughts went back to the security guards back at the train station. The rest of the calls were from various underworld figures in need of her services. "Fuck, I'm missin' all kinds of money."

She removed her phone charger and plugged in her cell phone. Once she saw the power light indicate it was charging, she removed her pink velour sweatsuit and matching pink thong and satin bra. She donned her black outfit once again, picked up her clean clothes, towels and complimentary soap and headed for the showers.

She showered, dressed and made her way to the dining car. She didn't realize how hungry she was until she watched a woman bite into a grilled chicken sandwich. The sound and smell of hamburger patties cooking on the grill nearly made her drool.

"What can I get you?" the middle-aged Spanish cook asked as she flipped a burger pattie.

Trenda scanned the laminated menu. "Let me have the cheeseburger meal and a Sprite."

Trenda paid for her meal, then took a window seat in a booth and waited for her food. The sun felt good on her face. As the scenery sped by, she daydreamed. *It feels damn good knowin' I ain't gotta deal wit' Darius no more.* She went into her purse and removed her compact mirror. She then studied the cut on her cheek. *Fuckin' Piper. The more I look at this cut, the more I hope that bitch is dead.*

The cook rang the bell on the counter and announced, "Order number 114 is ready!"

Trenda woke out of her daze and retrieved her food. She added mustard and mayonnaise to her cheeseburger. *I sure hope this little money I have is enough to get me by until I get on my feet. I heard California is expensive as hell.* She opened her bag of Lays Potato Chips and poured them on her plate. *I'm gonna need a car, a place to stay and—*

The sight of an Amtrak policeman and a conductor entering the dining car made Trenda squirt ketchup on her potato chips by mistake. They stopped four tables from her and asked the couple for their identification. *Oh shit! What the hell's goin' on?*

She fished in her purse for her sunglasses in the hope they would hide her attention-grabbing eyes. The cop and conductor scanned the car, then went to a booth on the opposite side of the car.

Nervousness replaced her hunger as she nibbled on a ketchup-stained chip. A familiar face came into view. Box entered the dining car. *Hmmmm, he might come in handy; the cops would be lookin' for a woman travelin' alone if they were lookin' for me.* She smiled and waved at him. "It's about time you got here."

Box gave her a confused smile as he walked past the conductor and cop. They were busy checking the ID's of a pair of college-aged kids. He wedged himself into the seat across from her. "I thought we were going to meet for breakfast?"

Trenda gave him a smile, glanced at the cop, then back to Box. "I like a late breakfast."

Box adjusted his glasses as he smiled at his new friend. "I see." He glanced at her plate. "I've never seen anyone eat potato chips with ketchup."

She looked over his shoulder and watched the cop scan the car again. "That's how we do it in B-More."

His eyes enjoyed how good she looked in pink. "Oh, is that where you're from?"

Trenda took a bite off the tip of her pickle spear. She noticed for the first time how wide his shoulders were. Even though he had a belly, it looked as though he'd worked out quite a bit back in the day. "Yup... Born and raised. Where you from?"

He turned his head after Trenda caught him looking at her breasts. "El Cerrito, California."

She smiled and arched her back slightly, giving him a better view of her twins. "Is that by L.A.?"

He glanced at her titties, then scratched his forehead. "No, it's about fifteen minutes from Oakland."

That's real good to know. She watched the cop and conductor head their way. "I wonder what happened. Why you think that cop is checkin' folks?"

Box turned around and eyed the pair. "They're doing random ID checks. You can blame that on 9/11."

She looked into his glasses. "What do you mean?"

"It's a part of heightened security. They like to know who you are…make sure you're not on their 'Known Terrorist List.'"

She felt her heart crawling into her throat as the cop and conductor approached. *I sure hope he's right!*

Box nodded and smiled at the officer as they checked the ID of the Korean couple across from them. "Do you need to see our ID's, too, Officer?"

Shut the fuck up! Trenda yelled in her mind. *He wasn't even gonna check ours!* She then took a bite of her cheeseburger and gazed out the window, hoping to avoid eye contact with the cop.

The alabaster-colored officer glanced from Box to Trenda. "No, that won't be necessary. We're done here."

Cool! Cool! She took another bite of her burger. *I just hope Mr. Box can keep his damn mouth shut.*

Box stood up. "I'm going to go get a sandwich. I'll be right back."

She nodded as she chewed a mouthful of food. *He sure is a wide body.* She watched him walk toward the grill in his red polo shirt and black slacks. A pair of conservative black loafers adorned his large feet. *He dresses just like a white boy.*

She watched the countryside rush past as she enjoyed her food. "Mya…Hey, Mya…can you hear me?"

Trenda happened to look his way as she took a sip of her soda. *Oh shit! I forgot what name I gave him!* "Yeah, sorry I was busy daydreamin'."

He gave her a smile. "Do you want anything while I'm up here?"

She shook her head as she tossed a few chips into her mouth. Unfortunately, his pleated slacks concealed the slightest hint of his package size from her scrutiny. Once he returned with his tuna melt, the train pulled into the Chicago station. After pouring his Doritos onto his plate, she noticed he made sure none of the chips touched his sandwich. "So, what you doin' on this train, Box?"

He used his napkin as a bib. "I'm on my way home from a business conference in D.C." He closed his eyes, lowered his head and said a silent blessing. He then looked back at her. "Where are you on your way too or from?"

Trenda finished swallowing a bite of burger. "I'm relocatin' to California."

He looked at her over his glasses as he held his sandwich. "Really? Job transfer?"

"You could say that. What do you do?"

"I'm a systems analyst for a large retail company."

She glanced at the invisible braces on his teeth. "What is that?"

He held up one finger and motioned for her to hold on as he swallowed a bite of food. "I make sure all the cash registers stay online. I also go out and set up the cash register and computer systems for new stores."

"You ride around doin' that all the time?"

"Most of the time. Sometimes I telecommute from home."

She took a sip of soda. "Why are you on the train? Wouldn't it be quicker if you flew?"

He gave her a bashful grin as he rubbed his forehead. "I don't like to fly...I hate it."

She smiled at his boyish manner. "Oh...so you scared to fly."

He picked up a chip and nibbled it. "I wouldn't call it *scared*. I'd say I have an aversion to riding inside a flying coffin."

She laughed. "A big ol' man like you scared of flyin'. That's funny!"

He blushed and opened his can of root beer. "Say what you will, but remember; there are no emergency lanes in the sky to pull over into if something goes wrong."

For a moment, she forgot her worries and enjoyed

their banter. "You must be damn good at your job if they gonna let you catch a train instead of fly. If I was your boss, I'd want your ass on the job as quick as possible."

He grinned. "Well, I guess I'm lucky you're *not* my boss!"

She bit her pickle spear. "You still didn't answer my question. You must be one of the best at your job."

He sipped his soda, then wiped his lips. "I'm pretty good."

She let her eyes rest on his wrist. *I bet you gettin' paid real good if you can afford that Bvlgari watch.* "I bet your wife is real happy when you hand her over your paycheck."

He choked on his mouthful of sandwich. After composing himself he replied, "Excuse me?"

She grinned as she wiped potato chip crumbs off her breasts, drawing his attention to her sexy rack. "Dang, don't die on me, baby!"

"I thought I heard you say something about me having a wife."

Trenda glanced at his ring-less fingers, then back into his face. "I did."

Box peeled the bread crust off his sandwich. "The only Mrs. Bockman close to me is my mom. I don't have a wife, and if I did, she'd have to be a true goddess to have me hand her over my cash like that."

Trenda placed her elbows on the table and leaned over her plate, giving the big man a magnificent view of her cleavage. "And why no wife, Mr. Box?"

He blinked his eyes and looked away from her chest. "A lot of reasons." He focused on the scratch on her face instead of her luscious breasts. "But it may happen one day."

I bet if I pulled one of my tits out, you'd gimme everything you got. She gave him a flirtatious smile. "I know a big, fine man like you has got a girlfriend."

"You could say that."

Trenda took a swallow of her soda. "Does she travel with you?"

"No. I usually travel alone or with co-workers." He sat back in his seat. "My turn; are you married? Attached?"

She pushed her shades up on her nose. "I ain't got no man. I'm free, single and able to mingle."

Even though the train's air conditioning was on, Box had to wipe a bead of sweat off the side of his face. He looked into her shades. "I bet you left a lot of broken hearts back in Baltimore."

She chuckled as she let her foot brush against his shin under the table. "I plead the fifth."

Box flinched as though she'd rubbed his left nut. To get his mind off the dancing dong in his pants, he changed the subject. "What do you do for a living, Heartbreaker?"

She looked out the window as Middle America's landscape whizzed by. "I do hair and stuff."

He removed the napkin from his shirt, balled it up and tossed it on his plate of scraps. "Oh, you're a cosmetologist. Did you go to school for it in Baltimore?"

She continued to stare at the passing scenery. "Yeah, I

went a few years ago." Thoughts of how she dropped out of cosmetology school three months in, after finding out she could do hair better than her teachers, played in her mind.

Box stood and pointed at Trenda's tray. "Are you done?"

She looked past him and did a double-take. *Oh shit, there goes the cop again.* She then drained the last of her soda and placed the empty cup on her tray. "Yeah, I'm done, thanks."

He placed her tray on top of his. "Can I ask you a question?"

She watched as the cop walked toward them. "Yeah, go ahead."

"How did you get that scratch on your face?

Trenda gently touched her slightly swollen cut. "I was fake boxin' with my nephew and he scratched me by accident with his watch."

He leaned in for a closer look. "You don't want it to get infected. Did you put any kind of ointment on it?"

The cop stopped at the counter and ordered a soda. "Yeah…as a matter of fact, I gotta get back to my room and put some more on it."

He smiled at his reflection in her dark shades as he picked up their trays. "Okay, well, if you get bored, I have a DVD player in my laptop and a bunch of movies to watch."

"I'll think about it." She let her eyes fall on the cop as he paid for his drink. "Where can I find you later?"

He nodded toward the front of the train. "I'm in room D-12, two cars that way."

She slid across the blue vinyl bench seat, stood up and gave him a sly grin. "Oh, you think you're slick; you're tryin' to get me in your room. I almost fell for ya 'innocent teddy bear' act."

He shook his head. "I assure you that's not what I meant. As a matter of fact, if you wish, we can watch the movies up here."

She studied his backside as he turned and took their empty trays and placed them on the grill counter. Something about his mannerisms and thickness intrigued and warmed her. She then looked away from his behind and caught sight of the cop looking at her as he turned his can of Coke up and finished it. "Hey, I gotta go. Do you have a cell phone?"

He turned from the counter after he and the cop exchanged a glance. "Yes I do."

She pulled a pen out of her purse and removed a napkin from the dispenser on the table. "Lemme have it in case I decide to call you later about the movie thing."

"510.555.9656. What time should I expect your call?"

Why the fuck is that cop just hangin' around the grill if he ain't gonna order no food? She took a couple steps backward toward the exit. "I dunno…maybe I'll surprise you. Bye."

"Sounds good! I'll catch you later." He watched her turn around and walk down the corridor. He then turned and walked back to the counter and stood next to the cop. "What's up, Officer?"

The cop leaned back on his elbows, on the counter. "Man, you are one lucky dude! She is *hot!*"

Box continued to stare at Trenda's pink velour-covered, heart-shaped ass until she exited the door at the end of the car. "That, she is, my man…that, she is." He winked at the cop. "It's one of the perks that come with my job; you get to see a *lot* of nice sights."

Eight

"Fuck!" Darius yelled after slamming his fist down on the hot, black hood of his patrol car. "Are you *sure* they were talkin' about me?"

His partner, Tyrone, hocked up a wad of phlegm and spat it onto the blacktop. "Hell yeah, I'm sure! I met up with our boy, Terrence, in Internal Affairs earlier today after the briefing. He told me they got your ass on video!"

Darius placed his hands on his hips as he stared up at the bottom of the freeway underpass they'd parked under. "Did he say what I was doin' on the tape?"

Tyrone watched a large rat run along the curb, then disappear into the gutter across the street from them. The broken windows of the abandoned textile factory they stood in front of looked like accusing eyes. "He told me you was gettin' your dick sucked by some broad in a blonde wig."

Darius dropped his hands, cocked his head and looked at his slim, charcoal-colored partner through squinted eyes. *"What?"*

Tyrone removed his hat and rubbed his low-cut afro.

"Man, he said they got you doin' baby, pullin' your gun on her and slammin' her on the floor." He replaced his cap on his head as he looked Darius in the eyes. "Accordin' to the time stamp on the video, it happened during the time *we* were supposed to be on patrol."

Darius shifted his bottom jaw from side to side, grinding his teeth as he analyzed the information he'd just received. *How the fuck did she tape us without me knowin'?* "Well, that ain't as bad as I thought…a lot of that sounds like circumstantial evidence to me."

Tyrone leaned back on the patrol car, exhaled loudly. "That's not all; they also got you on tape admittin' you extorted her out of money she was gonna use for a drug transaction. Since the ho put *my* name in it, I'm sure they are gonna investigate me, too." He turned and glared over the roof of the car at Darius. "I *told* you that bitch Trenda was scandalous when you *first* started fuckin' with her."

Darius scowled at him. "Quit panickin', scary-ass!"

The sound of a car skidding to avoid an accident overhead briefly silenced them. "Quit panickin'? How the hell you gonna explain the goddamn video?"

Darius walked a few steps away, while drumming the fingers of his right hand on his thigh. He froze. "Role play."

Tyrone gave him a perplexed look. "Role play? What the hell you talkin' about?"

A thin smile crossed his lips. "Lots of people practice sexual role play. I can claim that's what we were doin'."

Tyrone stared off into the night as he contemplated his partner's words. "Okay, so how are you gonna explain being on tape when *we* were supposed to be on patrol?"

Darius broadened his smile. "Who's to say her camera timestamp wasn't wrong? People do make mistakes, cameras do malfunction."

The patrol car radio called out their unit number. Tyrone shook his head as he opened the driver side door and got into the car. "That sounds all good, but we still have a problem."

"What the hell are you talkin' about now?" Darius asked as he entered the car.

After responding to a request from the dispatcher to check out a domestic violence call, Tyrone started the engine. "They also want to bring Trenda in for questioning, see if she wants to press charges."

Darius adjusted his hat as they pulled off. "In that case, we'll have to get to her before they do."

Nine

Trenda met Box in the café car to watch his collection of the Dave Chappelle Show DVDs. "He is a damn *fool!*" she said with a laugh as she and Box watched Dave Chappelle perform a skit with Ashy Larry.

Box wiped tears of laughter from his eyes. "He sure the hell is!" The feel of Trenda's thigh touching his in the booth they shared had more of his attention than the comedy playing on his laptop. He looked out the window and saw a large, brown, full moon keeping pace with the speeding train. "I order every season that comes out on DVD."

After the skit ended, Trenda lifted her arms over her head, yawned and stretched. She looked around the car and saw they were two of the only five people still in the café car. "What time you got?"

Box checked his watch. "I have five after eleven." He smiled into her hypnotic eyes. "I hope it's not past your curfew."

She looked at him out the corner of her eye with a devilish grin as she let her hand fall on his surprisingly firm thigh. She then slowly removed it. *Hmmmm, he's a lot more solid than he looks.* "Don't worry; I told daddy not to wait up for me."

He nearly snapped the DVD in half as he tried to put it back in its case after feeling Trenda's hand on his leg. "I have another DVD of his show if you want to watch it."

She turned toward him and leaned back against the window. "Do you have a room or just a seat?"

He gave her a blank expression as he zipped up his DVD case. "Huh?"

Trenda maintained eye contact with him. "Do you have a room here on the train or just a seat? My ass is gettin' sore sittin' on this hard bench seat."

"I, uhhh… I have a room."

Hmmmmmmm, I ain't fucked a man big as him in a long time. He might just get lucky. "Why you hesitate? You don't want me to visit?"

He nervously adjusted his glasses, then scratched his beard. "I didn't hesitate; I just wanted to be sure I understood what you were asking." A gleeful smile stretched his face. "You *do* want to come back to my room, correct?"

She read the lust and desire in his body language. She then leaned closer and placed her hand on his forearm. "Yes, Mr. Box. That's exactly what I said. I can't sit through another DVD on this hard-ass seat."

Blood rushed to the stiffening organ in his pants. "Cool!" He then pointed toward the outlet under the window. "Can you unplug the laptop power cord, please?"

She watched with an amused grin on her face as he

shut down and packed up his laptop with light speed. "You want me to carry your DVD case?"

He stood and placed the strap of his black laptop case on his shoulder. He then picked up the black leather DVD case. "No, I've got it."

Her top rode up, revealing her flat stomach as she slid across the bench seat and stood. *Damn, that cut on my shoulder still hurts.* After catching him eying her, she stretched and yawned again, giving him a good look at her abs. After adjusting her clothes, she said, "Let's go before I fall asleep on you."

After following Box to his room, he stopped before opening the door. "Ummmm, can you wait out here for a minute? I want to make sure the place is presentable."

She crossed her arms over her breasts, cut her eyes at him and chuckled. "What? I already know you got a woman. You ain't gotta hide the picture of her you have on the nightstand."

He laughed as he unlocked the door to his room. "You should be on the Dave Chappelle show with all the jokes *you* have!"

He opened the door just wide enough for him to slip inside. "Don't have me waitin' out here all night."

He stepped inside. "Just give me a minute."

She smirked, checked her watch and nodded her head as he closed the door.

Moments later, he opened the door, stepped aside and let her inside. "Sorry about the wait."

"You must of had a whole lotta pictures to hide as

long as it took you." She eyeballed his spacious room. It looked to be twice the size of her roomette. "Why do you have a room this big if you're travelin' alone?"

She took a seat on the sofa next to the window. "I got lucky; this was the only room available at the time my trip was booked."

"Yeah, right." She gave him a smirk, peeled back the curtain and looked out the window. The glowing lights of an unknown city flashed by as the train sped westward.

"What you want to watch now?" Box asked as he set up his laptop on the table across from them.

She took her eyes off the moon as it chased the train. "Do you have any scary movies?"

He opened his DVD case and rifled through his collection. He stopped and removed a DVD. "Have you ever seen *Jeepers Creepers?*"

She shook her head, closed the curtain and sat back on the sofa. "No…but I hope it's not one of those fake-ass Jason movies."

He chuckled, pressed play and sat down beside Trenda. "It's better than that."

As the movie began, she pointed at the wall-mounted light. "Why don't you turn that off so we can see the screen better?" He stood and turned off the light. *Damn, he got a big ol' booty!*

As the first killing took place in the movie, she felt her eyelids getting heavy. A continuous loop of dull pain from her injuries coursed through her body. Moments later, the sound of her inner voice replaced the sound of the movie dialogue. Worries of where she was going to live in California, for how long and if Piper was still alive ran through her mind like a track star.

Box gently elbowed her in the side. "Mya…Mya, wake up."

She opened her eyes and tried to focus on the screen. "I'm awake…I was just restin'."

He grinned. "It sounded more like you were pretending to be a buzz saw."

She rolled her eyes as she pulled down her top, which had rode up above her navel. She noticed his eyes were riveted to her exposed flesh. "I *know* you're trippin'. I don't hardly snore."

He blinked and quickly took his eyes off her sexy stomach. "If you say so; besides, I guess I wouldn't really know without spending the night with you."

She looked out the corner of her eye into his glasses. She read his desire to fuck her like a billboard on his face. "Are you askin' me to spend the night here with you?"

He avoided her gaze. "That's not what I meant by my comment, but you *would* be more than welcome to stay here tonight."

She gave a slight grin as she watched the movie reflect off his glasses. "C'mon now. Do you think I'm the kinda girl that would sleep with a stranger I met on a train a couple of days ago?"

"You wouldn't have to sleep in the same bed as me."

He pointed up at a rectangular-shaped section of the wall above their heads. "That folds down to another bed."

You sure give up easy. She contemplated his offer. "Okay, that'll work, but I wanna be on top."

Her innuendo-filled reply made him grin. "I wouldn't have it any other way."

She yawned and stretched in her seat. "I'm too tired to finish watchin' the movie. I'm ready to go to sleep."

He stood up, turned on the light and walked over to the laptop. "That's cool. Maybe we can finish watching it together one day."

She rubbed her eyes as he shutdown the laptop. "Now how are we gonna do that with you livin' with ya woman?"

He chuckled as he placed the laptop in its black leather case. "I told you I *had* a woman; I didn't say I *lived* with a woman."

She paused as she processed this new information. She knew a possible meal ticket when she saw one. "Bullshit! How long y'all been together?"

He glanced over at Trenda as she bent over to untie her white Adidas tennis shoes. "We've been together for three years now."

Trenda kicked off her shoes and wiggled her unpainted, pretty toes. "Now, how y'all go that long without one of y'all movin' in with the other?"

Box walked over to the closet and placed his laptop inside. "We agreed to not move in together until we were really ready for it."

Trenda picked up her shoes, stood and put them against the wall, under the window. She nearly lost her balance as the train ran over a particularly bouncy stretch of tracks. "I'm not tryin' to be all in your business, but don't you think three years is long enough to know whether or not y'all are ready?"

For the first time, Box showed her an emotion other than lust and bashfulness. "I'm pretty sure I'm ready, but Meagan…" He paused, took a deep breath, held it, then exhaled. "She decided she wants to finish school first. She's at U.C. Berkeley working on her masters in molecular and biochemical nutrition."

Damn, she sounds like one real boring bitch. And with a name like Meagan I bet she a white girl. She watched Box fold down the upper bunk. "What is molecular whatever-the-hell you said?"

Box walked over to the closet and removed the spare blankets and pillows for Trenda. "It's the study of the effects of nutrition on diseases such as cancer, diabetes, etcetera."

Trenda yawned. "Okay, enough. You makin' my head hurt." Box nearly went into cardiac arrest as he watched Trenda unzip her pink velour top. "Well, I'm going to bed. Talk to you in the morning."

For a moment, his mouth moved like a fish trying to breathe air. "Uhhh…wow…okay." The sight of her pink lace bra-covered cleavage made his balls tickle and his dick straighten out. He turned and looked out of the window in order to conceal his condition. "I guess I'll turn in, too."

I knew you'd like that. She watched him attempt to hide his stiffness. She then walked over to the bed. "Can you help me up?"

He whipped his head around. "Huh?"

She pointed at the upper bed with her thumb. "How am I supposed to get up there?"

Box walked over to the end of the bed. "You climb up here by standing on the edge of the bottom bed and pulling yourself up."

Trenda yawned. "I'm too tired to do all that. Come over here and lift me up."

He fought to hide a smile as he scratched his forehead. "Okay."

As he walked over, Trenda turned toward the bed and placed her hands on top. "Grab me by the waist and lift."

Both his pulse and breathing quickened as he wrapped his big hands around her small waist. Once she was halfway up, he had to push her up the rest of the way by placing his hand on her soft ass. That treat left his palms sweaty with a yearning to pull those pink pants off her. "Are you going to be okay up there? Are those two blankets enough?"

Trenda leaned over the bed. "Yes. I'm gonna be all right." She then kissed him lightly on the lips, then tucked herself in. "I had fun tonight."

Box slowly opened his eyes after the soft kiss. After a

quiet moment, he grinned. "It was my pleasure…believe me."

After Box turned off the lights and climbed into his bed, Trenda lay on her side listening to the *clickety-clack* of the train. *I just might be able to get ol' Box to let me stay at his place for a minute until I get myself together, if I can figure out a way to deal with his girlfriend issue.* Trenda then drifted in and out of troubled sleep as stress-filled thoughts of her dilemma refused to let her rest.

An hour later, after tossing and turning, Trenda's eyes fluttered open. *What the hell is that?* She lifted her head off the pillow and listened. Below the sound of the train clacking on the tracks and the intermittent blows of the train whistle, Trenda heard a low grunting sound and covers rustling. She then quietly leaned her head over the edge of the bed and looked. In the dim light of the city the train rolled past, she caught a brief glimpse of Box, on his back with his eyes closed, stroking his dick underneath his covers. *Oh shit!* She then quickly and silently lay back down. *I can't believe he's down there jackin' off!*

Ten

At 2:00 a.m., back in Baltimore, as Trenda lay in her bunk fascinated by the power of her pussy, Darius—with Tyrone riding shotgun—slowly cruised down Pratt Street in search of their best informant, "Thin Tim."

"What makes you think Tim's tweaked-out ass is gonna have any info?" Tyrone asked as he and Darius cruised the areas Thin Tim was known to frequent.

Darius slowed for a red light, then sped through it once he saw no approaching vehicles. "If anybody knows how to find a dope-runnin' bitch, it's Tim's dirty ass." He looked over at his partner as they bounced through a deep pothole. "Did you forget the reason why we don't lock him up?"

Tyrone let his right arm dangle out the window as they drove through the Harbor area. "I know he's been in the streets longer than I can remember and knows every thug, pimp, ho and dope dealer in the city, but half the time he's too fucked up to get any useful information—"

Darius silenced Tyrone with a wave of his hand as he

mashed on the gas pedal. "Ahhhh, there's that nappy-headed bastard!" Darius exclaimed as he turned on the red beacon in the grill of their unmarked patrol car and swooped up to the curb.

Tyrone jumped out of the car and stood in the path of the tall, lanky, bright-skinned, fifty-something, dreadlock-sporting, paranoid man. "Awwww, shit. What the hell I do, now?" Thin Tim yelled as he turned around and automatically placed his hands on top of his matted hair.

"Now who said you did anything?" Darius asked as he walked around the front of the patrol car while pulling on his tight, black leather gloves. "We just wanted to stop by and make sure you're okay."

The smell of body odor, gin, and hopelessness wafted off Thin Tim and into Tyrone's nose as he patted down their snitch. The lint and naps in Tim's unkempt beard made Tyrone nauseous. "Goddamn! When's the last time you took a *bath?*"

Tim looked over the collar of his filthy navy pea coat. "Why you always tryin' to clown somebody?"

"Shut the fuck up and stand still!" Tyrone shouted as he stood behind Thin Tim and placed him in handcuffs. Tyrone then looked over at Darius. Darius gave him a slow head nod. Tyrone stealthily reached into his pocket and removed a small plastic bag containing six crack rocks. He then reached into the left pocket of Tim's jacket. "Uh-oh! What's this?"

"What's what?" Tim asked in a bewildered tone.

"What you got there, Tyrone?" Darius asked as he walked over and examined the dope in his partner's hand.

"It looks like about twenty years' worth of jail time for our parolee friend," Tyrone said as he placed the bag of crack on the roof of the car.

A few onlookers, mostly vagrants, standing in front of the ESPN Zone stopped to gawk at the scene. Panic stricken, Thin Tim looked across the street at the small crowd and yelled, "Hey! Hey y'all! These cops is tryin' to set me up!"

"That was the wrong move," Darius said as he opened the back door of the patrol car and shoved Tim into the backseat. Thin Tim cringed as Darius leaned inside and glared at him. "Now we have to take you somewhere *private* and question you."

Fear flooded into Thin Tim's dirty face. The last time the two cops took him to a *private* place, he found himself coughing up blood as the dirty duo took turns kicking him in the stomach. "I'm sorry, man! I'm sorry! I was scared, man! We ain't gotta go nowhere! We can talk right here! C'mon, Darius, *C'mon, man!*"

Darius gave him an evil grin as he backed out of the car. "Too late, son." He then slammed the door, looked at Tyrone, pointed at the baggie on the roof of the car and said loud enough for the crowd to hear, "Yo, Tyrone. Grab that evidence so we can take him in."

"Got it," Tyrone replied as he grabbed the dope and put it in the left breast pocket of his shirt. He then entered the car and looked at his partner. "Where we gonna take him?"

Darius started the car and pulled from the curb. "We're gonna take him to the 'Lighthouse.'"

After hearing where the cops were taking him, Thin Tim quickly sat up and put his face inches from the metal screen that separated him from the officers. The "Lighthouse" was the name given to an abandoned two-story house in West Baltimore. After being taken over by drug addicts, homeless people and dope dealers, it was transformed into the biggest crackhouse in the city.

The term, "lighthouse," came from all the tweaked-out crackheads walking around with their eyes wide open, or in street terms, having their "high beams" on. Not only was it a den for tweakers and dope dealers, it was also a place one could dispose of a dead body—permanently. After Darius, Tyrone and a squad of officers raided the place eighteen months ago, they discovered four of the original six fifty-five gallon drums of hydrochloric acid that the dope dealers keep in the basement. They used the acid to destroy evidence in case of a raid or to make enemies disappear. A week before the raid, Tyrone suggested to Darius they confiscate two of the drums for their personal use. Darius agreed. They rented a U-Haul, rolled the drums into it and stashed them until it was safe to bring them back.

It was rumored in the streets that even though the "Lighthouse" had been boarded up and the acid removed, Darius used the house to beat information out of informants and perform clandestine and illegal transactions.

"Not the 'Lighthouse'! I heard what y'all do to folks in there!" Thin Tim yelled as his spittle sprayed through the metal screen.

Tyrone slammed his left fist against the barrier. "Shut the fuck up before I roll your stankin' ass out on the freeway!"

Ten minutes later, they pulled up to the cyclone fence that surrounded the Lighthouse. It stood in the middle of four other abandoned homes. Darius looked in the rearview mirror and watched as Tim rocked back and forth in his seat, mumbling to himself. He then looked over his shoulder at his prisoner. "You have a couple of choices to make, Thin Man. I need to find somebody and I'm sure you know where I can find her." He stopped at the driveway entrance. "Tyrone, get out and open the gate."

Panic consumed Tim as he watched Tyrone open the gate. "What you want from me, man? I don't know shit!"

After Tyrone waved him through the fence, Darius drove over the broken glass-strewn, dark driveway and around to the back of the house. He then killed the engine and looked over his shoulder at a now terrified Thin Tim. "I'm not in the mood for games or your usual bullshit." He looked out the back window and saw Tyrone's silhouette approaching. "I'm looking for a female drug runner and I'm sure a dope smoker like you knows where I can find her."

As Tyrone opened the back door, Tim blurted out,

"Man, I don't smoke no mo'! I just drank, now. Man, I don't know nothin'!

Tyrone grabbed him by the arm and pulled the frail drug addict out the car. "Get out and stand still."

Darius got out of the car and walked over to the rear door to the house. The tattered remains of yellow and black crime scene tape flapped in the mild, chilly breeze. A sign warning not to enter the condemned property was barely readable in the lightless area where they stood. A pair of two-by-fours nailed over the door, prevented entry. He then removed his heavy black flashlight and shined it in Thin Tim's face. "If I have to go through all the trouble of finding something to pry these boards off, I'm gonna be mad as hell."

Thin Tim licked his chapped lips as he fought to avoid the glare of the light. "Man, why we even out here? What y'all want from me?"

Darius walked over to the car, reached in, and removed a manila envelope from the front seat. He then looked at Tyrone. "Here, hold the light for me."

Tyrone took Darius's flashlight and shined it on the envelope. Tim mumbled to himself as he watched Darius reach into the envelope. From the envelope, Darius pulled out a blown-up print of a mugshot. "You know who this is? Her name is Trenda."

Tim barely glanced at the photo before shaking his head. "Naw, I ain't never seen her before."

Darius exhaled loudly, then grabbed a fistful of Thin

Tim's hair. "Look again, muthafucka!" He jammed the photo in Thin Tim's face. "Take a real good look; your health depends on it."

Thin Tim wailed as Darius pulled his hair tighter. "I don't know! I don't know! I don't know, man!"

Frustrated, Darius tossed the picture on the hood of the car and looked at Tyrone. "Go get the bucket."

Tyrone smirked. "Aw shit, Tim. You done pissed him off now."

Thin Tim slid to the ground and whined as Darius let go of his hair. He quickly rolled over after nearly landing on a huge dead rat. "I'm tellin' you, I don't know nothin'! *Nothin'!*"

Darius stood over Tim and watched as Tyrone walked over and looked behind the overgrown hedges that lined the back fence. Tyrone's flashlight beam bounced until it landed on a white plastic five-gallon bucket. Darius grinned as Tyrone carefully grabbed the handle of the bucket and walked back to the car. "Tim, it looks like we are gonna have to give you a little 'act right' juice."

Thin Tim rolled away from the cops and the bucket and sat with his back against the rear wheel of the patrol car. He watched as Darius cautiously removed the lid from the bucket. "What you doin' wit' that?"

Darius studied the contents of the bucket with the beam of his flashlight as he spoke. "I'm sure you heard about the drums of acid they found in the basement." He turned his gaze to Thin Tim. "We saved a little for our own use."

As Thin Tim tried to scoot away, Tyrone stomped on his leg. "You try to move again, and I'll shoot you in the ass!"

"Bring him over here," Darius said as he stood over the bucket. "I think ol' Tim looks kinda thirsty."

Thin Tim's eyes grew to the size of dinner plates. "No! No! No! Help! Somebody help meeeeeeeeee!"

"Shut the fuck up!" Tyrone said as he dragged Thin Tim by the collar and shoved him in front of the bucket.

Darius said, "You got one more chance to answer my question before I give you the strongest drink you *ever* had."

Thin Tim froze with terror, eyes locked on the bucket, as his bottom lip shivered. "I-I-I don't kn-kn-knooo-ooooow…"

Tyrone shined his light on the trembling man. "Think hard, Thin Man."

This is takin' way too long, Darius thought as he scanned the ground with his flashlight. His beam landed on the dead rat. He bent over and picked it up by its long skinny tail. "Hey, Tim, have you ever seen what acid does when it gets on you?"

The sheer horror of the question paralyzed Thin Tim's vocal chords. He sat bug-eyed watching Darius.

Both Tyrone and Thin Tim watched as Darius took the rat by the tail and dunked it halfway into the industrial-strength acid.

A minute later, Darius pulled the rat out. "Oh shit!" Tyrone yelled as the acid-soaked rat dissolved and smoked. "I'm gonna fuckin' throw up!"

Thin Tim shook with terror and slobber formed on the corners of his mouth as he watched the rat liquefy in front of his eyes. "P-p-please don't acid m-m-me," he said in a terrified whimper.

Darius watched as the skull of the rat became visible. He then dropped the remains of the rodent into the bucket. "Okay. How about you take another look at the picture?"

Tyrone picked up the picture off the hood and handed it to Tim. "Take a *real* good look."

Darius winked at his partner as he shined his light on the picture. "Tell me what you know, Tim."

Thin Tim studied the picture for a full minute as his gin-fogged brain searched for information. Trenda's unforgettable green eyes jostled his memory. "I…I think I seen her before…I think I seen her at Griff's junk yard."

Darius grinned. *"When?"*

Tim licked his lips as he stared at the picture. "I was over there a couple nights ago lookin' for work. She was talkin' to Griff about her car…" He looked up at his captors. "I swear that's all I know, I *swear!*"

Darius's grin expanded as he put the lid back on the bucket. "See, Tim, that wasn't that bad, now was it?"

Thin Tim sat in silence with his back against the rear door of the car. "Can I go now?"

"Sure!" Darius wiped his gloved hands on Thin Tim's jacket. "Turn around so I can get the cuffs off."

Tyrone made sure the lid was on securely, then took the bucket back to its hiding place. Once he returned,

Darius handed him his cuffs. "Time to get back for shift change."

Thin Tim stood and rubbed his wrist as the cops got into the car. "Ain't y'all gonna gimme a ride back?"

Tyrone looked at Tim as he started the car and turned on the headlights. "Sorry, I ain't got time." He then went into his shirt pocket and pulled out the bag of crack and tossed it to Thin Tim. "Here you go. Have fun."

Darius smiled as he took off his gloves and stuck them in the glove compartment. "Oh, yeah! That was *all* good! All we gotta do now is visit ol' Griff." He tapped Tyrone on the shoulder with the back of his hand. "I'm gonna have to find another dead rat just in case we need to bring Griff out here for a 'private' questioning."

Tyrone laughed as he reversed out the driveway, then shifted to drive and headed for the freeway. "I gotta admit, I thought you was out ya damn mind when you told me about this crazy-ass plan with the rat and acid."

"It's called 'Rat Soup.' I got the idea from this old detective from the Bronx I met a few years ago. The hardest part was finding a big enough rat."

Tyrone chuckled. "Shit, I bet you can find all the rats you want inside the 'Lighthouse.'"

Darius continued to smile as he sat back in his seat. "I can't wait to visit ol' Griff tomorrow."

Tyrone noted the time. "Man, it's almost quittin' time; let's go grab a couple of hoes after work, go to my apartment and have a few drinks to celebrate?"

Darius grinned as he shook his head. "Nah, man; the hoes I'm down with, but drinkin'? You know I'm the first to admit I can't hold my liquor. That shit always gets me in trouble. That's how I ended up proposing to Beverly's ass."

Laughing hard, Tyrone slapped the steering wheel. "You a straight fool!"

After watching the car back down the driveway and disappear, Tim walked around to the side of the Lighthouse and removed a board from one of the downstairs windows. All the serious dope heads knew about this hidden entrance.

After entering the house and finding the battery-operated lantern he'd stolen from a hardware store and stashed it there, he looked at the bag of rocks. The two weeks prior to this night, he'd managed to fight off the temptation to smoke the Devil's Candy in his hand.

Thanks to Darius, temptation won the battle. Tim found a soda can, which a previous visitor had used as a makeshift crack pipe, and smoked himself back into the grip of his hellish addiction.

Eleven

Trenda reached into her pants and caressed her pussy after witnessing Box pleasuring himself. *Mmm-mmm, shit…damn that turns me the fuck on!* She was so worked up, her movements cause the bed to creak. She ceased her actions and listened. She heard the rustling below her stop also.

The sound of the train's whistle filled the night, several cars in front of them. Trenda quietly slid out of her pants and tossed the covers off. The freaky diva inside her took over as she swung her legs over the edge and eased down onto the floor.

Box's attempt to fake sleep almost made her laugh. She gazed at his tent pole as he lay on his back. Trenda steadied her feet to compensate for the rocking motion of the train. She then unsnapped the back of her bra, removed it and tossed it on her bunk. She rubbed the moist patch on her panties for a moment before grabbing his dark gray blanket and snatching it off of him.

He did a brilliant job of fluttering his eyes, pretending to be awakened from a deep sleep. "Mya? What the…"

He rubbed his eyes as he focused on the image of her beautiful breasts. "What are you doing?"

Trenda played with one of her hard nipples. "I had a feelin' you needed help with *that.*"

She pointed at his rigid, throbbing meat. Embarrassed at his hardness, he attempted to cover it with his hands. "I…I don't know what—"

Trenda closed his mouth with her hand as she got on her knees. "You talk too much." As she wrapped her hand around his stiffness, she thought, *his dick ain't all that long, but it's thick as hell!*

As he lay there, his face full of thrill and shock, Trenda sandwiched his meat between her soft mounds. Her freaky inner-child took over as her eyes closed with tingly satisfaction. "Mmmmmm…yesssssssss…nice fat dick," she whispered.

Pleasure-filled moans escaped Box as he enjoyed his first tit fuck. Trenda's passion for oral gratification kicked in as she licked the head of his dick each time it surfaced from between her sacks. Box began pumping his hips as he rushed toward Cum City. Trenda, sensing he was close to nutting, relaxed her throat muscles and took his entire joint into her mouth. His fuzzy pubic hairs tickled her cheeks.

Box muttered a string of unintelligible words as he stiffened up, ready to shoot. Trenda's head bobbed furiously as she sucked him like the expert she was. She then stopped and held his dick. "I want you to watch this." She slowly stroked him.

Box gazed at her with half-closed eyes and panted, "Don't…stop…please…I want…you."

She gave him a freaky look. "You wanna fuck my mouth, baby?"

He tried to fuck her fist. "Yessss…pleaseeeeeeeeee…"

She rubbed his dickhead on her lips. "Watch me."

As Box tilted his head forward, Trenda sucked him as she looked him in the eyes. That was one of her big turn-ons; making her sex partner lose control. Once she tasted his pre-cum, he could no longer watch. His body was overcome with pleasure. "Ohhhhhhhhhhhhhhhhhh Myyyyaaaaaaaaaaaaaaaaaaaaaaaa!" She jacked his rod and let his spray of sperm cover her pink tongue.

She moaned as his hot sperm hit the roof of her mouth. As his stick twitched in her mouth, she gently massaged his balls as she sucked every drop of cream out of him.

"Oh shit! Oh shit! Oh shit! Oh shit!" he repeated as the best blow job of his life came to an end. "Oh, Mya… wow! That was *great!*"

You damn right it was. She wiped her mouth with the back of her hand. "You liked that, Mr. Box?"

"Yesssssssss, yes!" He tried to catch his breath.

She stood up, picked up her bra and put it on. "I'm glad you did."

He opened his eyes in time to see her reach for, and put on, her pants. "Hey, where are you going? I thought you were going to spend the night?"

She put on her jacket and sat down. "I was, but I really don't like sleeping on a top bunk."

He watched as she put on her shoes. "You can sleep down here with me."

Trenda chuckled as she finished tying her shoes. "C'mon now. You know damned well we can't both fit in that little-ass bed." She then walked over and rubbed his sweaty forehead. "Maybe we'll run into each other on another train ride one day."

"But, Mya...wait." He attempted to get up. "I don't want you to leave."

She smiled at him knowing her "oral magic" had worked once again. "I gotta go. Night, night."

Twelve

The following day as Trenda's train pulled into the Jack London Square station in Oakland, California, Darius got a briefing from Tyrone over a late lunch at the Cheesecake Factory at the Baltimore Harbor. "I just talked to Terrence and he told me shit is heatin' up."

Darius looked at him as he finished off his roast beef sandwich. "What's goin' on now?"

Tyrone sat back and burped into his fist. "You remember Trenda's roommate they found the night Trenda disappeared?"

"Yeah. Ain't she the one they found knocked out in her apartment?"

"Yup. Her parents are sweatin' the department to find Trenda. They want her charged with attempted murder on their daughter."

Darius knew that Piper's family was wealthy and well connected politically. He also knew the police chief would do all he could to find Trenda since elections were coming up. "You had any luck findin' Trenda?"

"Nope. I checked all my sources and it's like she evaporated." He picked a piece of beef brisket out of his teeth. "You tried askin' Griff, yet?"

"No, but I'm gonna go check him out when I leave here."

Tyrone looked around to be sure no one was in earshot. "You know they're still investigatin' you. Terrence told me the only reason they haven't come after you yet is because they need to get Trenda's testimony so they have a solid case against you."

"Fuck them haters," Darius drank the last of his lemonade. "I'm gonna find that bitch. She'll turn up somewhere."

"You might wanna do that, homeboy. He also said they're gonna pull you in next week and most likely put you on administrative leave."

Darius couldn't stop worrying about what Tyrone had told him over lunch. He knew the chief would love to see him fired or put in jail. They hadn't got along since Darius filed and won a discrimination suit against the department four years ago. He also knew that if they did put him on administrative leave, they would watch him closely and restrict his movements. He put those thoughts aside as he pulled into the driveway of "B-More Auto Salvage." He needed to focus on getting the information on Trenda he needed from Griff.

As Darius got out of his car, grateful to see the late afternoon sun after the past few rainy days, Julio hopped off the large forklift he was driving and walked up to the pearl-white Escalade while wiping his oily hands on a red rag. "Can I help you wit' somethin'?"

Darius picked up a photo off his seat then got out and removed his dark shades. "Yes, I need some information."

Julio walked around the customized SUV. "What kinda information?"

Darius stepped between Julio and his vehicle then showed him the picture. "Have you seen this woman before?"

Julio glared at him. "Why the fuck you askin' me?"

Darius brushed aside his black leather jacket, exposing the badge clipped to his belt. "Because I can, punk." He then held the picture inches from Julio's nose. "Now, answer the goddamn question."

Annoyed, Julio glanced at the photo. "Nah…I ain't seen her before."

Darius then remembered that Thin Tim had seen her at the junkyard at *night*. "What time do you get off work?"

"In about an hour. I work from eight to five." He then looked over at the beat-up Dodge sedan dangling from the forklift's blades. "Hey, I gotta get back to work. I ain't got no more info for you."

Darius then looked over at the long, silver Airstream trailer across the yard. "Does anybody live in that trailer?"

Julio exhaled loudly. "That's the owner's. He lives in there."

Darius recalled hearing about Griff's shifty ways in precinct reports. It was rumored that he was involved with stolen cars and peddling bootleg movies and CD's. "Where is Griff?"

Julio pointed across the yard as he walked back to his forklift. "He's over there runnin' the car crusher."

Darius put his shades back on and walked over to the loud, giant machine. He looked up into the glass-enclosed operator's booth, ten feet over his head. Inside, Griff smoked a fat cigar as he moved levers and pressed buttons. Darius waved his hands as he yelled, "Hey! Griff! Yo!"

Griff looked down at the waving man. He opened the window of the booth and yelled, "What you want?"

Darius removed the badge from his belt and held it up. "I need to talk to you."

Griff shook his head as he shut down the car crusher. Darius watched the hefty man climb down the ladder of the machine. After getting on the ground, Griff looked at Darius's badge, then into his shades. "What you need to talk to me about?"

Darius watched as a Griff's old German Shepherd, Bluto, came from behind the mobile home and walked over to them. "I'll make this quick." He held up the photo of Trenda. "When's the last time you saw her?"

Griff took two quick puffs off his cigar as Bluto sniffed Darius's pant leg. "I don't know what you talkin' 'bout. Who the hell is she?"

Darius looked around and saw a few customers walking around the yard, inspecting the wrecked cars for parts. He needed a place to interrogate Woodsy in private.

"Follow me," Darius said as he walked around behind the flat bed truck Griff used to bring junk cars to his yard.

Reluctantly, Griff followed him. Once they got behind the truck, Griff said, "You wastin' my time. I told—"

Darius grabbed him by the lapels of his greasy coveralls. "I know all about your crooked-ass. If you don't stop bullshittin' me and tell me where this bitch is, I'm gonna have my boys come through here and see how many of these goddamned cars are stolen."

Before Griff could speak, they both heard an angry growl. Bluto bared his teeth at Darius. "Easy, Bluto… easy," Griff said. "He don't like folks fuckin' wit' his master."

Darius let go of Griff as the dog took a step toward him. "You better call him off before I put a hole in him." Darius slowly reached for the pistol in his shoulder holster.

Griff looked at the dog. "Bluto! *Go home!*"

The dog gave Darius one last menacing glare, then turned and walked back toward the mobile home. Griff took a puff off his cigar, ground it out on the fender of the truck and put it in the breast pocket of his overalls. "I don't know what you talkin' 'bout. I run a legit business."

The loud sound of an air chisel cutting through metal got Darius's attention. He let go of Griff and looked over the hood of the truck. The sound came from behind the wooden, grease-stained doors of a large, ragged garage near the back of the junkyard. He looked at Griff. "What's going on in that garage, Griff?"

The defiant look drained from his face. "Nothin'."

Darius walked toward the garage. "Let's go see what that, 'nothin' noise is."

Griff hurried behind him. "You got a warrant?"

Darius continued walking. "For what?"

Griff hurried past and stood between the garage door and Darius. "I know my rights. You can't just search my property without a warrant."

Darius balled his fist and hit him in the stomach. He watched Griff fall to the wet, oily dirt. "How's that for a warrant, fat man?" He pushed Griff to the side with his foot as he tried to catch his breath, and slid the garage door open. He grinned and shook his head. "Griff, Griff, Griff…now why would you have your men working on a vehicle out of sight of the public eye?"

The startled pair of workers stopped dismantling a fairly new Trooper SUV as Griff struggled to his feet. "Ain't no law…" he fought to get his breath back, "against it."

Darius walked around to the back of the vehicle and read the familiar license plate. He then looked at Griff. "How about I run these plates and see who the owner is?"

Griff grimaced and looked at his workers. "Y'all get outta here. Go unload those cars off the flatbed." The two black men placed their tools on the engine of the fenderless and hoodless vehicle, gave Darius a curious glance and left.

Darius looked inside and saw a blonde wig on the floor

where the passenger seat used to be. *You must have been in one hell of a hurry to get away, Trenda.* He stepped back and looked around the garage. Air bags, leather seats, chrome rims and other expensive car parts—in remarkably good condition—crowded the cluttered garage. "Griff, tell me where Trenda is or I'm gonna call the fellas from the Regional Auto Theft Team down here and have them go over your inventory with you."

"Fuck!" Griff glared at Darius. "How do I know you ain't gonna keep harrassin' me even if I do tell you?"

Darius walked over to a rack full of top quality in-dash CD and DVD players and picked one up. "You don't." He walked back over and stood in front of Griff. "But I guarantee if you don't, every time you open your eyes, you're gonna see the world through prison bars."

Griff removed the unfinished cigar from his pocket, put it in the corner of his mouth and chewed on it as he pondered his future. "She was here a couple days ago tryin' to sell me her truck. I bought it and dropped her off on North Charles Street. I ain't seen or heard from her since."

"Where was she going?"

"I dunno; she didn't say, and I didn't ask."

"Where did you drop her off?"

"I told you I dropped her off on North Charles Street."

Darius grabbed a handful of Griff's thick beard. "Think hard, muthafucka. Did you drop her off at a house, business, movie theater, what?"

Griff broke free of his grip and rubbed his sore chin. "Owww, fuck!" He glared at Darius. "All I remember is droppin' her off by a big Laundromat on North Charles and East Madison."

"What time was it when you dropped her off?"

"Fuck, I dunno…it was kinda late…around midnight."

Darius looked at the expensive combination in-dash CD/DVD player in his hand. "If I find out you're lyin', I'm gonna come back, put you in the trunk of one of these cars and run it through the car crusher. You got that?"

Griff narrowed his eyes and mumbled, "Yeah, I got that."

Darius pulled the cigar out of Griff's mouth, flicked it away and shoved him against the stripped SUV. "I didn't hear you, fat-ass."

"I *said* I heard you."

Darius let go of Griff, tucked the CD/DVD player under his arm, went into his jacket pocket and handed him one of his cards. "Call me if she shows up or contacts you. I'll be back to check on you real soon." He looked at the stacks of chrome rims in the far corner. "Oh, and make sure you get me some nice twenty-six-inch rims for my Escalade. I'll be expecting them next time I see you."

Griff huffed. "When the hell is that gonna be?"

"When I fuckin' feel like it." He patted Griff on the side of his jaw a couple of times. "And don't forget the tires to go with the rims." Darius then left the garage, walked to his Escalade and put the confiscated CD/DVD player inside.

Half an hour later, Darius pulled up to the intersection of North Charles and East Edison streets. *Now where is that Laundromat Griff was talking about?* He slowly drove up North Charles and saw the Sudz N Dudz Laundromat on his right. *Bingo!* He parked in front, got out of his car and looked around. *If she sold her truck to Griff, she had to be desperate for cash.* He looked at the bus schedule posted on the bus shelter. *She is most likely trying to get out of town with all the heat on her.*

A blue and white sign pointing in the direction of the Amtrak station caught his eye. *I wonder…*he jumped back in his car and sped off to the train station.

"How can I help you, Officer?" asked Dorothy McMurray, the silver-headed manager on duty, as she offered Darius a seat in her office. Photos and paintings of the evolution of the trains over the years hung on the walls of her office.

He put his badge away and took a seat on the wooden seat across from her antique desk. "I need to see the security video tapes from last Friday night."

"Certainly, but may I ask why?"

"I'm trailing an attempted murder suspect. We have reason to believe the suspect boarded a train here on the way out of town."

She placed her hand to her mouth in shock. "Get out! *Really?*"

"Yes. She's very dangerous. I need to find her as quickly as possible."

She put on the glasses that hung on a chain around her neck and stood. "Please, follow me to the security room."

He followed her out of her office and across the station. Late afternoon sunlight illuminated the huge, intricately designed stained glass section of ceiling. Across the hallway, next to the stainless steel, light rail ticketing machines, they stopped in front of a door marked SECURITY. She unhooked a key ring from a belt loop on her dark blue pants and unlocked the door. He followed her into the room. Twelve monitors recorded the entire terminal—inside and out—from every conceivable angle. A rack full of VCR's blinked and whirred. On the wall behind them was a wall full of shelves, loaded with labeled VCR tapes. "Just a moment. Let me search for it."

I'm glad this old broad is cooperating. He gave her a well-practiced, insincere smile as she scanned the rows of tapes. "I really appreciate your help, Mrs. McMurray."

"No trouble at all! With all the craziness going on in the world, we must work together to lock up these nut jobs. Do you have a particular time of night you're looking for? These tapes record in four-hour blocks."

"I need to see the tapes from about eight to midnight."

She smiled and pulled a tape off the bottom rack. "Ah! Here we are!" She placed the tape in one of the VCR's, picked up a remote control off the desk and pressed PLAY. "I hope you find who you're looking for."

Darius pressed STOP on the tape. "I'm sorry but can I have you step out the room, please? For the sensitivity of this investigation, I can't disclose the identity of the suspect. I hope you understand."

She nodded. "I understand, Officer Kain." She handed him the remote to the VCR. "If you would, just place the tape back in the case, turn off the VCR and lock the door behind you. I'll be in my office if I can be of further assistance."

He waited for her to leave, then pressed PLAY. He scanned the faces of the people entering the train station on the tape. *Shit! This is gonna take forever!* He impatiently fast-forwarded the tape in small increments. "Ha!" He paused the tape after spotting a stunning and sexy woman beating a baseball cap against her leg after entering the station. "I got you, bitch." He watched her walk up to the ticket counter. *I wish this tape had audio.* He made note of the clerk's face that assisted Trenda and checked his watch. *I wonder if he works tonight?* He rewound the tape, put it back in its case and shut off the VCR.

He walked to Mrs. McMurray's office. "Did you find the person you were looking for?"

He shook his head. "No…there was no trace of the suspect."

"I'm sorry to hear that."

He gave her a false, disappointed look. "Thanks for your help. I'll be sure to note in my report how helpful you were."

She beamed as he left. "If I can be of any further assistance, don't hesitate to ask!"

He walked to the lobby and went to the ticket window of the agent he'd seen Trenda buy her ticket from. "Excuse me. I was wondering if you could help me."

The frilly clerk gave Darius a flirtatious look. "I'll certainly try."

Darius slid him the photo. "Do you remember seeing this woman a couple nights ago?"

The clerk looked at the picture, smacked his lips and slid it back to Darius. "Yes…I saw her the other night."

"Do you remember where she was going?"

The clerk blushed as Darius smiled at him. "I can't tell you that."

I knew this faggot muthafucka was gonna pull this shit. Darius looked over his shoulder and saw no one behind him. He then broadened his smile, softened his eyes, placed his hand on the clerk's as it lay on the counter and sweetened his voice. "Are you *sure* you can't help me?"

The clerk giggled like a schoolgirl. "Nooooo, I can't… I really wish I could but I could get in trouble."

Darius rubbed the clerk's hand. "C'mon, now. I won't tell." He looked around and saw a family enter the train station. He was running out of time. "How about you tell me," he read the clerk's name badge, "Orlando, and I come back and we go have a drink when you get off?"

Orlando laced his fingers in Darius's, smiled and whispered, "Are you *serious?*"

The family walked up behind Darius. He let go of Orlando's hand and licked his lips. "You know I am."

Orlando wrote a few lines on a blank train ticket, flashed his tongue ring and slid the ticket to Darius. "There's the information on your train, sir. Enjoy your trip!"

Darius placed the ticket in his inside jacket pocket. "Thanks." On the way out of the station, he removed the ticket and read it:

She took a train to the Jack London Square station in Oakland, California. Oh, and just for the record, my chocolate hunk, I loooove to spoil my man. I get off at one in the morning. My number's 410.555.9868. Cum back and get me.

Darius grimaced as he ripped up the ticket and tossed it in a trash can in the parking lot. *Sick faggot fuck! I'm tempted to come back all right—come back and strangle your gay ass!* He absently wiped the hand he'd use to hold Orlando's on his pant leg as he got in his Escalade. *So, that bitch went to the West Coast, huh?* He started the engine. "That ain't far enough, Trenda. Not far enough at all."

Thirteen

Three days after leaving Baltimore, Trenda's train pulled into the Jack London Square station a little after 10:00 p.m. She shouldered her bag and walked out into the cool night air. Tendrils of fog danced in the starry sky. *So this is big, bad Oakland.* For a Monday night, there was a lot of traffic in the busy Jack London Square area of downtown Oakland. She looked around and spotted the Waters Edge Hotel within walking distance. *The first thing I need to do is find me a room.*

"Hey, Mya! Wait up!"

Trenda whipped her head around and saw Box hustling his way toward her, with his cell phone to his ear. She smiled. *I knew he would turn up sooner or later after I put these lips on him.* "Wassup, Mr. Man?"

He slowed his stride as he closed in on her and put away his phone. He pushed his glasses up the bridge of his nose and returned her smile. "I've been looking for you all night! How are you?"

She adjusted the collar of her dark green, velour, Baby Phat sweatsuit as the cool air caused her nipples to rise.

"I've been around. I thought you would be halfway home by now."

"Now why would you say that?"

"You know you have to get home before your girl starts blowin' your phone up."

He shook his head and smiled as he eyed her rigid nipples. "You kill me with that! I don't have to punch a relationship clock."

Even in the dim light cast by the energy-efficient street lamps, she could see the growing lump in the crotch of his tan khaki pants. "Sure you don't." She moved her head from side to side, stretching her neck. "Well, Mr. Box, I'm tired. Thanks for keeping me company on the trip."

He unglued his eyes from her tits. "Where are you going to stay?"

"With my cousin. I'm waiting for her to get here. She's gonna pick me up in a few minutes."

"Is there a way we can stay in touch—" His cell phone rang.

Trenda laughed and pointed at the phone clipped to his belt. "Ask *her* if it's cool for us to keep in touch."

His smile waned after reading the number on the caller ID. He then let the call roll to his voicemail. "You are a real comedienne." He took a step closer to her. "I'd *really* like to see you again, Mya."

She looked down the street and saw the lights still on in the Barnes & Noble bookstore a few blocks away. She turned back to him. *He is just beggin' to get pussy whooped.*

She gave him a flirty smile. "I'm not in the business of home wrecking," she pinched his hairy cheek, "but you are cute…like a big ol' teddy bear."

He let go of his suitcase, grabbed her hand and kissed it. "I want to see you again. You won't be sorry if we hook up, I promi—" His phone rang again. "Shit!"

She removed her hand from his as he angrily ignored the call and put the phone back on his hip. "You need to go handle your business, sweetie." She looked at her watch. It was 10:21 p.m. "I have to go meet my cousin at Barnes & Noble."

"Can I have your number?"

She zipped up her jacket, ending his view of her cleavage. "No…but I have your number. I might surprise you with a call one day."

Dejection camped out on his face. "How can I change that 'I *might* call' into an 'I *will* call'?"

The blare of the train's horn as it prepared to leave the station briefly deafened them. "Your odds are good; you left a good taste in my mouth."

For a moment, she thought he was going to pass out from the shock on his face. "Uhhh, wow!" He blushed like a teenager. "That's uhhh…that's real good to know."

A taxi pulled up to the curb. "Hey, Mr., did you call for a cab?"

She looked at Box. "That must be your ride. I'll holla at you later."

The cabbie got out, opened the trunk and waited as

Box put his suitcase, garment bag and laptop inside. "Don't forget about me."

She turned away from him. "Go home before your girl beats your ass."

After the cab rolled past her, she cut across the street and headed for the Waters Edge Hotel. *Damn, it's gonna be nice to sleep in a real bed.* As she walked past Barnes & Noble, the smell of coffee coming from the Starbucks upstairs from the book store filled her nostrils. *If I wasn't so tired, I'd go get me a cup. After that long-ass train ride, all I wanna do is get some decent sleep, on a decent bed.*

She felt the comfort of her butterfly knife in her jacket pocket as she crossed Jack London Square en route to the hotel. The salty sea air coming off the Bay replaced the aroma of fresh brewed coffee as she approached the lobby doors of the hotel. She entered and crossed the well-lit lobby and stopped at the reception desk. The sound of a hip-hop song at a very low volume greeted her instead of a person. *Where is the receptionist? I just know there has to be somebody workin' tonight.* She spotted a dome-shaped silver bell on the counter next to a rack full of brochures and maps of local events. She rang it twice.

A split second later, a woman dressed in a navy blue skirt, white blouse and navy blue blazer emerged from the French doors to Trenda's left, which opened into the large bar/lounge area. "I'm sorry for the wait. I had to unlock the kitchen door for the food service delivery."

She opened a drawer and placed a card key inside. She tossed her shoulder-length hair over her shoulder. "I'm Lollie. May I help you?"

Her L'Oreal Sea Fleur-colored nails went well with her cognac-brown flesh. "Yeah. You have any rooms available?"

She typed a few strokes on her computer keyboard. "Name?"

I better stick with my alias for now. "Mya Collins."

"Smoking or non-smoking?"

"It don't matter—whichever one is cheapest."

She looked up from her screen and grinned. "I heard that." She typed a few more strokes. "I have a smoking room down on the first floor and a few other rooms on the upper floors."

"The first-floor room will work. How much is it?"

"$179 per night."

Trenda did a double-take as she rummaged through her bag for her wallet. "*Dayum!* Is that for *one* night?"

Before the receptionist could answer, a huge, acne-faced security guard entered the lobby from outside. "Hey, Lollie! How's it goin'?"

Lollie looked at the large white-faced clock mounted on the wall behind the reception desk, then back at the guard. "Where the hell have you been? You were supposed to be here fifteen minutes ago. I had to leave the desk and go let the food serviceman in. You know I'm the only one here tonight."

A crimson hue filled his alabaster face. "Sorry 'bout that. I saw some kids messin' with cars in the back parking lot. I chased 'em out. It took a while for me to check the cars to make sure they didn't get vandalized."

She rolled her eyes. "Next time, call me on your walkie-talkie and let me know what's going on."

He slapped himself on the forehead. "Awww, man! I left it in the back of my truck. I'll be right back!" The large ring of keys hooked to his belt jingled loudly as he hurried out to his truck.

Lollie shook her head and returned her attention back to Trenda. "I apologize. Usually we are much better organized, but the other girl that usually works with me went on maternity leave last week and the manager got sick and went home early."

As nice as your tits are, you could nurse the hell out of a baby. "It's all good. Now, how much did you say the room is?"

"It's one-hun—"

The guard came back carrying two sodas. "Hey, Lollie! I got you a Sprite!"

She huffed. "Jason, can't you see I'm with a *customer?*"

He let his gray eyes roam Trenda's curves. "Ohhh, I'm sorry!" He placed the soda can on the counter in front of Lollie. "I'm gonna go check on the deliveryman. I have my walkie-talkie now so buzz me if you need me."

Trenda removed her wallet and put her bag on the floor next to her. "They need to give you a serious pay raise."

"That's what I keep telling my boss." She smiled, picked up the soda and turned back to the computer screen. "Now, let's get you taken care of. Did you want the room?"

Trenda tapped her wallet against her palm. "I dunno… that price is a little rich for my blood. Especially since I only plan on stayin' for one night."

Lollie stood and leaned on the counter. "Did you just get in town?"

"Yeah. This is my first time here. I'm from Baltimore."

"Really?" Lollie's eyes lit up. "My grandparents live by Druid Hill Park!"

"No shit? I used to hang out there all the time when I was a kid. That was the spot!"

After ten minutes of small talk, the women found they had a lot in common. "I hope you don't mind me asking, but how did you get that cut on your face?"

"My ex-boyfriend. He's the reason I decided to get away so fast. He's one of those jealous, controlling assholes."

Lollie crossed her arms across her chest and shook her head. "I can't stand bastards like that."

They heard the sound of Jason's dangling keys as he left the kitchen and crossed the lounge. Trenda yawned as Lollie walked back behind the counter. "Let me quit runnin' my mouth so you can go get some sleep."

"I am tired, but I think I'm gonna have to find a cheaper place."

Jason entered the lobby and smiled at Lollie. "You okay? Want me to go get you something to eat?"

She began typing and read the screen. "No thanks, Jason. Why don't you go make sure that exit door on the third floor is closed tight? I found it open a few times last week."

He hitched up his utility belt. "Will do! I'll be back in a few."

Once he was out of sight, Trenda chuckled. "You know his ass is sprung on you, right?"

Lollie grinned as she finished typing. "Oh yeah, he's been trying to take me out for the past six months. Even after I told him I'm not down with the swirl, he's still tryin'."

"Don't knock it; he might become your own personal ATM card."

They both laughed. "Shit! His broke ass can barely afford to put gas in his raggedy pickup truck." Lollie stood, leaned over the counter and lowered her voice. "Check this out, if you are only gonna stay one night and can check out before eleven in the morning, I'll let you stay for sixty dollars—cash."

Ohhhh, my girl is a straight hustler! Trenda recognized Lollie's game. "I'm down with that. How you wanna do this?"

Lollie looked at the clock on the wall. "Meet me by the ice machine down the hall in five minutes and I'll let you in the room. I can't give you a card key though, so you'll have to prop the door open if you have to leave the room."

Trenda picked up her bag. "Cool." She then walked outside. Across the street from the hotel, a line of cars played loud music in front of the movie theater. *What's that all about?* She continued toward the ice machine as one of the cars—a yellow Mustang—pulled into the middle of the street and began burning rubber in a circular pattern while the crowd yelled and danced. Trenda stood captivated as she watched the spectacle.

"Do the youngsters in Baltimore 'go dumb' like these fools?"

Trenda jumped at the sound of Lollie's voice. "No! What the hell are they *doing?*"

Lollie opened the door of a room across from the ice machine. "They are starting up a 'sideshow.'"

"*Sideshow?* What's that?"

Lollie looked around, pushed the door open and waved Trenda in. "That's when a bunch of knuckleheads, with nothing else to do, get together somewhere in the town and just start acting and driving crazy."

"Don't they worry about the police?"

"Shit no. The cops are too busy chasing murderers and dope dealers." Lollie closed the door and turned on the lights. "As a matter of fact, the police station is only a few blocks up the street."

Trenda put her bag on the queen-sized bed, then sat down beside it. The well-designed and nicely insulated room muffled the loud sound of the sideshow revelers. She took her wallet out of her bag. "I really appreciate you hookin' me up."

Lollie walked over and peeked out of the eggshell-colored drapes. "Don't sweat it. All you have to do is make sure you don't use the phone and leave before ten. As long as you do that, it's all good. I have a housekeeper I work with that will clean it up, no questions asked, for a few bucks."

Trenda grinned, removed sixty dollars from her wallet and handed it to Lollie. "Thanks for the hook-up, girl. I'm likin' Oakland already."

Lollie tucked the cash into her bra. "Don't sweat it." She checked her watch. "I gotta bet back inside before Jason thinks I've been kidnapped. If you're not busy Wednesday night, you oughta go to Fats with me."

Trenda unzipped her jacket, revealing her white satin bra. "What's *Fats?*"

Lollie glanced at Trenda's impressive breasts. "It's the hottest club in the Bay Area. Wednesday night is Ladies Night."

"I might just do that. You got a number?"

Lollie walked over to the nightstand, picked up the complimentary notepad and wrote down her number. She handed it to Trenda. "Here you go. That's my cell number. Give me a call about nine. I'll pick you up."

"Thanks, I'll holla at you." Once Lollie was gone, Trenda stripped off her clothes, pulled back the covers, fell back on the comfy bed and burrowed under the covers. As her eyes tried to close, her cell phone rang. She rolled toward the nightstand where her phone lay. "Who the hell is this?" She picked up the phone and read the caller ID. "What the fuck Griff doin' callin' me this late at night?" She shut the phone off. "He can wait until tomorrow."

Fourteen

As Trenda fell asleep, Darius and Tyrone sat in their unmarked patrol car going over the files on Piper Langford's case. Tyrone shook his head as he read her medical reports. "Damn! Trenda fucked her *up!*"

Darius took a swallow of his Dunkin Donuts coffee. "Yeah, Trenda hit her in the back of the head so hard, she gave her a small skull fracture. It messed up Piper's vision…she's gonna have to wear glasses from now on."

Tyrone stuck the reports back into the folder and placed it on the dashboard. "Her rich-ass daddy is raisin' all kinds of hell. I heard he got his golf buddy, the mayor, involved."

"Yeah…I saw Captain Kelly and that evil Internal Affairs investigator, Mrs. King-Bey, walkin' to his office together. I could tell they were talkin' about me by the way they got all quiet when I passed them up."

Tyrone tossed his empty coffee cup out the window. "I heard they are gonna bring us in for questionin' in a few days. Shit is gettin' hot. If they find Trenda, we are done."

Darius picked up the folder off the dashboard and went through the papers. "I think I have a backup plan to make sure they don't find her…did you read the psychological profile on Piper? She has some serious violence issues."

He handed Tyrone the three-page psychological profile he had managed to obtain on Piper. Tyrone scanned the sheets. "Damn…she tried to stab her third-grade teacher with a pencil, hit a girl in the head with a bat in seventh grade, tried to run over her boyfriend in her senior year of high school, and threatened to kill her college professor after he gave her a B-minus on a final. This Piper chick has issues."

Darius nodded. "She has issues and an influential family that kept her out of jail. I'm gonna make use of her 'issues' with your help."

"What you mean with *my* help?"

"I'm gonna need you to pay a visit to Piper and give her some information on Trenda I'm sure she would love to have."

"Why you want *me* to go?"

"Because, dumb-ass, she saw *my* picture in that video, remember? She might fuck around and come at me and I'll have to hurt that crazy bitch. Besides, I have a plan."

Darius waited as Tyrone let that information simmer in his mind. He knew his partner didn't have much choice. Tyrone exhaled loudly. "So, what's this *plan?*"

Trenda woke up refreshed a little after nine. The cut under her eye and her sore shin felt much better. The wound on her shoulder still ached with vigor. Pissed that she had no clean clothes left, she showered and put on the pink sweatsuit she wore a few days ago. She stood in the mirror, combed her short afro and inspected her cut. *At least it's starting to scab over…please don't leave a scar!* She went to the nightstand, unplugged her phone and checked Griff's message. "Trenda! That muthafucka, Darius, came by my place lookin' for you. I dunno what kinda shit you in, but I don't need you bringin' me no mo' heat. Do me a favor and stay the fuck away from here 'til you get yo' shit straight."

Trenda rubbed her hand through her hair. *I knew that cockhoundin' bastard Darius was gonna start some shit.* She then exhaled, packed up her stuff and left the room. Outside, the crisp morning air blowing off the estuary greeted her. The not unpleasant scent of salty sea air surrounded her. Halfway across the plaza, the aroma of eggs, bacon and toast rode the air. She followed her nose and entered Momma's Café.

The hole-in-the-wall eatery had a reputation for having the most massive and tasty omelets in the city. After being seated and ordering a Denver Omelet, Trenda sat back and admired the quaint café. Copper pots and kettles hung from the rafters of the rustic-style restaurant. Pictures of the mothers of many of the happy patrons adorned the walls. One would think a woman ran Momma's Café, but the owner was actually a giant black man named Jesse Martin who served as owner and head chef. His recipes, handed down from his Lake Charles, Louisiana-bred mother, had won numerous awards.

So busy looking at the decorations, Trenda failed to notice the admiring stares of a middle-aged man across the room from her. After reading a plaque on the wall from the mayor, Trenda's eyes met her admirer's eyes. She gave the walnut-colored man a glint of her emerald eyes and white smile. *Hmmmm…sexy black man…I love a man with a little gray hair on his temples.*

The mid-sized man adjusted the color of his charcoal gray suit, folded his copy of the *Oakland Post*, stood and walked over to Trenda's booth. "Hello, lady." He extended his manicured hand to her. "Please excuse my staring at you, but didn't we meet at the Guitars and Sax's jazz concert last month in Sacramento?"

Trenda smirked and shook his hand. *The game don't change; just the date and location.* "No, handsome…I just got in town last night."

He was genuinely shocked. *"Really?* I mean…it would be impossible to mistake those eyes." He dropped his stare. "My name's Walter Secrease…and you?"

She noticed the lack of a ring on his ring finger. "I'm Mya." She favored the scent of his cologne. His diction told her he was an educated man. She sat back and watched him adjust his burgundy tie. "So, how was the concert?"

He gave her a puzzled look. "Hmmm? *Concert?*"

"Yes…the concert you claim you saw me at."

"Ohhh…*that* concert…well…" He took a deep breath and smiled. "You got me. I used that as a line to get your attention."

She took a sip of her water, folded her hands on the table and looked in his ebony eyes. "Well, it didn't work…but your cute dimples did."

His smile expanded. "That's good to hear! I was hoping I wouldn't have to take off my jacket and flex for you."

"Don't assume…I might just ask you to do that." The waitress arrived with her meal. Walter stood aside as Trenda's food was served. She sprinkled hot sauce on her omelet. "Did you already eat, Dimples?"

"Yes. I was getting ready to leave until I saw you."

She chewed a small bit of her omelet. "Am I holding you up or are you gonna sit down and keep me company?"

He beamed. "You must be a mind reader." He walked over to his table, got his paper and briefcase, returned and sat across from her. "So, what brings you to Oakland, Mya?"

"I needed a change from the D.C. lifestyle so I hopped a train and here I am."

"Are you always that spontaneous?"

She sipped her orange juice and licked her lips. "When it comes to most things, I am…why do you ask?"

He sat back, laced his fingers and placed them in his lap. "I asked because I'm in a spontaneous mood."

She read a twinkle of devilment in his eyes. "You gotta be more specific, Dimples…what is it you want?"

He checked his watch and grinned. "I had a meeting to attend this morning but I've decided I'm not going. I'd rather take you for a ride and work on our relationship."

She cocked her head. "*Relationship?* I heard you brothas in Cali were different but *damn!* You movin' *waaaay* too fast for me."

He laughed. "I don't believe in beating around the bush—I like the direct approach."

She watched him laugh as she added jelly to her toast. "I'm serious…what do you think my boyfriend would say if he heard you talkin' like that?"

He shook his head. "I know you don't have a man… no way would he let you come way out here by yourself. You might have *had* a man, but I'll bet my first born you are single."

"I see…what's your first-born's name?"

"I have no idea. He/she hasn't arrived yet."

"You tryin' to tell me, that a man your age, and as handsome as you are, has no kids?"

He stroked his salt-and-pepper goatee. "Not all fifty-year-old men have kids, no matter what your favorite talk shows have you thinking."

Her jaw dropped. "*Fifty!* I was thinking that maybe you were in your late *thirties!*"

"You can thank my gym membership, no smoking, no drugs and my daily jog around Lake Merritt for that."

She finished her hash browns. "Okay, Dimples. So let's say I agree to go with you. What would be on our agenda?"

He hunched his shoulders. "I have no idea…we could start by getting in my car and driving. See where we end up."

Her pussy senses were tingling. Something about Dimple's confidence made her clit wiggle. She pushed her half-eaten omelet away from her. "Okay, Dimples. Let's take a ride." She stealthily eased her butterfly knife out of her bag and slipped it in her pocket. *He might be a little charmin' but I'll be damned if I let him get me somewhere way out and try and rape me.*

Trenda got her wallet and summoned the waitress. Once she arrived, Walter handed her a twenty. "Keep the change."

They exited the café and he walked her across the street. Among the many cars parked along the curb, she mentally tried to guess which one was his. She spotted a new-ish, silver, convertible BMW with a license frame that read: Secrease Funeral Homes. (510) 555-8888. He slowed his pace as they approached the car. "Let me put your bag in the trunk."

"Death business must be good these days."

He gave her a curious look as he closed the trunk. "What?"

She pointed at the license plate frame. "Is that where you work?"

He looked at the license plate. "You could say that. My

brother and sister help me run the family business." He walked her to the passenger side, clicked the electronic keypad, unlocked the door and opened it for her. "What do you do for a living?"

She eased into the supple gray leather seat. "I used to do hair back in D.C."

He grinned and rubbed his short haircut. "Cool! I was looking for some new hands to put in my hair!"

"Yeah, well, first I have to find a salon that's hirin'."

"I see…" He closed the door, walked to the driver's side and entered the car. "There's plenty of hair salons out here in the Bay Area."

After he started the car, she lowered her window. "Before I find me a job, first I have to find a place to live."

He removed a pair of dark shades from inside his jacket pocket and put them on. "Damn…you really did just up and leave, didn't you?"

Her mind flashed back to the image of Piper sprawled on the floor of her kitchen, twitching. "Yeah, I seriously needed a change in my life."

He lowered the convertible top, then removed a cell phone from his hip. "Let me make a quick call; then we are out of here."

She listened as he called someone named Byron and informed him to have the meeting without him and he would check in later. She lowered the visor mirror and checked her face. She fingered the cut on her face. *It looks a hell of a lot better than it did a few days ago.* She closed the visor as he wrapped up his call. "Where are we goin', Dimples?"

"Let's see. Since you are new in town, I feel obligated to help you get yourself settled. How about we go find you a place to stay?"

She looked at him out the corner of her eye. "Hold up, Mr. Man. I didn't say I needed *you* to take care of me…I can find a room on my own."

He smiled, looked over his left shoulder and pulled into traffic. "Relax, my red-headed friend. I don't do this for *every* fine woman I see in a café. I just happen to be in a very good mood after closing a big deal."

"Oh really? What kinda deal?"

"We just finalized a deal to open up two more funeral homes in Los Angeles and one in San Francisco today. That's what the meeting I was supposed to attend is about, closing the loose ends."

She could almost smell money on him. "That's all good. How many funeral homes do you have?"

He drove them north on Broadway, into the heart of downtown Oakland. "We now have five. I run the combination funeral home and crematorium here in Oakland and the other funeral home in San Jose. My brother and sister are going to run the two new locations in L.A."

While sitting at a red light, an AC Transit bus pulled next to them. The burly driver looked into the convertible, made eye contact with Trenda and gave her a wink. She smiled, then turned to face Walter. "Okay, Dimples, where is the woman that helps you spend all ya cheese?"

He laughed aloud. "You are the epitome of a hardcore, East Coast sista. I'm going to have to teach you how to mellow out."

They drove past several blocks lined with car dealerships. "Don't give me that shit. Quit tryin' to change the subject. Where is yo' woman?"

He shook his head as he pulled to the curb. "You ever heard the saying, 'Don't look a gift horse in the mouth'?"

She turned from him and watched as they stopped in front of the Hotel Oakland. "Why you stoppin' here?"

He shut off the engine. "You need a place to stay, right?"

She looked up at the sixty-year-old, fifteen-story-tall, historic hotel. "You must be trippin'! You better find me a Motel Six! I'm not tryin' to spend all my money at once. I bet it cost a grip to stay here."

He exited the car. "You should spend more time enjoying life instead of always looking for flaws in everything."

She got out before he could open the door for her. "I'm not playin'. I'm on a serious budget."

He removed her bag from the trunk, handed it to her and waved his hand toward the entrance. "Please…just come inside."

Walter nodded to the uniformed door attendant, let her enter the brass and glass revolving door, and then followed. She took in the ambiance of the majestic lobby. A huge crystal chandelier hung from the tan, vaulted ceiling. A large multicolored wall tapestry hung on the wall next to the registration desk. Well-placed paintings and small sculptures gave the lobby an elegant feel. The young Lebanese woman at the counter greeted them with a smile. "How may I help you?"

Walter smiled and took Trenda's hand. "Do you have any vacancies?"

"Yes we do." She looked from him to Trenda. "This is a non-smoking hotel; is that okay?"

He let go of Trenda's hand, reached inside his jacket pocket, removed his wallet and looked at Trenda. "Well?"

Trenda was no stranger to receiving favors from men. The look in Walter's eyes reminded her of Reverend Swearington, the husband of her mother's best friend. She recalled how, at the age of sixteen, he used to gaze at her when no one was looking. She could read the lust in his eyes as they examined her well-developed breasts. Once, as he drove a vanload of kids to the Six Flags amusement park, he continually glanced in his rearview mirror at her. Trenda found she liked the attention the short, skinny, high-yellow, forty-eight-year-old man paid her. She purposely and repeatedly made eye contact with him, sometimes stretching in her seat giving him a nice view of the tight T-shirt covering her womanly tits.

Inside the amusement park, he did his best to stay close to the sexy teenager. While standing in line to get on the roller coaster, he managed to get paired with her. Once the ride started, he let his hand fall on the part of her thigh her denim shorts didn't cover. She recalled how the feel of his hand made her virgin pussy quiver. She made a meek effort to remove his hand, but he instead let it creep between her thighs. As the roller coaster sped over the rails, she screamed along with the rest of the kids—although her scream was from passion. The Reverend rubbed the hot spot between her legs fast and hard as she reached her first orgasm. As the roller coaster approached the end of the line, she looked at him and saw a nervous grin on his sweaty face. She looked in his lap and saw a dark stain near his zipper.

She saw him quickly untuck his shirt to hide the stain, dig in his pocket and come out with a fifty-dollar-bill. He pushed it in her pocket just as their car stopped for them to get off. She gave him a shy smile, hopped out of the car and went to join her friends. From that moment, she knew men were meant to be her playthings.

"Mya? Is that okay?"

Trenda shook off the flashback. "Yeah, that's cool. I don't smoke."

The receptionist did her thing and minutes later produced a pair of electronic card keys. She placed them on the counter. "How will you be paying for the room?"

Trenda gave him a crooked grin. "Well?"

He opened his alligator-skin wallet and placed a Platinum Visa card next to the room keys. "I'd like to pay for two weeks in advance."

Trenda glanced at the invoice as it printed out. *Goddamn! The rooms here are two-hundred-twenty dollars a night! Dimples just spent over two grand and don't know me from shit!* After he signed for the purchase, he attempted to pick up the cardkeys. She intercepted them. "I'll hold on to *both* of these, thank you."

He smirked as they walked toward the elevators. "I didn't expect you to give me a key to your room just because I paid for it."

She pressed the button for the eighth floor. "Bullshit! What man would pay for a room—an *expensive* room— and not expect some sort of compensation?"

"You're right; I do expect something from you."

She crossed her arms. "I'm listenin'."

He checked his watch. "I expect you to hurry up and put that bag away so we won't be late for our next stop."

The elevator doors parted and they stepped inside. "*Next* stop?"

"Yes. This is just the first leg of our journey."

The elevator swiftly carried them to the eighth floor. "When did this turn into a journey? I thought this was just a spontaneous moment?"

He followed her out the elevator. Recessed track lights in the ceiling illuminated the plush, light gray carpet and eggshell-colored walls. "Our moment isn't ove—" His cell phone rang. He flipped it open and looked at Trenda. "Hold on one sec."

She crossed the hallway and looked into the chrome-framed mirror mounted to the wall. She listened as he tried to answer a flurry of questions. *Sounds like Dimples is needed at the meetin' after all.*

He told the person he was talking to, to hold on. "Hey, Mya, I have to run across town for a while." He pressed the button to call the elevator, went inside his jacket pocket and removed a gold-plated business card holder. He ejected a card and handed it to her. "Meet me in the lobby at six so we can go to dinner. You can reach me at the number on the card."

Before she could answer, the elevator arrived. He put the phone to his ear as the elevator doors opened. He stepped inside, pressed the lobby button and rejoined his conversation. She hitched her bag up on her shoulder as he waved at her through the closing doors. She gave him a smirk, then walked down the hallway to room 8011. After entering the room, she placed one cardkey in her bag and the other on the coffee table. She placed the bag on the ottoman in front of the leather wingback chair, grinned and looked around the impressive room. *Walter, you just might have earned a piece of pussy.*

She picked up her bag and opened the door to the bedroom. A pair of mahogany nightstands flanked the king-sized bed. Two gold lamps sprouted from the wall over the bed. She opened her bag, removed her dirty clothes and put them in the clothes hamper in the closet. The adjoining bathroom was huge. She stood in front of the dual marble sinks and inspected herself in the large lighted mirror.

I have gotta get some more clothes. She returned to the bed and removed her cell phone and charger. She turned on her phone and plugged the charger into the outlet next to the bed. She attempted to check her messages and found her phone service was interrupted. "Shit! I forgot my bill was due last week." She checked the cash in her wallet. "I had better get outta here and handle my business."

On the way out of the hotel, she spotted a sign in the lobby pointing to the laundry room. She also made note of the sign pointing to the pool and spa. *Damn! This joint is straight up five-star!*

Several hours later, after paying her cell phone bill and purchasing a few new outfits, Trenda returned to her room. She changed into a new pair of tight, bell-bottom jeans and form-fitting white blouse. Once she'd put away the rest of her new clothes, her phone rang. She answered without checking the caller ID, thinking it was Walter. "Hello?"

"Hey, bitch…remember me?"

Piper's heavy voice chilled her ear. She hung up and sat heavily on the bed. The phone rang again. *Piper.* Trenda shut the phone off, lay on her back and exhaled. As it had all her life, trouble found her again. From taking the blame for stealing hair relaxer so her friend Sandy wouldn't get in trouble with her abusive father to being beaten by her mother for bringing home a stray cat and feeding it—trouble seemed to have always had her on speed dial. She closed her eyes. "I'm sure glad there's a few thousand miles between me and that nutty ho."

Fifteen

Two hours before calling Trenda, a stranger knocked on Piper's door. She adjusted her new eyeglasses and looked into the peephole in her door. "Who is it?"

Darius's partner, Tyrone, stepped back so she could get a good look at him. *I sure hope this crazy plan works...* "My name's Eric. I'm looking for Piper Langford."

She opened the door and studied the dark brown man eye-to-eye. "How do you know me?"

"We have a mutual friend...Trenda Fuqua."

The rage he saw behind Piper's glasses was unmistakable. "That bitch is *not* my friend. What do you know about her? Do you know where she is?"

Tyrone looked up and down the hallway. "Can we go inside and talk?"

Piper studied him a moment longer, then stepped aside and let him in. She motioned toward her sofa. "Have a seat."

He watched the bulky woman flop onto the loveseat across from him. Tyrone mentally went over the script he and Darius had formulated. "I'm gonna get straight to the point; Trenda used me. We were supposed to get married next month but instead, she conned me. She managed to get the passwords to my bank accounts and credit cards. She pretty much drained all my money and fucked up my credit. I also found out she returned the engagement ring I gave her and kept the cash...told me she was havin' it resized. She is fuckin' *scandalous.*"

Piper's face soured. "*Married!* She was going to *marry* you?"

He gave a solemn look and nodded. "Yes...she accepted my proposal a few months ago."

Piper's right eye twitched. "How could she do that? I didn't even know she liked men until I saw her on video giving this cop a blowjob. We had been lovers for over a year!"

Yeah, this big bitch is gettin' worked up now! Tyrone feigned shock. "*What?* She told me you were just a friend she shared an apartment with. No wonder she never let me come here to visit. We always had to stay at my place when it came time for us to be intimate."

Piper rose to her feet. "She didn't tell you about *us?*"

"No, nothing more than her letting you move in with her."

Piper slammed her beefy fist on top of an expensive Bose speaker, causing it to fall off its base. "That bitch! This is *my* place! I let her homeless-ass move in with *me!*" She paced the floor. A tear puddled behind the right lens of her glasses, then ran down her cheek. "I gave that cunt everything. *Every-fucking-thing!*"

He wiped his hand down his face. "I can't believe she played both of us! I should have known what kind of person she was by the way she talked about you."

Piper walked over and loomed over him. *"What?"*

He scooted back from her. "Well...I don't think you want to—"

"Tell me, goddammit!"

I'd better get up before her fat ass pins me down. He eased up off of the sofa. "She used to always tell me how you were such a...fool... she bragged about how she had you pay for all her stuff. I told her she was wrong for doing it, but she said that's the only thing you were good for... made me wonder what she said behind *my* back."

She reeked with fury. "I'll kill that fucking cunt! After all I did... goddamn her!"

Tyrone watched in horror as she picked up an ink pen off of the coffee table and repeatedly jabbed it in her thigh. He then went into his back pocket and removed a folded piece of paper. "I see we want the same thing... I want her ass to *pay.*" He un-folded the sheet of paper and held it out to Piper.

She stopped stabbing her thick thigh and glared at him. "What the hell is that?"

"I did some investigatin' and found out where she went." She dropped the pen, snatched the paper out of his hand and began reading it. "That's the information on the train she took to Oakland, California a few days ago. I was gonna go find her myself, but I have to go to Florida and take care of my mother for a while. She's in the late stages of cancer."

Piper held the paper as if it was the map to a treasure. "That's okay; I'm going to go find her myself. I *might* leave her alive long enough for you to spit in her face before I kill her ass."

He saw a small, dark stain blooming under her tan stretch pant leg covering her thigh. *Shit! This broad is nutty as a Snickers bar!* "Good! She deserves whatever she gets." He watched as Piper mumbled to herself while staring at the sheet of paper. "Uh…I'll check with you later."

Piper looked at him with eyes of the insane. "You do that."

He cleared his throat. "Okay…my cell phone number's on the paper. Keep me posted." He slowly walked away as she stared at him. Once outside the door, glad the cell phone number was one of the two dummy accounts set up for them by Darius, he hurried out the apartment and called his partner. "Man, that broad is *certifiable!* I damn near feel sorry for Trenda."

The following morning, Piper woke up early with the slip of paper Tyrone had given her still in her hand. She unfolded the crumpled paper as she walked over and logged onto her computer. "I'm coming for you, bitch." She navigated the internet until she came across a listing of Oakland area private detectives. She settled for the firm with the most impressive website and dialed their number.

"Dickerson Investigations, Nancy speaking, may I help you?"

Piper pulled her robe closed over her huge naked tits. "Yes, I need to find a missing person."

"Okay, let me get you over to one of our investigators."

"Get me to your *best* investigator."

"Well…*all* of our investigators are former federal agents and are all quite qualified."

A vein on Piper's forehead began to throb. "Look, I want the best. I want the investigator with the *best* success rate. The cost is of no concern."

After a pregnant pause, Nancy cleared her throat. "Although all of our agents have impressive success ratios, I think Mr. Martin would be able to assist you. I'll put you through to him. What's your name, ma'am?"

Piper sat back in her chair and waited to be connected. *Funny how fast you can get what you want when money is mentioned.* "Fine. My name is Ms. Langford."

Seconds later, a baritone voice spoke. "Hello, Ms. Langford. I'm Hank Martin. I understand you need help finding a missing person?"

After an hour-long conversation, Piper emailed Hank a few pictures of Trenda, provided him with the Amtrak train information, gave him the number of her Platinum American Express Card, and told him to put a rush on finding her. "Like I told your receptionist, I don't care how much it costs, I want her found."

Hank looked at his computer screen and saw that her credit card was valid and grinned. "I just moved your case to my top priority. I'll report back to you within seventy-two hours. Good day, Ms. Langford."

Sixteen

Trenda did her best to shake off the phone call from Piper, but that anger-filled voice haunted her. Instead of letting it handicap her, she got up, gathered up her dirty laundry and went downstairs to the laundry room. While waiting for her clothes to finish, she went into the lobby, picked up one of the complimentary copies of the *Oakland Tribune*, and scoured the want ads. *I'd better find me some kinda job until I can get my hustle on.* None of the minimum wage jobs appealed to her. The majority of the other jobs required a college degree she lacked. She sighed, folded the paper and put it back on the large, round coffee table. She removed her cell phone from her small Coach bag. *That bitch probably has filled up my voicemail.* Relief washed over her once she saw that Piper had left her no messages. A grin fixed her lips once she saw it was almost five. "Time for me to get ready for dinner with Dimples."

After gathering her laundry, she went to her room, put the clothes away, showered and stood naked, trying to decide what to wear. She settled for an ankle-length tan, denim skirt, a copper, tight, short-sleeved V-neck sweater and a pair of sexy copper pumps. As she put on her gold hoop earrings, the phone on the nightstand rang. She answered. "Hello?"

"Hello, Red! I'm starving so hurry and get your butt down here to the lobby."

She chuckled at how he had picked up the nickname people in her family called her because of her severely red hair. "And what makes you think I'm going with you? I might already have a date, Mr. Man."

"Well, if that's the case, he'd have to come eat at the bar because I have reserved a table for *two* at Dorsey's Locker. I hope you like soul food."

The thought of greens, yams, smothered steak and cornbread made her stomach giggle. "You're lucky I like soul food…I'll be down in a minute."

Ten minutes later, after packing her butterfly knife, wallet and cell phone in her bag, she stepped off the elevator and strolled into the lobby. Walter slowly rose from the couch across from the reception desk, admiring his date. "Hmmmm! You clean up *well!*"

She put a hand on her hip and let the other dangle her Coach bag on her side. "I *always* look good."

His eyes lingered on her cleavage. "I agree…" He removed her hand from her hip and held it. "Now I get to go show you off."

She allowed him to lead her out to his car. After letting her in, he got in and drove them to the locally famous soul food restaurant. A mostly Creole staff greeted them and sat them in a cozy booth near the back of the room. The low lights gave the place a cozy and romantic feel. She gazed at the pictures and oil paintings of Black cowboys, entertainers and sports figures that decorated the walls and rafters. She picked up the menu. "This place smells like my granny's kitchen on a Sunday after church."

He unfolded his white cloth napkin and spread it on his lap. "Oh, so you were raised in the church?"

She briefly looked at him over the menu. "Why? You surprised?"

"Kind of. You sound a little too edgy to be a church-girl."

"How are church-girls supposed to be? Like those girls on *Little House on the Prairie?*"

He smiled and picked up his menu. "Not exactly. I see you as more of the 'Aunt Esther'-type from the *Sanford and Son* show; preach the gospel one minute, slappin' you upside the head with the Bible the next."

She lightly kicked him on the shin under the table. "Don't get hurt up in here, okay?"

A gorgeous, freckle-faced female server broke up their fun. She placed a small basket of fresh cooked cornbread squares on the red-and-white checkered tablecloth. "You folks ready?"

Trenda's smile waned as she watched a pair of Oakland Police officers enter the front door. *Oh, fuck! I wonder what they want?*

Walter gave Trenda a curious look. "What's wrong?"

She covered her face with the menu. "Nothin'. You go ahead and order. I'm still tryin' to decide what I want."

He studied her a moment longer as the server waited patiently. "I'll have oxtails, greens and macaroni and cheese."

She lowered the menu enough to spy on the cops as they looked around the room. Suddenly, a short, heavy-set, grandmotherly-looking woman emerged from the kitchen. Trenda watched as the cops broke out in smiles and took turns hugging her. *Cool, looks like they're just here to eat.* She was surprised to see Walter watching her intently. "What's wrong with you?"

"You looked like you were ready to jump up and run!"

She gave the menu a final glance. "You are straight trippin'." She addressed the server. "I'll have smothered steak, green beans and yams."

The server scribbled on her pad. "Can I get you guys anything to drink?"

He let his eyes fall from Trenda's face to the wine list on the table. "Do you drink red wine, Mya?"

"Yeah. It's okay."

He turned to the server. "Can we have a bottle of Monticello Pinot Noir?"

She scribbled their beverage choice. "Great! I'll be back shortly with your order."

Trenda reached into the red plastic basket, grabbed a square of warm cornbread and took a small bite. "This is pretty good!"

Walter looked over his shoulder as the cops picked up

their call-in order and left. He turned back to Trenda. "Did those policemen make you nervous?"

The piece of cornbread she was buttering broke in half and fell on her plate. "Hell no…why you say that?"

He stared at her for a moment, then got a piece of cornbread out the basket. "Because your eyes got as big as hubcaps when they came in."

She avoided his eyes and nibbled her cornbread. "Whatever." Even when she wasn't sought by the law, her fear of police was hard to mask. She had seen the ugly side of cops for most of her life. On occasion, she'd been arrested for no reason and released in exchange for a hand job, or in extreme cases, fellatio. Once word got out about how good her mouth was, bad cops up and down the Eastern seaboard hounded her—none as much as Darius. She gave him a defiant look. "Takes more than a couple of cops to make me nervous."

He chuckled at her hardcore look. They made small talk over the meal and a bottle and a half of wine. Two hours later, after discussing the cremation process, another cop strolled in. She did her best to remain calm and not tip off Walter she was scared as shit. Anxiety awakened her need for comfort. Her favorite form of comfort was a nice stiff dick. She kept Walter's attention away from the officer by reaching across the table and touching his cheek. "Did you get these cute dimples from your mother or father?"

He took her hand and kissed it. "You can thank my late mother for them."

She rubbed her thumb on his hand. "Sorry to hear about your mother."

"It's okay. She lived a long full life. She passed away five years ago at the age of ninety-nine."

"Wow! Is your father still around?"

"Nope…he passed a year after my mother. He was one hundred and two."

She sensed his good mood waning. She changed the subject. "Well, I'm full. Thanks for the food. Are you ready to leave?"

He removed the napkin from his lap, wiped his mouth and tossed it on the table. "Yes. Are you sure you don't want to try their peach cobbler?"

She rummaged through her purse for her compact mirror. "I'll pass. My ass is already wide enough."

He shook his head and grinned as he reached for the bill. "You have *got* to be kidding. You have a body any woman would die for."

She smiled, then applied a fresh coat of copper lipstick. "I bet you say that to all your girlfriends."

He removed his credit card and placed it on the table along with the bill. "No, I can honestly say I don't say that to *all* my girlfriends."

Her smile widened as the cop left with his meal. "Well, at least you're honest. That's a good sign. I like to keep it real in everything I do."

He summoned the server with a wave of his hand. "I'm glad to hear that. Makes it a lot easier when both parties are on the same page."

She looked him in the eyes. "And just what page are you on, Mr. Secrease?"

He stood and took her hand. "Depends on which book you're talking about."

"I'm not sure if you read the same books I do. Maybe we'll find out back at my room."

He grinned broadly. "I sure hope so."

Twenty minutes later, they arrived at her hotel. Walter pulled into the underground parking garage and opened the door for Trenda. She looped her arm in his as they talked about his life back in D.C. She fed him lie after perfect lie about how she was raised in New Jersey and moved to D.C. after her parents divorced. She amazed him with tales of how she had to drop out of college after her mother hurt her back at work and had to go on disability. He shook his head in amazement as she unlocked the door to her room. "It sounds like you have seen a lot."

She kicked off her pumps and turned on the light. "Been through a lot, too." She picked up the TV remote and handed it to him. "Have a seat. I'll be right back."

He sat on the sofa, put the remote down, put his hand on her hip and ran it down her curvy thigh. "Hurry up and bring all this back to me."

Her mild wine-buzz helped cracked the door open for her inner nymphomaniac to peek her head out. She allowed him to stroke her thigh a few times as she gave him a half-smile. "You ain't ready."

He placed his other hand on her round mound of an ass and pulled her to him. "Bet."

She put her hands on his shoulders. "You better be careful, Dimples…you keep rubbin' on me and I might have to test that fifty-year-old heart."

He caressed her soft backside. "In that case, it's a good thing I just had a physical last week and was given the okay for strenuous activities."

She loosened his tie, removed it and tossed it on the floor. The firm grip of his large hands ignited her furnace. "You talk a good game."

He found the zipper on the back of her skirt and unzipped it. She unbuttoned his shirt and massaged his shoulders. He eased the skirt down over her bulging hips. The sight of her black boy-shorts made his lump jump. "Damnnnnnnnn," he whispered as she stepped out of the skirt. "Your legs are *flawless.*"

Her eyes narrowed and she switched into "Freak Mode." She broke his grip, removed her earrings and put them on top of the TV. She then faced him and slowly pulled her tight shirt over her head. A satisfied smirk filled her face as his eyes fixed on the black satin bra covering her big, perky tits. She slowly rubbed them as he hurriedly unbuttoned the cuffs of his shirt. "Like what you see?"

He licked his lips. "I sure do. Do they taste as good as they look?"

She watched him remove his shirt and toss it to the floor. His wife-beater showed off his fit and trim physique. "I don't know; let me see." She unstrapped her bra and let her luscious breasts free. As Walter gawked at her, she lifted one to her mouth and sucked the nipple. "Mmm-mmm, tastes good to me…"

"Oh, shit!" He stood and tried to grab her. "My turn."

She stepped forward and pushed him back down on the bronze- colored sofa. "Not so fast…" She stepped back and sucked the other nipple. The way his eyes followed her put a tingle in her valley. "I'm not done yet."

She proceeded to lick and suck her hard black nipples as Walter's hand fell to his lap and gripped the log behind his zipper. She loved to tease. Making men's knees buckle was her specialty. She slipped a finger in her mouth, then into her panties. She watched Walter gulp hard and kick off his shoes as she fingered her wet opening. He stood, unbuckled his pants and let them fall to the floor. "Shit, Mya!"

She tossed her head back and let her narrowed green eyes lock on the bulge in his navy blue boxer briefs. "What's wrong, Dimples?"

He stepped out of his slacks. "I'll give you two guesses but the first one doesn't count."

She walked over, placed her hand on his chest and pushed him back on the sofa. "Does it have anything to do with this?" She placed her hand on the swelling below his navel.

He closed his eyes as she gently caressed his package. "I think you are about to find out."

She moved in to kiss him on the neck. "What do you—"

Before she could finish, he quickly stood, grabbed her by the waist and flipped her onto the sofa. In another quick move, he removed his boxers and fell between her legs. "Enough of this teasing shit."

She looked into his eyes and read the burning lust in them. *This fool done lost his mind!* "Easy, baby. We got all night."

He ignored her as his breathing increased. He reached between them and yanked off her boy-shorts. She only had a second to see his black snake before he positioned himself and slammed inside her wet box. She watched with a mixture of passion and annoyance as his eyes closed in ecstasy. Rarely did Trenda give her pussy to any man. She enjoyed sucking a dick almost more than she did penetration. Thus, her pussy was in great shape, nice and tight. It had been eaten—by men and women—almost more than it had been fucked. The feel of his above average-sized penis slamming into her produced a waterfall in her vagina. His energy surprised her. Just as she'd almost accepted him taking her, he pulled out, stood and picked her up. "We need more room."

She put her arm around his neck. "I see you can be a bad boy."

He gave her a cold look. "You damn right." He carried her into the bedroom of the suite and tossed her onto the bed. "Bend your ass over."

She narrowed her eyes, nipples and clit throbbing. *I see he wants to be The Man.* She grabbed a pillow, put her ass in the air and looked at him over her shoulder. "Like this, Daddy?"

She watched as he gazed at her soft ass and pussy.

"Yesss…just like that. Daddy likes that." He crawled behind her, lined his dick up with her wet lips and slid inside. He gripped her hips and fucked her hard and fast.

She laid her head sideways on the pillow. *He is fuckin' like the Energizer Bunny. I got something for his wannabe bad boy ass.* She lifted her head and looked back at him. "Is that all you got? Fuck…me…*harder!*"

He gritted his teeth as a bead of sweat ran down his nose. "Shut up and give me my pussy!"

She pushed back to meet his every stroke. "C'mon, Daddy…fuck your nasty bitch good!"

His guttural moan told her she had pushed his buttons. His grip tightened on her hips as he pounded harder. She used her pussy control and gripped his dick. "Fuck yes! Shit, this pussy…is…*good!* I love…fucking…my nasty bitch!"

She reached back and rubbed her clit. "More! Tear this pussy up, Daddy!"

The bed rocked and shook with each violent, pleasurable stroke. She felt his hands grip her ass cheeks firmly. He huffed and puffed. "Daddy…is about to…teach you… a lesson…for being…a bad…bitch!"

She almost laughed. *Listen to this proper-talkin' fool tryin' to sound all hard.* "What you gonna do—"

A split second later, she felt his dick pop out of her and land on her ass hole. The coat of her woman juice on his junk acted as a natural lubricant. "Time to punish you." He pushed a little harder and his dickhead disappeared inside her tight ass.

Oh helllll no he didn't! She gripped the apricot-colored bedspread in both hands as he pushed deeper in her anus. Having her ass reamed was nothing new; but it was normally reserved as a treat for deserving lovers. Her clit fluttered as the pleasant pain stoked her fire. "Mmm-mmm, Daddy...take...that...assssss..."

His pleasure was so intense, he could no longer utter a decipherable phrase. He pounded her ass while pulling her hard nipples. "Ohhhhhhhhhhhmyyy Goddddd! MYAAAAAAA!"

She enjoyed the feel of his heavy balls hitting her swollen pussy. "Yesssssss...let your bitch...know...how you...like this ass..."

She felt him tremble and grip her hips tighter. His dick felt like a steel fist as he fucked her faster. He moaned as the first drop of pre-cum leaked into her ass. "Oooooooooooooooooo fuck! Gon-nnnaaaa cummmmmm!"

Trenda bit down, and screamed into the pillow as his hot juice pumped into her. She climaxed as he held her tight and convulsed. He then collapsed on top of her, catching his breath. Moments later, she felt his rod fall out of her. She gently rolled him off of her. "Damn, baby! It felt like you nutted in me for five minutes!"

He wiped sweat off his forehead and tried to catch his breath. "That was some of the best ass I've *ever* had!"

"Thank you, baby." She stood and felt his warm sperm leaking out of her. "I'm glad you enjoyed yourself, but you really wore me out. I need to take a bath and go to sleep."

He wiped his face, then checked his watch. "It's barely eleven o'clock." He reached for her hand. "How 'bout we shower together, take a nap and have round two?"

She eased her hand out of his and stroked his cheek. "I'm sorry, honey. I know that once my head hits the pillow, I'm done for the night. Can I get a rain check?"

His half-flaccid, sticky-dick moved as he looked at her full lips and firm, perky tits. He took a deep breath through his nose and exhaled. "I guess a rain check is better than a solid, 'No.'"

She pressed her hands to his chest as he tried to get out of the bed. "Hold on...let me clean you up."

He placed his hands on her curvy hips. "Damn, Mya... your body is...mmmmmmm..."

She looked in his lap and saw his dick growing. *Oh, no, my brotha; we are done for the night.* She smiled and backed out of his grip. "I'll be right back." She walked into the adjoining spacious, gold and white bathroom. She removed one of the neatly folded white washcloths off the gold rack next to the shower stall. She looked into the green eyes in the mirror as she lathered up the washcloth and smirked. *Let's see, I'll fuck him again in a few days but make him wait for some of this monster head. Gonna have to get Mr. Dimples sprung real good since he don't mind openin' his wallet.* Pleased with her plan, she went to wash him off and send him home.

Seventeen

The following morning, Trenda went out to breakfast. *Damn, that dude must really love this cafe*, Trenda thought as a middle-aged, gray-haired man took dozens of shots of Momma's Café. *And that's the biggest lens I have ever seen.* She turned away from the photographer, entered the eatery and read the want ads over breakfast. She folded the classified section, placed it on the table and exhaled. *Sometimes I wish I would have gone to college…*images of the beatings she took from her parents soured her mood. Although she was an A student in junior high school, it still wasn't enough to please them. Her parents believed everything the media told them. She was routinely accused of things she didn't do. Most of the time it was just because her parents thought all kids were into sex and drugs. Her room was searched without warning on a regular basis. They just knew they were going to find drugs or condoms. Sometimes they would stage their raids while she had company, embarrassing her to no end.

By the time she got to high school, she started making

their prophecies come true. Her motto became, "I'm damned if I do and I'm damned if I don't." After the many commando raids by her parents, she became skilled in the art of sneaking and stashing. The only reason she experimented with drugs was to get back at them. She would bring her weed home and hide it in the hollowed-out middle of her Bible. She would grin as he parents searched everywhere in her room except for the Bible laying in plain sight on her nightstand.

Sneaking boys *and* girls in and out of her room became a game to her. She became so brazen she would have sex while her parents held Bible study in the living room down the hall from her bedroom. She had her first girl-on-girl sexual experience as a sophomore. One afternoon after field hockey practice, she and her friend Tracy were the last to shower. Tracy couldn't keep her brown eyes off Trenda as the soap suds covered her sexy, mocha-brown body. Trenda knew of the rumors of her being a lesbian, but she paid it no mind. Tracy, six inches taller than Trenda and a few pounds heavier, moved closer and closer. By the time Trenda noticed, Tracy was inches from her with stone-hard nipples. Trenda read the freaky desire in her eyes. Seconds later, her inner nympho took over. She bent over and sucked Tracy's waiting tits. Tracy moaned and fingered Trenda's hot pussy. Trenda returned the favor and they fingered each other until they climaxed. They enjoyed each other for another three months until Tracy moved away to Utah.

Trenda felt a tickle in her twat as the memory faded. She took a sip of tea and her phone rang. She looked at the unknown number, hesitated, then answered. "Hello?"

"Hey, girl! Wassup? This is Lollie."

Trenda relaxed at the sound of a friendly voice. "I'm eatin' breakfast. What you up to?"

"Gettin' ready to run around for a while. Did you find a place to stay yet?"

"Kinda…I'm stayin' at the Hotel Oakland for a minute."

"Damn! You're goin' straight first class, I see."

Trenda smiled. "I have a new friend to thank for that."

"Oh really? Sounds like you found a Suga Daddy."

"I don't know yet, but so far so good. I still need to find me a job though. You know you can't count on a pussy-whooped man forever."

Lollie laughed. "You got that shit right! That reminds me; I might have a job for you if you're interested."

Trenda set her fork down. "Hell yeah! What you got?"

"Remember I told you about Pam, the girl I normally work with who is out on maternity leave? Well, after I bitched to management about how overworked I am, they asked if I know of someone that could cover for Pam. It's only until she comes back in about six months, but at least you'll have something until you find a better gig."

Trenda barely let her finish telling her about the job before she said, "Hell yeah I'll take it! When can I start?"

"Cool! I'll give you the manager's number and you give him a call. He will hook you up. It only pays ten bucks an hour to start, but the job is easy as hell. The only fucked-up part is your days off are scattered. I have Wednesdays and Saturdays off. The good thing is they are cool about you taking other days off—without pay—if there is somebody to fill in for you."

"Girl, I owe you big time! Thanks a lot."

"Don't sweat it. The manager's name is Jeff Wright. His number is 510-555-6776. He's expecting your call. It'll be good to have somebody to talk to at work besides Jason's horny ass."

Trenda laughed as she took a pen out of her purse and wrote down the number on a napkin. "I told you if you give him a taste, he'll pay your rent."

"Bullshit! I'll use a carrot before I'd fuck that weird bastard. Hey, you still gonna come to Ladies Night at Fat's with me tonight?"

Trenda recalled her offer. "Oh, yeah. Can you still come pick me up?"

"Yeah, I can do that. I'll swoop you up around nine. The dress code is casual so you ain't gotta get all fine."

"Girl, you a nut! Give me a call when you are on your way and I'll meet you at the curb in front of the hotel. Thanks again for the job info."

"Like I said, don't trip. We gonna kick it, I promise. Peace."

"One love." Trenda hung up with a grin as the mid-morning sun warmed her face through the restaurant window. For the first time in years, she felt like things could finally be going right in her world. She had a new friend she felt she could trust and the beginnings of a new lifestyle. She thought about the troubles she'd left behind in Baltimore. "Fuck you, Darius; fuck you, Piper. Y'all ain't ever gonna see me again."

Eighteen

That same afternoon, thirty minutes before the start of his graveyard shift, Darius entered the police officers' locker room. "What the fuck is this?" he asked himself as he removed the envelope taped to his locker. He opened the envelope and read the note inside.

Officer Kain, report to Captain Kelly's office at the start of your shift.

He looked around at the other officers filing into the locker room before folding up the note and putting it in his pocket. *I wonder what the hell is going on?* He looked across the aisle at Tyrone's locker. It had no note, but there was no sign of Tyrone. Usually both he and Tyrone arrived a half hour early. He removed the cell phone from his hip and called Tyrone. Once it rolled to Tyrone's voicemail, he hung up. He closed up the phone and put it back in its belt holster. *I don't like this.* He headed out the locker room and to the elevators.

While waiting for the elevator, Terrence from Internal Affairs rounded the corner. Darius did a double-take. "Yo, Terrence, what's goin' on?"

Terrence stopped then looked around. "Man, the shit has hit the fan. Do you know the girl Piper Langford that Trenda cold cocked? Her father had the mayor to call Captain Kelly personally and demand he find out who assaulted Langford's daughter."

"I wonder if that has anything to do with the note I found on my locker telling me Captain Kelly wants to see me."

Terrence looked around nervously. "I'm willing to bet it does. Your partner is already in Kelly's office with one of our agents."

"Please tell me it ain't that cold-hearted Ms. King-Bey."

Terrence nodded. "That's the one. I suggest you say as little as possible…you might wanna get yourself an attorney since they saw you on video. I think they are going to put you two on administrative leave."

The elevator arrived. "Good lookin' out."

"Watch your ass, Darius…watch your ass."

He stepped inside and watched Terrence walk away as the doors closed. On the way up, he wondered what his grandfather, Floyd Kain, would think if he saw the grandson he raised having his dick sucked on tape by a known felon. While on duty no less. He recalled how he was raised in New York as a child. After his heroin-addicted mother overdosed and left him with his father, a big-time pimp, he grew up watching how his father handled women.

At the age of ten, a dope addict murdered his father

in a robbery attempt. Darius watched the entire event take place from the backseat of his father's Jaguar. The junkie shot Darius's father in the head as he tried to get out of the car. His father's favorite prostitute, Suga, jumped out and ran, leaving Darius. The junkie then pointed the gun at Darius and pulled the trigger. Fortunately, the cheap pistol jammed. The junkie took Darius's father's watch and wallet before running off. From that point on, his grandfather, a former Baltimore police chief, moved him to Baltimore and raised him.

Many of his grandfather's friends in law enforcement still helped Darius out as a tribute to the love they had for Floyd. Darius went on to join the police academy as soon as he was able. His hatred of lowlifes did little to keep him from morphing into one himself.

Before getting to the eighth floor of Captain Kelly's office, he had an epiphany. He grinned and pressed the button for the fifth floor. He exited and headed for the Human Resources office. Before entering, he called his brother in Hackensack, New Jersey. *Damn, I hope his spot is available!* "Wassup, Pete?"

"Not much, bro. What up?"

"Hey, is anybody renting out your vacation cabin in Avalon?"

"When?"

"Right now."

"No, it won't be booked for a few weeks, around May first. Why? You know somebody that wants to rent it?"

Perfect, Darius thought as he brainstormed. "Yeah…I wanna use it for a week or two."

"Cool, but I'm gonna have to charge you a lil' somethin'; this economy is cuttin' into my profits."

"No worries…but I need you to keep this on the down-low—I don't want Beverly to find out."

"Ahhhh, I see! You're trying to sneak some pussy…boy, don't have Beverly come up there and tear my shit up!"

"I got this; don't trip. I'll meet up with you later, get the keys, and give you your pay. Peace."

Satisfied his alibi was in motion, he entered the office and smiled at the middle-aged Human Resources supervisor. "Hey, Cathy, how have you been?"

She returned his smile. "I have been great, Darius. How can I help you?"

"How much vacation time do I have on the books?"

She typed his info into her computer. "It appears you have two weeks available."

"I wanna take both weeks, starting today."

She adjusted her cat-glasses. "You sure you want to use it all?"

He knew that if he took vacation, he would be under none of the restrictions he would be if he were placed on administrative leave. "Yup, both weeks."

She punched in the necessary information and printed him out a vacation verification slip. "Here you go. Are you going anyplace in particular?"

He folded up the sheet and put in his pocket. "Yes, gonna go to Jersey and stay in my brother's beachfront rental. Spend the next couple of weeks enjoying the sound of the waves."

"Have fun, Darius."

He smiled. "I'm gonna do my best." He left and went back to the elevators. At the eighth floor, he stepped off and walked down the corridor leading to Captain Kelly's office. He straightened his Pierre Cardin shirt, then knocked on the door. Captain Kelly's baritone voice sounded. "Come in."

He pushed the door open and walked inside. He nodded at the solemn-faced Tyrone. He glanced at the attractive hot chocolate-colored woman seated next to Tyrone, then to Captain Kelly. "Wassup?"

Captain Kelly cleared his throat, ran his large brown hand through his gray hair and looked into Darius's eyes. "We have a problem." He looked in the direction of the Internal Affairs investigator. "Agent King-Bey?"

The petite, slightly graying woman rose from her seat. She walked over and extended her hand to Darius. "Hello, Officer Kain. I'm glad you made it."

He looked into her brown eyes and shook her soft hand. "Thanks." He walked over and sat down in the last vacant chair across from Captain Kelly's desk. "So what's this all about?"

An hour later, Darius and Tyrone exited Captain Kelly's office. On the way to the elevator, Tyrone grimaced. "I knew it! I *knew* you fuckin' with that bitch Trenda was gonna get us in trouble!"

Darius pressed the elevator button. "Shut the fuck up.

You ain't no better; out there beatin' on those hoes like you some kinda pimp when they don't wanna suck you or fuck you for free." He followed Tyrone inside. "Now, quit trippin'. I told you they ain't got shit without Trenda's statement. They can't prove me and her weren't involved in a sexual role playin' game. Anyway, all they got you on anyway is suspicion of being an accessory."

Tyrone glared at him. "Did you forget Trenda mentioned me robbing her? How about Diamond? Did you forget how he choked to death on his own blood after we beat his ass in the Lighthouse? That bitch was there, remember? I sure as fuck didn't." He pounded his fist on the elevator wall. "This thirty-day suspension is nothing compared to what'll happen if they find her and she snitches."

Darius relived that night when he and Tyrone kidnapped the area's largest heroin dealer, Diamond, and ended up beating him to death after he decided he wasn't going to pay their new extortion rates. Unfortunately, Trenda was riding with Diamond when he and Tyrone forced them into the back of their patrol car. Trenda never asked what happened inside the Lighthouse while she was locked in the patrol car, but Darius knew she was smart enough to figure out what had happened— especially after she had watched them stuff Diamond's carcass into his car.

The following day, the media reported that Diamond's body was found burned to death in the front seat of his car, blocks away from the Lighthouse. "Relax…you're still getting paid. Consider it a month-long paid vacation.

Besides, our voices were so muffled on that video that they need a statement from Trenda or else all they can do to us is discipline us."

"I don't see how you were able to file for vacation today, right before this meeting. You skated on getting put on leave like I did."

"That was pure luck; I ran into Terrence on the way to Captain Kelly's office. I'm gonna find Trenda before they do. They have no idea she's in California."

"How can you be so damn sure? For all you know they could have her locked up already and be waiting to build up enough evidence to fire our asses or throw us in jail. What if they find her and she tells them *everything*... including information about our 'side jobs'?"

Darius shook his head. "As bad as the captain wants me gone, he would have let Agent King-Bey grill us alive. They have nothing. Trust me. I can tell by how pissed off he was when I handed him my authorized vacation slip."

Tyrone mulled it over as the elevator came to a halt. They stepped out and entered the parking garage. "You take shit too lightly. Not everybody has a wife with a good job to fall back on, and a grandfather that left them a large chunk of money."

Darius swung around, grabbed Tyrone by the front of his Morehouse college sweatshirt and pushed him up against a concrete pillar. "Don't you *ever* bring up my family again, you hear?"

Tyrone tried, but couldn't break Darius's grip. "Get your fuckin' hands off me!"

Darius glared at his partner a moment longer, then let go. "Just keep your mouth closed and lay low. I'm gonna give you a call later."

Tyrone straightened out his sweatshirt and pointed at Darius. "You had better be careful about who you grab on! I ain't one of them dope fiends or hoes you like fuckin' with."

Darius smirked, turned and walked toward his Escalade. "Like I said, I'll call you later, partner."

Nineteen

Fifteen minutes before her appointment, Trenda walked through the lobby and found the manager's office. "Thanks for working me into your schedule and interviewing me this afternoon, Mr. Wright," Trenda said as she stood and shook hands with the manager of the Waters Edge Hotel.

The lanky, middle-aged man's blue eyes sparkled in appreciation of Trenda's sexiness. "No, thank *you!* It would be great to have you come aboard. You come highly recommended by Lollie." He opened a manila folder on his desk and glanced at the applications inside. He then closed it and returned his eyes to Trenda's tight gray sweater. "I do have a few others I was considering for the job, but what the hell." He smiled and did his best to keep his eyes on hers and not the outline of her impressive nipples. "I'd like to formally offer you the job, Mya."

Trenda returned his smile, adjusted her short charcoal skirt and shook his hand again. "I really appreciate this. What's the next step?"

"Come in tomorrow morning at eleven and meet with Connie, our HR person. She will have a few forms for you to fill out. Once that's done, come to my office and I'll get you set up to train with Lollie."

She shouldered her black purse. "Great! I'll be here at 10:59 in the morning."

"I look forward to it. Have yourself a great rest of the day, Ms. Collins."

Trenda sauntered out, making sure Mr. Wright got a nice view of her swaying hips. *This is workin' out cool!* She exited the building, pulled out her cell phone and called Lollie. "Hello, Lollie, guess what; I got the job!"

Lollie laughed as she sat in the manicure shop having her nails done. "I told you, you would get it! Now we really gotta celebrate tonight. Remember, I'm gonna pick you up at eight."

"Cool. I'll be ready." Trenda hung up and walked to the bus stop on Broadway. While waiting for the bus, her cell phone rang. She read "Secrease Funereal Home" on the caller ID. "Hello?"

"Hello, Sexy Red! What are you up to?"

"Not much, Mr. Man. Just leaving a job interview. What's goin' on?"

He smiled, leaned back in his chair and put his feet up on his desk. "No wonder I couldn't find you. How did it go?"

She sat on the bus stop bench. "It went well. What did you mean when you said you couldn't find me?"

"I stopped by the hotel this morning with intentions

to take you to breakfast with me. Unfortunately, when I got there I got no answer when I knocked on the door."

Trenda's smile faded. "So, you just showed up this morning without callin' me?"

"Well, yes. I wanted to surprise you."

Oh hell naw, this fool got shit twisted. "Uhhh, Mr. Secrease, I really do appreciate what you did for me, but I'm not real cool with you just showin' up on my door-step unannounced."

"Hmmm, I had no idea my little surprise would cause so much drama."

Trenda was no fool. She knew she had to be diplomatic in her approach. "It's all good, I just hope that from here on, you can give me a lil' heads-up. You feel me?"

"No need to be paranoid. I assure you I have no in-tention of stalking you. Anyway, where are you? Are you free to hang out with me for a while?"

This fool is lyin' his ass off. I can already tell he's one of those possessive brothas. "I'm kinda busy right now; can I get with you later?"

He paused, then sighed. "Okay. I was hoping to take you to Sausalito with me for a late lunch."

She read a mix of disappointment and annoyance in his voice. "I'm sorry, Boo. I have a second job interview to go to. As a matter of fact, I have to get movin' so I won't be late. I promise I'll make it up to you, okay?"

"Okay. Call me when you're done. I'll be waiting. I've been craving a taste of you all day."

She smiled at his admitted horniness. "Is that right?

Well, in that case, let me get goin' so I can help feed that craving. I'll call you later." She hung up, saw the bus approaching and got to her feet. She rode the bus back to the hotel thinking of how she wanted to further wrap Mr. Secrease in her web of pussy. Back at the hotel, she picked up a copy of the *Oakland Tribune* and a copy of the *Classified Flea Market* from the lobby and took them to her room. She entered her room, kicked off her shoes, turned on the TV, sat on the sofa and began scanning the papers' classified sections. *I need to find me a cheap ride. I hate not having my own transportation.*

She circled a few promising car ads, then yawned. The low hum of the room's heater coupled with the sound of Oprah's voice and the muffled sound of the traffic below her suite caused her to nod off. She put the papers on the coffee table, stretched out on the sofa and slept.

She awakened three hours later to the sound of her cell phone ringing. She sat up and picked her phone up off of the coffee table. She read the name on the caller ID, grinned, then answered. "Hello?"

"Wassup, girl? It sounds like you either just woke up or just got some dick!"

"You are half right. Just finished takin' a nap and need some dick."

Lollie laughed. "You are a natural *fool!* It's about ten to seven. I'll be there at eight to get you. I'm about to drop my sister off in El Cerrito, then I'll be heading your way. Are you gonna be ready?"

El Cerrito...now why does that name sound familiar?

"Yeah, that's cool. I'm about to get ready now. I'll meet you in front at eight." She ended the call and walked back to her bedroom. A smile etched on her face. *Now I remember; Mr. Box lives in El Cerrito!* The memory of the sweet taste of his cum almost made her salivate. She stripped off her clothes, entered the bathroom and started the shower. *I'll have to call up my teddy bear and see how he's doing.*

Forty-five minutes later, after a hot shower, Trenda stood in the bathroom mirror admiring how nice her jeans made her hips and ass look. Even the scratch on her face was healing well. It was barely noticeable. The cut on her shoulder looked better, but was still a bit sorer than it should be. She went to the closet and put on her new Triple 5 Soul, form-fitting navy blue hoody. It fit her like a mini skirt over her tight jeans. She sat on the bed and pulled on her black Steve Madden Latchh Boots. After packing her butterfly knife into her boot, some cash in her front pocket, she put her fake ID, room key, and cell phone in her small black leather purse. On the way out, she gave herself the once-over in the mirror mounted over the room's desk. She smiled. *Trenda, you are ready to get ya party on!*

Five minutes after exiting the hotel, a black Nissan Pathfinder on large chrome rims pulled up to the curb. Trenda took a step back until she recognized Lollie's cute chocolate face. She walked up to the window. "Damn, I didn't think you would be rollin' like *this*."

Lollie tossed her freshly blow-dried hair over her

shoulder. "I might be a broke bitch, but I still ride like I'm ballin'!" They laughed as Lollie unlocked the door. "Get on in."

Fifteen minutes later, they pulled into the parking lot of the local hot spot, Fats. The club was a one hundred-year-old Victorian house that was converted into a restaurant/nightclub a decade ago. Situated on the border of downtown and the ghetto, the club drew a mixed economic crowd. Trenda followed Lollie down the side of the club. A line of people waited to enter a side door, which led into the club. The front door took you upstairs to the seafood restaurant. The food was almost as legendary as the club's female deejays. Lollie pulled down the hem of her burgundy sweater dress. It fit her like a condom. She fished through her small burgundy Juicy Couture purse, which hung from her shoulder, for her ID. "What you think so far, Mya?"

Trenda's mind was on the knife in her boot and the burly bouncer at the door with the metal detector wand. She noticed that when he talked with the women trying to get in, he only waved the wand from their tits to their crotch. She looked from the bouncer to Lollie's round ass. "What do I think about what?"

"What do you think about my town so far?"

"So far it's all good! I got a job, the weather is way better than in Baltimore and I've met some cool people…hell, I might just make this my new home."

Lollie opened her purse for the lusting bouncer to

inspect. "That's real cool! I need me another runnin' buddy."

Trenda looked up into the bouncer's eyes and gave him a flirtatious smile. "How you doin' tonight, muscles?"

The bouncer barely glanced in her purse. He instead focused on her eyes and tits. "I'm real good…especially now that you just showed up."

She stepped closer to him and opened her purse. "I hope all the bouncers here in the Bay Area are as sweet as you!"

Her hypnotic eyes and smile successfully distracted him. His wand dangled at his side. "Where you from?"

She closed her purse. "Jersey. I just moved here a few weeks ago. Maybe you can recommend a few places where I can have some fun?"

He glanced at the line of people waiting to get in. "Yeah, holla at me on your way out." He winked at her. "I'm sure I can help you out with that."

Trenda walked away. "Thanks, boo. I'll be lookin' for you later."

So smooth was her move, no one noticed she got away from the bouncer unscanned. The cityscape-painted walls vibrated from the bass rumble of the music. The tall, bronze Amazon-like DJ shook her six-inch blonde Mohawk to the beat. Lollie took Trenda by the hand. "C'mon, let me buy you a drink to celebrate your new job!"

Trenda basked in the lusty gazes of the men. "Sounds

good to me. Let's do this." She followed Lollie to the unique bar. It was all chrome and glass, adding to the old building's modern look. A gigantic fish tank full of colorful, tropical fish sat on display behind the circular bar. Three bartenders navigated the bar. Trenda sat down on one of the chrome and leather barstools. She watched Lollie sit down and adjust the cups of her black bra. "I like that dress!"

Lollie swept her hair back and smiled. "Thanks. I got this from Old Navy a while back." She waved to the heavyset Asian bartender. "What you drink?"

Trenda scanned the shelves around the enormous fish tank. "I dunno; I might just have a glass of wine."

Lollie shook her head. "Hell no, not tonight."

The bartender came over and placed his hands on the bar. "What can I get you ladies?"

Lollie opened her purse and removed her wallet. "Bring us two Mojitos, please."

"Ohhh! I ain't had a Mojito in a *long* time." Trenda barely heard her phone ring as she rocked to the music. *Who in the shit is callin' me?* She took her phone out of her purse and saw she had missed a call from Walter. *I'll call you later, baby.* She put the phone back into her purse.

Lollie smiled. "That's right; turn that phone off, girl! We're here to have some fun."

The pair of hotties turned down half a dozen dances before their drinks arrived. Trenda read the room and saw a few thuggish men in the crowd. The same kind of men she did dirt with back in Baltimore. The familiar itch for the excitement and thrills of the street life gripped her. Something about the danger of running pounds of marijuana or kilos of cocaine from place to place was damn near orgasmic in intensity to her. She watched a short dark man with a mouth full of gold teeth approach. He reminded her of the first person she delivered drugs for—her first boyfriend, Ishmael. After promising to buy her a leather jacket if she delivered an ounce of cocaine to a customer in D.C., she gave in and did it. He bought her a bus ticket and sent her on her way. The danger of getting caught kept her aware, alert and intoxicated. That feeling never left her. It really became an addiction after she started getting paid to make those deliveries. The dark man walked up and stood in front of Trenda and Lollie. He flashed his gold grill. "Wassup, hotties?" He studied Lollie's long legs. "I'm Geno. Most folks call me King Gee. Can a King buy his Queen a drink?"

Lollie waved her glass at him. "No thanks, King. I'm good."

He looked at Trenda's tits, then her face. "How 'bout you, sexy?"

Trenda took a sip of her drink. "Oh, no thanks. I'm not good at being second choice."

King Gee held his hands up and feigned shock. "C'mon now, baby! I could only choose one of you ladies at a time."

Trenda lifted her eyebrows. "Looks like you shoulda made a different choice."

He cocked his head, removed his oversized sunglasses and read her green eyes. "Where you from, baby? It sounds like you from back east."

"Virginia."

Lollie glanced at Trenda, grinned and took a sip of her drink. Trenda returned her grin as King Gee split his gaze between the two sexy women. He turned back to Trenda. "I thought that's where you was from. I got folks back there. I can tell that accent anywhere." He held his glass of Hennessy high enough for both women to see his large, diamond-studded, G-shaped ring before downing the liquor. "Why don't you ladies come sit wit' me and my folks at my table?"

Lollie set her drink down, placed her hand on Trenda's thigh and tossed her hair back. "No thanks, Playa. Me and my girl are just gonna chill right here."

He watched Lollie pat Trenda's thigh and grinned. "Oh, I see…y'all *together*." He placed his glass on the bar next to Trenda. "I'm feelin' that. Ain't nothin' wrong with some girl-on-girl lovin'."

Lollie removed her hand, traded her grin for a glare and pointed at him. "You really need to get out of our business and go on back to your table."

He smirked. "Baby, you betta be cool; you don't know who you fuckin' wit'."

Trenda crossed her leg, giving herself easy access to the knife in her boot. "Look, *Gina*, you are fuckin' up my buzz. You needs to go."

He snapped his head toward Trenda. "*Gina?*" He grabbed his crotch. "Shorty, my name is *Geno* and I'm all man! Don't make me pull this muthafucka out and show you."

Trenda bounced her crossed leg as she watched one of Geno's friends approach. "That shit-colored suit is bad enough; don't pull out your tired little dick and embarrass yourself some more."

Lollie laughed. "That's *clownin'!*"

King Gee grimaced and took a step toward Trenda. "Bitch, don't get ya ass beat up in here!"

She eased her hand toward her boot as King Gee's friend wrapped an arm around him and pulled him back. She looked Geno in the eyes. "Call me another bitch."

The bartender waved frantically for the bouncer. The people on the small dance floor looked over to see what was going on. Lollie got out of her seat, stood in front of the restrained, angry King and looked at his friend. "You had better talk to your drunk-ass friend before I call my brothers down here to handle his ass!"

A pair of large black bouncers ran over and stepped in between Lollie, King Gee and his friend. Trenda remained seated and calm. Threats from wannabes like King Gee didn't faze her. In the circles she ran in, his type were a dime a dozen. She had left plenty of men like him leaking blood. As the bouncers escorted King Gee and his friend back to their table, he glared at Trenda. "We ain't done, ho. We got business!"

Trenda downed the rest of her drink, smiled and showed him her middle finger. "Whatever."

Lollie fixed her hair and looked at Trenda as the folks on the dance floor went back to partying. "I'm sorry, girl. That fool is always here actin' like he's runnin' shit. Usually this spot is real cool."

Trenda shook her head. "Don't trip. I ain't gonna let that trick mess up my night." She waved to the bartender. "This round is on me."

While standing near the dance floor, halfway through their second drink, a pair of men approached. Lollie adjusted the hem of her short skirt. "We got company on the way."

Trenda nodded and sipped her drink. "I see."

The two average-looking, late twenties-aged men smiled, split and each addressed one of the women. The shorter of the two light brown men offered his hand to Trenda. "Hey, lady, wanna dance?"

Trenda watched the other dude repeat the same offer to Lollie. She smiled, placed her drink on a vacant table and took his hand. "You must know this is one of my favorite songs."

Trenda and Lollie captivated not only their dance partners but also all those around them. They danced with each other almost as much as with the men. The way Trenda moved was like watching a hypnotist swinging a coin. Her body melded with the music. She had a move for every beat of every song. Even the sexy dancer

Lollie had to admire the way Trenda's body undulated. By the end of the third song, Trenda's dance partner showed signs of exhaustion. He wiped his bald head with his sweat-soaked handkerchief. "Damn, baby! You give a brotha *serious* workout."

She winked at him as she sauntered off the dance floor. "Yes I do."

He licked his lips, grinned and attempted to follow her to her seat. "I wanna hear more about your workout routines."

Trenda saw King Gee glaring at her from the dance floor as he danced with a young blue-eyed, blonde-haired woman dressed in the finest of urban street wear. She rolled her eyes at him and looked at her dance partner. "Maybe some other time, sweetie. I'm gonna go to the ladies room."

"How 'bout I wait for you right here?"

She watched Lollie and her partner exit the floor. "Not tonight, baby. I'm just here to kick it with my girl."

He removed a pen from the inside pocket of his suit jacket. "Can I give you a call later just in case you change your mind?"

She picked up her drink, saw all the ice had melted into the last of her Mojito and put the glass back on the table. She read the pleading in his horny eyes. "Give me your number instead."

He sighed. "Okay, I'll be right back. I'm gonna go find a piece of paper. Don't you go anywhere!"

She looked over his shoulder and waved Lollie over. "I'll be here."

She watched Lollie go through a similar separation anxiety issue as she tried to escape. After accepting the man's phone number, she finally got away. She sat next to Trenda. "Damn, you ever run into a dude that can't take a hint?"

Trenda elbowed Lollie in the side and nodded toward King Gee and his alabaster friend on the dance floor. "There's one right there. That fool's been givin' me the evil eye all night."

Lollie looked at him just as he caught sight of them. He pulled the blonde closer to him and gave them a smug, see-what-y'all-missed-out-on look. "Oh, no! I just *know* he don't think we care about him and that skank!"

Trenda made eye contact with him and laughed. "I actually think he does." She saw his smug look transform into a scowl. She kept her eyes on him, made sure he was watching, then leaned over to Lollie. She then held her thumb and forefinger about an inch apart. "I guess that gray-girl don't mind him having a little dick."

Lollie bent over and laughed. "That's fucked up!"

Trenda laughed as King Gee stopped dancing, grabbed his girl by the wrist and headed toward them. Trenda let her hand dangle next to the boot containing her knife. "Looks like little dick has something else to say."

Lollie stopped laughing, stood and looked around. "Where the fuck the bouncers at? I ain't about to let this fool get all up in my face again."

Trenda sat calmly nodding her head to the music. "Don't worry. If he starts some shit, I'll give him some shit."

Something about the calmness in Trenda worried Lollie. She spotted a bouncer leaning on the bar and waved to him. Meanwhile, King Gee stopped a few feet short of Trenda. His date gave them a nervous smile. The odor of brandy ran out of his mouth, and a bit splashed out his glass as he spoke. "I see you still ain't learned how to respect a man." He staggered, grabbed his belt buckle and glared at her. "Maybe I need to take this off and give yo' ass a whoopin' and teach you some manners."

Trenda continued to nod her head as her fingers slipped inside her boot and touched the knife. She looked at the blonde. "You might wanna take this drunk back to your table before somethin' happens to him."

King Gee snatched his hand away from his date, swayed and yelled, "Bitch! I'm gonna ki—"

A pair of huge black arms grabbed King Gee and dragged him away from Trenda. The bouncer held him tight. "That's enough, Geno. Time for you to go."

Geno grimaced at the laughing Lollie and tossed his drink at her, soaking the front of her skirt. "Laugh at that, ho!"

"You muthafucka!" Lollie yelled as she pulled at the fabric of her skirt, trying to prevent the alcohol from soaking through to her skin. "You better hope I don't see you again, I'm gonna have my brothers kill yo' ass!"

As the bouncer struggled with King Gee, Trenda eased the knife into her palm, hiding most of the knife in the sleeve of her shirt. *Let that sorry punk get loose and come at me now, I'll gut his ass right here.* Two other bouncers joined the first one, and they managed to hustle King Gee out of a side door of the club. She slipped the weapon back in her boot, removed the napkins from under their drinks and handed them to Lollie. "C'mon, let's go to the bathroom and get you dried off."

The crowd parted like the Red Sea before Moses and let them through. Inside the women's restroom, the aroma of brandy filled the air as both Lollie and Trenda attempted to dry Lollie's skirt. Lollie slammed the wad of paper towels to the floor in disgust. "Of all the years I've comin' here, this is the first time I've *ever* had to deal with this kinda bullshit!" She looked at the Australia-shaped brandy stain on the front of her dress. "I could *kill* that muthafucka!"

Trenda shook her head as the stain began to set. "You are gonna have to go soak that in water so it won't be ruined. Let's get the hell out of here."

Lollie touched her expensive purse and stomped the floor. "Awww, shit! That bastard got brandy on my fuckin' Juicy Couture!"

Outside the club, Trenda shook her head at the light rain that greeted them. "What the fuck else can happen? Now we gonna get rained on to top everything off." Surprised at Lollie's lack of a response, Trenda turned and found her glaring at someone or something across the street. "What you see?"

Lollie continued to glare. "That faggot-ass Geno."

Trenda looked across the street and saw Geno pleading his case with one of the bouncers as his female friend held an umbrella over his head. The remainder of his small entourage hovered around them. She grabbed Lollie's arm and gently pulled. "Fuck that trick. Let's bounce."

Reluctantly, Lollie began walking with her. In the parking lot, she stopped in front of a fairly new, red, convertible Saab. "I wish I had a brick to throw through his goddamn windshield."

Puzzled, Trenda cocked her head. "What you talkin' about?"

Lollie pointed at the oversized red letters across the top of the windshield at the roofline: KING GEE. "He likes attention."

Trenda looked around and found they were alone. She grinned. "Too bad it has a hole in that pretty peanut butter top."

Lollie gave her a confused look. "What are you talking about? That top looks new." Trenda bent over, removed the butterfly knife and flicked it a couple of times. Lollie's mouth hung open. "What the hell?"

Trenda placed a finger to her lips. "Shhhh." She then walked over and made a two-foot-long incision in the convertible top. The puddled rain on the roof leaked onto the plush tan leather interior. She whipped the knife closed, tucked it back in her boot and smiled. "Ahhh, now I feel better."

Lollie finally managed to close her mouth. "Girl, you are *crazy!* Let's get the fuck out of here!"

Twenty

Once she was satisfied no one was following them, Lollie broke out in a fit of laughter as she drove them away from the club. "Where the hell you get that knife? How did you get it in the club?"

Trenda grinned and removed the blade from her boot. "This is my friend, 'Baby.' Baby takes *good* care of momma."

"You ever cut anybody?"

Trenda rolled the knife between her palms. "Yeah, a few fools."

Lollie stopped at a red light. "You ever cut anybody real bad or kill anybody with it?"

Trenda thought back to that summer night four years ago when she was attacked in a cheap, North Carolina hotel by a dope dealer named Phillip "Phil Good" Rawlins. After delivering ten kilos of booger sugar to him, he decided to give her a tip along with her regular payment—his hard dick. When Trenda declined his offer and demanded her cash, he caught her by surprise with a backhand slap. Once she fell to the floor stunned, he pulled up her summer dress and prepared to invade her coochie. He made the fatal mistake of allowing Trenda the opportunity to reach into her purse, which landed within arm's reach, and get Baby.

All Phil Good heard was three clicks as Trenda whipped Baby open and jabbed him twice in the side of his neck, hitting his jugular vein. She didn't hang around long enough to see if he survived, but the red lake around his body gave her reason to suspect he was well on his way to Hell. She was so scared she left the dope and her money behind and drove fifty miles before she realized her dress was drenched in blood. She pulled over behind a church, stripped, got a change of clothes out of her "Travelin' Bag" and stuffed the dress into the church's garbage dumpster. She recalled looking up at the illuminated stained glass window above the church's back door and seeing a weeping, crucified Jesus staring down at her. She still believed that was the only illuminated window in that entire, darkened church that night...

Trenda let the memory dissipate; it reminded her too much of her estranged family. "Not that I recall."

The rain increased in intensity. Lollie sped up the windshield wipers. "Damn! It's pourin' out here. I know the freeway is gonna be bad on my way back home."

Trenda put Baby back in her boot. "You live far from here?"

"Kinda. I stay in Hercules. That's about a good half-hour ride from here on the freeway."

Trenda saw her hotel a few blocks ahead. "Why don't you stay in my room tonight? Fuck tryin' to drive in this weather. I have plenty of room."

Lollie nodded and smiled as they arrived at the Hotel Oakland. "Oh, that sounds *cool!* Plus, I don't need to be drivin' with this alcohol buzz anyway."

"Good." Lollie pulled into the guest parking lot. Both women got out and hurried across the lot in the downpour. Trenda opened the door and ushered Lollie into the warm lobby. "You ever stayed here?"

Lollie gazed at the extravagant interior. "Hell naw! This place is *way* out my budget."

Trenda led her to the elevators. She pointed at the sign toward the pool. "You can even go late-night swimming in the indoor pool."

Lollie folded her arms across her chest, slanted her eyes and smirked at Trenda. "Mya, how the hell you pull this off? You straight dissed my hotel about its room rates."

Trenda summoned the elevator. "I told you I met a new friend the other day."

Lollie shook her head. "I meet men almost every day and they ain't springin' for plush hotel rooms just because of my good looks." She pursed her lips. "You whipped that cat on him, huh?"

Trenda gave her a broad smile. "Kinda."

On the way to Trenda's suite, she filled Lollie in on how she earned Walter's favor. After entering the suite and looking around, Lollie sat down on the sofa and pulled off her pumps. "Damn! You *worked* him."

Lollie unzipped her top and turned on the TV. "Nah, he's just grateful for the pussy. Not stingy like most brothas." She noticed the stain in Lollie's skirt. "You wanna take that off and soak that stain?"

Lollie looked down at the front of her skirt. "Yeah, let me do that." Trenda's clit vibrated as she watched Lollie undress. Her chocolate ice cream-colored body radiated sexy. The diamond stud in her navel reflected a bluish-red sparkle into Trenda's probing eyes. She longed for Lollie to remove her black thong and bra. Lollie draped the skirt across her forearm. "Which way to the bathroom?"

Trenda got up. "This way."

In the bathroom, they talked while Lollie filled the sink with hot water and used one of the face towels to soak and scrub the stain. Lollie looked at her watch. "I can't believe it's only half past eleven. Shit, my buzz is comin' down. I wish I had another drink."

Trenda went into the bathroom's closet and removed a tan, Hotel Oakland terrycloth robe. "Hey, you know I got a wet bar."

Lollie smiled as she squeezed all the water out of the skirt she could. "Awwww, shit! Now you talkin'!"

Trenda handed her the robe. "Hang your skirt up on the shower door. It should be dry by morning."

At one in the morning, after more girl talk and half a bottle of Gran Patron Tequila, Trenda got up, turned up the volume on the room's compact stereo system and undressed down to her red bra and G-string. Lollie clapped her hands and whistled as Trenda danced to the hip-hop song on the radio. "Oooooh wee! I see why Mr. Walter is spendin' so much money on you!"

Trenda turned around, staggered, grinned, bent over and made her ass cheeks clap. "My grandma always said, 'Use what you got to break 'em and shake 'em!' "

Lollie, in her drunken state, laughed so hard she rolled off of the sofa, onto the floor. Trenda laughed with her as she tried to pour herself another shot. She missed the glass on the first try and tequila spilled onto the table. Both girls paused, looked at the mess Trenda made, then fell out laughing again. Lollie wiped tears of laughter off of her face. "Mya…sit your ass down…you don't need no more of that fire water."

Trenda set the bottle down, picked up the overflowing shot glass and downed the alcohol. She showed Lollie the empty glass, grinned, then threw it across the room. After it exploded against the refrigerator, Trenda laughed and nearly tripped over the coffee table. "That's how big girls do it!"

Lollie's robe fell open as she howled with laughter, on her back, on the floor. "You are out your damn mind! You gonna fuck around and get us put out!"

Trenda dropped to her knees, swayed, then fell onto the floor next to Lollie. They both lay on their backs on the thick beige carpet, giggling. Trenda rolled over on her side and got a nice look at Lollie's enticing cleavage. "I been meanin' to ask, is Lollie your real name?"

Lollie chuckled. "No...I *hate* my real name. It's Ingrid... Ingrid Slawson."

Trenda laughed. "*Ingrid?* Are you serious? That sounds like some old white lady's name."

"I was named after my great-grandmother. She was German."

Trenda's eyes bulged. "What? How the hell you have a white great-grandmother as dark as you are?"

"My three brothers are all light-skinned. It took a long time for my father to believe I was his kid. He used to argue with my mother about it until he found out traits from your ancestors can skip generations." She grabbed a handful of her glossy hair. "But I definitely got my great-grandmother's hair."

Trenda put her hand in Lollie's mane. "You gonna have to let me whip it up for you one day."

Lollie closed her eyes as Trenda stroked her hair. "You know how to do hair?"

"Yeah...just because I don't have any don't mean I can't do hair."

Lollie laughed. "I didn't say that, crazy. I'm just surprised. You don't look like a hairstylist."

Trenda saw Lollie's hard nipples jabbing at her bra. She grinned. "Don't let the smooth taste fool ya!" She massaged Lollie's scalp. "Where did the name 'Lollie' come from?"

Lollie relaxed her neck muscles as Trenda massaged her head. "My daddy used to say I had a big ol' head and a skinny body, just like a lollipop, when I was little, so he started calling me 'Lollie.' "

Trenda's eyelids drooped from a mixture of the tequila and her building heat. "He sure can't call you that now, you thick as *hell!*" She let her hand move from Lollie's scalp to the back of her neck. "You got a boyfriend?"

Lollie cracked her eyes open and smirked. "I had one up until a couple months ago."

Trenda inched a little closer. "What happened?"

Lollie rolled back onto her back. "He had too many hang-ups for me."

Trenda gently placed her hand on Lollie's shoulder and began massaging it. "What kinda hang-ups?"

Lollie yawned. "Whenever I tried to do something new in bed, he freaked out. All he wanted to do was the same old positions—missionary, doggy style, stuff like that."

Trenda's thigh brushed against Lollie's. "Ain't nothin' wrong with those positions."

"I know, but sometimes that shit gets boring. I like to experiment."

"What kinda experiments?"

Lollie moved her shoulder in sync with Trenda's massaging hand. "All kinds of stuff. I remember one night I tried to lick the spot between his balls and ass and he jumped out the bed, got dressed and went home."

Trenda's nipples rose to the occasion. They ached to be touched, sucked. "Mmmmm…I love lickin' the taint. I can make a man nut by doin' that."

Lollie bent her knees and slowly opened and closed her legs. "I tried to do that to him, but he swore somebody must have turned me out since I had never tried it on him before."

The slow movement of Lollie's chocolate thighs mesmerized her. She let her hand move down the side of Lollie's upper arm. "Don't you just hate men like that? Way too insecure."

"I know. I really found out one night after we showered together." She sucked in a long, deep breath, and exhaled, causing her tits to rise and fall inches away from Trenda's face. "I scrubbed his balls and ass real good, but wouldn't let him touch me. I had never seen his dick that hard. Anyway, I led him to the bed and began kissing all over him. When I rolled him over and tried to lick his ass, that fool damn near had a stroke. He had the nerve to call me a pervert. I cussed him out and we broke up that night."

Trenda's forearm brushed against Lollie's tits as she rubbed Lollie's tricep. "Goddamn, girl! You freaky like *that?*"

"Damn, my head is spinnin'." Lollie placed her arm over her eyes and hiccupped. "Oh hell yeah. When it's on, it's on; everything goes."

Trenda couldn't tell if it was the alcohol or her heat that gave her a head rush. "That's what I'm talkin' about." She let her hand move to Lollie's right tit. "I like it all."

Lollie moaned as Trenda rubbed her rock-hard nipple,

then her body hitched twice. She quickly sat upright. "Oh fuck! I'm gonna throw up!"

Trenda rolled over on her back as Lollie jumped up, wobbled, then ran to the bathroom. "Shit!" She rubbed her swollen pussy. "I guess we ain't gonna get to play tonight." She eased up to her feet, steadied herself against her dizziness and went to assist her buddy.

Twenty-One

After helping Lollie through her regurgitation episode, Trenda helped her to the bedroom and tucked her in. It only took seconds for the drunk, chocolate goddess to fall into a coma-like sleep. Trenda got in beside her and passed out. At eight in the morning, the rude ringing of the room's telephone awakened Trenda. It took a moment for her to remember where she was. She smiled, reached over the sleeping Lollie and picked up the cordless phone. "Hello?"

"Good morning, stranger. What are you up to?"

"Hey, Walter, Wassup?"

"Not much, just wondering if you were ready for breakfast."

Trenda squinted and strained to read the yellow numbers on the nightstand clock. "Oh…breakfast." She yawned and stretched. "That does sound good, but by the time you get here I won't have much time. I have a job orientation at eleven."

"Well, it's a good thing I'm here in the lobby. If you hurry and get dressed, we can make it to Momma's Café and get a bite."

She ran her hand down her face and watched Lollie sleep. "Do you plan all your dates like this? Or do you just do this with me?"

He chuckled. "I just do it with you. All my other dates know the routine; I still have to break you in."

His confidence made her grin. "Well, Mr. Secrease, I have to tell you something; I have company."

He paused. "Company?"

Trenda forced her legs to swing over the edge of the bed. "Yes, company. You're welcome to come on up, though."

"Hmmm, are you sure?"

Trenda stood and stretched. "I wouldn't say so if it wasn't cool."

"Okay, if you say so. I'll be up there in a few minutes."

Trenda hung up and tossed the phone on the bed next to Lollie. *Damn, that Patron is some good shit! I ain't even got a hangover.* She walked over to the closet and grabbed one of the complimentary robes. She went to the bathroom, relieved herself, washed her face and brushed her teeth. She looked at her red eyes in the mirror. *I'll take a shower after Walter gets up here.* She reentered the bedroom and saw Lollie buried under the covers, snoring. A second later, she heard a knock at the door. She left the bedroom and closed the door. "Just a minute, I'm comin'."

The pleasant aroma of Walter's cologne greeted her at the door. His ever-present grin was gone. "Are you *sure* I'm not intruding?"

She tightened the belt on her robe, gave him a puzzled

look and stepped aside so he could enter. "Why are you trippin'?"

He stepped inside and scanned the room. "Because." He walked over to the kitchenette, bent over and picked up a piece of her shattered shot glass. "It seems like you have been busy with your *company*."

She blushed as she vaguely recalled some of the previous night's details. "Oh that…I guess we got a lil' bit out of control."

He walked over to the coffee table, put the top on the half-empty bottle of tequila and picked up the shot glass next to it. "Is this *his* glass or yours?"

She read the jealousy in his face, smiled and shook her head. "That belongs to—"

They both turned to the sound of the bedroom door opening. A naked Lollie stepped out. "Hey, Mya—"

"Oh shit!" Walter quickly covered his eyes and turned around.

Lollie jumped back behind the door. "I'm so sorry! I didn't know you had company, girl!"

Trenda smirked at Walter. "Is that the 'him' you were referring to?"

He kept his hand over his eyes. "Funny."

She swatted him on the ass. "I'll be right back." She went into the bedroom and watched Lollie pick her robe off of the chair next to the bed. "My bad. I thought you were still knocked out."

"I was until I got up to use the bathroom. I damn near panicked; I forgot where I was." She moved her hair out her face and grinned. "Who is that cutie pie I just gave a free peepshow to?"

Trenda laughed. "That's Walter. He wants to go to breakfast."

"You guys have fun. I have to get outta here. I forgot I have a doctor's appointment at ten."

"Yeah, I have to go sign some papers at the hotel at eleven."

Lollie smiled. "Oh yeah! I almost forgot you on the team now. Most likely they are gonna have me train you."

"Yup, that's what Jeff said." She ran her hand through her short hair. "I gotta get back in there with Walter."

Lollie stretched and yawned. "I was gonna ask if it's okay if I take a quick shower."

"Yeah, that's cool. I checked your skirt this morning; the stain didn't set."

Lollie smiled, untied her robe and let it hit the floor. "Cool! I'll be done in a few minutes and leave you two alone."

Trenda licked Lollie's trimmed pussy with her eyes. "You ain't gotta rush. There's another bathroom down the hall."

"Okay, see you in a few." Lollie walked into the bathroom and shut the door.

Trenda opened the bedroom door and found Walter sweeping the broken glass into a copper dustpan. "What you doin', man? They have maids to do that."

He poured the shards into the stainless steel garbage can. "I can't stand a mess."

She gazed at the outline of his manhood in his khaki pants. That, along with the image of a naked Lollie, moistened her. She walked over, took the broom from him and tossed it onto the floor. He shook his head. "What are you doing?"

She walked up and rubbed against him. "I'm hungry."

He looked at his watch. "Well, if you hurry and get dressed—"

She shook her head and rubbed his crotch. "I want this for breakfast."

His eyes widened. "What are you *doing?* Did you forget about your company?"

Trenda ignored him, unzipped his pants and got on her knees. "She can get her own breakfast." Trenda reached inside his pants and pulled out his throbbing piece. After a couple of quick strokes, she sucked the brown head into her mouth. The feel of the swollen veins on her tongue made her pussy tremble. She gave him long, slow sucks as she stroked the shaft.

He closed his eyes and forgot all about Lollie in the other room. "Mmmmmmmmmmm, Myaaaa…fuck…" She relaxed her throat muscles and let him fuck her in the mouth. Her lack of a gag reflex allowed her to take his dick until she felt his pubic hairs against her face. She heard him whimper while she held his rod in her throat. She eased it out of her mouth, spit on it, then sucked him fast. He gripped the edge of the refrigerator. "Sssuckk it ouuttt!"

Trenda let her lips and tongue rub his sensitive, quivering dickhead. At the same time he grabbed the back of her head, she tasted a bit of pre-cum. She gripped the back of his thighs and forced his dick deeper into her throat as she herself came. She felt his legs shake as his hot, creamy love juice filled her mouth. She moaned and swallowed every drop. She kissed the tip of his dick, licked her lips and stood. "Mmmm, you had a lot for me."

He panted and leaned against the refrigerator. "Damn! That was...*damn!*"

She grinned, tucked his log back in his pants and zipped him up. *Another satisfied customer.* She took his hand and led him to the sofa. "Wait here. I'll be dressed in a minute."

He leaned back, closed his eyes and smiled. "No problem...no problem at all."

They both turned around at the sound of the bedroom opening. Lollie stepped out wearing her skirt. She combed her hair with her fingers and gave them a shy smile. "Sorry for busting in on you guys." She looked at Walter. "I don't always go around flashing strangers."

He stood and offered her his hand. "My name is Walter. Now that we are no longer strangers, you have nothing to be sorry for."

Trenda observed the way Walter and Lollie smiled and locked eyes. She also noticed how long he held her hand after shaking it. She folded her arms over her chest and grinned. *Looks like a love connection startin' up.* "Watch out, Lollie; looks like he's ready for another peek!"

Lollie blushed as Walter released her hand. "Did anybody ever tell you, you are crazy?" She picked her purse up off the coffee table. "I have to get going. I'll call you later."

Walter's eyes lingered on Lollie. "It was nice to meet you, Lollie, even under the 'special circumstances.' "

Once again, their eyes synchronized. She smiled. "Same here..."

Trenda walked her to the door. "I'll call you once the orientation is over."

"Okay, do that. My shift starts at three. I'll be waitin'." She looked over Trenda's shoulder. "Bye, you two!"

Trenda closed the door, turned and walked over to Walter. "What do you think of my friend?"

He tried to look uninterested. "She's cool."

Trenda glanced at the lump next to his zipper. "I'm glad you think so. I'll be right back." Trenda entered the bedroom, stripped and got in the shower. Her nipples perked up. *Walter and Lollie...*

Twenty-Two

T wo days later, Piper paused in the courtyard of the University of Maryland and answered her cell phone. "Hello?"

"Hello, Ms. Langford, this is Hank Martin. Are you free to talk?"

Piper took a seat next to the fountains in front of the Tawes Fine Arts Building. "Yes. What's going on?"

"I have a bit of good news for you. I think I found Ms. Fuqua."

Piper set her purse down and a sinister grin covered her face. "You did? Where?"

"I found her staying at the Hotel Oakland. It appears she is staying in a room paid for by someone by the name of Walter Secrease. It's booked for two weeks. I'd like to email you a few photos I took of her to verify it's her. Do you have access to the internet right now?"

It sounds like she found a new dick to suck by the name of Walter. Piper angrily unzipped her bag and pulled out her laptop. "Yes, I can use the wireless connection here at school."

"Great! I'll send them right now."

Piper chewed her thumbnail as she waited for the laptop to boot up. "Okay, I'm booted up. Give me a second."

"Take your time."

A mixture of pain, lust and rage blanketed her mind as she zoomed in on the five pictures of Trenda on her screen. One of the pictures showed Trenda in front of a restaurant, seemingly looking directly at the camera. Piper dug her fingernails into the palm of her clenched right hand. "Yes…that is definitely her."

"I was surprised at how many people I spoke with recognized her picture; I think her unusually green eyes stuck with them."

"I bet they did. I'm glad you found her."

"Very good! I can transfer you over to Nancy to complete this investigation. Thank you for choosing Dickerson."

"Wait! I want you to keep your eye on her until I get there."

"Well, that will incur extra expenses."

"I don't give a damn! You have the number of my credit card; I want you to keep your eye on her until I get there."

"Okay, when will you be arriving?"

"I'm going to book a flight to Oakland as soon as I get home. I hope to be there in a day or so. Stay on clock, Hank."

"I'll do that. If anything changes, I'll give you a call."

"You do that." She hung up, put away her laptop and hurried to her next class.

"Are you sure you can't stay these last two weeks and complete your finals, Piper?"

Piper shook her head as she handed him her last assignment. "No, I have an emergency situation to take care of."

He scratched his stringy, gray hair. "That's a shame… you are so close to getting your degree."

"I know. Maybe I'll return next year and finish."

"But this program is *very* exclusive. The waiting list is already two years long."

Piper thought about the past few days since her fight with Trenda. A mixture of fury, heartbreak and insanity fueled her bipolar condition. She pushed her thick glasses up the bridge of her nose. "Well, I guess this fucking degree will have to wait then, won't it, professor?"

He adjusted his wire-frame glasses and gave her a nervous, nicotine-stained, toothy smile. "I see…if it's because of your 'incident'…"

She glared at him and took a step toward him. "That's none of your goddamned business!"

His eyes bulged. "I meant you no harm, Piper. I simply meant that—"

The image of Trenda sucking Darius's dick filled her head. She pointed at him. "I don't need your sympathy… I don't need a damn thing from you or anybody else!"

He recalled hearing about her violent history, took a few slow steps away from Piper and opened the door to his office. "I think it's time for you to leave, Ms. Langford."

She took her time leaving. Stopping at the threshold, she looked back into his scared face. "I'll see you when I get back." Outside, in the last grayish light of the cloudy late Friday afternoon, she removed her cell phone from her backpack and called Johns Hopkins Hospital. "Hi, Mom."

"How are you, sweetheart?"

"I'm fine. I just wanted to let you know I'm going to be out of town for a few days…a few of my sorority sisters are going to celebrate spring break in San Francisco."

Her mother put down the patient's chart she was reading. "I don't think it's a good idea for you to be going that far so soon. You're still healing, honey."

Piper rubbed the small knot on the back of her head, under her layered haircut, as she crossed the student parking lot. "I'm fine, Mom."

"You may feel fine, but I still think it's too soon. You have suffered a serious concussion. Your eyesight hasn't even returned to normal yet."

Piper rolled her eyes. *Damn, Mom, I fucking know that.* "It's okay, I'm getting used to my glasses. My headaches are even getting better."

"Piper, you need to rest. Why don't you come stay with me and your father for a few days instead? We can go do some serious summer clothes shopping."

Piper removed her keys and opened the door of her

Range Rover. "No, I really want to get away for a while. Besides, you and Dad are way too busy these days."

"That may be true, but we are never too busy for our baby."

Her right eye twitched with agitation. She longed for the day her parents stopped treating her like a toddler. "Mom, I'm going to San Francisco. I'll give you a call once I get there."

Her mother paused. "Okay, but your father isn't going to be too happy."

"Mom, it's only gonna be a few days…it's not like I'm moving there."

"He may need to have you here as the police investigate your case. You know he has every cop in the city working on it."

Piper put the keys in the ignition, sat back, closed her eyes and exhaled loudly. "I know…I hear from them almost every friggin' day. It seems they aren't getting anywhere."

"These things take time. And the more accessible you are the better. You never know when they may catch that little whore, Trenda, and need you to identify her."

These fucking dumb cops have no idea she is on the West Coast, Mother. "She could be anywhere. If they do catch her, I'm sure they can find a way to hold her until I can make a positive ID."

"Why are you so hell-bent on going to California? Did you meet a boy there?"

Piper almost laughed out loud. *If you only knew I haven't been with a man in over ten years, you would have a stroke.* "No, Mother. I did not meet a boy there. I just want to get away from all this crap for a while."

Her mother sighed. "Well, if you just *have* to go, at least promise you will call me once a day so I can know you're okay."

Piper started the engine and turned on the wipers. She'd made it to the car just as a spring shower erupted. "Okay, I'll call."

"When are you leaving?"

"In a couple of days. I have a few things to take care of first."

"Don't forget to pack your medicine and eye drops."

Piper felt her blood pressure building. "Mother, I *am*... I know what I need. Talk to you later." She folded her phone closed, tossed it on the passenger seat and turned up the speed of her windshield wipers. "I swear she gets on my last nerve sometimes." Back at her apartment, she went to her desk and found the sheet of paper she had gotten from Tyrone with Trenda's information on it. She dialed the number.

"Hello?"

She picked up the picture of her and Trenda celebrating Trenda's birthday last year at a popular local Mexican food restaurant. She recalled how she ate Trenda out for hours that night. "Eric?"

"Yes, that's me. Is this you, Piper?"

"Yes. I just got off the phone with a private investigator I hired to find Trenda. He found her still in Oakland. I'm going to book my flight there tonight."

Tyrone put down his hamburger and swallowed the French fry in his mouth. "When are you leaving?"

She scowled at the picture, then placed it back on the table, face down. "I'm hoping to leave in a day or two. The sooner the better."

He folded his hamburger in a napkin and tossed it back into the bag with his fries. "Piper, can I call you right back? I need to make a quick call."

"Whatever. I have things to do."

He listened to her hang up on him. "What a bitch!" He then picked up his food, walked past the life-sized cardboard image of a Burger King and called Darius. "Yo, Piper is getting ready to book a flight to Oakland."

Darius watched as Griff's workers mounted a set of expensive chrome rims onto his Escalade. "Did she say when she was leaving?"

"She didn't. But she did tell me she hired a P.I. that found Trenda in Oakland. I told her I was gonna call her back in a minute."

Darius walked across the oil-stained floor and exited the garage. He flipped up the collar of his leather jacket in an attempt to ward off the chilly breeze and last gasp of the short spring shower. "Call her back and tell her you might be going to Oakland, too, lookin' for Trenda. See if she'll give you all her travel info."

"Man, I really don't feel like talkin' to her crazy ass again…she sounds like she is ready to snap."

"You want this shit over, don't you?"

"Yeah, but…you don't know how twisted this Piper chick is. She is literally out her damn mind."

Darius spit the toothpick out of his mouth into a dirty puddle of rainwater. "Do I need to remind you of what will happen if Internal Affairs finds Trenda before we do?"

Tyrone hesitated, then exhaled loudly. "Okay, okay. Lemme call her back. I'll hit you up later."

"Cool." Darius disconnected and tucked the phone into the pocket of his jacket. *Don't get soft on me now, partner. We are in way too deep for you to pussy-out now.* He walked back into the garage just as Griff's men lowered his Escalade from the lift and checked the tightness of the lug nuts on his new rims. He looked at Griff as he opened the door and got into the vehicle. "Your boys do good work; you need to give 'em a raise."

Griff glared at him in silence and gnawed on the butt of his cigar. He then turned, pressed a button on the wall and the roll-up door began opening. He stood to the side as Darius reversed and saluted Griff on his way out. Griff removed his cigar and spat in his direction. "You gonna get yours, crooked muthafucka."

Darius, fueled by adrenaline, sped across the wet, four-lane Harbor Tunnel Thruway, en route to the Baltimore

Harbor area. He needed to relieve some stress so he could think clearly and plan his next move. In a particularly insalubrious neighborhood, he soon spotted the solution to his stress relief issue. *She ain't half as good as Trenda, but what the fuck.* He removed the portable red siren light from his glove box, plugged it in and placed it on the dash. He then slowly rolled up to the curb behind a pair of big booty females strolling down the sidewalk, sharing a large, red-and-white umbrella. He tapped the horn and both women stopped and looked at the shiny Escalade. He lowered the passenger window. "Good evening, ladies."

Both women frowned and shook their heads. The dark-skinned woman in the long black wig leaned over. "What you want? We ain't doin' nothin'."

Darius quickly scanned the area. Satisfied the coast was clear, he turned his attention to the slim woman with the gold front teeth. "C'mon now, Cherry, you know I'm just checkin' on you."

She rolled her eyes and chewed her gum faster. "Uh-huh, sure you are."

He waved her to the side. "I need to speak to your friend, Constance."

Reluctantly, Constance the "Cum Catcher," as she was known in the streets, exhaled cigarette smoke, bent over, swiped her shoulder-length blonde hair behind her back and looked into the window. "Yeah, what do you want with me?"

Darius looked into her blue eyes. "I need to ask you a few questions." He patted the empty passenger seat. "C'mon…take a ride with me."

She furrowed her brow and pulled at the hem of her lime-green micro miniskirt. "Why are you fuckin' with me? All I'm doin' is walkin' down the street with my friend. Is that a crime, now?"

He gave her a serious look. "No it's not, but I bet if I was to search you, I'd find a joint or weed seed on you. You know it would look real bad if your probation officer found out about that, wouldn't it?"

Constance looked over at Cherry and grimaced. "I had better go. Even though I'm clean, I'm sure 'Officer Friendly' here would magically find some contraband on me."

Cherry stepped back from the car and adjusted her extremely short, bright yellow shorts. "Yeah, you right. He is good at that trick."

Constance flicked her half-smoked cigarette into the street, tucked her pack of Newport cigarettes into her thigh-high black boots, opened the door and got inside. "So, what do you want to talk to me about?"

He removed the beacon from the dashboard and put it back in the glove compartment. "I'll tell you in a minute. We're gonna go someplace *private* and talk."

Constance sat back and crossed her arms over her huge tits. "Oh, I see you are taking me to the 'Lighthouse.'"

He grinned and sped off. "I see you have a good memory." Twenty minutes later, he unlocked the gate at the

"Lighthouse" and pulled around back. He unzipped his pants, looked over and watched Constance remove a red scrunchie from her small black purse and tie her hair back into a ponytail. He stopped her before she bent over into his lap. "You used to run with Trenda…she ever say anything going to California?"

She cocked her head. "What?"

"I said, did Trenda ever say anything to you about going to California or mention having any friends or relatives there?"

"No…why are you asking me anyway?"

Darius grabbed her by the back of the neck. "Look, bitch, I know you and her were tight. I busted both of you together a couple of times for possession on one of her drug runs. Don't fuckin' play with me."

Fear replaced her boldness as she read the anger in his glare. "Owww! That *hurts!*"

His dick swelled once he saw her cockiness evaporate. He kept his grip on her neck. "The pain stops when you tell me what I wanna know. Now, answer my fuckin' question."

He added pressure to his grip. She winced. "No…she never told me anything about going to California or anywhere else."

He held her neck and read her face for signs she was lying. Satisfied, he eased off the pressure and pushed her head into his lap. "Make yourself useful."

The feel of her lips on his swollen head made him lean back in his seat with pleasure. Normally, a blowjob would put him in a good mood, but as he fucked Constance in the throat, a sense of doom shadowed him. The thought of getting fired, or worse, going to jail, fueled his thrust. He ignored Constance's gags and forced his knob deeper into her mouth. The image of his cute but boring-in-bed wife taking half his shit made him pump harder with frustration. Seconds later, he shuddered and squirted thick, sticky woo juice down the Cum Catcher's throat. She gulped it all down and sucked out the residue.

He released her head and she sprung up, gasping for air. She grimaced and wiped her mouth with the back of her hand. "Can we go now?"

He looked into her face and watched the blood slowly leave her flushed face. He put away his sperm worm and zipped up. "Sure can."

He started the car, turned on the headlights and drove out to the street. After locking the gate, he drove a few blocks and stopped at the corner bus stop. She stopped applying her red lipstick and looked at him. "Why are you stopping?"

He put the car in "park," reached into his pocket, pulled out some cash and tucked a five-dollar bill into her bra. "This is where you get off. I gotta go."

She glared at him. "This is fucked up!" She got out, slammed the door and walked away.

Before he pulled off, his phone rang. He looked at the caller ID and answered. "What's the latest?"

"I just got off the phone with Piper. She is flying out to Oakland tomorrow afternoon."

Fuck! That crazy bitch is movin' fast! "Okay, good lookin' out. I'm gonna go home and see if I arrange to get there around the same time."

"What you gonna tell ya wife? You know Beverly ain't gonna be happy with you just up and flyin' across country."

"I'm gonna tell her I'm going fishing with my brother. Besides, we have been on bad terms for a while now; she most likely won't give a damn."

"I sure hope that works. Worrying about this shit is making my ulcer act up."

He pulled into his driveway, thankful his wife's car wasn't there, parked, and got out of the car. "Like I keep tellin' you, quit trippin' and just lay low. I'll holla at you later." He went into the house, logged onto his computer and purchased a round-trip ticket to Oakland using his alias, Thomas Reed. He then printed out pictures of both Piper and Trenda. He picked up the briefcase next to his desk and put the pictures inside. He then walked over to the huge safe in the corner of the den and removed a few items borrowed from the Baltimore PD's Crime Investigation Unit office. He packed the equipment into his briefcase. Once done, he sat back and stared at the walls of his den. The large framed picture of his grandfather seemed to stare at him. He shut down his computer and turned his back to the picture. "I sure hope you can forgive me for what I'm about to do, Gramps."

Twenty-Three

Saturday morning, her first day working solo after three days of training with Lollie, Trenda met with Alberta Flores in the Barnes & Noble parking garage. "Like I told you on the phone, young lady, this car has always been garaged. My late husband also kept all the maintenance records."

Trenda let her hand glide over the roof of the ten-year-old, brown Honda sedan. She then kicked the left rear tire. "It's okay…but the tires look a little worn."

The seventy-ish Mexican woman bent over slightly, adjusted her glasses and inspected the tire. "I agree they are a little worn, but they were replaced only two years ago." Whe stood up straight and smiled. "This is a very nice car for the price. Fifteen hundred is very good price."

Trenda knew the car was worth the money, but her years of hustling made her have to haggle. "I dunno… I'm supposed to meet another guy later on who has a nice BMW for about the same price." She watched the old woman's confident smile weaken a little. "And he says it has new tires."

The old woman turned away from Trenda and ran her

hand over the fading paint on the hood. "Okay, young lady. I can tell you like the car but like to wheel and deal." She looked back at Trenda. "I'll take off two hundred dollars."

Trenda grinned and removed the wallet out of her purse. She pulled out ten one-hundred-dollar bills. She held them out to the woman. "I'll give you a thousand."

The old woman looked at the money in Trenda's hand for a few moments. She shrugged her shoulders and exhaled. "Okay, you have a deal."

After dropping the old woman off at home, Trenda drove back to the hotel, smiling all the way. Now that she had a car and job, all she needed was a permanent place to live. Although she could probably seduce Walter into booking the hotel for her for a while longer, she had never been one to want to depend on anyone for shit.

She checked the time and saw she had about three hours before her shift started at one. She sat on the bed and counted her remaining cash. *Damn, after the train ticket, three hundred dollars in new clothes and a grand on this car, I'm down to my last thousand bucks.* She put a hundred in her wallet and the rest back in her Travelin' Bag. *I'm gonna have to save like hell to get a place of my own. I doubt a thousand dollars is gonna go far out here when it comes to finding an apartment.*

She went to the desk, sat down and opened the phone book. "Let's see where the nearest DMV is so I can get this car put in my name." She browsed the listings and found a few close by, but only one open on Saturdays.

She smiled at the listing in El Cerrito. She got her purse and removed her cell phone. "Time to see how my friend is doing." She scrolled through her many numbers and found one labeled "Box," and dialed.

"Hello?"

"Hey, Mr. Box. How are you?"

"Uhhh…I'm great…who is this?"

She walked over to the window and let the warm spring sunshine warm her face. "Oh, I keep you company on the train and now you don't know nobody?"

His smile reached through the phone. "Hey, Mya! How are you? Wow! Where have you been?"

"I've been here and there. What are you up to, sir?"

"Right now I'm trying on a pair of shoes. Boy, it's good to hear from you! Are you still in the area?"

"I sure am. Why aren't you out workin'?"

"I'm on my last couple of days of vacation. Did you find a job yet? Are you free right now?"

She picked up the desperation in his line of questioning. "Yes and maybe."

"Yes you found a job and maybe you are free?"

"Bingo."

"Cool! Did you find work as a hairdresser?"

Trenda turned from the window, walked over to the closet and picked out her work uniform—blue blazer, white blouse, blue slacks. She opted for the slacks instead of the skirt option. "Not yet. I'm a reservation clerk at the Water's Edge Hotel. It's just somethin' to keep me goin' until I find a better job."

"That sounds great! Hey, how about we get together this morning? I would love to see those emerald eyes again."

She put her uniform on a hanger, put her wallet into her purse and picked up her new car keys. "That can happen. I was thinking of going to the DMV out there in your town to take care of some business. Is that close to you?"

"Sure is! I live about five minutes away. Right now, I'm at the Hilltop Mall. I can meet you there in fifteen minutes. Or we can meet at the Starbucks in El Cerrito Plaza if you want."

She carried her uniform with her as she closed and locked her door. "Okay, I can do that, but you're gonna have to give me some directions."

Twenty minutes later, Trenda pulled into the El Cerrito Plaza strip mall. *Cool, there it is!* She smiled at the sign directing her to the El Cerrito Department of Motor Vehicles a quarter-mile away. She parked, got out and looked at her new ride. "Runs pretty damn good." She put on her shades, adjusted her tight, peach Baby Phat blouse and headed toward Starbucks. Dozens of senior citizens and a handful of high school-aged kids traversed the small but modern mall. She grinned as a pair of high school boys stared at her as she walked by. She could feel their young eyes on the jiggle of her white denim-covered ass. *Horny lil' bastards.*

She crossed the parking lot and angled towards the

Starbucks. Several people sat outside the coffee house sipping expensive coffee and enjoying the warmth of the spring sunshine. As soon as she got ten feet from the door, a familiar face opened it for her. "Hey, Mya! Good to see you again."

She eased past the grinning big man and entered. "It's good to see you, too, Mr. Box." She looked at the Macy's bags in his hand. "Is that how you spend your vacation, shoppin'?"

He looked at the bags and laughed. "I wish. I needed a new pair of shoes for work." He motioned for her to have a seat and pulled the chair out for her. "So, what do you think of California so far?"

She sat back and placed her purse on the table. "It's cool, but way more expensive than I thought."

He placed his two bags on the floor next to his seat. "Yes, it is that, but you get used to it." He stood up. "Can I get you something?"

She turned her head and read the huge menu board on the wall, behind the young baristas. *Poor baby, he even dresses like he's goin' to work while he's on vacation.* "I'll have a small iced coffee."

He adjusted the collar of his tie-less, white dress shirt, reached into the back pocket of his dark green Dockers and removed his wallet. "Is that all? Can I get you a sandwich or something?"

"No thanks, sweetie. I just ate a little while ago."

He let his gaze leave her tits. "Okay, I'll be right back."

She watched the thick man walk over to the counter and place his order. His broad shoulders made her want to wrap her legs around his neck. Her closet "Chubby Chaserness" made her study his hefty frame. He returned with two iced coffees. She stroked his hand gently as he handed her, her cup. "Thanks, baby."

He blushed from her touch and looked into her face. "I see your cut is almost healed. It doesn't look like it's gonna leave much of a scar."

She touched the healing wound. The cut on her shoulder still wasn't healing as quickly as she hoped. "Yes, thank God."

After listening to a ton of subtle hints dropped by Box wanting to see her again, Trenda removed her phone and checked the time. Box frowned. "Do you have to leave?"

She set the phone on the table and finished off her coffee. "Yeah, I gotta get to the DMV and then to work. Hey, can you give me directions back to Jack London Square?"

He pointed at her phone. "Do you have GPS service on your cell phone?"

She gave him a clueless look. "GPS? What's that?"

"It stands for Global Positioning System. It allows you to punch in the address where you want to go and the phone gives you step-by-step directions."

"You mean like Yahoo maps?"

He smiled and shook his head. "It's better than that." He pointed at her phone. "May I?"

She handed the phone to him. "Go ahead."

He flipped her phone open, pressed a few buttons on the keypad and nodded. "Cool. You do have it available on your phone. All you have to do is contact your carrier and subscribe."

She took the phone and read the screen. "You mean to tell me I can type in an address—anywhere—and the phone will tell me how to get there?"

He smiled. "Yes indeed, I'll show you." He removed his phone, logged on his GPS service and punched in the address for the Oakland Coliseum. He handed her his phone. "Take a look."

She laughed as a robotic female voice told her to "turn left" as she read the small map on the display. "This is so damn cool! I *gots* to get this!"

"You should. It will really help you get around since you don't know the area that well." He grinned and took her hand. "It will also make it a lot easier for you to come see me."

She gave him a flirtatious smile. "Yes, it sure would." Moments later, after calling her phone carrier, her service was activated. She input the address to the Water's Edge Hotel and was thrilled to hear that female robotic voice again. She stood, walked over and gave Box a kiss on the lips. "Thank you, teddy bear. I have to leave but I will give you a call later."

He almost floated out of his seat after tasting her lips. "You are very welcome, beautiful. I can't wait to see you again."

She hoisted her purse up on her shoulder. "Keep that

faith, baby." Twenty minutes after leaving the DMV with her temporary registration, pending a smog check, and with the help of her new GPS service, Trenda pulled into the employee parking lot of the Water's Edge Hotel. She smiled at her phone in amazement at how accurate the GPS was. "This is gonna come in real handy." Her phone rang as she prepared to get out of the car. "Hey, Mr. Secrease! I was just thinkin' about you." She got out, opened the back door, got her uniform off the backseat and bullshitted with Walter as she walked into the hotel.

Twenty-Four

Saturday afternoon, while Piper devoured the lunch served to her in her first-class accommodations, thirty thousand feet in the air above Ohio, Trenda changed into her work uniform. *I wish I had Saturdays off like Lollie, but shit, I ain't complainin'; at least I got a damn job.* She buttoned the top button of her blouse and pulled on her blue blazer. She checked herself in the full-length mirror mounted behind the dressing room door. "You look square as I-don't-know-what."

Not even her conservative uniform could mask her sexy frame. She'd already caught twice as many men eyeballing her, than the number of men that lusted for Lollie. Although she was grateful for the job, the lure of the fast money to be made in the streets beckoned her. During a lull between incoming and outgoing guests, Trenda used the calculator on the computer and added up how much she would make per pay period. She shook her head at the estimated amount. "Shit…it's gonna take forever to save up enough money to get my own place."

She watched Jason pull into the special security guard

parking stall in front of the hotel. She chuckled to herself thinking about how intimidated Jason was by her. She noticed he had also started dressing better since she had arrived. A car blasting a hip-hop song grabbed her attention. A customized Buick sedan pulled into the passenger drop-off area and parked. She watched as the driver, a lanky, young black man, got out, leaving his skanky, but cute, female passenger inside.

Everything about his mannerisms screamed street soldier. His urban wardrobe, outrageously overpriced athletic shoes, gaudy rings, sideways baseball cap and his golden teeth told Trenda all she needed to know. She reflected on how she used to deal with men and women just like him on a regular basis. Most times, they were the ones paying her to move their illegal products for them. Paying her *very* well. She sighed at the amount of money she had fucked off in the past. Having no kids or man to answer to, she had wasted thousands of dollars on frivolous shit, not once considering investing her cash as many of her "associates in high places" had suggested.

The same D.C. lawyer she often fucked for profit, many times, offered to set up an investment account for her after he jokingly calculated how much he had spent on her. She watched the street soldier try to con Jason into letting him park in the passenger-unloading zone. She looked at the amount in the calculator on the computer screen again. All at once, regret she had ever left her lifestyle back in Baltimore hit her like a lead pipe to the face. All the calls to her cell phone from folks needing her services made her grind her teeth in disgust at all the money she was missing.

She closed the calculator and watched Jason grin and shake his head, refusing the cash the street soldier flashed. Trenda had no doubt he was the kind of guy she could hook up with and get her hustle on. She knew that if she showed him a little interest, let him lust for her and maybe sucked him and fucked him real good a couple of times, she could easily learn his connections and set up her own enterprise. After a couple more unsuccessful attempts at keeping his prime parking spot, he hopped back in his extravagant car, turned the music up extra loud, and sped off in search of a new place to park.

After parking his car, the lanky thug got out and called his "Boss," King Gee. "Yo, King! You ain't gonna believe who I just ran into over here at the muthafuckin' hotel?"

"What you talkin' about, fool?"

"You know that breezy the security guard showed you they taped cuttin' the top of your ride?"

"You mean that green-eyed ho?"

Lanky grinned broadly and began pacing as he read the excitement in King Gee's voice. "Yeah! Yeah! *That* bitch! She is workin' here at the Waters' Edge Hotel. I even saw her leave after her shift and followed her to her car. I got her license plate, too!"

"Good lookin' out…I'm gonna break you off a lil'

reward money when I see you. Don't let on you know who she is…I have a special surprise in mind for that biotch…"

Trenda watched Jason adjust the badge on his security guard jacket before entering the lobby. He looked just like a cop. That thought made her feel a little better about leaving Baltimore. Darius was in Baltimore. Just the thought of one more night of letting him sexually abuse her was enough to make her current situation look pretty damn good. She didn't even want to think about the fact that the Island Boys gang was also looking for her. Jason lowered his gaze as he approached the counter. It was amazing how he reacted to Trenda versus Lollie. He looked at Lollie as if she was a princess, but he *acted* as if Trenda was the Queen. She barely heard him say, "Hi, Mya."

She made herself busy moving items around behind the counter. "Wassup, Jason?"

He adjusted his cap. "Not much. You know, just patrolling the place."

She sat down in her seat. "What did that dude want you were talkin' to?"

"He wanted to park in the passenger zone while he booked a room. He claimed he'd only be a minute, but you know how that goes; let one person do it and everybody will want to do it."

Trenda looked over his shoulder and watched the thug

enter the lobby while talking on his cell phone. "It looks like your friend made it back."

Jason stepped aside as the young thug approached the desk. "I guess he found a place to park his 'pimped-out' ride."

Five feet from the counter, the thug did a double-take and hung up his phone after getting a good look at the sexy green-eyed hotel receptionist. His date took notice of Trenda and did her best not to show how intimidated she was by Trenda's undeniable sexiness. Trenda closed the calculator on her screen, removing the depressing image of the peasant wages she was earning. She smiled and greeted the pair. While checking them in for what she deducted was to be a freak session, her thoughts returned to her living conditions. She caught the thug's girlfriend staring and smiled, as she turned away, embarrassed. Trenda activated a pair of electronic room keys and handed them to the man. "Enjoy your stay."

The thug's date tugged his arm after tiring of the way he fawned over Trenda. "C'mon, Peanut, let's go."

He took the cards and grinned. "I have a few folks that might be lookin' for me later. I hope it's a'ight if we party a lil' bit."

"It's okay as long as you and your 'folks' don't destroy the place." She looked over at Jason. "I'd hate to have to send my hit man up there to quiet y'all down."

Jason hitched up his belt and produced a shy grin. "You folks just enjoy yourselves."

The hours crawled by. Her irritated mood did little to

help pass the time. As soon as her lunch break arrived, she turned the reception desk duties over to her Asian co-worker, Elena, grabbed her purse and hurried outside. The springtime, late afternoon sunshine helped heal her sick mood. She walked over to the railing next to the estuary and took a deep breath of the salty sea air. She thought about stealing Peanut from his hoodrat girlfriend. "Fuck no. don't you even go there, Trenda," she told herself. "You are supposed to be tryin' to change your life, remember? Not using another fool to get your money hustle on."

The loud blare of a horn across the water caused a flock of scavenging sea gulls to take flight. Trenda looked toward the sound of the horn and saw a drawbridge split open to allow a large sailboat to pass between it. A different sound caught her ear. She dug into her purse and retrieved her ringing cell phone. The caller ID read: "Secrease Funeral Homes." "Hey, honey, wassup?"

"Everything is good, sexy. I was hoping we could hook up tonight so you can help me celebrate my birthday."

A seagull landed on the railing five feet from her, begging for a treat. "Oh really? Is today your birthday?"

"No, it's actually tomorrow, but I want to get an early jump on it."

She turned away from the sea gull's black, pleading eyes. "What are you doing at work if you are celebrating your birthday?"

"What makes you think I'm at work?"

"Have you ever heard of this new thing called 'caller ID'?"

He chuckled. "I have got to remember that! I'm just here catching up on some paperwork until you get off, then I'm coming to take you to dinner."

"I get off kinda late for dinner, don't you think?"

"Nine o'clock is perfect for a birthday dinner. I hope you eat sushi."

"Yeah, it's okay."

"Why do you sound like that? You sound as if somebody died."

Sunset stole the last warm rays of sunshine. She checked the time on the giant clock on the Tribune Building and saw half her lunchtime was gone. "I'm cool…just been stressin' a little bit."

"Sorry to hear that; I hope this bit of news makes you feel a little better. I called the hotel and extended your stay another two weeks."

Trenda looked up into the twilight sky, smiled and shook her head. The similarity between Walter and Dennis, the D.C. lawyer she used to date, tickled her. The biggest difference between the two was the fact that Dennis was shy about fucking, where Walter had no problem taking a piece of pussy. She walked toward the hotdog cart in the center of the promenade. "Walter, I can't let you keep spendin' your money on me."

"Look, Mya, let me worry about how I spend my money. I know exactly what I'm doing. To some, it may seem as though I am throwing my money away on a, pardon my French, 'piece of ass,' but to me, it's called enjoying my life. I have no kids, no wife, no drug addictions and no bills. To be blunt, the money I spent on you so far, I made back in less than half a day. Now, enough of you worrying about me. Come help me bring in my fifty-first birthday the right way."

Trenda looked at the fat hotdogs in the vendor's steamer. Her pussy and mouth watered. "Okay, okay. Give me time to get home and get changed and you can pick me up at ten."

Twenty-Five

"Thank you for flying Jet Blue," the friendly-faced Caucasian flight attendant said as Darius departed his flight out of Newark International Airport. He'd booked the flight and rental car under his alias, Officer Kenneth Barnes.

"Thanks." He checked his watch and hurried out of the boarding area. "I hate fucking flying." He played "Bumper Cars" with people, wheelchairs and garbage cans in his haste to get to the American Airlines boarding gates. Once there, he stood in front of the digital display that showed the status of their flights. He set his briefcase down, removed the piece of paper with Piper's flight number on it from his pocket and scanned the board.

Once he saw that flight number 1131 was due to arrive in forty-six minutes, he relaxed and exhaled. "Cool…I have plenty of time to get my shit before that fat bitch's flight arrives." The combination gift shop/convenience store to his right caught his eye. He went inside. "Yeah… this'll work," he said as he plucked a pack of red rubber bands off the rack next to the toiletries and carried it to the counter.

After his purchase, he made his way to the Jet Blue baggage claim area and grabbed his two bags. As he bent over to pick up his duffle bag, a little black boy tugged on the pant leg of his faded jeans and pointed at his waist. He wiped his long dreads out of his face. "Wow! Is that a real police badge, mister?"

Darius pulled his New York Mets jersey down over the badge he wore clipped to his belt. He had forgotten to remove it after showing it to security in order to explain why he had a firearm and a few other hard-to-explain items in his luggage. He forced a smile. "Yes it is, young man."

The boy's brown eyes widened. "Whoa! Did you ever shoot anybody?"

Darius looked around and squatted down in front of the boy. He placed a finger to his lips. "Shhhh! Don't say it too loud; I don't want the bad guys to know I am looking for them."

The boy went numb with awe. "Can I see your gun?"

Darius looked at the clock mounted above the luggage carousel and saw he had only half an hour until Piper's flight arrived. He stood and looked around. "Where are your parents?"

The boy looked around, then pointed toward the bank of pay phones thirty yards away. "My momma's right there on the phone."

"How old are you, little man?"

He grinned and held up four fingers. "This many!"

He looked over at the extremely young-looking, tall woman dressed in a Chicago Bulls sweatsuit, identical to the boy's, running her mouth on the phone. *Where the hell is Child Protective Services when you need them? It's a goddamn shame she's not watching this boy. If I wasn't on my current mission, I'd arrest her ass.* He looked down at the boy. "You want to do me a police favor?"

The boy grinned. "Yeah!"

"I want you to go over there and keep an eye on your mom until I get back, okay?"

The boy beamed. "Okay!"

"What's your name?"

"LaMarcus!"

Darius stood straight and saluted the boy. "Okay, now you are *Deputy* LaMarcus." Darius looked behind at LaMarcus and winked at an old black couple behind the boy as they enjoyed the way he handled LaMarcus. He looked back at the boy. "Okay, go on. I'll check on you in a little while, Deputy."

LaMarcus giggled, ran over to his mother, tapped her on the thigh and began telling her about how he had gotten deputized. The woman took the phone off her ear and covered the speaker as she listened. When she looked over at Darius, he smiled and waved as he headed toward the Hertz Car Rental booth to get the keys to his blue, rented Chevy Malibu. LaMarcus's mother gave Darius a grin that said she wanted to become deputized in a whole different fashion. She motioned with her finger for him to come to her. He smiled, tapped his watch and shook his head slowly. *Bitch, you are too skinny and way too ignorant for me*, he thought as he picked up his pace and hustled to Hertz.

Half an hour later, flight 1131 touched down. Piper rummaged through her carry-on bag in search of her cell phone. 'Many of the off-boarding passengers and flight attendants gawked at the linebacker-sized black woman departing the first-class section. She ignored all the flight attendants' pleasantries as she exited the plane. *As much as I'm paying, he'd better answer his goddamn phone*, Piper thought, as she headed to baggage claim. After the fifth ring, she checked her watch. *It's not even ten o'clock yet; that bastard Hank had better pick up.* She hung up once his voicemail kicked in. *I'll deal with him later. I need to get a car and get to my hotel so I can go find my little red-headed ho.*

Several yards away, next to a large concrete pillar, Darius pulled down the bill of his New York Mets cap and discreetly watched the hefty woman make a beeline from the American Airlines boarding gate straight to the baggage claim area. *Well, it should be easy enough to find her in a crowd.* He stealthily trailed her as she got her bags and rental car. As soon as she went to the Enterprise Rental Car desk, he hurried out to his car so he could track her from the Enterprise parking lot.

A short time later, he followed her white, rented Nissan Maxima into the five-story parking garage of the Hyatt hotel in the middle of Downtown Oakland. He kept his distance and watched her back into a parking slot next to a gray minivan, half a football field from the elevators. He parked a few rows away from her and waited for her to get on the elevator. *So far, so good.* He got out his car, opened the trunk and opened his briefcase. Inside, he removed a three-inch-long, P-Trac Pro, GPS Tracking device. He held the tiny device and turned it on.

I can follow your ass to the moon with this, Piper. He looked around, waited for an Asian family of five to enter the elevator, then closed the trunk and walked over to Piper's rental car. He took a quick look around as he removed a small leather case, containing lock-picking tools, from the side pocket of his loose-fitting jeans. *Good, this van is just enough cover to avoid the security cameras from seeing me.* In less than two minutes, he picked the trunk lock, peeled back a corner of the quarter panel insulation, placed the tracking device snuggly inside and closed the trunk. He grinned as he got back in his car and started the engine. *If shit keeps going this smooth, I'll have time to find Trenda, silence her and spend a little time doing some real vacationing.*

He drove around the corner and booked a room at

the low-budget Cypress Inn. He tossed his bags onto the eons-old, pale-green bedspread and grimaced. "I swear if I catch a fucking disease from this nasty-ass room, I'm gonna put a bullet into that shit-breathed check-in clerk." He walked over to his second-story window, pushed aside the dingy, piss-colored curtains, looked out at the clear, warm night and studied his view of the pool area of the five-star Hyatt Hotel.

The streets crawled with activity as clubgoers, hustlers, taxicabs, police cars, players, and other people of the night traveled on Broadway. He watched the hotel a little longer, then closed the drapes, walked over to the bed, opened his bag and removed the pistol and rubber bands. "Let me get you ready for action." After opening the packet of rubber bands, he wrapped nearly all of them around the grip.

Since the previous owner of the pistol had filed off the serial number, and the rubber bands would make pulling fingerprints off the grip impossible, the gun was the perfect, untraceable murder weapon. After putting the gun in his bag, he went into his briefcase and removed a top-of-the-line BlackBerry. He logged into the tracking software he'd used in a stakeout a few months back and was pleased to see the small, blinking red triangle indicating Piper's car. He went back to his briefcase, removed the mugshot picture of Trenda from the manila envelope, and grimaced. "Game on, bitch…"

Twenty-Six

"Shit!" Trenda said as she examined the run in her one and only pair of stockings. "And it's ten minutes to ten; I don't have enough time to go buy a new pair before Walter gets here." She opened the long split up the side of her designer, ankle-length, body-hugging, backless, halter-topped, black evening gown she'd found at the Goodwill store down the street from the hotel a few days ago, and examined her smooth bare leg. A confident smile curled the corners of her mouth. "Fuck the stockings; I'm sure Walter will appreciate not having to fight with taking them off."

She was extra horny. Stressful situations usually brought the freak out in her. Sex served as a form of escapism for her. She watched her braless nipples grow as she admired herself in the bathroom mirror. The thought of tasting Walter's log again made her slit sweat. "Girl, you a straight freak." As she applied a coat of brick-colored lipstick, she heard a knock at the door. She checked her watch, ten o'clock on the nose. *He is the most punctual man I have ever met.* She patted down her growing afro and walked barefoot to the door. "Who is it?"

"Your chauffeur."

She opened the door and enjoyed the way his eyes bulged as they traveled over her. "You look *fantastic!*"

"Thank you." She stepped to him, wrapped her arms around his neck and pressed her lips to his. He accepted her tongue for a short but intense kiss. She backed off and wiped her lipstick off his lips. "Happy Birthday, baby."

He adjusted his bright red tie, composed himself and followed her inside. His eyes locked on her rolling buttocks. "That's the best birthday greeting I have gotten all day."

She went into the bathroom and reapplied her lipstick. "It had better be." She picked up her tube of lipstick, turned off the light, walked back into the sitting area, sat next to Walter on the sofa and crossed her legs. "So, where are we eating?"

He followed her bare thigh all the way to her brick-red painted toenails. "Since it's kind of late, I figured we could go to Kimiko's in Alameda and have some sushi."

She picked a piece of lint off the lapel of his black Italian suit jacket. "That sounds real good, but I don't like raw fish."

He chuckled, took her hand and kissed it. "They also have tempura."

She wrinkled her nose. "Tempura? What's that?"

"It's batter-dipped shrimp, prawns, vegetables or fish that's fried."

"That's more like it!" She pulled her black pumps from

under the coffee table and slipped them on her feet. "Let's get goin'."

She enjoyed the view of the city and star-filled sky while riding with the top down in Walter's BMW. He glanced at her. "Is that too much air on you?"

She let her arm dangle out the window. "Not at all." She wiped an imaginary lock of hair out of her face. "I love to feel my hair blowin' in the wind."

He laughed. "I see. I wouldn't want it to get caught in any low-hanging branches."

"Funny." She smiled and thought back to when she used to wear her hair well past her shoulders. That and the combination of her eyes and extraordinary figure sometimes brought her *too* much attention. There were times she would rather starve than go get something to eat just to avoid being harassed by lusty men and women. Five years ago, after being approached by five different men in ten minutes while trying to get to a restroom in the mall, she went home and cut it all off.

At half past eleven, a waitress politely informed Walter and Trenda that they would be closing in thirty minutes. Walter put down the last piece of California Roll and patted his belly. "I think I overdid it. I can't eat another bite."

Trenda put her glass of sake up to her lips and looked at him over the rim. "Are you sure about that?"

He cocked his head. "What do you mean?"

She put her glass down, looked him in the eyes, licked

her lips and asked again. "Are you *sure* you can't eat anything else?"

He grinned and placed his hand on her bare thigh. "I think I can make room for a little dessert."

She placed her hand on his and guided him to the hot, bald, leaking oasis between her panty-free legs. "I have a lot of dessert for you."

He let his fingertip trace the moist slit. "I think it's time to get out of here."

On the way back to the hotel, Trenda reached between his legs and grasped Walter's swollen mass. The feel of its firmness under the fabric of his slacks turned up her burners. She nuzzled his neck and licked the inside of his ear, then whispered, "I am gonna fuck you crazy."

The car ran over several lane marker bumps as Walter swerved from his sexy distraction. "Keep that up and we won't make it back to the room."

Trenda continued to rub his crotch. It had been a while since she actually wanted to have her pussy dug out by a real dick. Usually a tongue or dildo would suffice, but with all the tension she had been suffering, she yearned for release. Just as she started unzipping his pants, a cell phone beeped. She looked up. "Is that your phone or mine?"

Walter did his best to speak coherently. "Has to be yours; I turned mine off as soon as I picked you up."

Trenda picked her purse off the floor, got her phone and saw she had a text message from Lollie. *"Hey, girl! Wassup? What you into tonight?"*

She leaned back in her seat, released her grip on Walter's junk and typed a reply. *"Hey, baby girl! I'm out helpin' Walter celebrate his birthday. What you into?"*

"Shit…bored as hell. I just got back from Fats. They had to close early because a few knuckleheads started fightin'. But I can catch you later. I don't wanna mess up you guys' groove."

Trenda glanced at Walter as he impatiently waited for a red light. A wicked smile filled her face. She sent another text. *"Come by my room in twenty minutes."*

"What? You want me to come by tonight? Don't you two have some celebrating to do?"

Trenda turned slightly away from Walter to keep him from reading her conversation. *"Yeah…come by and have a drink with us. He's cool with it."*

"Okay…if you are sure I won't be in the way. I ain't tryin' to be a third wheel."

"Cool! Bye." She shut off her phone, dropped it into her purse and resumed caressing Walter's chunk. "How you feelin', baby?"

He ran a yellow light, six blocks from the Hotel Oakland. "I am gonna go bananas with you teasing me. I can't tell you how many laws I have broken trying to hurry and get to my dessert."

She smiled, let him go and gathered herself as he pulled into the parking garage. *If all goes well, you are gonna have the mother of all birthday gifts…*

In the elevator to her room, Walter ran his hand through the split in her skirt and massaged her wet clit.

Trenda nutted on his finger twice before the elevator stopped at the eighth floor. They kissed, groped and stumbled all the way to her room. After she fumbled with getting the cardkey to work, he smiled and took it from her. "You are taking *way* too long."

Trenda checked her watch. *I gotta stall him for another ten minutes.* She waited for him to open the door and took her time walking in. She watched him take off his jacket, undo his tie and toss them onto the sofa. Before he could take off his shirt, she walked over and grabbed his hand. "C'mon, let's have a drink first."

He grabbed a handful of the ass under her tight dress. "I don't need a drink." He spun her around and pulled her close. "All I need right now is a double shot of you."

The feel of his lump pressed against her almost made her forget her plans. She resisted the urge to drop to her knees and suck the color off his prick. She grabbed him by the arm and pulled him to the wet bar. "We have to have a birthday toast. What do you want to drink, birthday boy?"

He stood behind her as she bent over and removed two shot glasses from the cabinet under the small sink on the wet bar. "Do you have any of that Gran Patron left?"

She bent back over and felt him grind on her ass. His firmness made her clit tremble. She found the half bottle of tequila and placed it on the counter next to the glasses. "It's your lucky day."

He kissed the side of her neck. "I see." He opened the bottle and poured both of them a healthy shot of tequila.

He eased back just enough for her to turn around facing him. He gave her a glass and held his out to her. "Happy birthday to me."

She pressed her breasts against him, smiled, and held her glass up. "Happy birth—" They both heard a knock at the door and froze.

He looked from the door into her eyes. "Are you expecting company?"

She grinned and slipped out of his arms. "Kinda." She ignored the puzzled look on his face, then went to the door and looked through the peephole. *Right on time, Lollie.* She opened the door and admired how good Lollie looked in her pink, mid-thigh-length skirt and black leather jacket. She stepped back, laughed and let her in. "I just know you didn't come over here in that bad-ass skirt wearing *house shoes!*"

Lollie, oblivious to the man standing by the wet bar, took off her jacket and stepped out of her fluffy, pink slippers. "Hell yeah! I wasn't about to wear my pumps just to come see y—" She saw Walter out the corner of her eye and paused. "Uhhh, hi, Walter, long time, no see." She smiled and pushed her hair out of her face. "Happy birthday!"

He beamed as his eyes involuntarily found her impressive breasts. "Thanks. I'm glad we could meet under more comfortable circumstances."

Lollie grinned, removed her jacket and handed it to Trenda. "Oh yeah...the last time was a *little* unusual."

Trenda stood back and read the reaction on their faces.

The pheromones in the air were as thick as London fog. She grinned. *Oh, yeah, I'm gonna make this happen.* "You are just in time to have a birthday drink with me and Walter."

Lollie wiggled her toes in the thick, champagne-colored carpet and looked from Walter to Trenda. "Are you guys *sure* I'm not interrupting?"

Trenda stepped out of her black pumps, bent over and picked them up. "Girl, please. Quit all that drama and sit down somewhere." She looked at Walter. "Do you mind if she has a drink with us?"

He was already getting a third shot glass out for Lollie. He smiled as he poured a dose of Patron into it. "I would be hurt if she didn't."

Trenda carried her shoes over to the sofa, put them under the coffee table, sauntered over to Walter and picked up two of the full shot glasses. "Bring the bottle in here, sweetie."

Lollie shook her head, laughed and made the sign of a cross as Walter walked in carrying the half bottle of Patron. "Oh, shit!" She looked at Trenda. "Now you *know* I don't need to drink any of that goddamn tequila."

Trenda grinned, removed her hoop earrings and placed them on top of the TV cabinet. "You need to quit it; you handled that shit like a pro."

Walter walked over, stood between the women and handed each a glass before picking up his own. "Join me in a birthday toast, ladies." They held their glasses in position. "To new friends and new memories…" They clinked glasses and tossed back their alcohol.

Trenda put her empty glass on the coffee table. "You guys sit down while I turn on some music." She picked up the TV remote, turned on the television and turned to the cable service's music channels. As she scanned the music they had to offer, Lollie and Walter struck up a conversation about how the club scene had changed over the past few years. Trenda found the classic hip-hop and R&B station and settled on that. She looked at her guests and grinned. *They sure look mighty cozy with each other.* She adjusted her dress's halter-top, sat down next to Walter and held up her empty glass. "Hey, birthday boy, I'm a lil' dry over here."

"Oh my bad. I'm going to have to do a better job because I definitely want a good tip." He ripped his eyes off Lollie's womanly goodies, picked up the bottle and refreshed all their drinks.

After the first two shots, Trenda and Walter were plenty buzzed after the sake they'd had with dinner. Lollie downed a third shot and her buzz was evident. She rose from her seat, picked up the TV remote and turned up the volume. "Ohhh, I love this song!" she said while bouncing to the sound of, 'Sexy Motherfucker' by Prince. She tossed the remote to the captivated Walter as she went to the middle of the floor and danced.

Trenda's eyes bounced in unison with Lollie's tits. She smiled and got up. "That song still sounds good as hell!"

She clapped and danced her way over to Lollie and joined her dance.

Walter looked as though he'd just entered his private suite in Heaven. He leaned forward on the sofa with the largest smile known to mankind on his face. He pursed his lips, furrowed his eyebrows and inhaled with pleasure at the sight of Trenda's bare leg as it emerged from the split in her dress.

While in the midst of a Prince triple play, the music station immediately mixed in Prince's song, "Soft and wet." Lollie and Trenda howled with delight. Lollie watched as Trenda broke it down, shaking and wiggling her body as she crouched inches above the floor. Lollie tossed her hair back and grinned. "I'm gonna show you how we do it 'Oakland style.'" Lollie pulled her skirt up just below her crotch, giving both Trenda and Walter a glimpse of her black thong, as she wiggled her way to her knees. Once there, she bent backward until the back of her head touched the floor, putting all the business under her skirt on display.

Walter jumped off the sofa and clapped furiously. "God Daaa-aaaaayum! You sure you didn't break your back?"

She eased up onto her knees, still moving to the music and smiled. "It takes a whole lot more than that to break *my* back."

Trenda's nipples rose like Walter's dick. "I see you talk a gang of shit with a lil' alcohol in you."

Lollie laughed and hitched up the spaghetti-strap of

her skirt, which had fallen over her shoulder. Her nipples were as excited as Trenda's. "Hey, don't let my smooth taste fool ya!"

Trenda looked at Walter and saw a broomstick growing down the leg of his light-gray slacks. He looked like a kid that had been given keys to Santa's toyshop. She bounced her way over to the table to the sound of "Lady Cabdriver." She took Walter's hand. "C'mon, birthday boy. It's your turn to show us what you got."

He hesitated. "I don't dance. Besides, I'm having a *great* time just watching you two."

Lollie smiled, shook her head and took his other hand. "I ain't tryin' to hear that tonight! You better get your butt over here."

With Pleasure in one hand and Delight in the other, he was powerless. He allowed them to situate him between them in front of the coffee table. Trenda picked up the remote and increased the volume as "Short but Funky," by Rapper "Too Short" fueled the groove. Walter bobbed his head as the women danced seductively in front of and behind him. Trenda worked her way behind him, wrapped her arms around him and rubbed her body against him while rubbing his chest. She stood on her toes and whispered in his ear. "Loosen up…it's party time."

He smiled as Lollie worked herself over and jiggled her body inches from his. "Okay!"

Lollie locked her eyes on his, smiled, then spun around

and placed her firm, round ass directly on his ultra-hard dick and ground on it. Trenda lowered her hands, took his hands and placed them on Lollie's waist. "If you gonna ride, you better hold on, cowboy!"

Lollie tossed her hair back and yelled, "Yeeee-haw!"

Walter got with the program. He wrapped his arms all the way around Lollie's small waist and rode her ass like the Lone Ranger. Trenda chuckled behind his back. *Now this is my kinda party!* She unbuttoned his shirt while rubbing her body against his from behind. She watched Lollie bend over and touch her toes as Walter held fast and enjoyed. Trenda's heated up. She pulled Walter's shirt off his shoulder and kissed it repeatedly. He took one hand off Lollie, reached behind and put his hand under the split in Trenda's dress. His fingers found a pleasant, wet, bald surprise. She licked his shoulder. "Mmmmmm, that's what I'm talkin' about."

The song changed from Too Short to "Saturday Love" by Alexander O'Neal and Cherelle. Lollie, feeling the heat behind her, turned around and faced Walter. He eased his hand out of Trenda's pussy and put it back on Lollie's hip. Lollie looked over his shoulder at Trenda. Trenda winked at Lollie letting her know everything is good. *I know you two are sprung as hell on each other.* Trenda then let go of Walter, walked up behind Lollie and danced up against her. She then whispered in Lollie's ear, "Go for it, girl…He ain't my man."

Walter smiled and pulled Lollie closer, then looked from one to the other. "What are you two up to?"

Lollie put her arms around his neck and grinned. "Nothing."

Trenda grinned like a mischievous imp. "She might not be up to nothin', but I am definitely up to something." She pulled down one of Lollie's shoulder straps and then the other. That was the first time Trenda had seen Walter truly shocked. He took a step back as Trenda placed her hands on Lollie's tits. Trenda felt Lollie tense up for a second, then relax as Trenda rubbed her hard nipples under the pink fabric. Trenda looked into Walter's shocked and lust-filled face. "Don't you want a taste of these?"

He was tongue-tied. "I, uhhh…hmmm…"

Trenda uncovered Lollie's chocolate breasts. She read the caution and lust in his eyes. She smiled and reassured him all was good. "I think you do…"

Lollie covered her love bags with her arms out of reflex, then slowly let her arms fall. She looked at Walter through the half-closed eyes of a horny freak. "You like?"

Trenda took Walter's arm and helped him out of his shirt. He took both hands and cupped Lollie's right breast. "Yes…I like a whole lot." He lowered his head and suckled her black, erect nipple.

Trenda rubbed her own twins as she watched Lollie lean her head back and enjoy Walter's sucking. Trenda went to the table, poured a shot of Patron and picked up the glass. She poured half the shot in her mouth, walked over to Lollie, took her by the hair and pressed her lips to Lollie's. Lollie resisted at first, then caved in and opened her mouth. Trenda let the half-shot of Patron run from her mouth into Lollie's. Lollie greedily swallowed it down and sucked the remainder off Trenda's tongue. Trenda unlocked lips with Lollie and poured the rest of the shot into her mouth, and repeated her trick on Walter. He, too, accepted the drink and licked the inside of her mouth clean. She smiled, grabbed Lollie's left breast and offered it to Walter. "This one needs some attention now."

Both Walter and Lollie moaned in unison as he went to work on her tits. Trenda enjoyed her roll as the sexual orchestrator. She refilled the shot glass and poured a trickle on Lollie's areola, which Walter eagerly cleaned up with his tongue. Walter licked the last few drops of tequila off Lollie's nipples, then kissed his way up to her neck. Trenda walked up behind Lollie, reached around and caressed her tits. She purred like a satisfied kitty as Walter and Trenda worked on her.

Trenda watched Walter grab a handful of Lollie's hair, lean her head back and kiss her full lips. As they tongue-wrestled, Trenda moved around, undid Walter's pants, and let them fall to the floor. She rubbed the bulge in his burgundy, Michael Jordan-endorsed, boxer-briefs as he stepped out of his trousers. She gripped Lollie's ass while massaging Walter's tool. *Mmmmmm, it's time for business.* She moved behind Lollie and eased her skirt down her smooth thighs, to the floor. She took both of them by the hand and led them to the bedroom. "Time for you to open your presents, birthday boy."

Twenty-Seven

B y the time Trenda turned on the small lamp on the desk across from the bed, Walter and Lollie stood next to the bed, completely nude, trying to suck the taste out of each other's mouths. Trenda's pussy perspired at the sight. *They look good together…* "Mmmm, I want some of that…" She walked over, eased between them and they engaged in a three-way tongue fest.

Walter put one finger in Trenda's bald snatch and another finger in Lollie's hairy cat. They wriggled and wet his digits while rubbing each other's tits. He inserted a second finger into each vagina. "Mmmm, my favorite; wall-to-wall pussy."

Trenda slid off his fingers, leaned him back on the bed and stood next to the bed looking down at him. His dick looked like a black Washington Monument. She grabbed the swollen head and stroked it slowly. She turned to Lollie who watched as she rubbed her pink clit. "C'mon… suck it. I see your mouth waterin' for it."

Lollie grinned, got on her knees between Walter's legs, swept her hair back and kissed the tip of his penis.

Walter's toes gripped the thick carpet as Lollie slowly took him into her wet mouth. Trenda watched his eyes roll back with pleasure. The slurping sound of Lollie's suction increased Trenda's heat. She peeled off her dress, let it fall to the floor and crawled into the bed. Lollie stopped sucking and jerked him slowly. "You want some of this?"

Trenda shook her head. "Not yet…you keep doin' what you doin'."

Walter opened his eyes to the sight of Trenda tossing her leg over his face. Her pink pussy looked down at him. "Oh yeah! Feed me, baby."

Lollie licked her lips as Trenda placed her pussy on Walter's mouth and soaked his moustache. Lollie gripped his dick tighter as she stroked him. "Oh, shit! That looks sexy as fuck!"

Trenda looked over her shoulder at Lollie and smiled. "Get back to work on that dick." Walter ate Trenda's pussy like a lesbian. His tongue tickled and teased her clit while Lollie sucked the meat off his dick. Trenda had multiple orgasms in and on his mouth. She sensed Walter getting close to busting a nut and hopped off of him. She looked into his wet face. "Not yet, baby."

He tried to speak, but Lollie's magnificent head turned his words into unintelligible mumbles. Trenda eased Lollie off the dick. "Enough suckin'; time for fuckin'." She stepped back and watched Lollie straddle his pole, take hold of it and gobble it up with her wet wonderland.

Trenda watched Walter simultaneously try to knock a hole in Lollie's uterus as she tried to break his dick off at the root. *Now that's what I call fuckin'.* Lollie slowed down and teased his dickhead with her swollen pussy lips, giving Trenda the opportunity to join in the action.

Trenda worked her way to Walter's balls and sucked his cum-heavy nut sac. Walter yelled with ecstasy overload. "Ohhhhhh-hhhh, fuck! Shiiiiiiiiiiiiiiiiiiiiiit!"

Lollie rubbed his meat-helmet against her wet, wet clit. "I am… gonna…mmmmmm…gonna…cummmmmm… oh fuuuuuuuuu-uckkkk!"

Trenda moved out of the way and rubbed Walter's balls, allowing Lollie to grind her way to a massive orgasm. Trenda read the unmistakable contortions in his face, signaling he was about to nut. He gripped Lollie's hips and thrust faster and harder. Trenda massaged his balls faster. *Oh, yeah, here we go…*she felt Walter's legs stiffen, and heard Lollie shriek with delight, as he shot cum inside Lollie's hot hole. Overwhelmed with passion, Trenda slipped his ejaculating dick out of Lollie, sucked the last drops of semen out of his hose, and licked it clean. She then looked up, saw a few drops of white, creamy cum leaking out of Lollie's twat, and licked her lips. *Ahhhh, seconds!*

Twenty-Eight

The following morning, after three hours of sleep, Piper hopped out of the comfortable queen-sized bed in her suite, put on her glasses, picked up the handset of the phone on her nightstand and dialed. *You had better answer, asshole.*

Three rings later, she heard, "Hank Martin, how can I help you?"

She let the goldenrod-colored bedspread fall from her huge boobs. "This is Piper Langford. How are you, Hank?"

Her unusually chipper tone shocked him. "Hello, Ms. Langford. Good to hear from you. How are you?"

"I am wonderful. What do you have for me?"

She heard the volume of a radio talk show being turned down along with papers rustling in the background. "If you can give me a second…ahhh, here we go. I was able to track Ms. Fuqua up until approximately midnight last night where she entered the Hotel Oakland."

Piper grabbed the complimentary ink pen and pad. "Do you have the address?"

"Sure do. It's 801 Broadway. Oh, by the way, she wasn't alone last night. Just thought I'd let you know."

Piper squeezed the handset. Her tone shifted from pleasant to irritated in the space of a heartbeat. "That's not surprising. Do you know who the hell she was with?"

"According to the license plates of the vehicle they rode in, it belongs to Walter Secrease, the same gentleman who paid for the room."

Piper squinted as a beam of morning sunlight sprung from between the gap in the reddish-brown drapes and bounced off her glasses. "I assumed that. What other fucking information did my money buy?"

Ten minutes later, Piper received an email containing a picture of Walter, a picture of his car, the plate number and the location of his Oakland funeral home. After getting what she wanted, she rudely hung up on Hank, walked over to the closet and put on her Hyatt hotel robe. Not until she stood and saw her face in the mirror, on the wall, over the desk, did she notice the tears running down her face. She removed her glasses and brushed them away. She saw a hallucinated image of Trenda laughing at her in the mirror. "Just wait, you bitch."

She walked over to the desk and picked up her toiletry bag. Inside, she scrounged around until she came across a small bottle of Xanax pills. She popped the top and looked at the four remaining pills as she walked over to the bathroom sink. *God, I hate the taste of these nasty fucking pills.* She placed the bottle on the counter next to the sink. *The hell with this, I'm going to have room service bring me up a glass of orange juice to wash them down.* As she turned from the counter, the wide sleeve of her robe knocked the bottle of pills into the sink. "Oh fuck!" She watched the four peach-colored pills roll down the drain. She grabbed the empty bottle and hurled it across the room. She watched it harmlessly bounce off the drapes and roll under the desk. *The hell with it. I'll do without them for now. I have much more important business to take care of.*

Sitting on the bed, she ordered breakfast from room service. She sat and picked at a hangnail on her right thumb, thinking about doing harm to Trenda, until blood ran down to her wrist. A knock at the door broke her psychotic moment. She rose from the bed, caught a glimpse of herself in the mirror and suddenly laughed aloud as she wiped the blood onto her robe. "Damn, Piper, tuck that big tit back in your robe before the bellboy gets a free peek."

By ten in the morning, Piper had eaten, showered and dressed. She tore the sheet of paper that contained the information she had gotten from Hank off the notepad and tucked it into the pocket of her navy blue Addidas sweatsuit. She used both hands to pull her foot up high enough into her lap to tie the laces of her white Addidas tennis shoes. She huffed and puffed after the effort it took to tie her shoes.

Trenda has never got out the bed before noon; I have plenty of time to catch her still in her room. She grabbed her room cardkey, rental car key and wallet and tucked them into her pockets before exiting her room. She had to pick up a few things before paying her friend a visit. After stopping at the reception desk, she used the hotel computer to download and print the pictures Hank had sent her.

In the BART station parking lot, across the street from the Hyatt, Darius yawned and stretched while sitting in the driver's seat of his rental car. "I sure hope I don't have to stake out Piper's ass all day." He picked up the BlackBerry off the passenger seat and sighed at the sight of the blinking, unmoving small red triangle. *It's bad enough I've had to sit here and chase off the begging panhandlers since six this morning. I don't need to be here for the next shift of bums to come through.*

He watched as a mild breeze caused the myriad of flags from different countries, mounted around the roof perimeter of the Hyatt, flicker and dance. *My hunch about Piper had better be right, or else I'm wasting a lot of valuable time.* He reached down to the floor in front of the passenger seat and picked up the black gym bag. *Something tells me she's gonna silence Trenda for me.* He unzipped it and picked up the silencer-equipped, snub-nosed .38 pistol he had "borrowed" from a crime scene several months ago. He flipped open the cylinder, inspected the hollow-point rounds and put the weapon down. *But just in case…* It belonged to an unsolved murder case in West Baltimore.

Next to the gun, box of ammo, three sets of handcuffs,

bulletproof vest, lock-picking tools, roll of duct tape and a black ski mask, he found his sunglasses. He put on the shades, zipped up the bag and put it back on the floor. He watched a young black couple walk out of the hotel, hugged up. He looked at the grinning cola-colored brother and thought, *I sure hope that pussy was worth it. That looks like one hell of an expensive hotel to use for fucking a chick as average looking as your girl is.*

He reflected on how he made sure to use the cheapest motels possible for his unsavory trysts. The only woman he'd ever taken to an expensive hotel was his wife—on his honeymoon in Hawaii. Even then, he'd bitched about the cost. Of all the women he'd fucked with and fucked over, Trenda was the only one that gave him a serious challenge. He loved her fiery ways. The more she defied him and his authority as the law, the more he desired her. No woman had ever satisfied his out-of-control sex drive the way Ms. Fuqua did. He had joined the ranks of those whom had fallen under the spell of her unforgettable "Magic Clit."

He grinned at the memory of how he had actually called her name while making love to his wife six months ago. Of course, when she pushed him off of her and cussed him out, he did the only thing he could do: deny, deny, deny! He did a piss poor job trying to claim the name Beverly sounded like Trenda under the circumstances. He told her, her pussy was so good he couldn't speak clearly.

Although she didn't buy his lie, she did calm down a bit after he did a Kobe Bryant and gave her a "shut up" trinket—a six-grand, mother-of-pearl and diamond Versace watch, which, he removed from a bag of loot he and Tyrone had recovered from a snatch-and-grab jewelry store robbery. He had no problem stealing the watch in order to keep his wife from divorcing him.

The idea of ruining his flawless public image with the ugliness of a divorce was more than his gigantic ego could bear. That, along with his allergy to doing prison time, helped pave the road on which he currently traveled. A road that currently had him three thousand miles from home, prepared to commit one of the most heinous acts imaginable.

While Piper debriefed Hank Martin and Darius sat behind the wheel of his car having a bag of corn nuts for breakfast and fending off beggars, Trenda was awakened by a few strands of Lollie's hair tickling her ear, as they lay back-to-back. She gently brushed the hairs off the side of her face and thought about the previous night's triple play. She looked over Lollie's shoulder and saw her and Walter were asleep in a lover's embrace.

Last night was far from the first time Trenda had given away a lover to a deserving friend. As far as she could remember, she always had a talent for hooking people up. Her kidneys told her it was time to tinkle. She eased out of the bed, picked her robe off the floor and went to the bathroom. She had no memory of how the nearly empty bottle of Patron ended up on the hallway floor or of how her dress wound up, balled up, under the bed.

She closed her eyes and slowly rotated her neck as she did her business on the toilet. A tingle shot threw her as she wiped her kitty and flushed. *I'm still horny. I need a thick, stiff one inside me.* That was one of the rare times she craved penetration. She almost regretted not letting Walter fuck her last night. Usually a finger, tongue or dildo would suffice, but in that instance, she needed to feel a hot, living hard dick stretching her pussy walls. After a nice hot shower, she stood at the sink, picked up her toothbrush, applied toothpaste and began brushing her teeth. *I guess I could just let Walter fuck me, but now that I have officially given him to Lollie, that's a no-no.*

Although Trenda had made many men leave their women for her, she had never *knowingly* slept with any of her friends' men. After brushing her teeth, she headed back to the bedroom. On the way, she chuckled at the array of clothing strewn about the hotel room: Walter's jacket across the sofa, Lollie's pink dress on the floor in front of the TV, her black thong dangling from the tall, artificial plant next to the sofa and three pairs of shoes scattered around like chips on a bingo card. She eased the door open a bit, peeked into the bedroom and saw Lollie and Walter still tangled up. He lay on his side, facing her, with his leg sandwiched between her smooth thighs. She recalled getting out of the bed, sitting on the edge of the dresser, and fingering her pussy while watching Lollie and Walter fuck.

She pushed the door open a little further. It creaked, causing one of Walter's eyes to open. His lips formed a smile. "Good morning, you."

Trenda tightened the belt of her robe and returned his smile. "Good morning to you, birthday boy."

Lollie stirred, opened her eyes and immediately unwrapped her legs from Walter's and pushed back from him. "Oh…hey, Mya."

Trenda chuckled and shook her head. "It's all good. You ain't gotta let him go on my account." She turned her attention to Walter. Puzzlement replaced his normally cool demeanor. "You ain't gotta trip, either. I saw how y'all was feelin' each other the first time you met. I knew right then y'all needed to be together."

Walter and Lollie looked at each other and exchanged small smiles. Even though the smile exchange confirmed what Trenda proclaimed, they both ignored what she had said and instead traveled down the road of denial. Lollie swung her legs over the edge of the bed and used the bedspread to cover her body as though she hadn't fucked them both all night. After not being able to locate a robe, she gave up the charade, stood up and grinned. "That's your hangover talking."

Trenda swatted Lollie's bare bottom as she walked toward the bathroom. "That's some bullshit and you know it."

Walter enjoyed the spectacle as he absently rubbed his well-satisfied penis. "Mya," he patted the bed next to him, "come here and quit harassing folks. You need to learn how to live in the moment every now and then and enjoy life."

Trenda turned away from his smiling face, walked over to the sliding patio doors, spread the earth-toned drapes and peered outside. Her face welcomed the warm sunlight. She opened the glass doors, stepped outside, looked down at the swimming pool and watched a maintenance man check the PH level in the pool. *Lollie and Walter make a cute couple.*

For the first time since she was a teen, she found herself wishing *she* could wake up in the arms of a man she cared about. She watched an elderly couple walk past the pool area, hand-in-hand, seemingly very happy to be together. *I wonder what it feels like to be that close to someone? I bet they still fuck, too…as a matter of fact, I bet they make love…* Trenda found herself very uncomfortable with this new line of thinking. The closest she had come to falling in love was back in her junior year of high school. The BMOC at the time, the state wrestling champion, a huge, grizzly bear-shaped brother named "Big Paul," nearly stole her heart. His size, confidence and gentleness appealed to her. Even though all the other jocks, and most of them with a much better physique than Paul's, practically fought for her affection. Something about his gut and kindness *almost* stole her heart—that was until she hooked up with the uncle of her best friend.

The lure of that married man's willingness and ability to spoil Trenda with material shit made her soon forget Big Paul's huge heart and small wallet. *It's cool that Walter likes to spend money on me, but he ain't my type. It's a blessing that he and Lollie hit it off; will make it easier for me to break loose from him.* She turned around at the sound of Lollie's laugh. She walked back into the room and watched as Walter grabbed her and pulled her down on top of him. "Uh-oh! Time for another round I see."

Lollie turned toward Trenda, smiled and tossed her hair out of her face. "Will you please tell your friend to let me go?"

Trenda grinned and stood with her arms crossed. "Nope. My dog ain't in that fight. You're on ya own."

Walter placed his hand behind Lollie's head and smiled at her. "See, even your buddy agrees with me. You might as well give it up and just relax."

Trenda walked over to the closet and picked out some clothes. "I need to go take care of some business; you guys just lock up when you leave."

Walter placed his hand on Lollie's head and stroked her hair. He then looked at Trenda. "So, where do we go from here?"

Trenda stood at the edge of the bed, next to Lollie. "It depends…" She read the questioning look on Lollie's face. "It depends on how you two want to handle this. I have no problem keeping the status quo—with a few adjustments."

Lollie brushed her hair out of her face and sat up on her elbows. "You don't feel funny about what we did last night? I mean, I thought you and Walter were…"

Walter threw his arm across Lollie's abdomen. "What kind of 'adjustments' are you talking about?"

"Let's keep it real. I can tell by the way you and Lollie got down that y'all are feelin' each other something fierce. I think you two might have more in common than just fuckin' each other to death." She looked at Lollie and grinned. "And Lollie, girl, you ain't gotta trip. Even though Walter and me did kick it once, it ain't gonna happen again. I don't mess with my friends' men." She tickled the smiling Lollie's chin. "And as much as you have helped me out—both of you—it's the least I can do to try and pay you guys back."

Walter shook his head. "You don't owe me anything, Mya. I—"

Trenda cut him off. "No…no…I always pay my debts. No matter how long it takes. It's just how I am. All I ask is that I can keep this room for the next two weeks since it's already paid for. By then, I will find somewhere else to stay, even if I have to live out of my car. I've done it before and can do it again if necessary."

Lollie relaxed and leaned back onto Walter. "You won't have to live in a car as long as you know me. I can show you how to work the hotel where you can always find room if you need one. Hell, you can even stay with me for a while if need be. And since we are 'keepin it real,'" she looked into Walter's grinning face, "I *am* feelin' Mr.

Secrease and do intend on keeping him around for a while." Her gaze found Trenda. "I'm even good with the idea that you two have fucked. Actually, it's kind of sexy to me. I don't think I am nearly as wild as you, girl, but I do likes to get my freak on, too."

Walter cleared his throat. "Uhhh, ladies. Do I get to have a say in all this?"

They both looked at him. Trenda shook her head, stood and began putting on her clothes. "No…and if you want to keep that dick satisfied, you would be wise to keep your mouth closed. It's not every day you wake up with two fine bitches and the chance to keep one of them as your personal 'dick emptier.'"

Both Lollie and Walter laughed aloud. Lollie shook her head. "Girl, you are a damn fool!"

Twenty-Nine

"It's about goddamn time," Darius said once he spotted Piper pulling out of the hotel's parking garage. He checked the blinking light on his BlackBerry and started his car. "C'mon, Piper. Lead me to that half-slick bitch."

Fifteen minutes later, Piper pulled into the parking lot of a Manuel's Cutlery Shop on Broadway. "That is one of our finest carving knives, ma'am," the gray-haired cashier said after ringing up Piper's purchase of a ten-inch, extremely sharp serrated knife. "You could slice up a reindeer with it!" he said with a huge smile.

One short bitch is all I need it to cut up, she thought as she paid for her purchase. "Thank you, sir." On her way to the Hotel Oakland, she smiled with glee at the thought of using the knife to pop both of Trenda's green eyes out. *Yes…the last thing she is going to see is the smile on my face…*

"What the hell is she doing here?" Darius said after following Piper into the cutlery shop's parking lot. His patience with Piper leading him to Trenda was growing thin. Each moment Trenda walked around free, was another moment closer to his ruin. *Captain Kelly would cut her any kind of deal he could to get her to snitch me out,* Darius thought while watching Piper enter the store.

He switched the BlackBerry from his tracking software to his phone's call log. *That's another issue; I haven't heard from Tyrone yet. I need to find out if he heard anything new about our case from Terrence. And I also need to make sure he doesn't buckle from the captain's pressure. He's my boy, but he can fold up like a card table if you press him too hard.*

Ten minutes later, to his pleasure, Piper exited the store. While discreetly following her, he mentally worked on his exit strategy once Trenda was dealt with.

Piper tapped the carving knife against her leg as she drove to the Hotel Oakland. "It's time to pay the Piper, bitch," she said as she pulled into the Hotel Oakland's parking garage. "Oh shit!" She slammed on her brakes after passing up a silver BMW backing out of a parking stall. "Is that the car?" She quickly sorted through the pictures on her front seat she had gotten from Hank. She whipped a quick U-turn as she held the picture of a silver BMW. "Fuck yes! That's' it! I can't tell for sure with that tinted back window, but it looks like he had a passenger."

Weaving in and out of traffic, trying to catch up with the BMW, Piper almost caused a heap of accidents. An "Out to Lunch" sign hung on the logical part of her brain. Never once did she let go of the carving knife as she maniacally maneuvered her rental car down the streets of Oakland. The BMW was two blocks ahead of her. "C'mon, fuck!" Piper yelled at the slow traffic in front of her. After running her second consecutive red light, she caught up with the BMW and pulled alongside it at a four-way stop sign. She then turned her wheels toward the car just in case she had to ram it if he tried to get away.

"This nutty broad is gonna kill somebody with her crazy-drivin' ass," Darius said as he did his best to keep up with Piper and yet remain unnoticed by her. "Trenda must be inside that car." He used one hand to pick up his bag containing the pistol and put it on the passenger seat.

"Do you know this woman?" Lollie asked as she turned her attention away from the large woman in the car next to them. "She sure is staring hard at your car."

Walter leaned forward, looked past Lollie into the face of the staring woman. "No, I don't know who she is." He lowered the passenger window. "Can I help you?"

The woman continued to glare at them, eyes searching

for something. She glared at Lollie. "Is Trenda in there with you?"

Lollie hunched her shoulders. "Who?"

Is this bitch deaf? Piper thought as she gripped the carving knife handle tighter. "I said, is Trenda in the backseat?"

Walter shook his head. "I can't hear you and don't really have time to chat. The cars behind us are getting pissed off. Goodbye."

Before throwing her car into park, and jumping out, Piper caught movement in her rearview mirror. "This is your lucky day, ass-hole," she said as a motorcycle cop made his way toward them between the line of drivers waiting behind them. She slammed the blade of the knife six inches deep into the passenger seat, turned on her blinker and made a right turn just as the cop reached her rear bumper.

After giving Walter a chirp with his siren, the cop waved at him to move. Walter and Lollie looked at each other as he took off. He shook his head. "What the hell was her problem? Have you ever seen her before?"

Lollie shook her head in return. "Hell no. I don't know who that big woman is. And who was she looking for? Some body named Kendra or Brenda?"

"I don't know, but I tell you what; I sure as hell am glad she isn't looking for me! She looks like she's a few eggs short of a full dozen."

"What are they talking about?" Darius asked, three cars behind the BMW. "Whatever it is, it must be damned important for them to ignore all these horns blowing behind them."

His police officer mentality took over. As soon as the motorcycle cop passed him, Darius followed the BMW until he was able to make a note of the license plate. "If he was important enough for Piper to stop traffic for, I need to find out who he is."

Thirty

The Sunday morning sunshine gave Trenda a warm caress as she exited the hotel. Her freshly cleaned, pink velour sweat suit was a perfect outfit for that spring morning. The chime of nearby church bells informed her it was eleven o'clock. A low rumble in her belly informed her it was time to eat. She made a U-turn en route to her car. "It's not that far. I think I'll walk."

Halfway between the hotel and Momma's Café where she was going for breakfast, Trenda slowed her pace as she approached one-hundred-and-ten-year-old St. Augustine's church. She adjusted her dark shades and watched the last folks trickle in trying to make the eleven-thirty service. *This looks like daddy's church.* The huge, brick church boasted of the largest congregation of Episcopalians in the city. The modern digital marquee, erected above the twelve-foot-high solid oak doors, displaying service times and upcoming events was a blemish on the magnificent ancient architecture.

A wave of melancholy washed over her. She recalled how she actually used to love going to church. Each

Sunday she looked forward to the feeling of comfort in God's house. That was before puberty hit and the devil in her hormones took over. At the age of twelve, her development began. By the time she was a teen, the looks she received from men had changed from "she's a cute kid" to "mmmmmm, shit, she is sexy!"

Her regular skirmishes with her parents also began. She recalled her father's favorite Bible quote: REVELATION 22:12:

Behold, I am coming soon! My reward is with me, and I will give to everyone according to what he has done.

She had heard that quote more times than she cared to remember. *My period must be getting ready to come down*, she thought as her somber mood encased her. She rubbed the spot on her arm where her contraceptive implant was located. *It's almost time for me to get a new dose.* Bitchiness and extreme horniness were warnings that her monthly was on the way. After passing through the shadow of the church, the sunlight made her feel a little better.

The pancakes, bacon and scrambled egg breakfast she enjoyed at Momma's Café worked a miracle on her mood. After pushing back from the scraps of her meal, she took her cell phone out of her purse. After returning her many, many voicemails and missed calls from her most important clients, she set the phone on her table. *Fuck... I have turned down almost five grand worth of work since I left.*

The sun beaming through the café window warmed

the side of her face. *Oh well, I gotta get used to that anyway if I'm really serious about tryin' to live a square lifestyle. Even though running that briefcase of coke from B-more to South Carolina would have paid for a couple months of bills for me, I can't let that big money tempt me.*

A husky man, in his finest church suit, walking past the window, reminded her of Box. She smiled and picked up her phone. *I wonder what my big-boo is up to this fine Sunday morning?*

After three rings, his familiar voice sounded. "Hey, Mya! How are you? I was wondering when I was going to hear from you."

"Well, today is the day. What you up to, Box?"

"Not much. I just got back from visiting my mother's church in Vallejo. What's on your agenda? Did you go to church today?"

What's with all these religious messages today? I know it's Sunday but damn! "No, I didn't make church today. I'm just tryin' to enjoy my day off before I have to go back to the plantation tomorrow. I was kinda wondering if you wanna hang out or somethin'."

"That sounds real good to me!"

Trenda grinned and waved to the waitress to bring her check. "Are you sure about that? Did you get permission from Meagan to get out the house?"

"Don't tell me you are still on that 'needing permission' kick. I told you I answer to no one but God."

Trenda accepted the bill from the waitress, reached

into her wallet and placed a twenty-dollar bill on the table next to the bill. "Anyway, I'm out and about; do you want to meet at the Starbucks where we met when I went to the DMV?"

"Yes, let's do that. What time?"

She glanced at the clock on the café wall. "About twenty minutes."

"Okay, I'll see you then!"

After ending the call, Trenda stood, stretched and smiled. The warmth building in her pelvic area pepped up her mood. *Let's go see what Box is all about...*

As Trenda walked back to the hotel, got her car and drove to El Cerrito, Officer Kain was busy in his hotel room looking up information on Walter Secrease. The phone book ad for "Secrease Funeral Homes" laid open before him, on his hotel room's tiny desk. "Looks like this brotha has a few bucks," Darius said as he looked at the full-page ad. "At least I know where I can find him if need be."

The ad featured the business hours, location and the fact that they performed traditional burials at their four-acre cemetery. They also did cremations in their onsite crematory as well. After entering all the pertinent information about the funeral home into his BlackBerry, he went into his bag and got the second of two cell phones he and Tyrone used when they needed an anonymous conversation and dialed. "What's good, partner?"

"Well, besides having to worry about the possibility of losing my job *and* ending up in jail, everything is pretty goddamn good."

"Easy, homeboy. Hold on to ya panties. Have you heard anything from Internal Affairs?"

"Not a word. They just 'requested' I be available in case they need to contact me. I wish I had thought of goin' on vacation right before all this shit went down like you did. How the fuck you get so lucky?"

Darius stood in front of the mirror next to the TV, picked up his brush off the desk and gave his hair a few strokes. "It's called handling your business." He put the brush down and rubbed his eyes. "Anyway, I was just callin' to get your status. For the time being, we'll only talk on these phones; I don't wanna take any chances. They might have our regular phone lines tapped."

"I wish you would quit talkin' to me like I am some new-booty rookie! If you think about it, I have been on the force a year longer than *you*, homeboy."

Darius furrowed his brow. "*What?* I just *know* you ain't goin' there! You are the one that was always cryin' about how broke you were when we first became partners almost ten years ago. Did you forget about that stripper you fucked from Savannah who got pregnant and is suing your ass for child support and your other baby momma that is collectin' from you? It was *me* that hipped you to the game and helped you make enough extra money to dig your ass out of bankruptcy and get your ex-wife's lawyers out your ass!"

"Yeah, well—"

"Yeah well my ass! Don't forget it was *you* that begged *me* to bring you into my side hustle. Besides bein' a rapper or ball player, where the hell else could a broke and horny muthafucka like you make an extra ten grand a month and free-fuck every prostitute in Baltimore?"

"Man, this is different; it's not like some upset gang member wanting to get revenge on us shakin' him down. We can't just drop Internal Affairs in a tub of acid to get rid of them…and all this drama is behind *you* chasing that redheaded bitch's pussy."

The unaccustomed feel of losing control of a situation caused his words to dry up in his mouth. He'd watched Tyrone dispose of many bodies over the years without nearly this much concern. *Maybe I am taking this situation too lightly.* "You're talkin' too much…way too much."

"Whatever. I gotta go; handle *your* business and get rid of this problem *quick*."

Darius shook his head after hearing his stressed-out partner end the call. *That fool is comin' loose at the seams. I can't afford to have his ass freakin' out on me now.* He sat at the desk and looked at the ad for Secrease Funeral Homes again. *Fuck waitin' for Piper to do all the work. I'm gonna go do some recon work on my own.*

Thirty-One

Inside her car, just outside the El Cerrito Department of Motor Vehicles, Trenda smiled at the sight of the thick man standing near the entrance of the closed building. He stood in the shadow of the entryway looking up and down the sidewalk. "I bet he ain't ever been late for an appointment in his life."

Outside the car, it took mere seconds for the watchful Box to spot his desire. Trenda put a lil' extra sway in her already lethal sexy walk as she approached him. Leaving his spot in the shade, his smile grew with each step. "Hello, gorgeous one!" He opened his thick arms and offered her a hug. "Come here, you!"

A genuine smile curved her mouth as she walked into his arms. "Hey, big fella! Did you miss me?"

"More than the deserts miss the rain."

The smell of his cologne was pleasant. She smirked. "Okay…now I know you stole that line from a song I heard a long time ago."

"Guilty as charged." He gently released her. "But it fits! You sure have been on my mind."

A pair of teen-aged boys on skateboards whizzed past them. A rogue cool breeze briefly visited the smiling couple. Trenda adjusted her shades and watched the skateboarders use pedestrians, the DMV stairs and the curb as their personal obstacle course. "Now why in the world would you be thinking about me? I'm sure Meagan gets all your attention."

He rolled his eyes, then pushed the sleeves of his topaz-colored shirt up to the middle of his forearms. "Why do you have to bring her up? This is *our* time."

He is so thick! she thought as she ran her eyes over his body while putting her shades back on. "I'm just sayin'… I don't need you callin' out the wrong name one night. I'd hate to think of her doing an 'Al Green' and throwing hot grits on your ass."

Laughter erupted from him. "Oh my God! I cannot believe you went there!" He wiped sweat off his forehead. "Are you always this suspicious?"

She chuckled to herself as she watched him struggle with not looking at her tits. "I am a woman…suspicion is in our nature. Besides," she unbuttoned the top button of his shirt and gave his throat some air, "if we are gonna be the kind of friends I believe you wanna be, I need to know what kind of situation I'm workin' with."

It took a few moments for him to formulate his words. The unusually warm spring afternoon didn't account for all the heat he was feeling. His body language told Trenda all she needed to know; seducing him would be as easy as drawing a breath. "What do you mean when you say 'the kind of friends I want to be'?"

Smiling behind her shades, she walked up and wiped a bead of sweat off his forehead. "The kind that fuck…"

A nervous grin took shape on his face. "What…what did you say?"

She glanced at her watch. "Look. Enough of this drama. I saw a few motels on San Pablo Avenue on the way here. We are going to go to one, book a room and fuck." She crossed her arms and looked in his face. "Is there a problem with that?"

Licking his lips, he ran his hand over his head. "Wow! Boy…I uhhh…" He adjusted his wire-rimmed glasses. "God, you have no idea how long I have waited for this, Mya."

She took his large hand in hers. "Where did you park, sexy?"

"Right down the street." He walked her halfway down the block and stopped at a blue Prius. "Here we are."

Trenda lifted her shades and studied the car. "Is this one of those cars that gets a million miles a gallon?"

"Close." He opened her door and let her in. "It gets me from here to there a lot cheaper than most cars."

Reaching between his legs before closing the door, she squeezed his chunk. "Just make sure it gets us to the motel, baby."

Thirty-Two

"So this is the place," Darius said as the beacon on his GPS showed he was in front of Secrease Funeral Home. He pulled into the large, empty parking lot next to the sparkling white building. Tall Italian Cypress trees, standing like twenty-foot-tall missiles and well-trimmed hedges encircled the facility. It reminded Darius more of a Southern-style plantation mansion than a building of death.

The crematorium portion of the building was tastefully placed behind the building, hidden from view. The only giveaway was the chimney from the furnace, which peeked over the rooftop of the main building. He looked at the eaves of the building and at the lamppost in the parking lot. "Cool…I don't see any kind of security cameras in place."

After taking a second look around, he walked up to the large double doors and read the sign giving the business hours. He checked the door locks. "These are easy enough to break into…but then I doubt Mr. Funeral-man never had much need to worry about anybody breakin' into a fuckin' funeral home."

He made his way to the back of the building and checked out the crematorium. It, just like the main building, had minimum security set up. A row of white limousines and hearses sat across from the entryway into the crematorium. "Ahhhh, what's this?" he said after reading a plaque next to the door. It told him deliveries were only accepted during the week after three in the afternoon. "I bet that's when he does most of his body burning." He looked up at the tall chimney. "I'm sure he doesn't want to have the thing smokin' during the day if he can help it."

The sound of an engine got his attention. He hurried and ducked behind one of the Italian cypress trees, near the rear entrance. A beam of sunlight bounced off the bumper of an approaching white van as it rounded the building. The van stopped a few yards away from him, next to the entrance. The side of the van read, "Secrease Funeral Homes Transportation."

A pair of white smock-wearing men exited the van. The plump white driver removed his dark shades, wiped back his oily black hair and poured half a bag of M&M's into his mouth. After chewing them up, he looked over at his partner. "Man, all this overtime is kicking my ass. We haven't been this busy in a long time."

His partner stretched, yawned and shook his shoulder-length dreadlocks into place. "I know…" He then grinned at the M&M eater. "But it sure looks good on payday!"

"True enough. But this is the third straight weekend

we have had to work. Ever since Mr. Secrease bought that funeral home in Frisco, the cremation business has been off the charts. I will be glad when he has a crematorium built onto that spot over there across the Bay."

Dredlocks walked to the rear of the van. "I ain't gonna complain too much; at least we ain't gotta stay here late night cookin' these bodies."

The candy eater joined him and opened the rear doors of the van. "Yeah, I almost feel sorry for Mr. Secrease. Until he can hire a new mortician, he will be here every night this week himself. I don't see how he does it. I could never get used to that fucking smell night after night. That dude has bodies to burn all this *week!*"

Darius catalogued their conversation for later consumption. It took all his concentration to keep from being discovered. There was only a small space between the tree and the building. The branches of the tree continually brushed against his nose in the confined spot. *How long are these fools gonna be out here talkin'?* He brushed a spider off his forehead. *Fuck! This tree is full of goddamn bugs!*

Moments later, the pair of employees wheeled a covered body out of the van and into the crematorium. As soon as they entered the building, Darius dashed from his hiding place. A wicked smile filled his face as he hopped into his rental car. He couldn't believe his luck. *It really does pay to be in the right place at the right time!*

Thirty-Three

"I'm sorry, ma'am, but we can't give out that information," the nervous clerk said as the huge woman glared at her. "It's illegal for us to give out information on our guests without their consent."

Piper looked around the lobby of the Hotel Oakland, hoping to see Trenda. She turned her attention back to the Lebanese woman behind the counter. "All I want you to do is tell me what floor Mr. Secrease's room is on; I don't need the room number."

The receptionist put her foot a little closer to the silent alarm button. "I am sorry...I can't. I have already called his room and got no answer. If he was there, I could have informed him you were here and directed you to his room. Without his consent, I can't. Is there anything else I can do for you, ma'am?"

The desire to choke the receptionist to death tested Piper's restraint. "Fine. That's okay. I'll catch him later." She leaned over toward the nervous woman. "I'm his cousin from out of town. Don't tell him I asked about him; if so, you will spoil a big surprise, understand? I'd be *very* upset if you told him."

The meaning of her words was crystal-clear to the cowering clerk. Her foot hovered over the panic button. "Yes…I will not say a word."

Pissed off, she placed a call to Hank Martin. "Thank you for calling Dickerson Investigations. This is Hank Martin. I will be out of the office on vacation until May first. If you need any assistance, please contact the receptionist for referral to another qualified investigator. Thanks again for choosing Dickerson In- vestigations."

Her storm of anger turned into a monsoon as she yelled into the phone, "Fuck you, cocksucker!"

"Have you ever been here before, Box?"

"No, I can honestly say I have never been here to the Come On Inn even though I have lived in this city for almost ten years," Box said as they pulled into the motel's parking lot. The horseshoe-shaped motel encircled the parking lot. None of the patrons' vehicles were visible from the street.

Trenda rubbed his upper thigh before getting out. "Are you ready for this, baby?"

His breath caught in his throat. "Yes…more than you can possibly imagine."

He leaned over and pressed his lips to hers. She gave him a taste of her tongue. "Good. Let's go."

Sweat continued to coat his forehead as they walked

to the registration office. Trenda stopped several yards in front of the door. "Why don't you wait outside? No need on taking a chance on somebody behind the counter recognizin' you."

A puzzled looked etched itself on his face. "Now why should I do that? I told you I have never been here before."

"That may be true, but what if somebody that works here knows your girlfriend? I just know you don't want Miss Prissy to find out through the grapevine that her honey is hotel hoppin', now do we?"

He shook his head as he reached into his back pocket for his wallet. "You worry too much, Mya...now come on so I can get this room."

This poor man can't take his eyes off my tits long enough to think about what I just told him. She smirked. "Baby, you stay right here. I got this."

"No, no, no! No way am I going to let you pay fo—"

"Shhhh!" She placed her hand to his lips. "Keep arguing with me and we ain't gonna have much time to do this. Now, when I move my hand, just keep your mouth closed until I get back. You got that?" •

His eyes closed behind his glasses as he slowly nodded. She winked at him, turned and walked to the office. Even before she opened the door, the aroma of incense marched into her nostrils. A middle-aged couple of Arabian descent turned from the small TV behind the counter and checked out the visitor. The woman said something in her native language to the man. He frowned slightly, unhappy that his wife moved him aside preventing him from getting a better look at the hottie in pink. "How can I help you?"

The woman's English was good. Trenda expected much more of an accent. "I just need to get a room."

The woman sized up Trenda with her eyes as did her husband as he pretended to be interested in a cereal commercial on TV. "For how long? We do rent by the hour if that's all you need."

Trenda cocked her head. *Ain't this a bitch?*

Don't judge lest ye be judged.

Get outta my head, Daddy! She took a few seconds to calm down. *This old broad must think I'm a ho or somethin'.* "I need it for the whole day; is that a problem?"

The ice on Trenda's words made her back off the condescension. The clerk grew a fake smile. "No problem at all! I have a room located on the second floor. The price is only forty-five dollars—including tax. Is that okay?"

Trenda eyeballed her for a few seconds, then opened up her purse. *Even though this is cutting into my budget, it will come back to me plus interest,* she thought as she handed the woman three twenties, got her change and left.

She knew exactly what she was doing. Her experience with men taught her that by spoiling a man like Eli, who was used to being the spoiler, would just about guarantee her his heart and soul. There was a certain lawyer in

Washington, D.C. that could attest to her powers of enamourance. Trenda had broken that man down by simply buying him an iPod and loading it full of his favorite songs. The few hundred dollars she spent on that gift returned thousands of dollars in legal fees and other pleasantries. Her awesome pussy whipping of him was the icing on her seduction cake.

"Room 202," she said as she tossed the keys to Box. "This is your last chance to escape me, baby...once you fuck wit' me, you stuck wit' me."

Nervousness and arousal chipped away at what little cool he had. "I'll take my chances." The keys fell out of his hand.

She chuckled as she watched him bend over and pick up the keys. "Famous last words."

The concrete steps vibrated under Trenda's feet with each step Box climbed. The thirty-year-old motel was maintained just enough to be functional; not much of the budget went to glamorizing the place. She could feel his eyes burning a hole in her rump as she led him to the room.

At the door, she spun around and smiled as he inserted the key and opened the door. The fragrance of ancient PineSol and the ghosts of other unknown odors welcomed them. Trenda was all too familiar with the drab furnishings and color schemes of this class of motel. The boring earth tones and equally dull gold shag rug seemed to be universal in the cheap motel world. Standing next to the bed, she unzipped her top. "I bet you think this is the only outfit I have, huh?"

The room key dangled from his hand as he gazed at her. "What in the world are you talking about?"

She took off her velour top and draped it over the wooden chair under the desk. After that, she turned off her cell phone and dropped it into her purse. "Two of the last three times you have seen me, I have had it on… but don't trip; it has been to the cleaners. And once I get caught up on my bills, I am gonna get a whole new wardrobe."

As if his feet were planted in the carpet, he hadn't moved since closing the door and staring at Trenda. "I assure you I didn't give it a second thought." He pried his eyes off her tits and took a few steps toward her. "I see the cut by your eye is almost healed. How did you get that wound on your shoulder?"

She inspected the swollen, four-inch cut. It still throbbed from the slightest touch. "After I got cut playin' wit' my nephew, I tripped and fell against the corner of my sister's coffee table."

His eyes drifted back to her wondrous cleavage. "I hope nothing else on you is injured…"

"I guess you will have to find out for yourself." She then unfastened her black bra and tossed it onto the desk. Her hard nipples pointed at him. "Lose those clothes so we can take a shower."

"Uhhhh…okay…"

The lump in his trousers took away from his sweet look of innocence. The same look turned Trenda on. She placed the rest of her clothes on the desk while he disrobed. Even though his body was far from chiseled, it still fascinated her. His "love-handles" and slight "man boobs" made her pussy leak. *Damn, I like a thick man!*

Taking him by the hand, she led him into the bathroom and turned on the hot water. "We are gonna play a little game. I want you to stand here and watch me shower, and then I will get out and watch you. Are you game?"

As transfixed as he was by her nude perfection, she could have just asked him to eat a bowl of broken glass and he would have agreed. "Yes…yes I am game."

After spreading one of the large towels on the floor, next to the tub, to use as a rug, she picked up the small round bar of soap on the sink, unwrapped it and grabbed one of the white washcloths. "Oh…and no touching." She looked down at his immensely hard tool. "Me or that dick."

It both amazed and frightened her that she recalled so many of the quotes and proverbs her parents had bestowed upon her over the years. One of her mother's favorites jumped into her head as she watched her extremely horny date chew her up with his eyes:

Keep watch and pray, so that you will not give in to temptation. For the spirit is willing, but the body is weak!

MATTHEW 26:41

She dismissed the thought and climbed into the shower. The hot water added to her internal fire. The steam fogged up his glasses so badly he had to remove them. Even without them, Box was able to see he was witness to one of the sexiest shower scenes ever. Trenda started at her neck and worked her way down, using hands full of lather to soap up her tits. "You like that, baby?"

All Box could do was nod. He had not moved an inch since she had climbed in the shower. She soaped up her flat belly, then began washing her twitching pussy. "Does Meagan do this for you?"

"I wish…," he whispered.

His hands fell slowly to his crotch. Trenda pointed a wet and soapy finger at him. "No! Get your hands away from your dick." Feeling he was tortured enough, she rinsed off, took his hand and pulled him in the shower. "Okay, now you shower for me."

His grip tightened on her hand. "Stay in here with me…I…I want you, Mya…"

"That's against the rules, boo."

She escaped his grip, lathered up a washcloth and put it in his hand. He sighed heavily. "This is going to be the quickest shower on record."

As she toweled off, Trenda watched the heavy man clean himself. She could tell he was a little self-conscious of his body as she stared at him. He had no idea how fucking hot she was getting watching him. It took all her willpower to not take his swollen dick in her mouth as he prepared to wash it. *God, I am gonna fuck you good, Box…*

After he turned off the water in the humid bathroom, she slid the small, opaque window open, took one of the dingy white towels off the imitation-chrome towel rack and handed it to the soggy man.

The waning sunlight coming through the window sparkled in the waterdrops on his back as he began drying off. She couldn't help herself. She walked up behind him and wrapped her arms around him. It was as though she was holding a padded bag of cement. Beneath his pudgy exterior was a solid man. She kissed the middle of his wide shoulders, licking a few drops of water in the process. She felt as well as heard a sigh of pleasure resonate inside him.

Her hands circled his belly, rubbed his nipples. Caught up in her own desire, she laid her face sideways on his back and rubbed his chest. Her hands found his tools. She gently held his heavy balls. "Ohhhhhhhhhh, Mya…. mmmmmmmmm…"

"Mmmmmmm…we need to empty these…"

In a surprisingly agile move, he spun around, swooped her up in his arms and carried her to the queen-sized bed. "You have no idea how long I have wanted you."

She thought back to how she caught him jacking off on the train ride from Baltimore. She rubbed his bearded cheek. "I think I do, baby. Do you mind if I start callin' you 'Eli' instead of 'Box'? I like that better."

Finding his voice was difficult for the off-the-charts horny man. "Ahhh, sure...by all means."

Lying side-by-side, face-to-face, her lips found his, then their tongues touched. His kiss was tender, gentle and passionate. She could not recall the last time she was kissed like that by a man. Some of the women she had bedded were great kissers, but Box was by far the best-kissing man she had serviced.

Her head leaned back as he kissed his way down her cheek, to her neck and her waiting nipples. He rolled her onto her back and kissed, sucked, caressed her breasts. His caring and patient touch turned up her vaginal fire several degrees. She had to have him.

Now.

She pulled him up to her face. "Fuck me, Eli...," she whispered.

He was beyond words. Anything she wanted was hers. He gave her a simple nod.

As he rolled over on his back, Trenda stopped him. "I said I want you to fuck me."

He whispered, "I thought maybe you would want to be on top." He self-consciously rubbed his stomach. "You might be more comfortable...you know I am kind of... heavy."

A tear almost fell from her eye. *I bet that bitch Meagan makes him think that.* She rolled over onto her back, spread her smooth legs and pulled him to her. "No, I want to feel all of you...fuck me like you want to, baby... take what you want."

A shiver of delight and awe rocked his big body as he maneuvered his root between her wet pink lips. "Ooo-oooooohhhh…Oooooooo, Myaaaaaaa…"

The feel of his weight, heat and strength loosened Trenda's freak. She wiggled her hips in tune with his thrust, taking all his post inside her. As his dickhead found her G-spot, she pulled her legs back and gave him all the pussy he could want. Her moans overlapped his. What started as a quest to simply pussy whip him soon turned into a boatload of unexpected passion.

Each time his full weight rested on her and she could barely catch her breath, she had a magical orgasm. Her fingernails dug into his back and ass. "Mmmmmm, Eli… deeper, baby…yesssssssss…"

The big man pounded her wetness relentlessly. It was as though Trenda had given a life raft to a drowning man. She licked the side of his neck and ears, taking the opportunity to turn the heat up a notch by whispering to him how good he was fucking her.

Even though most of her moves were scripted from previous "pussy-whoopin'" sessions, a noticeable amount of genuine pleasure caused her to moan loud and long at times. After her umpteenth orgasm, she felt his body quiver and his pace increase. "Yesssssss, baby…gimme that cummmmmm…don't make me beg for it, baby… mmmmm."

His garbled reply sounded like part Martian, part animal. He came loud and hard. She wrapped her arms around him, pressed her thighs against his and coaxed a remarkable amount of sperm out of the shrieking man. Whoever was on the other side of the tissue-thin motel room walls was sure to have heard his moans of pleasure.

Damnnnnnnnnnnn! He shot a lot! she thought as a flow of lava-hot cum ran out her pussy down between her ass cheeks. *I bet his girl never lets him nut inside her like that…* after giving him a minute to catch his breath, she wiped his face with her hand and looked into his eyes. They told her he was absolutely, completely and thoroughly narcotized by her enchanted pussy. "You okay, boo?"

He shook his head slowly as he rested on his elbows, taking most of his weight off of her. "No…no, I am not." He kissed her soft lips. "That was the best sex I have had since…*ever!*"

"Uh-oh!" She grinned and rubbed his ass. "That's not good."

They rolled over on their sides, facing each other. "I mean it, Mya; you were *incredible!*"

"I'm glad you think so." She reached between them and caressed his package. "But I'm sure your girl takes good care of you."

He kissed her lips a few times. "No…not like you. You are all I desire in a woman, Mya…"

He had no idea of the minefield he was now walking. He had sprung open the gateway for Trenda to work her magic. She stroked the side of his face and exhaled loudly. "I am flattered you feel that way, but I don't wanna get too close to you right now."

The bed creaked as he propped himself up on one arm. "Why not? Did I do something wrong?"

"No, it's not that." She closed her eyes for effect. "I just don't wanna fall for you when my situation is what it is…"

"What do you mean? What's wrong, Mya?"

Her eyes opened slowly. "I really like you, Eli…but I am afraid of getting close to you when I might have to pack up and leave real soon."

He caressed the side of her face, looked deep into her green eyes. "Why do you have to leave? You have a job now…are you still having problems?"

A tiny bit of guilt jabbed her in the gut, but she proceeded anyway. "Yeah, but it doesn't pay enough for me to afford my own place…I may have to go back to D.C. and move in with my parents until I can get on my feet. It's way more expensive to live out here than I thought. Plus, I don't wanna come between you and your relationship. Do you understand, baby?"

The lovelorn look on his face almost broke her down. It looked as though that big man was about to drown her in tears. "I have been looking for you all my life, Mya," He gently caressed the side of her neck and whispered, "I know this sounds crazy, but I have dreamed of having a beautiful, sexy and fun woman like you…and I do not want to lose this dream."

That last-minute quiver in his voice moved her in a way she was unaccustomed to. The urge to flee before doing any more damage to this man beckoned, but she fought it off. "You are so sweet, baby…but what about your woman? I don't want you to do anything you will regret."

A long pause. "The only regret I will have is if I don't do all I can to make you mine."

She blinked and pulled his head down so they were cheek to cheek. "Eli…you are making me…" It was at this point that she knew her mission was accomplished. But something about putting the whammy on this victim didn't feel as good as it did in the past. *What the fuck is going on, Trenda? Why are you so concerned for this dude?*

"What? What do you mean, Mya? What am I making you do? I hope I didn't offend you in any way…did I?"

She kissed his lips. "No, baby…I was just a little overwhelmed…you are such a perfect man. Any woman would be glad to have you if she ain't crazy. I can deal with seeing you and seeing where we end up if you want…but to be honest, if I don't do something about finding an apartment, I will have no choice but to go back home."

Before speaking, he gazed into her eyes. "I can help… If you promise to keep seeing me, I will help you get a place. I can take care of the first, last and deposit to get you in. Will that help you stay in my life?"

Girl, you are too good at this shit! Her self-congratulation was unenthusiastic. *Why am I trippin'? He is just another pussy-hungry man, right?* Ignoring her thoughts, she replied, "I promise."

After giving her a broad grin and a sigh of relief, he kissed her long and deeply. "Thank you, Mya...you won't be sorry."

She smiled, rolled him over on his back and whispered, "Enough talkin'." She stroked him as she kissed her way down to his growing penis. "I need something creamy to drink."

Thirty-Four

"Piper?"

"Yes, Eric, this is Piper. I don't have a lot of time for pleasantries; did Trenda ever mention anything to you about a guy out here by the name of Walter Secrease?"

After sticking the gas pump nozzle into the tank of his black Lexus, Tyrone picked up the conversation with Piper. Just hearing her voice again put him on edge. "I think she said something about having a friend or cousin by that name out there. What's the latest? Did you find her?"

"I think so...I found that tramp running around with this Walter guy. He is paying for her very expensive hotel room downtown. I was hoping you had some information on him. I plan on paying him a visit at his place of work if I can't find his home address."

He leaned back against his car. "When are you gonna do that? Do you think he knows how to get in touch with Trenda?"

"Do you think I would waste my time on that fucker if I didn't think he could lead me to Trenda? I just told you he is paying for her hotel room, idiot! Use your fucking head. I am going to go to his business tomorrow. I need to get a few things together today before I go see him. Stay tuned."

The gas pump stopped seconds after Piper hung up on him. His frayed nerves did the cabbage patch on his mind. *How did I let myself get caught up in this shit? Now that Darius is out in California, this shit is now a federal crime if something goes wrong and we get busted!* "Fuck!" he said as he put the gas nozzle back and screwed on his gas cap. The overcast sky felt as though it was closing in on him—like a long prison sentence. The pussy in him emerged. "Mutha-fuck that…if shit goes wrong on Darius's end, I'm gonna do what I gotta do to stay out of jail." He hopped in his car and started the engine. "Even if I have to cut a deal with Internal Affairs…"

As he drove out of the gas station, he called Darius. "Tyrone…talk to me."

"Man, I just got off the phone with Piper. That broad is about to go off."

"What the fuck do you mean?"

"She just called to ask me about some dude named Walter Secrease. Says he is some buster Trenda knows. She told me he is paying for her hotel room. Does that name ring a bell?"

"*What?* Did you say he is paying for her hotel room?"

Distracted, Tyrone had to slam on his brakes in order to avoid rear-ending a taxicab. "Yeah…she said it was some expensive hotel downtown."

"Downtown where? Did she say?"

"Fuck, I dunno! Oakland, I guess. She hung up before I could get any other info. Man, you really need to end this shit…end it *real* quick. Shit is gettin' tense out here waitin' to see what Internal Affairs is up to. I can't take a crap without worryin' if they're watchin' me."

"Calm your ass down! All you have to do is keep your nose clean for a few more days and this shit will be over! Quit actin' like a fuckin' coward! Now…I'm gonna call you tomorrow. By then, this shit will be handled. Got it?"

"Fuck you!" Tyrone pulled over, spat out the gum he was chewing and opened the pack of Newports he had just purchased at the gas station. His stress made him dive headfirst off his eight-month-long stay on the no-smoking wagon. He fired one up, took a long drag, then exhaled. "Just get it done."

The sound of Tyrone smoking signaled Darius his partner was rapidly coming apart. *I have got to end this shit before that scary bastard gets caught slippin',* Darius thought as he walked back inside Moon's Chinese Café to finish off his meal.

While finishing off his lemon chicken, he sorted through the information Tyrone had given him on Walter. *So, Trenda has already worked that fool for a room…*a touch of jealousy hit him in the face once he admitted to himself that Walter was now getting his pussy. And head. Suddenly he was no longer hungry. After leaving a twenty on the table, he rushed to his rental car. He no longer felt the need to spare Walter's life if he got in the way.

Sunset, back at his motel room, Darius prepared for his next moves. Since Piper was going to visit Walter's place of business tomorrow, so would he. He removed one of the hollow point bullets from his pistol and absently spun it around on the desk as he worked out his plan. *I have to make sure Trenda ends up there, too. Some way, somehow I have to make sure she is at the funeral home when I get there.* A smile touched his face. *Or at least be there when Piper shows up...that would really make my day...*

After calling five expensive hotels and asking for Walter Secrease, and using his uncanny finesse, he was rewarded with the room number for Mr. Secrease in the Hotel Oakland.

After fucking Eli into a pussy coma, Trenda eased out of the bed to go to the bathroom. In the waning sunlight, she spotted his wallet on the floor. It had fallen out of his pants in his haste to enter her. Wallet in hand, she glanced at the sleeping man. He was knocked the fuck out. She flipped it open and examined the contents. Two hundred and eighty dollars in cash, four credit cards—including a platinum American Express card—a Chevron gas card, and several pictures.

Ignoring the cash and cards for a moment, she flipped through his pictures. *Hmmmm, so that's Ms. Meagan...* Trenda flipped through the half dozen or so pictures of

Eli and his girl. *If she ain't white, she is the next best thing,* she thought as she looked at the light-skinned, prim and proper-looking woman. Her hair bun looked so tight; it looked as though her forehead would split if she smiled. Behind her glasses was a pair of dark brown, no-nonsense eyes. Her modest and sensible clothes did nothing to accentuate her figure. *Poor baby, no wonder it's so hard for him to keep his eyes off me.* The pictures of them together showed they made a good-looking couple. In a few of the pictures, he actually looked happy—and so did she.

Normally, in a situation like this, she would dress and slip out, wallet in hand. However, this was his lucky day; he was a big enough catch to escape the Baltimore okeydoke. Besides, she had already committed practically every crime in the book—including being implicated in a murder or two. She exhaled and set his wallet on the desk. His cell phone glowed on the desktop next to his shirt. She picked it up and saw he had eleven missed calls. *I bet those calls are from Meagan.*

She walked over to the window and peeked out at the horseshoe-shaped parking lot and disappearing sun. The itch of her healing wounds reminded her of all the shit she had gotten herself into since running away from home all those many years ago. For an instant, she felt hurt because no man she knew of walked around with a picture of her in his wallet. *Be cool, girl. Don't fuck up this meal ticket.*

Even after her craving for penetration had been met,

she still felt an empty spot that needed filling. She tried to blame it on her oncoming menstrual cycle. But, in reality, it was the annoying replay of past events in her life that would not go away. The high concentration of drama she was currently wading through would not be ignored.

Another of her father's favorite proverbs filled her thoughts as she stared out at the first stars twinkling in the sky:

There are six things the Lord hates, yes, seven are an abomination to him; Haughty eyes, a lying tongue, and hands that shed innocent blood; A heart that plots wicked schemes, feet that run swiftly to evil, The false witness who utters lies, and he who sows discord among brothers.

—Proverbs 6:16-19

Thirty-Five

"Let's take it slow, baby," Trenda said as she tried to say goodbye to Eli after he pulled up behind the only car left parked in front of the DMV that evening; her car. Even after fifteen minutes of goodbye kisses, he was reluctant to let her leave. "I gotta go to work in a few hours. You will see me again soon, love."

His buzzing cell phone gave her the opening she needed. He grimaced after reading the caller ID. "Okay…I'd better let you go. Thanks for the *great* time, Mya."

Trenda opened the door and got out. "What are you gonna tell your woman when she asks why you didn't call her back?"

"What makes you think that call was from Meagan?"

She closed the door and leaned in the window. "Please, don't try to bullshit a bullshitter…we both know that was her. No way in hell you are gonna spend all day fuckin' and not check in on her. I bet you guys check in with each other at damn near the same time every day."

His slow response and blushing face confirmed she was right. "It's not *that* bad." He reached over and caressed her hand. "Now if it was you calling, you had better believe I'd pick up on the first ring, no matter what I was doing."

As he caressed her fingers, she eased her hand out of his. "Is that right? I'm gonna hold you to that. And believe me, I don't forget stuff like that."

"Damn, Mya." A sigh escaped him. "It's so hard to let you go."

C'mon now, man. "Don't worry, love. I'll give you a call tomorrow. Now get your ass home where you belong!"

Before he could reply, she blew him a kiss and walked to her car. Not until he heard her car engine start did he pull away. She smiled at his gesture. "I have had'em whooped before, but *this* one, *damn!*"

"The internet is a dangerous thing," Darius said as he read the information he found on the cremation process. The weight of the bulletproof vest under his gray, loose-fitting Nike sweatshirt and the pistol tucked behind his back made him feel more at ease while in Oakland. Even back in Baltimore they knew of Oakland's deadly reputation. He found the array of women walking around the Starbucks he sat in to his liking. It made it worth having to pay for the wireless internet service.

"That Walter has got to be one weird muthafucka to like doing this shit." Like a true cop, he did all the research he could on his query. That research included finding out how long the cremation process took, so he would have an idea how long Walter would work into the night.

Satisfied he had all the info he needed, he took a sip of his luke-warm coffee and grinned. "By this time tomorrow night, Trenda will be no longer be a problem."

One of Darius's weaknesses was his arrogance. He would sometimes get so caught up in his smugness he would lose focus, get sloppy. This was one of those moments. While working on his laptop, sipping his coffee and eyeballing the women in the coffee shop, he failed to notice the gorilla of a woman looking at him through the large plate-glass window, twenty feet from his table.

Instead of finding a place to get a decent meal outside of her plush hotel, Piper, in one of her psychotic mood swings, enhanced by her lack of medication, decided to enjoy an evening walk to the local BBQ restaurant. *Ahhhh! Tomorrow I will confront Mr. Secrease and convince him to get me access to Trenda.* She reached into her purse, stroked the large knife inside and smiled. *I'm sure he'd much rather assist me than become a human filet.*

With the crescent moon as her guide, she took her time strolling toward her dinner destination. For whatever reason, women's intuition or ESP, she was compelled to cross the street and check out the combination Starbucks and Barnes & Noble bookstore.

Whether it was the aroma of the coffee in the air or the lively look of the building that drew her, she would never remember. Once she saw the unmistakable face of the man in the video with Trenda, sitting on the other side of that window, her brain focused on one thing only: homicide. Even with his ball cap pulled down low on his forehead, she knew it was him.

Remarkably, even through her insane rage, she wasn't able to go inside and gut him as she so badly wanted to. The armed security guard standing just inside the coffee shop entrance proved to be a deterrent. "I'll wait out here until fucking Christmas for that motherfucker if I have to," she said through her clenched teeth.

While Darius was being stalked, King Gee and one of his boys sat across the street from the Water's Edge Hotel. They had a clear view of the hotel and the employee parking lot. "She oughta be pullin' up in a few," King Gee said as he stood next to the driver's side door of the stolen forest-green Ford Explorer his boy "borrowed" from some citizen in the sleepy suburb of Walnut Creek. "I been checking this place out all week. I know when all the shift changes happen. I was even able to con that hillbilly security guard into tellin' me what shift that ho works tonight."

The nappy-afro sporting, mulatto soldier grinned at his boss's ingenuity. "I bet she ain't even knowin' how bad she messed up when she fucked wit' the King!'"

King Gee made sure to keep his fingerprints off the stolen vehicle. The strong scent of marijuana escaped the interior of the Explorer. "Yeah, I got a wake-up call for her ass."

Ten minutes later, just before the 8 p.m. to 4 a.m. shift at the hotel was to begin, the two men watched a brown Honda pull into the employee parking lot next to the hotel.

The soldier pointed. "Hey! Is that her car?"

King Gee nodded and followed the car with his eyes. "Yup, that's her ass. You ready to do this?"

The soldier adjusted his black leather gloves and started the engine of the Explorer. "You ain't even gotta ask; they don't call me 'Nuts' for nothin'."

King Gee stepped back. "Hold on a minute. Wait about another fifteen minutes. Let's give the rest of the folks that might be startin' work with her to get here and park. We don't need any fools rollin' up as you do your thing."

Nuts offered King a fist bump. "That's hella smart, King!"

He grinned and tapped fist with his soldier. "That's why I'm the King, fool!"

"Wassup, Jason?" Trenda asked as she walked behind the reservation desk and logged in. "Is it busy tonight?"

Jason adjusted his utility belt, straightened his cap and glanced into her eyes. "Hey, Mya! It's been kinda quiet tonight. I bet it's gonna be crazy next Sunday though."

Trenda sat down behind the computer. "Why you say that?"

"Next Sunday is Easter. We usually get a big crowd of out-of-towners on that weekend." He struggled with trying not to stare at her. "What are you gonna do for Easter? Are you going to spend time with family or go to church?"

She stared off into space for a moment. *Damn! Easter already? I bet Momma and the rest of those stuck-up church wives are still gettin' stuff ready for the church's Easter dinner. I sure am glad I ain't stuck in the middle of all those nosey women. I used to hate havin' Momma volunteer me every fuckin' Easter to help cook. And Momma tryin' to make me feel good tellin' me how much everybody loved my sweet potato pies. And havin' to deal with them hatin' old bitties cuttin' they eyes at me all damn day. So many times I was tempted to tell them bitches how many of their husbands had tried to get in my drawers...*

Just like clockwork, as soon as the memories of her home life became too clear, too strong, she shut them off. She unbuttoned the three brass buttons on her navy-blue blazer and smoothed down her white shirt. "I dunno...I might just stay home and chill until I have to be back here."

The keys on his belt jingled as he leaned back against the desk. "Yeah, it sucks that we have to work the holidays. But the time-and-a-half pay helps take some of the sting out of it."

Lollie's copy of *Essence* magazine lay next to the keyboard. She gazed at the African-American actress on the cover standing knee-deep in some pretty blue water in a tropical paradise. *That's where I need to be…right there with nobody fuckin' wit' me. No hustlin', nobody huntin' me, no worries, nobody to please. Just me doin' me for once.* "Nah, not all money is good money; sometimes I'd rather just have some 'me' time."

"I still can't believe how we met," Lollie said while sitting across the table from Walter in Francis Ford Coppola's Café Zoetrope restaurant in San Francisco. They had become inseparable since Trenda, once again, had orchestrated another successful hook-up. "It feels like I'm in a movie or something."

Me neither; I can't believe I bounced out of one hot pussy into another so smoothly! Walter thought as he admired Lollie's beauty. But it was more than just her hot sex and beauty; the chemistry between he and Lollie was magnificent. He returned her smile as his fingers walked across the table, past his half-eaten plate of *Linguine alla Vongole*, past her glass of 2006 vintage, *Sangiovese, Borgo di Colloredo, Molise* wine and took her hand in his. "I know…it's crazy as I-don't-know-what. That friend of yours deserves a serious 'thank you.' This is the best blind date on record."

She wiped back the lock of her hair that had covered

half her face. "Yeah, Mya is a trip. She is one of the coolest females I know—with her freaky ass. I'm thinkin' about letting her move in with me until she can get her own place."

A huge grin filled his face. "Hmmmmm! Now *that* sounds like a great idea! Two sexy birds in one tree!"

"Don't get any ideas, Mr. Secrease. Your 'two-for-one' privileges have been suspended." She took a sip of her wine. "Until further notice, or *maybe* until your next birthday, this is a one-on-one hook-up. If you can't hang with that, let me know so I can tear up our contract."

They shared a chuckle as the waiter brought over a box for their leftover food and the check. "I was thinking of offering her an internship as a mortician. I'm not sure if she would be interested, but it would be good for her. I pay my interns well."

"Are you serious? I bet she would love that!" Lollie gave him a mock evil look. "I hope you don't try and fuck your interns."

Shaking his head, he laughed. "I'm sure I'll be too busy chasing you to worry about fucking the help."

She gave him a grin. "Good answer."

He took his wallet out of the inside pocket of his expensive black suit jacket. "Have you noticed anything odd about Mya?"

Lollie chewed her bottom lip while pondering his question. "She can be kinda distant at times…like she has a lot on her mind."

"Yeah, that's what it is…distant. I noticed that myself. When it comes to sex, she's a whole different animal, but other than that, it's like she is always looking for something. Like something is missing in her world. Why do you think she's like that?"

Lollie began boxing up her food. "When I ask her what's on her mind, she always just says, 'nothin'' and lets it go. It don't matter, though; she still my girl."

He finished the last of his wine. "I agree; she is good people. But I still think there is a lot more to our green-eyed siren than she lets on."

Under the table, before slipping her feet back into the purple pumps, which matched her tight purple dress, she rubbed her foot along his calf. "We can pick this topic up later; I get *real* horny after a good meal like this, baby. I hope you have a lot of dessert for me."

This girl is insatiable! Thank you, Mya! Grinning, he adjusted his purple tie, which matched her outfit. "Keep that talk up and you won't make it back across the bridge tonight. I'll have your sexy ass locked up in a hotel over here."

As he stood holding her leather jacket, prepared to help her put it on, she stood and gave him a good look at the outline of her hard nipples, which stood at attention. She flashed him a lust-filled smirk. "I dare you."

Thirty-Six

Ten minutes after watching Trenda enter the Waters Edge Hotel, King Gee tapped his soldier on the shoulder. "Time for you to go to work."

Nuts took two last puffs off his blunt and tossed it to the ground. "A'ight, I'll holla at you when I'm done."

As King Gee walked over to his Saab with the new convertible top, Nuts opened the red backpack sitting in the driver's seat. Inside, he removed two six-inch-long balloons, smiled and bounced them in his hand. *As soon as the gas in her gas tank eats through this balloon rubber, the Drano inside these balloons is gonna mix with the gas and blow her shit up!*

Along with the balloons in the backpack, there was a black ski mask, tire iron and a bottle of motor oil. He drove over and backed in next to Trenda's car. He double-checked the Chevy pickup truck on the other side of Trenda's car and made sure it was unoccupied.

The spotlight twenty feet from his stolen vehicle didn't bother him at all. Leaving the Explorer running, Nuts, the pyromaniac, pulled on the ski mask, grabbed the tire backpack and walked over to the Honda. Using the tire iron, he popped open the fuel door, unscrewed the cap and opened the bottle of motor oil. *This will make sure these balloons slide all the way down the fill tube and into the gas.*

The stuffed balloons were just barely slim enough to fit down through the fuel tank opening. But since Nuts had done this numerous times, he was proficient at knowing just how much catalyst to use. He inspected each of the balloons and made sure they were tied tightly. Before putting them into the tank, he got the rush he was seeking; the danger of the rubber dissolving too quickly and him being blown the hell up. The thrill of getting away just in time was so exciting to him it made his dick hard.

"Here we go!" he said as he quickly slid both balloons down the oil-soaked filler tube, ran and jumped in the Explorer. Instead of speeding off right away, his sickness made him tempt fate and stall for a few unnecessary seconds before smashing down the accelerator and jetting out the parking lot.

With each passing second, Piper became more agitated. It took a Herculean effort for her to enter the bookstore without running over and slitting Darius's throat. She watched him while pretending to be browsing the books.

Over by the cookbook section, near the elevator that conveniently took patrons to the underground parking garage, she saw a sign on the elevator door:

Elevator temporarily out of service. Please use the stairway east of the store entrance to access the parking garage. Thank you for your patience.

Her eyes went from the sign to Darius, thirty feet away. *Looks like he is finally ready to leave.* She hitched her purse up on her shoulder. *I'll wait for him outside.*

Outside the glass doors, she watched him walk over to the elevator and read the sign. A maniacal smile crossed her lips. "Yes! Bring your ass here!" She hurried her husky self over to the stairway, went inside and stood behind the door, in the blind spot of an unsuspecting victim. Since the bookstore was a couple of hours away from closing, there weren't many people leaving. She gripped the wooden handle of her carving knife and used the end to shatter the lone light bulb, mounted on the wall behind the door. Other than the dim light emanating from the flight of stairs below her, the stairway was as silent and as dark as a tomb. Perfect.

Damn, there are some fine ass hoes out here! Darius thought as he nodded at the security guard on his way out the bookstore. Five seagulls fought and squawked loudly over a scrap of food at the foot of a trashcan a few yards away from Darius. He stopped, stretched and sucked in a lungful of the Bay air. *One more day and this shit will be over! I am gonna fly back to Baltimore knowing Trenda is takin' a dirt-nap.*

Tossing his empty cup of coffee in the trash, he headed for the stairs to the parking garage. He walked over, pushed the door open and entered the dark stairway. "Damn, it's dark as he—"

A demonic voice whispered behind him. "She's mine…" It got louder. "She is *mine!*"

Before he could react, he felt several thumps on the middle of his back. "What the fuck?"

"Trenda is mines, you motherfucker! Trenda is *mine!*" she yelled as she continued slamming the blade into his back with the fury of a devil.

Darius felt a sharp pain in his left underarm as the point of the blade found a piece of flesh unprotected by his bulletproof vest. "What the fuck…is wrong…with you?" he yelled as he scrambled for the pistol behind his back. With only six square feet of space to work with, and the blade of the knife getting closer and closer to his neck and other exposed body parts, he knew he only had seconds to act.

If he moved too much, he would lose the protection of the vest. Obviously, she didn't know he was wearing it. She continued trying to open his back with the knife while yelling repeatedly that Trenda was hers. "I saw her sucking your ugly dick, you son-of-a-bitch!"

Finally, his hand found the rubberband-cover grip of the pistol. He pulled it, fell to the ground, rolled over on his back and scooted a few feet away from her. Even in that dim light he could see the saliva leaking from the corners of her mouth and the insanity in her eyes. He cocked the pistol. "Back off, fat bitch!"

She snarled like a werewolf. "Fuck you! *Fuck you!* I'm going to cut your fucking eyes out!"

As she brought the blade up again to follow up on her threat, he fired. The bullet went into her large right breast. She paused, touched the bullethole with her free hand, felt the blood and growled. "You shot me, you faggot!" She then brought the blade up again and ran toward him.

Fuck! Is this bitch for real? He fired three more silenced rounds into her chest. Still clenching the blade, she wheezed and fell to her knees. He scrambled to his feet as she tried to crawl toward him.

POP!

He put one final, muted slug in her back. The knife fell out of her hand and she stopped moving. Just like Nuts, this scenario was very familiar to Darius. Thinking fast, without bothering to check and see if she was dead, he kicked the knife away from her and moved her body over behind the door. *If anybody tries to push the door open, her big-ass will block them, givin' me a little extra getaway time if I need it.* He then ripped off her watch and gold chain, picked up her purse and poured out the contents. *Looks like she got robbed to me.*

After going through the spilled contents of her purse, he grabbed her wallet and pulled out the cash. *Time to get the fuck out!* Grabbing the knife, he tucked it under his sweatshirt, and ran down the three flights of stairs to the parking garage.

He nearly jumped out his skin after hearing a loud *"BOOM!"* followed by a second *"BOOM!"* once he opened the door leading into the parking garage. "What the hell was that?" He pulled down the bill of his cap, lowered his head and calmly walked to his car.

Thirty-Seven

The way of the wicked is as darkness:
they know not at what they stumble.
—PROVERBS 4:19

Pussy twitching, body sore, Trenda eased herself into her seat behind the reservation counter. *Shit! It feels like I been at the gym workin' out all day!* Thoughts of the feel of Eli's weight on her and the warmth of his sperm pumping into her chiseled a small smile onto her face. *For a big dude, he knows how to work what he got!*

Even though everything was quiet at the desk, she was on edge. A by-product of her hustling lifestyle was a heightened sense of self-preservation. A sort of "spidey-sense," if you will. *I wonder where Jason went?* she thought after scanning the lobby. The only other person she could see was an old Asian man waiting for the elevator.

While counting out the cash in her register, she thought, *I don't know why I'm so jumpy. If anything, I should be dozing off after fuckin' with Eli all day.* She fiddled with the over-starched collar of her blouse. *I wonder what Lollie and*

Walter are up to? I bet money they are still gettin' their freak on. Just as she picked up her cell phone in order to give Lollie a call, the registration desk phone rang. "Hello, thank you for calling the Edgewater Hotel, how can I help you?"

"Is this that bad-mouthed lil' bitch?"

Trenda furrowed her brows. The gravelly voice on the other end of the conversation sounded very familiar. *"Excuse* me?"

"You heard right, bitch. I told you once you needed to learn proper manners."

"I ain't got time for games, muthafucka. If you have somethin' to say to me, come say it to my face."

"Calm down, ho. I was just callin' to offer you a ride home when you get off work."

"Look, asshole, I don't need shit from a punk muthafucka like you. I got my own ride home."

"You sure about that?"

"Hell yeah, I'—" Before she could finish cussing him out, he hung up on her. After hanging up the phone, she spotted Jason entering the lobby from the swimming pool area. She waved him over. "Hey, Jason, come here for a minute."

"What's up, Mya? Everything okay?"

She pulled her keys and "Baby" out of her purse. She slid the knife into her pocket before he got to the counter. "Can you watch the desk for a minute? I need to go get something out my car real quick."

"Sure I can!" He smiled and adjusted his crowded utility belt. "It's kinda dead right now anyway. I'll hold down the fort."

"Thanks, sweetie." She rounded the desk and strolled to the front door, Jason's eyes nailed to her wondrous ass. *I swear I can't enjoy a single fuckin' day without some kind of drama!*

At half past eight, the bells atop the St. Augustine's church tolled in the distance as she stepped outside the hotel. The lights seemed too bright, the conversations too loud and the distance to her car too far. In the past, she usually would recognize these signs, stop and analyze the situation. Is this a trap? A police sting? A hit? Her intuition was seldom wrong.

Unfortunately, her combination of fatigue and seething hatred of King Gee blinded her. She calmed a slight bit once she saw her car 100 yards away. "It looks okay… maybe that sorry asshole was just tryin' to fuck with my head."

At fifty yards from her car, she saw a Ford Explorer speeding down Broadway toward the freeway. She slowed down and looked around. *No sign of his ass.*

Thirty yards away from the Honda, she stopped, looked around, reached into her pocket and wrapped her hand around Baby.

She walked ten more yards toward her car. Seconds later, she saw a flash, heard a boom and felt herself flying through the air. The exploding Honda sprayed burning gasoline and debris on the pick-up truck next to her car. A piece of the shrapnel pierced the gas tank of the truck and it, too, exploded.

The initial blast tossed her twenty feet away, and rudely deposited her onto the hard parking lot asphalt.

Thirty-Eight

"Holy shit!" Jason yelled as he ran out of the lobby toward the sound of the explosions. Outside, he ran toward the dancing flames coming from the employee parking lot. A crowd began assembling a short distance from the fire. He removed his walkie-talkie and called in the emergency to his company dispatch. Channel two—located in Jack London Square—already had a news crew out investigating.

A tall, slim black man whistled and waved at Jason. "Hey! Hey! There is a woman over here on the ground! She's out cold!"

Jason ran over and fell to his knees next to Trenda, who lay on her side. The news crew quickly followed, filming. "Stand back, please!" he ordered the crowd. After placing his hand on her neck, he was relieved to feel a pulse. Her breathing was shallow, but consistent. Using his flashlight, he inspected her. Other than a penny-sized scrape on her left wrist, she looked okay. Careful not to move her, he took off his jacket and covered her torso.

The wail of an approaching fire truck mixed with the murmur of the growing crowd and the crackle of the fire-engulfed vehicles. Several employees of the hotel scrambled to move their cars out of harm's way. Jeff, the manager on duty, ran across the lot, paisley tie flapping in the wind. He stopped next to Jason and leaned over Trenda. "What happened?"

"I dunno! I was watching the counter while Mya went to get something out her car. The next thing I knew, I heard a loud explosion!"

Jeff's steel-gray eyes looked at Jason, bewildered. "Holy-fucking-shit!" He turned his gaze to Trenda. "Is she okay?"

"I think so…it's hard to tell. The paramedics should be here any minute."

To their relief, Trenda's head moved from side-to-side slowly. A moan escaped her mouth. "Easy…easy, Mya," Jason said as he gently held her shoulders.

Jeff stood and waved the firefighters over. "We have a victim here!"

"Owww, shit!" Trenda said, rubbing the side of her head, as her eyes fluttered open. She squinted, fighting off the glare of the TV camera as she pushed off Jason's jacket. She tried to sit up, but found Jason restricted her. "What are you doin'? Let…me…up!"

Before Jason could release her, two burly firefighters carrying paramedic rescue gear squatted down next to Trenda. "Just relax, ma'am," the balding firefighter said as he used Jason's jacket as a pillow and eased her head back down onto it. "Let us check you out first."

Gazing at the crowd around her, she asked, "Why do you have to check me out? What happened?"

Baldy checked her eyes with his penlight. "You were knocked unconscious by an explosion."

After two minutes of looking around in silence, she asked Jeff, "What happened? Why do I smell so much smoke? What's burnin'?"

Concern clouded Jeff's eyes. "You don't remember your car exploding?"

She shook her head slowly as the ambulance crew ran over pushing a gurney. "No...is that what's burnin'? Why am I on the ground? Somebody tell me what happened!"

The balding firefighter looked up at Jeff. "She's perseverating... I think she has a concussion. We need to get her to the hospital."

Stress ran through Darius like the bulls in Pamplona as he stood in the bathroom of his motel room, looking at the gash under his arm Piper had given him. It was short but deep. It took nearly the entire roll of toilet paper to stop the bleeding. He used some of the tissue to wipe off the blade of the knife. *With forensics being as good as they are these days, I am not gonna take a chance and leave some blood here for them to track me down with.*

After flushing down another bloody clot of tissue, he used one of the face towels as a bandage and taped it to his wound with some of his duct tape. Sweat formed on his head as he hastily packed his bags. He rolled up the knife in his bloodstained sweatshirt and put it in his duffle bag next to the pistol. He then inspected his bulletproof vest for blood. *Cool…it's clean.*

The sound of police sirens and speeding fire trucks filled the air. *Time to bounce!* He exited his motel room, tossing the cardkey in a nearby trashcan. "I was inches away from finding Trenda before that crazy bitch got in the mix and tried to kill my ass."

While sitting in his car, he called the airport and found out the next flight to Newark was four hours away. His stress level increased. *Be cool, bruh; be cool!*

After starting the car, he followed the signs to the Oakland Pier. The number of police cars he passed on the way as well as the CSI van told him they had found Piper. Displaying a remarkable amount of "cool" under the circumstances, he managed to make it to the pier with no problem.

At least something is working my way tonight, he thought as he pulled into the deserted parking lot. He was the only person who had an interest in the pier that night. He got out and walked along the boulder-lined shore until he spotted a basketball-sized rock. He took the rock back to the car, opened his duffle bag, removed his bloody sweatshirt, tied it around the rock, and put it inside his duffle bag.

After looking around, he got out, carried the bag of evidence to the edge of the pier and heaved the sweatshirt, gun, knife and bullets into the calm water. In the glow of the pier's night-lights, he saw the items splash and immediately sink. *That cold saltwater should take care of those bloodstains on the sweatshirt real quick.*

Feeling better, he took the ski mask, stuffed it into a nearby trashcan, and left the pier. As he neared downtown Oakland, he scanned the radio for a news station. Minutes later, he found a local talk-radio station on commercial break. He heard that a robbery victim had been found dead in a Jack London Square bookstore. A sinister smile grew on his face. "Now *that's* how you handle ya business!"

Feeling a bit of relief, he decided to find a place to hang out until his flight left. Police cars zipped up and down Broadway as he drove away from the action. A few miles south of the murder scene, he spotted a club called The Spot. "That'll work," he said as he parked and went inside.

The bar portion of the club was half-full of patrons. He took a seat at the bar and looked at the many TV monitors bordering the bar area. Every screen showed a live shot of a black news reporter with a background featuring a half-dozen police cars and a few fire trucks. He waved to the extremely sexy, middle-aged, African-American bartender. She smiled and placed a napkin in front of him. "What can I get you, babe?"

Darius looked from the sexy silver streak in her hair, to her large tits and back to the TV screen. "I'll have a double-shot of Hennessy with a cranberry back." He turned and nodded at the TV. "What happened?"

She glanced at the screen. "They had a murder and somebody's car blew up down in the Square...they're trying to see if the two are linked."

"Is it always this exciting down here?"

She poured his cognac. "Sometimes...but not always *this* exciting."

The surrounding patrons murmured about how violent Oakland was getting as they watched the breaking news footage. His drink arrived. "Here you go, babe. That'll be five dollars. Do you want to pay cash or use a card and run a tab?"

Darius took a long swig. "Cash...I have to get moving soon."

After taking his money, she picked up a remote control and turned up the volume. They watched as the reporter held his microphone up to the mouth of a balding firefighter. As the firefighter pointed, the camera followed. As the bartender walked away to serve another customer, Darius watched as the cameraman followed the firefighter over to a small crowd of people.

As the last drop of Hennessy trickled down his throat, he slammed his glass down so hard it shattered on the bar top. On the TV screen, he saw a green-eyed woman with an oxygen mask on her face being wheeled to an ambulance. "Hey, what are you doing?" the bartender asked as she hurried over to Darius.

Ain't no way! Ain't no fuckin' way that's...I'll be damned! That's Trenda! So shocked was he, all he could do was stare at the screen as the bartender angrily cleaned up the broken glass. Finally, his vocal cords thawed out. "I have to go."

"You are going to have to leave the oxygen mask on, ma'am," the Vietnamese paramedic said to Trenda during her ride to Highland Hospital.

"I told you I'm oka—," was her muffled response behind the oxygen mask before a surge of pain from her headache caused her to black out. What seemed like an eon later, she awakened to the feel of something cold on the side of her head. Groggy and disoriented, she mumbled, "What the hell are you doin'?" to the elderly Mexican nurse applying the cold compress to the lump just above her left ear. It looked as though someone had cut a hard-boiled egg in half and stuck it under her skin.

The gaze from the nurse's warm brown eyes washed over Trenda's face as she used an ace bandage and gently wrapped the compress to Trenda's head. "Ahhhh! It's good to have you back in the land of the living. You were sleeping so good, I didn't want to wake you. How is your head feeling?"

Trenda reached for the bandage around her head and saw her arm sticking out of a light-green gown. "What the?" She pushed back her covers and saw her clothes had been changed. "Where are my clothes? How long have I been here? *Why* am I here?"

"Well, Ms. Collins, while you were asleep, thanks to the painkiller the doctor gave you, we needed to make sure you didn't have any other injuries other than the nasty concussion you suffered. You have been here since about nine last night; about eight hours." The nurse gently took Trenda's left hand and inspected the bandage on her wrist. She then looked at the healing cut near Trenda's eye. "I see you have a few other fairly new injuries. I had to clean up the one on your shoulder; it was mildly infected. It required five stitches to close it properly."

Trenda rubbed the new bandage on her shoulder. The cut no longer throbbed as much as it did prior to the nurse's treatment. "Are you serious? I have been here since last night?" She rubbed the bandage on her head as she tried to peek through the fog obscuring her memory of what had happened to her. All she could recall was going into her purse and getting her knife before leaving the hotel. *Oh, shit! That reminds me; where is Baby?* "Thanks for fixin' me up, ma'am."

The nurse put her hand on her hips and gave Trenda a mock scowl. "I am *not* old enough to be called 'ma'am.'" She tapped the name badge on her white smock. "Call me Gloria."

Trenda chuckled at the stern but friendly nurse. "Okay, Gloria, my bad. Can you tell me where my clothes and stuff are?"

Gloria wrapped a blood pressure cuff around Trenda's

arm and nodded to Trenda's left. "I put most of your things in that closet over there." She squeezed the bladder in her hand, inflating the blood pressure cuff. "I'll get them for you in a minute after I check on your roommate over here."

For the first time, Trenda noticed there was another patient in the bed across the room. All she could see was a leg in traction behind the curtain bordering their beds. Trenda examined the jade crucifix around the nurse's neck. It featured a gold image of a crucified Jesus. Jade was her favorite shade of green. "How long do I have to stay here?"

"Since your concussion falls between the simple and complex category, the doctor suggests we keep you under observation for the next twenty-four to forty-eight hours."

After looking at the bandage on her wrist, she looked at the window and saw the sun rising in the crack between the floral-pattern curtains. "I can't stay here...I am supposed to go to work. I can't afford to get fired."

Gloria noted Trenda's blood pressure numbers, released the air in the cuff and removed it. "Honey, the last thing you need to be concerned with is that job. You need to be more concerned with finding out why your car blew up." She shook her head, did the sign of the cross and kissed her crucifix. "If you had gotten any closer to that car..."

Ignoring the dull ache under the lump over her ear, Trenda, shocked, sat straight up in bed. "*What?* Did you say my car *blew up?*"

Thirty-Nine

"Oh hell no! What the fuck you mean, Piper is *dead?*" Tyrone asked as Darius sat in his rental car, outside the bar. "*What happened?*"

"I was watching the news and saw somebody shot her down in a robbery attempt."

A long pause as Tyrone took a long drag off his cigarette. "Oh really…is *that* what happened, partner?"

The sarcasm in Tyrone's voice spoke volumes; it was clear Tyrone had his doubts about Piper's demise. "Yeah, that's what I heard."

"I can't say I'm sorry to hear that. What about your other business? Is that taken care of?"

Scheming, Darius drummed his fingers on the passenger seat as Tyrone poured a vat of stress on his head. "Not yet…working on it now. It won't be long."

"I sure-the-hell hope not! I'm gettin' tired of havin' to worry about her gettin' away!"

Darius's tension volcano erupted. "Listen, scary mutha-fucka! I'm tired of you whinin' about this shit! Just sit your worried ass down somewhere and shut the fuck up!

All I need now is for one of the Internal Affairs snitches to see you acting like a pussy to know something is up… and quit smokin'! You look nervous enough as it is. That change in your behavior is sure to draw unwanted attention…Man up, son! This ain't your first picnic! I'll holla at you later. Keep the phone on."

After tossing the phone on the dash, he ran his hands down his face. "I don't know how many Guardian Angels you have watchin' over you, Trenda, but they ain't gonna always be there." He grabbed the phone and called Jet Blue reservations. Luck was with him; the next flight to Newark, New Jersey was leaving in two hours. "It's gonna be too risky to take her out in the hospital—especially without a gun." He started the car and headed for the airport. "That's okay…I'll just have to resort to plan B, draw you to me."

A devilish grin shaped his lips. "I think I have just the way to do that."

Forty

"That's right, hon. All that's left of that poor car is a smoldering shell. The police are still trying to figure out what happened. They say it burned too fast to be an electrical fire."

Trenda still couldn't remember what happened to her after leaving the hotel. All she could see was a wall of fog. The more she strained to remember, the more the knot on the side of her head ached. "Gloria, can you pass me my clothes?"

Gloria sat her clipboard on the chair next to the other patient, a white woman who looked to be unconscious, and walked over to the closet. Inside, she picked up a large plastic bag, walked over and sat it on the bed next to Trenda. A bit of the warmth left her eyes. "There you go."

"Thanks." She looked over at the other patient. "Is she okay? I haven't seen her move since I got here."

Gloria shook her head with a sad look on her face. "No…she was struck by a car last night while trying to run from the police during a prostitution sting and is now in a coma. Poor baby had no ID on her and her fingerprints are not in the system. The police think she may be a runaway. It's a shame no one has even tried to claim her."

"That's messed up." Trenda rummaged through her stuff. *Where is Baby?* She glanced over at Gloria standing a few feet away with her hand in the pocket of her smock. "Is this all? I think I'm missin' some stuff."

Gloria drew the curtain between the beds and walked over to Trenda's side. "May I ask you a personal question?"

A layer of tension coated Trenda. "Uh…okay…"

Gloria let her hand play with something in her pocket as she lowered her voice. "I am concerned about your variety of wounds. I have been a nurse for over forty years. I have seen just about everything you can imagine. Your cuts appear to have been made by the same weapon; I can tell that by the dimensions of the wounds. My instincts tell me the cuts you have are defensive wounds, most likely from a knife. Is there anything you would like to tell me? Do you need help? Is someone after you?"

The concern in those brown eyes was unmistakable. Even as Trenda's mind automatically searched for a lie as an answer, as she had been conditioned to do in these situations, there was something soothing about those soft eyes. "Kinda…I had a boyfriend I got into some mess with…"

Gloria continued probing with her eyes. "Well, that's not good. Maybe when Detective Winslow returns, you can tell him about your crummy boyfriend."

Trenda's eyes widened. *"Detective?* What detective?"

"Oh! That's right, you were asleep. A detective from OPD came by to get a statement from you. I told him you were heavily sedated and for him to return later this afternoon when you were lucid."

"Did he say when he was comin' back?"

Gloria continued to play with something in her pocket as she placed a hand on Trenda's head. "Can I share a little something with you?"

Trenda mentally flinched from Gloria's touch. Memories of how, under the football field bleachers, her ex-boyfriend from high school forcibly grabbed her by the hair and made her swallow his dick flashed in her mind. She recalled passing out from lack of air. Instead of getting her some help, her punk-ass boyfriend jacked off on her face and left her there. When she woke up minutes later and found herself alone and with the sticky mess, she almost stroked out with rage. Unfortunately for that ex-boyfriend the following day, the interior of his new Camaro Z-28, and the tires, were slashed while he was at football practice. His parents ended up taking the car away from him and selling it. He lost his super car and his superstar girlfriend on the same day. To this day she's still *very* particular about *anyone* touching her head. She gulped. "Yeah, sure…what you wanna tell me?"

Gloria took her hand out of her pocket, rolled up her left sleeve and showed Trenda her forearm. "You see that tattoo?"

Trenda looked halfway up the bottom of Gloria's forearm at a tattoo shaped like a small teardrop with a dagger piercing it. "Yeah…it looks like you had it for a while."

"Yes, I made that mistake sixty years ago when I decided to join a street gang in East L.A."

Trenda adjusted the cold compress on her head. "You look like you was a bad ass back in the day."

Gloria put her hand back in her pocket and fidgeted with the item inside. "Yes…but now I am a soon-to-be-retired nurse, great-great-grandmother, wife and lover of the Lord."

Trenda eased back on her pillow. *Oh great…now granny is gonna try and get me to join her church or some shit…* "Cool."

Gloria took a deep breath, pulled the object out of her pocket, and showed it to Trenda. "Is this what you were looking for?"

Trenda sat straight up. "Yeah! Where did you find it?"

Gloria looked over the butterfly knife in her hand. "I found it on you while I was changing you into your hospital gown…it looks like it's been through a few wars. I was lucky to find it just before the detective showed up."

Taking Baby from Gloria, Trenda quickly put it under the covers next to her. "You could say that."

Gloria peered into Trenda's eyes. "Normally, I'm supposed to report these things, especially in a case like yours, but the Lord told me to keep quiet."

"I appreciate that."

"Ms. Collins…I have to tell you, I am a bit concerned for you. It may be—"

Sensing a sermon coming, Trenda had enough. "Look, I don't mean to be rude, but I am not in the mood to be preached to. I do appreciate you giving me my property back, but to be honest, my life is my life. I have always taken care of myself and always will." She fluffed up her pillow, closed her eyes and laid her head down. "Now, if you don't mind, I wanna get some rest."

Gloria just stared at Trenda, crow's feet wrinkles framing her warm eyes. "Fine…but let me say one last thing before I go." She proceeded to unbutton her blouse and leaned close to Trenda. "You see this?"

Trenda opened her eyes. *What the hell is this old broad doin'? I hope she ain't some kinda old lesbian freak!* "Whoa! Wassup, woman?"

Gloria pulled her white bra down just enough for Trenda to see an ugly zipper-like scar between her breasts and a quarter-sized scar about four inches from her heart. "You see this? This happened to me one night about fifty years ago when I was about your age. Being too cocky, thinking I was untouchable, me and a couple of fellow gang-bangers went to a Halloween party on the border of our turf, and of one of our most vicious rivals. As expected, some of them were there—double the number we had actually. As we tried to escape, four of our five were shot to death. I alone survived. I was shot twice, point blank in my chest." She tapped the smaller scar. "This one bounced off one of my ribs and ended up missing my heart by an eighth of an inch. Good thing for me the gun was only a .22-caliber and not something more powerful."

Shocked at the display, Trenda stared at the wounds. "Damn…"

Gloria buttoned up her blouse, then took off her watch and showed Trenda an equally ugly scar on her wrist, hidden by her watchband. "Since the gun only had two bullets left, the heathens, in hopes of making sure I would die, decided to slit my wrist."

Trenda's mouth went dry. "No shit?" She sat up on her elbows. "How did you get away?"

Gloria put her watch back on and rolled down her sleeve. "I didn't; the scum just left me in an alley behind the house party." She fingered her jade crucifix. "This is what saved me; the love of our Lord."

Again, Trenda rolled her eyes and lay back on her pillow, the knot on her head reminding her it was there. "I'm glad for you but I need some rest. My head is startin' to hurt."

"Do you believe in God, Ms. Collins?"

"Not really."

She began unwrapping the bandage holding the cold compress against Trenda's head. "I didn't either until that Halloween night when I was shot. And believe me, I had done far more than my fair share of sinning before that night. I can tell by the looks of your knife that you've had it for a while." She rolled up the bandage and set it and the blue ice pack on the table next to Trenda's bed. "And chances are you have used it. I'm not here to judge, just here to do my job as a good Catholic and pass along a bit of the Lord's word."

Irritation gnawed at Trenda's patience. "Look…I told you once—"

Gloria lowered her voice to a stern but warm whisper and pointed a slightly shaky and wrinkled finger at her. "No, *you* look, *Trenda*."

Trenda nearly lost her urine. "Wha? *Who* did you call me?"

Gloria didn't flinch. "Yes, I know your real name; you were so relaxed from the sedatives you were on last night you gave me your real name—a few times. As it stands, I am the only one here that knows. I could have given that information to the detective, but I decided against it."

Trenda's mouth sought a reply, but all her brain gave her was, "Oh, shit!"

Unmoving, Gloria went on. "As I told you, I have unshakable belief in my faith. While I was lying in that alley with my blood running into the gutter and flipping between being dead and alive, a voice told me to go back in time and recall the faces of everyone I had stolen from, beat up, lied to, let down or otherwise hurt in my life. The guilt I felt was so powerful I couldn't close my eyes. Each time I did, as I was about to give in to death, the guilt of looking into all those faces forced me to keep my eyes open. Through the pain, I did my best to focus on the blurry stars overhead and the sound of a bird singing in the distance. What seemed like years later, the bird song grew so loud it began to hurt my ears. The next thing I knew, I was surrounded by flashing red lights; the bird song was an ambulance. My blurred vision was the result of my tears of repentance being spilled. And I finally realized that the voice I heard was the same one I often ignored while I was in the clutches of Lucifer."

Trenda couldn't stop looking into the old nurse's eyes. They reflected great wisdom and more compassion than Trenda had ever encountered. She was momentarily torn between wanting to give Gloria a tight hug and jumping out of the bed and running her ass off. "I see…"

Gloria finally broke her gaze, checked her watch and gathered up her clipboard. "Well, Ms. Collins, my shift ended about eight minutes ago; if your head gets any worse, use the button on your bed rail and call the nurse immediately. Other than that, use the ice pack as often as you can; it will help get that walnut on the side of your head to shrink." She smiled and brushed Trenda's forehead. "Just remember this, honey; no matter how rocky, lonely, filthy or dark the road is you travel, God allows U-turns."

With that, Gloria quietly left. The only sound in the room was the ventilator her unconscious roommate was connected to. Trenda lay staring at the ceiling in silence long after her Catholic devotee left.

Forty-One

Two hours after receiving her breakfast, Trenda had a guest. "Oh my God! Are you okay, Mya?" Eli asked after rushing into her room. "I saw a picture of you on the news last night and almost had a coronary!"

Trenda covered the remains of her breakfast with the stainless steel lid and allowed Eli to take her hand and kiss it. "Yeah, I'm okay…just a little headache."

That was the first time she had seen him in relaxed clothes; both his jeans and blue UC Berkeley T-shirt could stand a little ironing. *"Just a little headache?"* His eyes gave her the once-over. "I saw your car burning up and you on a gurney! What happened?"

"I still can't remember much after leaving the hotel to go to my car. They say it's because of my concussion."

He carefully caressed the side of her face. "It must be a pretty serious concussion. Usually they just send you home with some Tylenol and codeine and put you on bedrest for a few days."

She managed a weak smile. "How you know so much, Dr. Teddy Bear?"

He broke eye contact with her. "Well, you know, Meagan being in the medical field…"

She inconspicuously reached under her covers and tucked Baby just under her right butt cheek. "You are one lucky man to have a brainiac like her sharin' your bed."

"Not really…she is nothing like you." The infatuation in his face read like a billboard. "Not even close."

You have no idea how lucky you are she's not, she thought after visualizing Gloria's face. "You are way too sweet to me, baby. Keep that up and I am gonna get spoiled."

Hovering over her like a cuddly Sasquatch, he took her hand again. "Mya, I don't like the way things have been going for you; you deserve better."

"Well, I'm glad somebody does…thanks, Boo."

"What are you going to do about transportation? Have you contacted your insurance company yet?"

Regretting she hadn't yet insured the Honda, she shook her head. "No…"

"Do you want me to call them for you?"

Drawing in a deep breath and letting it go, she confessed. "No… I didn't have time to put insurance on it."

Head lowered, he shook it slowly. "Oh wow…that is bad."

"Yeah, I know, but shit happens."

"Does your family know what happened? Do you need to call them?"

The lump on her head began aching with stress. "Yeah, I called and told them I'm okay and there's no need for them to fly all the way out here from the East Coast."

He nodded. "Cool…at least they know you are okay—not as okay as I would like you to be, but okay."

Trenda noticed he seemed to be distracted. He was fidgeting more than normal. "Good thing is I found out this is a county hospital and I don't have to pay the bill since I don't have any medical insurance yet."

Holding her hand a little tighter, he looked at her in silence for a few moments. "Mya, I am leaving Meagan."

Oh-the-hell-no he didn't! "What are you talkin' about? How you gonna do that when she's your fiancée?"

"I never *officially* asked her to marry me. We talked about it a few times, but never set a date. She is too busy with school to really be ready for the kind of commitment I want." He leaned over and kissed Trenda's stunned lips. "Besides, my heart has found what it has been looking for…"

A bolt of pain shot from the lump on her head through her brain. "Eli, do you really think—"

He caressed the side of her face and gazed into her eyes. "I love you, Mya…and I want you to be with me."

No less than a thousand thoughts filled her cloudy mind. Ashamedly, most of them were thoughts of how to best take advantage of the man and situation. After all, this was by far not the first time she'd been the recipient of that love line. "Wait…hold up, baby…this ain't… no…think abo—"

He shook his head. "No…I have thought about this ever since you arrived. This is the first time I have truly felt this happy." He let go of her hand, went into the large side pocket of his jeans and pulled out an envelope. "I have to get back home and get dressed for work. I will be back to see you as soon as I get off about five-thirty or so. In the meantime, think about what I said; I am very serious, Mya."

"Eli, we need to really talk about this…I mean, this is pretty damn serious."

Smiling, he leaned over, laid the envelope on the table and kissed her again. "You will see just how serious I am when you see what's in the envelope."

She watched him lay it on the table and hastily leave. A tingle of fear touched her as she reached for the white envelope. *What have you done, man?*

As soon as he disembarked from his red-eye flight into Newark, New Jersey, Darius got in his Escalade and hurried to the vacation cabin in Avalon. After tossing his bags on the bed, he called his partner. "Hey, wake up! I'm back in town."

"What the hell? Do you know what time it is?"

Darius checked his watch. "I don't give a shit that it's four in the mornin'! You need to get up and get your ass over here to Avalon so we can go over the new plan."

"What new plan? What the fuck is goin' on *now?*"

The calming sound of the waves hitting the beach outside did little to ease the tension Darius now felt. "Just get your ass here…and bring some coffee…"

This was the first time Officer Kain had a loose end he couldn't tie up. And he did *not* like the feeling of helplessness.

Nope, not at all.

Forty-Two

The two items inside the envelope both chilled and thrilled Trenda. She could feel her pulse rapidly beating in the bump on the side of her head. Her hand shook as she reached for her unfinished cup of orange juice. "Damn, Eli...damn..."

She picked up Eli's personal check, made out to Mya Collins, for five-thousand dollars. Along with the check was a short note in some of the neatest handwriting she had ever seen:

Hey, sweetheart! This is just a little something to get you on your feet. I figured you could use this to rent out a chair in a nice salon and do hair, get another car and get a down payment on an apartment. Actually, I would prefer you just move in with me. I have plenty of room. And don't worry about paying me back; this is a portion of the cash I had put aside for my wedding with Meagan. You have no idea how good it feels to know I have finally found my Queen! I love you, Mya...

Is he for real? She stared at the check. *Five grand?* The hustler in her went to work calculating how to best take advantage of this windfall. As always, her thoughts went first to turning a profit, then turning the Trick. Just holding the check seemed to ease the pain in her head. *Fuck just renting a chair in a salon; I can probably get him to help me find a spot and open up my own shop...*

Not once did she think about Eli leaving his longtime girlfriend for her. The lure of fast cash had blinded her as it had for most of her life. She tucked the note and check back in the envelope, set it on the table next to her carafe of ice water and prepared to turn on the TV for the first time since she had arrived.

Although she rarely watched TV at all, as she flipped through the channels, she was drawn to an episode of the *Maury* show. She paused on the show just as a heavy-set black woman was crying and yelling at a white woman and a tall, slim black man. "I wonder what made her go off," Trenda said as she sat up in bed, preparing to go to the restroom.

After returning, Trenda climbed back in bed and continued to watch the show. She found out that the man had filed for divorce from the crying woman after reuniting with a former lover he ran into at a high school reunion. Out of nowhere, a shroud of depression descended on her. She remained transfixed on the black woman, now on her knees, crying her eyes out to the asshole of a man in front of her while his white lover looked on unsympathetically.

Anger swelled inside Trenda. "If that muthafucka had

done that to me—" Her eyes fell on the envelope on the table next to her. Fake or not, the sound of the woman crying and yelling on TV drowned out the sound of the hospital's PA system summoning various doctors and nurses to various places. It dimmed the great mood she was in after obtaining her ill-gotten gain. More of her father's words seeped into her mind:

Wise choices are choices that line up with God's Word. Wise choices are choices that are pleasing to God. Just choose to obey God and His Word and you will make the wise choice every time. God made us—He knows who you are and what you need to be happy and satisfied and blessed. Obeying His wisdom will bring you life, whereas succumbing to the temptations of the devil and your carnal, fleshly desires will bring death and destruction to your spirit, your mind and your body

—GALATIANS 6:8

No longer in the mood to listen to the suffering woman on TV, Trenda picked up the remote. Before she could change the channel, a pair of familiar voices greeted her from the doorway. "Hey, girl!" Lollie said as she ran over to Trenda's bedside and gave her a hug. "How you doin'? I just got word about what happened!" She looked Trenda over with concerned eyes as she handed Trenda her purse. "Are you okay?"

Before she could answer, Walter walked over and gave her a hug. "It sure is good to see you up and about! You had us worried like crazy!"

Trenda saw something different in both her friends.

The way their hands immediately found each other's as they stood next to one another and the glow that encompassed them, even though they were covered in worry, were sure signs there was a serious chemistry flow between them. Finally, Trenda broke her silence. She set her purse on the bed between her and the bed rail. "Thanks for bringin' me my purse. I'm cool…just had a lil' mishap."

Lollie put her hands on her sexy hips. "Bullshit!" She put her hand to her mouth, spun around and looked over at the hoisted leg of Trenda's comatose roommate. She lowered her voice to a whisper. "Sorry…I didn't realize you had company."

Trenda waved her off. "Don't worry about it; she is out for the count." She couldn't help but notice how cute the pair looked in almost identical blue jeans and T-shirts—it was the first time she had ever seen Walter dressed so casually. She gave them a slight grin. "I knew I was right; you two make a cute-ass couple."

Blushing, Lollie did her best to brush the compliment off. "Anyway…" She rubbed Trenda's forehead. "So what happened? How long are you gonna be here? I talked to Jeff and he told me to tell you to take all the time off you need. I think they are scared you are gonna sue them."

"Sue them? For what?"

Walter put his arm around Lollie's slim waist. "Well, they do have a certain liability since you were injured on the job, on *their* property."

Again, the scheming demon on Trenda's shoulder spoke to her. *Hell yeah! I can sue the shit outta the Water's Edge Hotel!* She thought a little deeper about it. *But they did do me a big favor by hiring me when I really needed the help...* "I'll have to keep that in mind."

"So what happened?"

Trenda scoured her memory of the event and came up blank. "The only thing I remember is walking out of the hotel to get something out of my car, then I wake up here."

Lollie did a double-take at the TV screen as the news at noon came on. She pointed at the screen and yelled. "Hey! Check that out!"

On the screen, they all listened to the news reporter speak. "We have breaking news! There's a possible break in last night's killing in Jack London Square. We have an exclusive interview with the woman that found the victim's body. More to come when we return."

Trenda sat up and asked, *"Killing?* What killing?"

Forty-Three

"You didn't hear?" Lollie asked as she turned from the screen back to Trenda. "Have you watched the news at all since you got here?"

"No…I just turned the TV on not too long ago."

After the dishwashing liquid commercial ended, they watched the TV screen in silence. The dark-haired news reporter spoke. "We here at Channel Two just got word that the woman that discovered the body of homicide victim, Piper Langford, heard her final words."

Trenda bumped the table next to her bed so hard as she jumped out, the carafe of water flew like a missile and nearly landed on her roommate's bed. "*What* did he say her name was?"

A blown-up picture of Piper filled the screen as the reporter continued. Walter watched as Trenda walked closer to the TV, the back of her hospital gown open for the world to see. "Piper Langford…do you know h—"

Trenda silenced him with her hand as she stared intently at the screen. The reporter spoke as a film shot of a woman in shadow—to avoid her identity being known—

spoke. "I was on my way to Barnes and Noble, you know, to get a book. I usually take the stairs from the parking garage, you know, to get a little exercise in, you know? And last night, when I got to the top of the stairs, you know, I saw the light was off…I looked down, you know, and saw that lady layin' on the ground. I bent over, you know, and asked her if she was okay…she wasn't movin' at first, you know, then she opened her eyes a little and I heard her mumble somethin'…I got closer, you know, and saw she was bloody. That's when I screamed for help…I heard her still mumblin'…to me, it sounded like she said two words; 'Baltimore…cop…' I could be wrong, you know, but that's what it sounded like, 'Baltimore… cop…' After that, you know, she just stopped talkin'…I think, you know, that's when she died…"

Lollie walked up behind Trenda and attempted to tie up her gown. Trenda nearly jumped to the ceiling. "Easy, girl…I'm just tryin' to close you up."

Trenda nodded as she tried to calm her rapid heart rate. *Oh muthafucka! Piper? Dead? This cannot be happenin'! What the hell was she doing here?* "Thanks…thanks, Lollie." She walked slowly back to her bed and sat down.

Lollie pointed at the screen. "Hey, Walter! That's that crazy broad that almost ran into us the other day!"

"I'll be damned! It sure is!" Walter walked over to the bed, bent over and looked into Trenda's face. "Hey… you okay? Did you know that woman?"

Trenda avoided his eyes and instead focused on the

pool of water around the light blue carafe on the floor. "No...I thought it was my friend Piper *Stanford*...a friend I went to cosmetology school with back in D.C. Did you say y'all saw that woman?"

He glanced back at the TV. "Yeah, she pulled up to my car as Lollie and I were on our way to breakfast. She kept asking if we knew somebody named Brenda or Kendra, or something like that."

Lollie cocked her head as she looked at Trenda. "Are you okay, honey?"

Trenda, not Brenda...that bitch was here lookin' for me! A frosting of panic coated Trenda. She picked up the ice pack and put it against the side of her head. "I'm good... just had a little ache from this lump on my head."

"You need me to go get the nurse?"

Trenda momentarily spaced out as the two words the dead woman spoke peppered her mind. "Baltimore. Cop." *Baltimore cop shot me, is what I bet she was tryin' to say.*

Darius.

If Piper had found me, then it would be a real good bet that Darius could have found me, too...knowin' how he operates. I would bet anything that he killed Piper...and if he killed her, then anybody else close to me... She looked at her concerned friends. *Oh shit!*

"Mya?" Walter said as he held her shoulders. "I'm going to go get a nurse. I'll be right back."

She grabbed his arm. "No...serious, I'm cool...I'm just kinda groggy from the medication they gave me earlier.

I just need to lay down and rest." The image of both her friends dying at the hands of that bastard Darius tied a huge knot in her stomach. She glanced at the clock on the wall. *According to Gloria, that detective is supposed to show up this afternoon…it's damn near one now.*

Lollie went to the bathroom, got a towel and began cleaning up the spilled water. "Jeff told me some folks from corporate are going to come by sometime today. I think it's probably the hotel lawyers. I heard they already took care of the owner of the truck that was parked next to your car that burned up. They ain't bull-shittin' about tryin' to get this mess squashed."

Damn! More people comin' by? "Did Jeff say what time?"

Lollie wiped off the carafe with the damp, white towel and put it back on the table. "No…he just said some-time today."

Trenda could almost hear the steady tick of time running out. "Okay…I'm gonna try and take a nap before folks start showin' up. Why don't you guys stop by later this evening? I could sure go for some Chinese food for dinner."

Lollie set the wet towel on the tray with the remainder of Trenda's lunch. "Okay…I called out today after I heard what happened to you." She gave Trenda a hug. "I told Jeff I had to be off so I could help you out since you have no family here…he was real cool about it. He told me I could take off all week if need be to help you get back on your feet."

That show of love nearly brought tears to Trenda's eyes. She was barely able to keep her voice from cracking. "Thanks, Lollie." She broke from Lollie, reached for Walter and hugged him tight. "Thank you, too."

Forty-Four

As soon as Lollie and Walter left her room, Trenda sprung from the bed like a Jack-in-the-Box. The same intuition she had counted on all her life—that she ignored before she was almost killed—kicked in. "Hurry the fuck up, Trenda!" she said to herself as she ripped off the hospital gown and poured her clothes on the bed.

After slipping into her wrinkled uniform and black loafers, she pulled back the covers of her bed and put Baby and the envelope from Eli in her purse. *Good thing Gloria is honest,* she thought as she unfolded the twenty-dollar bill in her pants pocket. Once dressed, she walked to the door, stuck her head out and looked around.

An Indian male nurse was busy in the room across from her checking the pulse of an elderly man. The nurses at the station to her right were busy with phone calls and a line of worried-looking visitors. Trenda looked to her left and spotted the "EXIT" sign mounted to the ceiling at the T-shaped corridor entrance. *Aight, let's do this!*

Without stopping, Trenda walked the twenty feet to

the corridor and followed the exit signs. She *almost* thanked God once she made it to the stairway without incident. As she walked down the stairs, the thought of Piper being dead slapped her with a steel fist of guilt. *She might have been a lil' crazy, but that girl would do anything for anybody…and now she is dead…dead because of me no doubt…*

The sunlight outside wasn't nearly warm enough to comfort the ache in her heart. As she raised her hand to hail a passing cab, she noticed the white hospital bracelet on the same wrist she had injured in the explosion. Using her teeth, she bit through it, removed it and tossed it to the ground. "Where to, lady?" the Middle Eastern cabbie asked.

"Will twenty dollars get me to the Hotel Oakland?"

The cabbie punched the coordinates into the GPS unit attached to his windshield and dropped the flag. "It'll be close…"

She closed the door and sat back. "Well, just get me as close as my money will travel; that's all I have—includin' your tip."

Leaving the cabbie the three dollars in change from her twenty, she hurried inside the hotel and straight to her room. A feeling of déjà vu surrounded her as she rushed to pack up her "Travelin' Bag" once again. "Fuck! I am gonna have to leave almost all my new clothes," she said as she changed out of her uniform and into some jeans and a light-pink Baby Phat shirt.

With less than eight hundred dollars left in her stash, the check from Eli gave her a measure of comfort. Her chest tightened as thoughts of her new friends invaded her busy brain. *No time…ain't got time for reminiscing right now.*

"Are you checking out, ma'am?" the young Lebanese woman at the registration desk asked as Trenda headed toward the lobby exit.

Trenda patted her Reebok bag. "Nah, I'm on my way to work out with my friend at Curves gym up the street."

The receptionist smiled. "Cool! I work out there myself! Maybe I'll see you down there one day."

Trenda's fake enthusiasm was award winning. "That would be real cool! I'll be looking for you, girlfriend!"

Five minutes later, after failing to find a cab, she put on her dark shades and began walking away from the hotel. She couldn't recall a time she felt more rotten inside. After walking nearly half a mile, she paused in the middle of the sidewalk and looked around. *Where in the world are you going, Trenda?* The unfamiliar landscape added to the lonely feeling she'd begun to feel. The pain from the bump on her head was no match for the hurt in her soul.

Normally, she always had a friend to turn to in even the most desperate times. Whether it was her street-walking friends like Constance, one of her former high-powered lovers, or crazy Piper, they had become her family. Now here, thousands of miles from her East

Coast comfort zone, she felt as vulnerable as a newborn baby.

Pulling herself out of her pit of doom, she looked over her shoulder and spotted an approaching, Richmond-bound, AC Transit Bus. She hustled to the bus stop a few yards away and waited. *I don't know where Richmond is, but I'm hoppin' on this bus anyway.*

As the bus pulled into traffic, Trenda walked to the middle of the bus and took a seat across from the rear exit doors. A pair of rough-looking brothas sitting in the back of the bus patted the seat-space between them as she turned to take her seat. The droopy-eyed man gave her a gold tooth-filled smile. "Hey, sexy! You oughta come on back here and keep us company."

Ignoring the offer, she sat down and scooted over to the window seat. *Why can't I go just one day without some pest like that buggin' me?* She thought of something Constance once said to her a couple years ago. After a man relentlessly tried to get Trenda's phone number as she and Constance were walking past Camden Yards, Constance laughed at her friend and said, *Red, you remind me of one of those Sirens I read about back in high school. You know, those beautiful women in Greek mythology that lured men to their death with their irresistible beauty and singing. I never heard you sing, but we both know you are one of the finest bitches in B-More!*

Leaning her head back against the backrest, Trenda found her eyes closing. The sound of the bus's engine accelerating and decelerating, along with its gentle rocking motion, nearly put her to sleep. During one of her nodding-off moments, the image of King Gee tossing his drink on Lollie's dress made her eyes shoot open. *Now I remember why I was going to my car! That asshole King Gee called and said something about my car...*

The veil of amnesia began to lift. Bits and pieces of the events leading up to the explosion became clear. As she stared out the window, struggling with putting the pieces together, the bus passed a sign saying, "Welcome to El Cerrito."

After a moment's thought, she pulled the cable signaling the bus driver she wanted to get off at the next stop. *Why am I trippin'? All I have to do is go ahead, hook up with Eli, and chill.* The bus slowed, pulled to the curb and stopped. Trenda grabbed her bag and exited the bus. *Even if Darius did kill Piper, knowin' him, he got the hell out of Dodge. He can't afford to hang around here.*

Now that she had a game plan, she began to feel a little better. Even the aches from her many injuries seemed to have subsided. She managed a small smile as she sat down on the bus stop bench, opened her bag and pulled out the envelope from Eli. She checked the time. *Yeah... I think I'll surprise him. He should be off work in about an hour; hopefully he'll stop at his house before goin' to the hospital lookin' for me.* She removed the check and read his address in the upper-right corner. *Now, let me call a cab...*

Half an hour later, she got out the cab a block away

from Eli's home. As she walked down the tree-lined street of Eli's quiet neighborhood, a familiar-looking blue car passed her by. She stopped next to a large oak tree. *Hmm-mmm…I see loverboy is goin' home a little early.*

Three houses up from where she stood, Trenda watched as Eli got out, hustled around his car and opened the passenger door. *Ohhh! What is this?* Even from that distance, she recognized the woman as the infamous Meagan. *Wow! She is a lot cuter than she looked in that picture in his wallet!*

The couple stood face-to-face, next to Eli's car, having what looked like a heated conversation. Trenda watched Meagan try and wrap her arms around his neck. The look she gave him as he wiped her arms off him was unmistakable; she was hurting. The heartbreak on her face was beyond sad. Trenda eased behind the tree, out of their line of sight. Her good mood dissipated. *Well, maybe it's for the best…after all, he did tell me he wasn't happy with her…*

Eli looked to be in a hurry to do something. He opened the trunk of his car, removed a red backpack, handed it to her and closed the trunk. At that moment, Trenda recalled the happiness they shared in the photos in Eli's wallet. *They look good together.* All of a sudden, the temperature seemed to have dropped a hundred degrees.

After wiping her eyes, Meagan walked over to the yellow Volkswagen across the street, hopped in and drove off crying, right past Trenda. No more than ten seconds later, Trenda saw Eli remove his cell phone and dial. Her phone vibrated in her purse. She took a deep breath, took her phone out of her purse and stared at Eli's name on the caller ID. She was surprised at how hard it was for her to answer his call. Before she could decide, the call rolled over to her voicemail. He then got into his car and drove off in the opposite direction.

I gotta go… She hitched her bag up on her shoulder and walked away from Eli's house. As directionless as a leaf in a windstorm, Trenda just followed her feet as they led her away. An ocean of guilt washed over her.

With the sun fading in the horizon, Trenda found herself trudging down San Pablo Avenue with no destination in mind. Her eyes fell to the ground in front of her as she walked. "You know damn well why you didn't answer Eli's call." Her angry conscience yelled in her mind. "You know he only broke up with Meagan because of *you*."

The blare of a bus's horn brought her back into reality. While walking with her head down, she had nearly stepped off the curb onto a busy intersection against the red blinking "Don't Walk" sign. She stood on the edge of the curb, watching a fast-moving cement truck hurtling her way. With the truck only seconds away from where she stood, a lifetime of thoughts went though her head, with the most recent developments leading the way. *It would be so easy to just step off this curb…* The cement truck got closer. *I bet I wouldn't even feel no pain as big and heavy as it is…*

Forty-Five

"I have no idea where she went," nurse Baker said as Dr. Rambis stood next to Trenda's empty bed. "I came in to check her vitals and see what she wanted for dinner and found her gone."

The young blond doctor exhaled loudly and looked over at Detective Winslow. "Well, detective, what now?"

The black, middle-aged, gray-haired detective, holding a notepad and pen, peeked behind the curtain at Trenda's former roommate. "What about her? You think she could tell us anything?"

The doctor walked over and checked the patient's chart. "Not a chance. It's a miracle she is even alive. She's been comatose for two days now." He tapped her body cast. "Good thing she is; or else she would be in a world of pain right now."

The detective cast his eyes on the quiet couple sitting and holding hands across from Trenda's bed. "And you two say you haven't seen her since around one this afternoon?"

Walter shook his head. "No…I even checked her room

at the hotel she was staying in. It appears she packed some of her things and left. The receptionist said she saw her leave the hotel around two. She said she was going to the gym to work out."

Worry covered Lollie's face. "I went to the gym and they said no one by the name Mya or fitting her description had been in today."

The detective scribbled a few notes. "Thanks, you two. Remember, if you see or hear from her, be sure to use the business cards I gave you and give me a call ASAP. And like I said, she is not a suspect; we just have some questions we need answered."

Walter shook the detective's hand. "Sure thing…if we hear anything, we will contact you."

"Thanks," he turned to the doctor and nurse, "same goes for you and the rest of your staff." On his way out, the detective took the plastic drinking cup off Trenda's food tray, poured the last few drops of water back into the carafe, removed a plastic evidence bag from his briefcase, put the cup inside, and carefully placed the bag back in his briefcase. Exiting the room, he took the same stairs Trenda had. *Why were you in such a hurry to leave, Ms. Collins?*

Forty-Six

The people walking in darkness have seen a great light;
on those living in the land of the shadow of death
a light has dawned.
—ISAIAH 9:2

Someone tapped Trenda on the arm. "Hey, lady, this fell out your bag," said a little girl holding the envelope from Eli.

Trenda stepped back and turned to the little girl just as the cement truck zoomed past, running the yellow light. Trenda looked at the cute little black girl. She had to be no more than four years old. Trenda managed a smile as she took the envelope from the little girl. "Thank you, sweetheart!"

"You're *pretty!*" the blushing girl said.

Trenda saw a teenage girl a few yards away, busy talking on her phone. She looked just like the little girl. She smiled at the shy little girl. "I'm not as pretty as *you!*"

The little girl looked down at the ground. "Nuh uh… my friends always call me ugly."

Trenda gazed at the brown-skinned little girl. Splotches

of eczema covered her arms and neck. The perm in her hair was in desperate need of a touch-up. Pity for the poor child welled inside her. *Kids can be so fuckin' mean!* She stooped down and gave the girl a hug. "Remember, you are a pretty princess and one day you are gonna grow up to be a beautiful queen." Without thinking, Trenda showed the girl her arm. "I used to have eczema when I was your age." She showed the girl the unblemished skin on her neck and arms. "See! It's all gone!"

The girl's eyes bugged out. "Wow! Is mine gonna look like that when I grow up?"

Trenda nodded. "It sure is, hon…you just wait and see. Let those bad kids say what they want, but me and you know what's gonna happen when you get older, right?"

A magnificent smile filled the girls face. "Yeah! I am gonna be a beautiful queen like *you!*"

Her big sister, still a few yards ahead of Trenda and the girl, turned around with the cell phone to her ear. "C'mon, Raven, leave that lady alone so we can get home."

A mix of emotions swirled inside Trenda as she stood up. "You are already beautiful…now go on so you don't get in trouble. And don't forget our secret."

"I won't!" The smiling girl ran off to join her sister.

Trenda stuffed the envelope back in her bag. A burst of satisfaction shoved aside some of the sadness and stress inside her. For the first time in her adult life, she felt fulfilled; as if she'd found her true purpose. *Even though I never had eczema, somethin' told me lyin' to that baby was the right thing to do…I think that is just what she needed…*

Trenda stood at the intersection contemplating what had just happened to her in the space of the last five minutes. *Me talkin' to that little girl might change her whole life…she might have enough confidence to handle anything now…what if—*

The thought of what she had considered before the little girl tapped her arm horrified her. Her head began to spin. Sitting down on the bus stop bench, she tried to calm her nerves. *What if I had been a fool and stepped out in front of that cement truck? Don't even lie to yourself; you know damn well you was serious about doing it…*

At the same time, her phone rang in her bag. It stopped before she could answer. After unzipping the bag, she checked her phone. Her caller ID was littered with missed calls from Lollie, Walter, Eli, Constance, her parole officer and a host of other people wanting her for one thing or the other. After shutting her phone off, she stood and looked at the post office behind her. *I gotta do this…*

The clock in the post office lobby read a quarter 'til five. *Good, I have fifteen minutes.* After purchasing a pre-stamped envelope, she walked over to the counter people used to address packages before getting in the cashier line. She then withdrew the envelope from Eli, from her bag. The agony she saw in Meagan's face earlier replayed in her head as she stared at the five-thousand-dollar check in her hand.

Taking a deep breath, she ripped the check into four pieces. *That's the fastest I have ever blown five grand…*She found the piece with Eli's address on it and addressed the pre-stamped envelope. After putting the pieces inside the envelope, she took the note Eli wrote to her, flipped it over, and using the chain-attached black pen on the desktop, wrote a note back to him:

Hey, Eli, check this out. I am flattered you like me as much as you do, and I can't lie, I like you, too, but Meagan is the right woman for you. I bet before I came along you guys were happy. Don't let a big butt and a smile (smile) ruin that for you. I am just a thorn in your side; not a rose in your garden. Do the right thing, take this money and marry that girl. I saw y'all arguin' today by your house. She loves your ass more than I ever could. I have to do this, teddy bear. You will never see or hear from me again...

One love, baby...

The pain in the shrinking knot on the side of her head felt a bit better as she licked and sealed the envelope. She reflected on the genuine joy on the face of the little girl as she dropped the letter in the mail slot. She walked outside and scanned her surroundings. An itch underneath the bandage on her left wrist, as well as the bandage on the infected cut Gloria treated for her on her right shoulder, reminded her of the serious jeopardy her life was in. Even with that knowledge, she had a bit more confidence that her story was not yet over. A few blocks to the north of her, she spotted a large Greyhound bus station sign.

Hoisting her Travelin' Bag up on her shoulder, she began walking...

Forty-Seven

*Repay no one evil for evil, but give thought to do what is
honorable in the sight of all. If possible, so far as it depends
on you, live peaceably with all. Beloved, never avenge
yourselves, but leave it to the wrath of God, for it is
written, "Vengeance is mine, I will repay, says the Lord."
To the contrary, "if your enemy is hungry, feed him;
if he is thirsty, give him something to drink; for by so
doing you will heap burning coals on his head." Do not be
overcome by evil, but overcome evil with good.*

—ROMANS 12:17-21

"Fuck this," Trenda said as she spun on her heels, and
headed in the opposite direction. "I ain't runnin'
away like a scared bitch." Instead of going to the
Greyhound station down the street and getting out of
town, she had unfinished business to tend to.

As her head began to clear and more memories of
how King Gee had blown her car up—damn near killing
her—filled her mind, the angrier she got. "I'm not about
to let that fake-ass pimp punk me...and I'm through

runnin' from Darius, too. I'm gonna handle my business with these fools or die tryin'."

In the distance, she spotted a bus heading toward downtown Oakland. Hitching up her bag on her shoulder, she walked to the bus stop across the street. The lump on the side of her head served as a reminder of how bad she wanted to get King Gee. "First thing I gotta do is find someplace safe to chill."

The bus sat at a red light about six blocks away. She removed her "Travelin' Bag," opened it up and took out her wallet. Her bankroll had dwindled down to her last seven-hundred dollars. *Shit…maybe I should have kept that check from Eli.*

Ripping up that five-grand check she had received from Eli still felt good to her. She knew it was the right thing to do. Shoving those thoughts aside, she focused on how to draw King Gee out so she could extract her revenge.

As the setting sun's light reflected off the post office windows across the street, the lights of the club Fats came to mind. She recalled how she and Lollie had had a good time there until that bastard King Gee had fucked up the groove. She took her phone out of the bag and dialed information to get the number for the club. *I wonder if they have anything going on down there tonight.*

According to the recorded message, on Monday nights they featured an amateur exotic dancer night from nine to closing. She hung up her phone—ignoring the many missed calls and voice mails—and put it in the bag, then stood. The bus was a block away. *I bet money that cock-houndin' bastard will be there.*

After taking her seat on the bus, she pulled her phone out of the bag and scanned the missed calls. She exhaled loudly at the five calls from her parole officer. *Ain't no need in me callin' her back now; she told me after I missed my first two meetings with her that she was gonna do everything in her power to put me back in the pen if I missed one more.*

The monkey on her back morphed into King Kong. She grimaced as she listened to her voice mails. She deleted the ominous messages from Mrs. Kennedy, her parole officer, as soon as she heard her voice. Two other messages were from some of her underground cronies back east offering her big bucks to do some "work" for them. Trenda almost choked up after listening to the worry in Lollie's voice in the messages she had left.

The bus passed a familiar sight, which made her do a double-take. "Oh, shit! There goes the motel me and Eli went to."

Reaching up, she pulled the cable signaling the driver she wanted off at the next stop. Once off the bus, she turned and walked back to the Come On Inn.

Half a block from the motel, she walked past Solar Beauty Supply. She paused to look at the goods on display in the huge plate-glass window. "Cool. They have just what I need."

The sign on the window told Trenda she only had about ten minutes before they closed for the day. "Hello, how can I help you?" asked the fast-talking, cheery, middle-age Filipino woman. Her hazel eye contacts gave her an exotic look. The tight jeans and form-fitting purple blouse she wore did wonders for her petite frame.

Trenda walked over to the wall of wigs on display. She touched a black, shoulder-length curly wig. *My hair ain't been this long in years.* The store was stocked with a high percentage of African-American hair care products. Trenda picked up a bottle of hair shampoo and looked at the black woman on the label. "This is a damn shame; all these black hair products, in this all-white neighborhood, sold by a Filipino woman."

The clerk stood a few paces behind Trenda. "That curly wig would frame the shape of your face nicely."

Trenda put the shampoo down and let her bag slide down her arm and rest by her feet. "Can I try it on?"

"Sure!" the clerk said. "I'll be right back."

As the clerk went behind the counter to get a disposable stocking cap, Trenda noticed the row of colored eye contacts in the glass counter next to the cash register. *I'll need a pair of those, too.*

"I can't *believe* you are serious about killin' a *preacher*… this shit is way outta hand now," Tyrone said as he and his partner, Darius, stood on the deck of the beachfront vacation rental owned by Darius's brother.

The smell of the Atlantic Ocean air usually relaxed

Officer Darius Kain, but tonight, with the cloud of doom hovering over his head, it made him want to upchuck. "Relax…I'm just gonna use him for an insurance policy. I'm sure that once Trenda finds out I'm putting a contract out on her daddy, she will turn herself in to me."

A pair of stray dogs descended from a sand dune, onto the beach, in search of a meal in the trashcan, ten feet from the deck. Tyrone flicked his burning cigarette butt at them. "Have you considered how many fuckin' felonies we are now mixed up in behind that ho?"

Darius looked into the red eyes of his dark-skinned partner's worried eyes. "Look, once she is dead, it's over. So go find yourself a pair of balls and quit whinin' like a lil' bitch."

Tyrone grimaced at Darius. "Fuck you! I ain't tryin' to go to jail. And what makes you think she's gonna turn herself into you just because you are threatening her father? From my count, she ain't had a relationship with her family in years."

Darius took a swig of his Corona beer and eyeballed his partner. *This fool is scared as a ho in church. I gotta calm him down before he does somethin' stupid.* "Check this out, Tyrone; how would you feel if I told you I had somebody trackin' Trenda right now?"

Just as Tyrone's beer touched his lips, he paused. "What are you talkin' about?"

Darius set his beer on the railing of the redwood deck. His gift of being a world-class liar served him once again.

"I wasn't gonna tell you until I got the first update from him," he gave Tyrone a sympathetic look, "but I said to myself, 'I can't hold out on my partner.'"

As he had done for many years, Tyrone bought Darius's line of bullshit. A pound of stress fell from his face. "Say what? You have somebody tracking Trenda?"

The sound of an oceanliner's horn sounded in the distance as Darius crafted his lie. "Yeah...as soon as my flight landed in Jersey, I called up a private eye in Oakland, gave her all the info I had on Trenda and told her to go to the hospital where Trenda is and keep an eye on her."

Forty-Eight

"Wow! Between this cute wig and these new dark-brown contacts, you will look like a new woman!" the Asian clerk said as she rang up Trenda's purchases. She looked into Trenda's green eyes as she handed her, her change. "If I had eyes as pretty as yours, honey, I would definitely show them off!"

"Thanks," Trenda said as she pocketed her change. "But you know it's good to switch up every once in a while, give the fellas a treat."

Game recognized game as the clerk smiled and winked in agreement. "Yes...you give one treat, get many in return."

Trenda smiled on the way out the door. "I'm counting on that." As the first stars began to twinkle, Trenda walked over to the Come On Inn motel and entered the lobby.

The smell of the incense in the air reminded her of the fucking she and Eli had done in the same motel a few days ago. *Damn, I love the way his weight felt on me while he was cummin'.* Moisture formed in her vagina as she relived the way she had handled Eli's heaviness. Thick men seriously turned her on. Being forced into submission by the weight of a heavy man made her insane with orgasmic desire.

She was shaken out of her reminiscence by the sound of an Arabic voice. "Can I help you?" the Arabian man behind the registration counter asked. His eyes locked on Trenda's body like a pit bull.

Homeboy is mighty bold now that his wife ain't around, Trenda thought as she approached the lusting man. *The last time I was here his wife had his ass in check.* "Yeah, I need a room for the night."

The balding, fifty-something, olive-skinned man placed both arms on the counter and leaned over toward Trenda. The black chest hair climbing out of the throat of his multicolored Hawaiian shirt made her think he was part werewolf. "I have room for you, my pretty friend!"

The three missing teeth in his smile was a bad look. "Your rooms are still forty-five dollars, right?"

He broke eye contact with her bosom and glanced down at the laminated room price sheet on the counter top. "Yes...yes." He went to the rack of keys on the peg-board behind the desk. "I have a vacancy on the second floor. Will that do, pretty lady?"

Trenda set her bag on the counter, removed her wallet and the cash. She looked at the black cat clock on the wall. Its eyes moved back and forth as the tail swung like a pendulum. It was nearly seven. Weary of his lustful gazes, she slapped the cash on the counter. "Can you just give me the key? I am in a real big hurry."

Realizing his flirtatious moves had no effect on the

green-eyed honey in front of him, he picked up the cash and handed her the key. "Checkout is eleven in the morning."

I'll be gone way before then, asshole, Trenda thought as she headed for her room. The next few moves she had to make consumed her thoughts. After entering the room and tossing her bags on the desk, she paced back and forth as she did when she was scheming. Stress caused the knot on her head to throb. *I need some Motrin and a nap.*

Seeing she had a couple of hours until amateur night began at Fats, she set the alarm clock on the nightstand to go off at ten, then stripped and got in bed. *I wanna be nice and rested when I see the King.*

After fifteen restless minutes tossing and turning, Trenda hopped out of the bed, naked, and paced the floor. "I can't even relax knowing that bastard tried to kill me."

A little past eight in the evening, in his office on the third floor of the Oakland Police Department building, Detective Winslow took a sip of his vending machine coffee. Twelve-hour days were the norm for him as the city's crime rates continued to climb. "Something here is definitely strange." He stared at the day-old newspaper story in the *Oakland Tribune* about the tragic murder of a prominent Baltimore businessman's daughter who was visiting the Jack London Square area.

He then turned his attention to the report he'd just received. The fingerprints he'd lifted off the plastic cup he'd retrieved from Mya Collins' hospital room belonged to a felon named Trenda Fuqua—coincidentally from Baltimore also. "One woman visiting from Baltimore gets shot to death; another woman who just arrived from Baltimore damn near gets killed by a car bomb. What are the odds of two women from the same town, on the other side of the country, being attacked less than one hundred yards apart, minutes apart?"

The ringing of his fax machine broke his concentration. Rising from the worn, wooden desk he had occupied for twenty-two years, Detective Winslow walked across the room and watched as the cover sheet informed him there was a three page fax to follow. While waiting for his faxes to finish printing, he stared out his corner office window at the nightlife in the Oakland streets below him he had patrolled and protected for his entire adult life. *Please don't let this be another, senseless, stupid black-on-black crime. The act of murder is unforgivable enough; but throw in black folks committing self-inflicted genocide, and that's when I really wonder if we will be around another hundred years...*

After briefly glancing at the wall full of commendations he'd earned over the years, he turned his attention to the now silent fax machine. "Let's see what we have here."

Removing the reading glasses from the breast pocket of his crisp white dress shirt, he began reading the first sheet. He shook his head. "Son-of-a-bitch! No wonder she was in such a hurry to get out that hospital; she is wanted by the Baltimore PD for aggravated assault on

Ms. Langford." Removing his glasses and rubbing the bridge of his nose, he looked at the third sheet, which was a mugshot of Ms. Trenda Fuqua. *Damn, she is one gorgeous criminal.*

He carried the papers to his desk, sat down and took a sip of his tepid coffee. While staring at Trenda's mugshot, he wondered, *could she have shot Piper, then had her car blown up as she was trying to get away?*

"That makes no sense," he said as he read Trenda's rap sheet. "There is a major piece of this puzzle missing."

Dressed in black jeans and a tight, black blouse, Trenda stood in the bathroom of her motel room, putting in her new dark-brown contact lenses. *Damn, these things are uncomfortable as hell.* She ran her finger over the healing scar underneath her eye. *I hope I can hide this cut under my cover-up makeup.*

Fifteen minutes later, the cut was nearly invisible. "Now for the final touch." She went and picked the wig and her purse off the desk and carried them to the bathroom. After pulling the curly wig on her head, she saw an entirely new person in the mirror. *Whoa! Is that me?*

She opened her purse and removed Baby. She flicked the butterfly knife a few times. It worked flawlessly. "Now, let's see if I can hide my Baby." Closing the knife, she slid it underneath the wig, on the right side of her head. She examined herself in the mirror again. *Cool... these curls cover up Baby just right.*

Forty-Nine

"What's wrong, baby?" Walter asked as he stopped kissing Lollie's navel. "This is the first time I have ever felt you not grab my head as I go for a clit meal."

Rolling over on her side, she scooted back against him. "I'm sorry. But I can't stop worrying about Mya. I wonder why she ain't returning my calls. She didn't show up for work and today is payday. What if somebody kidnapped her?"

He draped his arm over her and kissed her bare, chocolate shoulder. "I know what you mean." He paused to reflect on how nervous Mya seemed to be during their visit. The soft gong of the grandfather clock in his spacious living room chimed half past nine. The tone seemed to resonate throughout the silent, five-bedroom home. "Have you heard back from that Detective Winslow?"

Lollie breathed in a bit of the sandalwood incense fragrance from the stick burning in Walter's fist-shaped incense holder on his expensive oak dresser. "I think he tried to call me today but the call dropped and I had to start my shift at work. I might try and call him back tomorrow."

He moved a lock of her long, soft hair and kissed the back of her neck. "That's a good idea. Did she ever give you any indication she was in trouble?"

"Well, she did tell me she came out here to get away from her crazy ex-boyfriend. She said he's the one that gave her that cut under her eye…"

"If he's crazy enough to do that, he might be crazy enough to try and kill her." He rolled Lollie over to face him. "I think you need to tell Detective Winslow about her boyfriend. No woman deserves to be treated like a fuckin' punching bag."

The blooming feelings she had been growing for Walter blossomed when she saw the genuine care in his face. She pulled him onto her, between her warm thighs, rubbed the back of his neck and whispered, "Make love to me Walter, please?"

After leaving her motel room, Trenda walked south-bound on San Pablo Avenue—toward Oakland. No one that knew Trenda would recognize her as she now appeared. The wig, eye contacts and slightly less sexy clothes than she normally wore transformed her into a different woman. A homicidal woman.

The slight ache in the small lump on her head and the uncomfortableness of the bandaged stitches on the wound nurse Gloria repaired for her helped fuel the growing rage inside her. With each step she took, she dove deeper into her old self; the hardcore, down-for-whatever, Trenda Fuqua.

Most of the East Coast underworld was aware of her no-nonsense attitude. She had learned her enhanced survival skills from the dangerous and ruthless criminals that orbited her world. Right then, as she inspected the vehicles she walked past, those skills were being put to the test. *I need transportation.*

The fluorescent, red-and-white Albany Bowl sign glowed a block ahead of her. She picked up her pace and entered the overflow parking lot, half a block away from the bowling alley. She stopped at the darkest corner of the parking lot and walked over to a white, early-model Toyota Celica. *This will work.* After taking a good look around, she removed Baby from under her wig, curled the closed knife in her fist—with about an inch of the knife handle sticking out—and slammed it into the driver's side window.

The window shattered, spilling hundreds of pieces of safety glass to the floor and the black driver's seat of the car. Trenda looked around, saw no one noticed her, unlocked the door and wiped glass off the driver's seat onto the floor and ground. She tossed her Travelin' Bag on the passenger seat and pulled Baby from under her wig. "I hope I don't break my fuckin' blade doing this; I usually use a screwdriver." She flicked open Baby and jabbed it into the keyhole on the ignition switch. After a few minutes of twisting and turning the knife, the ignition switch popped out the steering column.

About fuckin' time, she thought as she cut the ignition wires and searched for the two she needed to start the car. *I'm sure glad I paid attention when I was rollin' with that fool Danny-Boy back in the Bronx when I went with him to hustle stolen cars back in the day.*

After the first two sets of wires failed to work, she found the right pair. "Yeah! There we go!" She closed Baby and tossed it into her bag. Shifting the car into reverse, she eased out of the parking spot, and checked to see if anyone noticed her. Once she was clear, she drove out of the parking lot and halfway down the block before she turned on the headlights.

Fifteen minutes later, she entered the crowed parking lot of Fats. A surge of adrenaline shot through her body like a bolt of electricity. "I knew his bitch-ass would be here," she said after spotting King Gee's convertible Saab parked next to a gold Mercedes. Since the parking lot was packed, she ended up parking around the corner.

Squads of women—as well as horny men—headed for the club to attend Fats' Monday amateur exotic dancer night. After watching what the women were wearing, Trenda went into her bag and swapped her white Adidas for her only other pair of shoes; a pair of black pumps. *This should be enough to get me inside.*

Using the inside trunk release, she popped the trunk and tossed her bag inside, next to a large, black, bowling ball bag. Before going inside the club, she pulled Baby out of the bag and tucked it back under her wig. As she walked toward the entrance, she saw a familiar face; it was the thug, Peanut, whom she had checked into the Waters Edge Hotel a week ago. She had a hunch he was the one that informed King Gee where she worked. *I wonder if this fool is gonna recognize me.*

Standing next to the same "thugged-out" Buick he had driven to the hotel, his eyes went from her face to her tits with light speed. "Hey, sexy! Come holla at a playa!"

"I wish I had the time, baby," she said with a forced smile and well-practiced Southern drawl. After successfully fooling Peanut, she moved to the end of the admission line. She studied how the bouncers were scanning the incoming guests. *Cool; they are still just barely waving the metal detectors on the women.*

The husky, West Indian bouncer smiled as she approached. "How you doin', sista?"

She returned his smile. "I'm real good."

He let the metal detection wand dangle at his side. "Are you here for the dance contest?" His long dreads danced as he nodded to a group of women in a shorter line to her right. "If so, you need to take your fine self over to that line."

"No, I'm just here to kick it and have a drink."

"Too bad." He lazily waved the wand over her tits and waistline. "I have no doubt you would bring the house down."

"Thanks, baby."

"Where you from? Texas? I'm diggin' that country accent," he said as she attempted to walk past him.

"No, Suga; I'm from Jacksonville, Florida."

He stepped aside, smiling. "Is that right now? I didn't know they grew 'em sexy like you down there!"

Whew! Made it! After giving him a wink, she entered the packed club. It only took three minutes for her to spot her prey. There tossing back a shot of brown alcohol at the bar was King Gee. The overwhelming urge to draw Baby, run over and slit his throat was awful hard to resist. *Calm down, girl...stick to your plan.*

I'm glad he finally took his scaredy-ass home, Darius thought as he watched Tyrone get in his car and leave. He flopped down on the overstuffed bronze sofa and finished off his fifth beer, leaned his head back and watched the ceiling fan overhead spin. *I can't afford to let this shit drag on any further. It's time to up the stakes.*

He got up, staggered over to the octagon-shaped mahogany kitchen table and picked up the disposable cell phone he used to communicate with Tyrone. *I'll get that bitch's attention.* He burped, then called Trenda's cell phone number. "Look here, you no-good ho, I'm through playin' games with you. Unless you want me to do your parents like I did that fool Diamond and your crazy roommate, I suggest you return this call by tomorrow, noon. I am pretty damn tired of you ignoring my calls.

Remember; I better hear from or see you by noon. Bitch."
After tagging the call as *urgent*, he sent the message and
hung up. A drunken grin filled his face. "Ignore me now
and see what happens!"

Fifty

The ratio of men to women in Fats had to be at least three-to-one. The turnout for their amateur pole dancer contest was always standing room only. Trenda bounced off numerous people as she worked her way to the far end of the bar King Gee was leaning on.

The men howled and whistled as the DJ introduced the first amateur dancer of the night. As the tall, ebony Amazon wrapped her luscious legs around the pole, Trenda beckoned the bulky Asian bartender with her finger. "What can I get you?"

Over the cranked-up sound of "Siempre Hay Esper-anza" by Sade—a stripper national anthem—Trenda leaned in so the bartender could hear her request. "Can you tell me what that sexy man in the pinstripe suit is drinkin'?"

The bartender smirked. "Oh, you mean King Gee? He is drinking his usual; Remy Martin, Louis the XIII cognac."

Trenda fished her bankroll out of her pocket, smiled

and winked at the bartender. "Send him a double shot on me."

Sometimes she was surprised by her own coolness under pressure. It was a survival skill she honed by living constantly on the edge of danger. The bartender went to the top shelf for the bottle of Louis the XIII. She plastered a fake smile on her face as the bartender tapped King Gee on the shoulder, handed him the glass and pointed her way. *That's right, muthafucka. Bring your ass down here so we can handle our business.*

After taking a sip of his drink, King Gee grinned, tapped one of his homeboys on the shoulder and whispered something in his ear. His friend gazed at Trenda, nodded his head, returned King Gee's grin and bumped fists with him. He adjusted the lapel of his "look-at-me" suit and made his way to Trenda. "The King is pleased by your gift, princess," he said as he took her hand and kissed it. "How did I earn this, sexy?"

Trenda almost threw up in her mouth as he took her hand in his sweaty hand. He smelled as though he had on cognac-scented cologne. The only person who eclipsed the venomous hate she had for King Gee was Darius. "Game just recognized game, baby." She could tell by his bloodshot eyes and slightly slurred speech that he'd had several drinks. "I heard about you all the way back in Jacksonville."

His eyebrows lifted. "Is that right? What's ya name, baby girl?"

Confident he didn't recognize her, she smiled and took a step closer to him. "Cleopatra."

He took a step back and measured her with his eyes. "You got the goods, Cleo, and that country accent is hot as a muthafucka. You dancin' tonight?"

Trenda gave him a seductive look, then leaned over and whispered in his ear. "Look, King, I ain't come all the way out here to bullshit. I wanna be down in your kingdom. Why don't you take me out to your car so I can lace you with some of this Southern head game?"

His eyes and dick bulged. He downed the last of his drink and set the glass on the bar. "Ohhh, I see...well, I think I *will* audition you."

Taking her hand, he led her through the crowd and out the exit door. The light breeze blew a mixture of alcohol and his cologne up her nose. *I swear if this mutha-fucka grabs my ass one more time, I'm gonna slice him open right here!*

A black-and-yellow sign that read "Smile, you're being videotaped!" caught her attention as they approached his car. She pointed the sign out to him. *I'll be goddamned! I didn't see this sign the night I cut his top. That must be how he found out it was me.* "Hey, daddy, let's pull around the corner; I ain't into givin' free shows."

"You sharp. I likes that." He opened the passenger door for her.

I wonder how much this new top cost him, she thought with a smirk on her face. *I bet he had to re-cover these leather seats, too.* Listening to him sing along with the new Too Short song playing on his CD player—at an excruciating volume—was sheer torture. As they drove around the corner, half a block away from where she had parked her car, she pointed. "There you go, park right there between those two big rigs, Suga."

"Good call," he said as they parked behind the Bay Area Imports auto dealership. The space between a pair of their car carriers was just big enough for the Saab to fit between. Also, as Trenda noticed, the streetlight above them was blown out. He reached over and rubbed her tits. "Yeah…come here and work ya work, baby."

She took his hands and smiled. "Wait…let's change seats. I don't want you breakin' your knees on the steering wheel as I bless you with these lips."

As soon as he got out, Trenda quickly pulled Baby from under her wig and stuck it in her back pocket. The wake from a passing tractor-trailer hauling a container to the Port of Oakland rocked the car as it drove past them. "I'll be right there, Cleo," he said while pissing on the front tire of the truck behind them.

"Hurry up, Suga…I'm gettin' hungry. Come feed me." She flicked Baby open and stuck it down between the driver's seat and the center console. *Bring yo' ass on!*

Once back inside, he took off his jacket and tossed it in the backseat. He then turned into an octopus. His hands swarmed her body. "Yeah, yeah…I might have to get some of this country pussy, too."

Easing his hands off of her, she forced herself to place

her hand on his forehead. "Lay back and let Cleopatra do her job."

The sound of him unzipping his pants made her nauseous. "A'ight, go 'head and show Daddy what you got."

She unbuttoned his shirt. "Mmmmmm, I wanna lick my way from your neck to your dick, baby."

"Do yo thang, girl," he said as he reclined the seat so he was practically lying flat.

Summoning up all her willpower, she kissed the side of his chocolate neck. He closed his eyes in ecstasy as she wrapped a hand around his stiffness and slowly stroked his knob. *Even though he does have a nice-sized dick, no way in the fuckin' world would I put my mouth close to it for this fool.*

Unfortunately for King Gee, he made a wrong move, which sped up the inevitable. "Bitch, don't play me; I can jack my own dick off." He put his hand on the back of her head and tried to force her down. "Use ya fuckin' mouth!"

"Get your hands off my fuckin' head!" Before he could react, Trenda grabbed Baby, pointed it just below the left side of his ribcage and used both hands to push it in and upward into his heart.

His hands immediately fell as his life ended. His face didn't have time to register pain he died so swiftly. Fuming with anger, she yanked Baby out of his lifeless body; with the quick death of the heart, only a couple of drops of blood leaked from the wound.

She used his jacket to clean the blood off Baby. A second

tractor-trailer flew by, rocking the car and snapping Trenda out of her anger-filled hypnosis. *Time to get the fuck outta here!* After making sure the coast was clear, she used his jacket to wipe her prints off every place she could think of that she touched. Once done, she used the jacket as a glove to open the door and got out. She tossed the jacket back inside and used her hip to close the door.

As she walked away from the crime scene, she folded Baby up and tucked it into her back pocket. "Come out, come out!" she said as she removed the brown contacts from her eyes, tossed them onto the ground and crushed them. She then snatched the wig off and stuffed it into the gutter opening behind the big rig behind the Saab.

The knot on her head ached as she did her best to casually walk the half-block to her car. *Whew! Now let me change clothes...*she opened the trunk, opened her Travelin' Bag and removed her pink sweatsuit. After changing clothes in the backseat, she started the car. *I need to get rid of this black outfit.* A few blocks away, she spotted a small church on her right side. In front, there was a hand-painted sign that said, "Help us, help the less fortunate. Cash and clothing donations gratefully accepted."

"I must be trippin' hard," she said after the hair stood up on the back of her neck as she tossed her outfit—including the pumps—into the large plastic drum on the porch of the church. "I need to calm down, ditch this car and get the fuck outta town."

She almost had a coronary as the church bell gonged, announcing it was half past ten. She couldn't shake the eerie feeling she felt walking away from the church. It felt as if a thousand pairs of eyes were watching her. *Quit trippin'! Nobody saw you; you ain't wanted by the law—ain't no law in leavin' a hospital that I ever heard of. Nobody knows your real name...shit!*

Nurse Gloria.

Nah, she ain't the kind that would snitch me out. Trenda did her damnedest to convince herself everything was cool as she got in her stolen car and drove off.

It worked.

For a minute.

Fifty-One

For each man's ways are plain to the Lord's sight; all their paths he surveys; By his own iniquities the wicked man will be caught, in the meshes of his own sin he will be held fast; He will die from lack of discipline, through the greatness of his folly he will be lost.
—PROVERBS 5:21-23

While listening to the threatening voicemail left by Darius, Trenda noticed the changing signal light ahead of her too late. The yellow light changed to red well before her front end entered the intersection. Her blood turned to ice as she looked to her left and into the eyes of a pair of Oakland Police officers, in a squad car, which sat between two other cars, preparing to make a left turn.

"Oh fuck!" she said as she saw the blue and red lights atop the cop car come on. "No! No!" she yelled while looking in her rear view mirror. The cops made their way out from between the other cars and made a U-turn—heading her way.

Instead of panicking, her survival instincts kicked in. *I have gotta get rid of Baby!* Her heart broke as she made a quick right turn, reached in her bag, grabbed the knife and flung it out the window, into a grassy, vacant lot to her left. Ten seconds later, the cop car sped around the corner in her direction.

A strange calmness settled over her as she realized she was busted. Like a drowning man, her life flashed before her eyes. The reality of doing some serious jail time made her wish Raven hadn't intervened when that cement truck was heading her way. "I am so fucked..." She pulled the car to the curb. *If I was in Baltimore, I would have made these fools chase me—but I don't know my way around here good enough to even try to run.*

After shining the bright spotlight into her car from behind, both cops got out and approached. Trenda leaned her head back against the headrest and waited.

Well, here we go, she thought as the cop with the thick blond moustache stopped at her window. "Hello, ma'am; do you know why I stopped you?"

"No." The light from his partner's flashlight caught her attention as it stopped on the broken glass on the passenger seat and floor, then on the dangling ignition switch. "What did I do?"

After a short conversation with his partner, over the roof of the car, he placed his hand on the butt of his pistol. "Please step out of the car, ma'am."

Fifty-Two

"She hasn't said a word since we arrested her last night," Sergeant Milken said as he and Detective Winslow observed Trenda via camera in the holding tank. "She definitely acts like this isn't her first time behind bars."

Detective Winslow rubbed the gray, five-o'clock-shadow on his chin. "Yup, Ms. Fuqua is no stranger to the penal system. I just got off the phone with the Baltimore P.D.; they would kill or die to have us extradite her back there."

"You gonna give her to them?"

Detective Winslow picked up his cup of coffee and sipped the black elixir. "Hell, I might as well; with the current budget crisis this city is in, it would save us money."

Sergeant Milken stuffed his hands into his pockets. "What about the Langford murder? Have you been able to connect Ms. Fuqua to the killing?"

"Nah, there was definitely a third party involved. There was no way Trenda could have shot her. There are plenty of witnesses that recall seeing her behind the reservation counter of the Waters Edge Hotel minutes before the murder happened."

"How come Baltimore PD wants her so bad?"

"They need her testimony in a big Internal Affairs investigation. They need Trenda to testify so they can put away a suspected bad cop. Plus her parole officer is anxious to get her off the streets for violating her parole by crossing state lines—not to mention stealing a car."

They watched as Trenda, in her orange jail-issued jumpsuit, lay on her back with her arm over her eyes. Sergeant Milken checked his watch. "Yeah, I guess you're right. We need to save what jail cells we have left for more serious criminals—like whoever murdered our friend, 'King Gee' last night."

"I can't say I'm surprised someone finally got to him—he had more than enough enemies." Detective Winslow walked over and turned off the monitor. "I'll get in touch with the city prosecutor and suggest they let her off with time served and just hand her over to Baltimore P.D."

"No disrespect but I wanna talk to my lawyer before I make any kind of statements, if you don't mind," Trenda said as she sat across from the soft-eyed brunette district attorney.

The D.A. closed the folder of information she had on

Trenda and pushed back from the gray metal table. "Well, that is your right, Ms. Fuqua," the chubby, but stylish woman said as she stood and offered Trenda her pale hand. "Good luck." She turned to the guard at the door. "Please allow Ms. Fuqua to use a phone before taking her back to her cell."

"Will do." The heavy-set Mexican prison guard escorted Trenda out of the interrogation room and to a room with a bank of telephones. The nearly six-foot-tall woman looked at Trenda. "Make it quick."

Ignoring the masculine-looking prison guard, Trenda dialed the number for Dennis Wilcox, Attorney at Law. "Well, well, well! Where have you been, my sexy redheaded friend? I have been looking for you with a flashlight in the daytime!"

The excitement in his voice told her just how bad he missed their monthly hook-ups. *I bet you have missed the way I used to put on a finger condom and suck your dick as I put my finger up your ass. I ain't ever heard a man cum so hard or squeal like you do.* Trenda turned her back on the guard. "Hey, Denny…I'm locked up in Santa Rita jail out here in California."

"*California?* What the hell?"

"Yeah, I got caught up in some drama…they are—"

"Hold it! What have you told them?"

"Nothin'…I wanted to talk to you first."

"Good. Let me make a few calls and see what's going on. In the meantime, just chill, okay?"

"Yeah. I heard they are gonna be shipping me back to Baltimore in a few days."

"Ahh, shit…okay. Sit tight and keep quiet. I'll be in touch with you soon."

Friday, four days later, Trenda found herself sitting between two Baltimore detectives on a flight to BWI Airport.

The last voicemail she heard from Darius still disturbed her. *I can't believe that muthafucka had the nerve to threaten my family!* Some unexpected turbulence jolted the plane as they made their approach. *I don't give a fuck what it takes, I'm gonna find a way to kill his ass.*

The scowl she wore ever since being arrested gave her a serious "don't fuck with me" look. After realizing she was looking at a *minimum* of five years in prison, a boiling vat of hate-flavored venom brewed inside her. After the plane landed, the white detective stood in front of her as the black one re-handcuffed her. "All right, Ms. Fuqua, let's go. And do not stop moving until we tell you to."

"What in the fuck?" Trenda said as a mass of camera flashes exploded inside the terminal. A flock of news reporters screamed and jockeyed for position, trying to get a statement from or picture of Trenda. "What is this all about?"

The black detective gripped her arm harder and hurried

her along. "You will find out once we get to Baltimore City Jail. Right now, *move!*"

Outside, an equally large wall of reporters surrounded the black van she was being ushered to. Once inside, the tinted windows allowed her to witness the circus up close. *This is bananas! Did I just hear one of them ask me how long I have been having an affair with Darius?*

Fifty-Three

"What a cluster-fuck this is," Attorney Dennis Wilcox, "the Fox," said as he stood behind the layers of reporters in the airport. The slickness of how he got more than ninety percent of his clients off led to him being called "Wilcox the Fox." It wasn't always meant in a complimentary fashion.

Being the product of a German father and West Indian mother, it was sometimes hard for one to tell if the fair-skinned, wavy-haired, irritable man was black or white. *Once Piper's parents got wind that Trenda had been captured, they ran their asses to the media, just like I knew they would, and started this circus. And once those media vultures learned Officer Kain and his partner were being investigated by Baltimore P.D.'s Internal Affairs—for a case possibly involving their daughter—the sharks came to feast!* A devious grin filled his face. "I do good work!"

Trenda paced the floor of the solitary cell she had just been stuffed into. *This is crazy! I can't believe that detective told me they had to lock me up by myself because of all the threats they received on my life.* She sat down on the hard mattress of her bed and held her head in her hands. *It's bad enough Piper's family wants me; but now with all this publicity, the Island Boys know where to find me. I'm sure all these gangsta-bitches in here are gonna be lookin' to take me out for the contract they have on my head.*

Minutes later, the sound of footsteps and jingling keys echoed in her ears. The sound stopped in front of her cell. She looked up into the brown eyes of a mean-looking female correctional officer. "All right, Ms. Fuqua, you have a visitor."

"A visitor? Who?" Trenda asked as she sat up on the stiff bed.

The thick Latina woman signaled for the officer controlling the cell doors to open Trenda's. "Your lawyer."

Minutes later, Trenda was escorted into a small, concrete room containing a rectangular wooden table with four chairs around it. The fluorescent lighting did a poor job of brightening up the rain cloud-colored room. The Latina guard addressed the light-skinned man sitting across the table from them. "She's all yours. I'll be back in about thirty minutes. If you need me before then, ring the buzzer by the door."

"Thank you, Officer Cortez." He opened the alligator-skinned briefcase that sat in front of him on the table. "You have been very helpful as usual."

She gave him a smirk and looked into gold, wire-rimmed glasses. "Anytime, Fox."

Trenda took the seat across from him and waited for the officer to close the metal door. She slumped down in her chair, exhaled loudly. "You know I'm broke and can't afford to pay you, right?"

His too-white smile almost blinded her. "Well, my friend, we'll deal with that later. First, how are you doing? Are you feeling okay?"

She rolled the cuff of her too-big jumpsuit up a few inches. "I'm cool…just tired of this cat-shit they call food in here."

Adjusting his blue-and-yellow power tie, Dennis shook his head and rustled papers in his briefcase. "Sorry to hear that, my friend." His smile faded as he picked up a small stack of paper-clipped sheets of paper. "I'm going to do all I can to change that."

Trenda didn't like the lack of confidence in his voice. "How bad is my case lookin'?"

Taking off his glasses, he tucked them into the inside pocket of his expensive navy-blue suit coat and looked her in the eyes. "Here is what you are looking at; your parole officer is working hard to get you the maximum penalty for breaking your parole. The parents of your late-roommate Piper are pressuring the mayor to have you charged with the murder of their daughter—or at least as an accomplice."

Trenda jumped up. "That's bullshit! That broad tried to kill *me!*

Dennis didn't miss a beat. "The Baltimore P.D. is looking to charge you with evading justice and aggravated assault against Ms. Langford—at a minimum." He placed the stack of papers back in his briefcase and looked at the angry woman in silence for a moment. "All totaled, they intend to put you away for a minimum of fifteen to twenty years—that is if you don't get found guilty of Piper's murder. In that case it's a wrap; life without the possibility of parole."

Trenda seemed to shrink further into her over-sized clothing. She was too stunned to be angry. Her mouth moved; only one word escaped. "What?"

"Yes, my friend, they want you *under* the jail."

Something about his nonchalant attitude didn't make sense to her. "How in the hell can they pin all that shit on me? I can see the parole violation, but I ain't had nothin' to do with that girl gettin' killed. And aggravated assault? It was self defense!" She pointed to the scratch under her eye. "See this?" She then pulled her sleeve up and ripped off the bandage covering her stitches. "And this? This is where that crazy bitch cut me when I was tryin' to get away!"

"Wow!" He put his glasses back on, got up, walked over and examined her wounds. "Did you tell any of the cops or your P.O. about this?"

She reapplied the bandage. "No…I ain't told them shit." Panic covered her as she began pacing the floor. "I can't go back to jail for this, Denny, I can't…" His well-known "Fox smirk" greeted her as she turned to him. "Why you ain't sayin' nothin'?"

Waving to her chair, he said, "Please, have a seat, my friend. I just wanted you to know what *we* are up against."

Trenda could smell the makings of a caper wafting off him. Since he never did *anything* for free—luckily, her fierce fellatio game was all she had to pay him in the past—it had to be something big. "What are you not tellin' me?"

Fifty-Four

"That tramp is a *liar!*" Darius screamed as he and his weeping wife watched the female reporter talking about his investigation on the six o'clock news. "I am gonna sue those fuckers for slander!"

Tears of anger and heartbreak rolled down her cheeks. "Please tell me this is not true, Darius...please...," she whispered through her soft sobs.

Before he could answer, their phone rang—for the hundredth time. He checked the caller ID. "It's your mother, again. You wanna talk to her?"

Beverly got up, wiping her eyes, and took the phone from him. "Hi, Mother...yes, I know..."

Her voice trailed off as she walked away from Darius, on her way upstairs. He kicked over their teakwood coffee table, littered with newspaper stories of his possible criminal and infidelity issues, in front of the TV. *How could that bitch be so stupid as to get caught in a fuckin' stolen car while she is on the run?* The loss of control over the situation stressed him to the point of panic. *And now I have to deal with this cryin' bitch here. If she wouldn't spend so much time reading those goddamn tabloid magazines, she wouldn't be so quick to believe every fucking thing she reads.*

It seemed that everyone on the planet had called him about the breaking news including his partner, Tyrone. *I had better return his call before he freaks the hell out.*

He glanced at his liquor cabinet. *Fuck that; that's the last thing I need.* After canceling his "vacation" stay at the beach house a week early because of the news drama, peace of mind eluded him. His killing of Piper was far less troubling than the aspect of exposing the public to the not-so-perfect life his gigantic ego required. The prospect of doing time wasn't very attractive to him either.

After grabbing his cell phone, he walked outside into the cool night air, the realization that he failed to tie up a loose string for the first time—Trenda Fuqua—cut a groove of fear in his icy heart. *Let me call Tyrone back before he has a goddamned heart attack.*

Ten days after her arraignment hearing, Trenda was still as hot as a .45 pistol that had been shot all night. *This is some bullshit!* she thought as she was escorted down the jail corridor to the same room where she spoke to Dennis when she was first locked up. A stone-like shell of bitterness, pain, hatred and desperation shrouded her. Her normal sexy walk had been replaced with a hardcore stride as she adjusted to her bleak surroundings. *These muthafuckas are straight tryin' to do me, but fuck 'em.*

I'm not about to let these fools break me. She allowed one of her father's frequent sayings to stick in her brain:

So that we may boldly say, The Lord is my helper, and I will not fear what man shall do unto me.

—Hebrews 13:6

"You know the routine, Fox; I'll be back in thirty minutes," Officer Cortez said after watching Trenda take a seat.

"Very good, Officer." Dennis smiled. "That will be plenty of time."

Trenda scratched her rapidly growing afro and watched Dennis set his briefcase on the table. "What's crackin'?"

He straightened the gold and diamond tie clip on his silk burgundy tie. "Well, my friend, we made significant progress yesterday."

Placing both hands flat on the table, she leaned forward with interest. "What you mean? Are you close to gettin' me outta here?"

"I can't promise you *no* jail time, but if we play our cards right, things could turn out quite favorably for you."

After hearing he couldn't promise to get her out, she sat back dejected and ignored the last half of his statement. "Damn, Denny, how long am I gonna be stuck in here? It's so borin' here in protective custody, I am tempted to ask them to put me in general population before I go stir crazy. And I am *real* tired of all these dyke-ass guards lookin' like they wanna rape me."

He shook his head. "No way...every gang in here has

a hard-on to collect the bounty the Island Boys have on your head. A few days ago, I spoke to a member of the Island Boys I am defending on another case and told him, what you told me, about Darius and his partner robbing you. I hope that takes some of the heat off you." He furrowed his eyebrows. "And there's no telling how many crooked C.O.'s Darius could be connected to in here. That bastard *allegedly* has one hell of a network of 'friends' among the correctional officers."

"I wouldn't be surprised...that fool is crooked as a barrel of snakes." Trenda scowled. "Oh, and good lookin' out tellin' your client what went down with Island Boys' money."

"Don't thank me yet; I just hope they believe it. Speaking of Officer Kain," he silenced his BlackBerry and tucked it back into the inside pocket of his gray suit coat, "he and his partner hired a very good lawyer— Arnold Medved. He is twice the asshole I am—and just as expensive."

"I don't get it; why the hell *they* need a lawyer?"

Dennis looked into Trenda's face with a smile. "Well, my friend, it turns out that Baltimore P.D.'s Internal Affairs Department is investigating Officer Kain and Officer Dash for extortion, dereliction of duty, corruption, and felonious, aggravated sexual battery against one Trenda Fuqua."

Standing, Trenda's mouth hung open like the entrance to a cave before she could speak. "Are you *bullshittin'?*"

Opening his briefcase, he removed a sheet of paper and slid it across the table to her. "Here are the official court documents of the charges against them."

Information overload made her dizzy. She eased back in her seat. "What the...fuck? How did I get mixed up in this?"

"It appears the P.D. found a video tape of Officer Kain allegedly forcing a young lady to have oral sex with him... on the same tape, they overhear him discussing extortion of said young lady and possibly admitting to other felonious crimes committed by he and his partner. They were really pissed to see all this took place when both officers were supposed to be on duty." He smirked at her. "Sound familiar?"

Her eyes bulged with shock as she covered her mouth with her hand. *Oh fuck! The tape! They must have found the tape I left at Piper's the night we had the fight!*

"Trenda? Are you okay?" he asked, rising from his chair.

She nodded. "Yeah...but..." She found she was still speechless.

"Let me further clarify. You, my friend, are in a very unique position. The D.A. and your P. O. both want to lock you up for violating your parole, crossing state lines and for assaulting Ms. Piper. The Baltimore P.D., on the other hand, needs your testimony in order to get alleged corrupt Officer Kain off the streets and behind bars."

Trenda let anger replace the shock on her face. "Let's do it! I'll testify against that muthafucka right now!"

He raised his hand and shook his head. "Not so fast, my friend. We have to be smart about this. I'm sure you are aware this is an election year for the mayor and the city is in financial distress."

"Yeah, so? I don't give a fuck about this city or the mayor."

"You might want to...you see, if we can prove the allegations of sexual battery charges against Officer Kain are true, the city can be held responsible for its employee. Meaning they could be sued for a substantial amount."

The hustler wheels in Trenda's mind began to turn, helping clear her head. "No shit, huh?"

His face became a bit more serious. "It won't be easy; Darius has loaded up with fellow officers and some of his late grandfather's friends who are very respected in the community as well as on the force." He pushed his glasses up the bridge of his nose. "They are going to go all out to make you out to be a worthless criminal that belongs behind bars. His lawyer, Medved, is well known for his ability to exploit any flaw in a witness he can find. And let's face it, with your record, and the situation with you and the mayor's friend's dead daughter, they have *plenty* of ammunition."

Her lantern of hope dimmed. "Fuck...I knew shit was too good to be true..."

Fifty-Five

"So you say you just got in town a week ago? No wonder I ain't ran across you on my patrol," Tyrone said to the tall, thick, fine, coconut-shell-colored hooker named "Cakes" that leaned against his Lexus. "That sexy accent is off the chain! Where you say you from?"

"I'm from the Motherland, honey. The other girls told me how things work here on the Baltimore track." She flashed him a sweet smile as she stood and rubbed his chest. The light from the street lamp on the corner reflected on her pretty smile. "I'm ready for you, Daddy... ready for you *and* your partner, Darius." She pulled a set of car keys out of her purse. "I'll meet you at that place you were tellin' me about—the Lighthouse—in thirty minutes." Cakes showed him the tip of her tongue. "Don't keep me waiting, baby."

"You ain't gotta worry, sexy." As he watched her walk away, his disposable cell phone rang. "Wassup?"

"Hey! I got your message. Where you at? We need to hook up so we can talk about our situation. We only have two days before the trial starts; I wanna make sure we are on point. I talked to Medved today and he told me that after he gets finished grillin' Trenda, ain't a jury in the world gonna care about her."

"Yeah! That's what I'm talkin' about! I'm out here by the Harbor. Let's meet up at the Lighthouse." His dick trembled as Cakes and her jiggling ass turned the corner. A lusty smile crossed his lips. "You might wanna get in on this; I have a hottie right here that is ready to be 'initiated' into the game. After that, we can talk shop. Meet me there in thirty minutes."

He understood Tyrone's code for breaking in a new prostitute well. The idea of busting a nut in a new piece of ass felt just like the stress relief Darius needed. "I'm on my way."

"That fool is late as usual," Darius said as he pulled up to the gate at the Lighthouse. He saw an extremely sexy, tall, woman rise from one of the Lighthouse steps she was sitting on. "But I see our guest of honor is already here."

Dressed in the same short red mini skirt, red stilettos and tight red half-top that got Tyrone's attention, she proved to Darius that arousal was not one of his many problems. She sashayed up to his car door. "Hi, Mr. Officer," she said, wiping back the flowing black hair of her cute wig. "I hope you have a taste for a piece of 'Cake.'"

Reaching out of his car window, he rubbed her large,

round ass. "As soon as I open this gate, I'm gonna break me off a *big* chunk of this cake, baby."

She backed out of his grip, smiled and walked to the gate. "I got it. Bring your fine ass in here so we can do this."

If it weren't for the stress he was under—and his horniness—he might have noticed the gate was unlocked as she pushed it open. He and Tyrone *always* locked the gate. *Always.* He pulled his Escalade all the way up the driveway and into the large backyard. He then saw Tyrone's car parked near the fence, a few yards ahead of him. *I wonder why she didn't tell me Tyrone was already here?*

As soon as he stepped out of his car, watching Cakes pull on a pair of gloves as she walked up the driveway toward him, he felt a strong arm wrap around his neck and a cold piece of steel against the side of his head. "Quit movin' or me blow hole in you head, blood clot," a voice whispered to him.

Terror chilled his blood as three ski-masked men emerged from the dark bushes and joined the man currently holding him. Cakes walked up and stood in front of the stunned cop. "I heard you and your partner robbed one of the Island Boys' associates a few weeks back." One of the men handed her a long, blood-stained machete. She held it inches from his face. "They hired me to get it back. Where is the money?"

For the first time he noticed her foreign accent. She had done a remarkable job of hiding it to this point. "I don't know what the fuck you talkin' about!"

"You mean you don't recall stealing a quarter-million dollars from my employer's transporter?"

Flashbacks surfaced of how he had talked Tyrone into pulling over Trenda and robbing her. He had been tipped off that she was hauling a large sum of cash for a client. After finding the duffle bag of money in her SUV, they took it anyway, even after she told him the money belonged to the Island Boys. Tyrone used most of his share to pay off the $65,000 in back child support he owed the mother of his daughter in Savannah, Georgia and to another baby-mama in Virginia. Darius was also aware that Tyrone blew most of the rest trying to keep up with his extravagant lifestyle. "Hell naw that wasn't me! Look, let me go now and I'll overlook this...I'll call it a case of mistaken identity."

Ignoring him, she ran the blade across his cheek, drawing blood. "So you're saying you don't have the money?"

"Oww, bitch! Didn't I just tell you I don't know what the fuck you're talkin' about?"

The man holding him pushed him to the ground. All four men cocked their pistols and aimed at Darius. "That's funny; your partner said the same thing." She snapped her finger and one of the men walked inside the back door of the Lighthouse. He came back minutes later holding what looked like a bowling ball in the darkness. She took the object from the man and held it up to Darius. One of the masked men shined a penlight on the object in her hand. "Are you sure you don't want to change your answer?"

Darius vomited on the forearm of his captor. "You sick fuck! Oh, *shit!*"

The object Cakes held was no bowling ball; it was the head of his partner. Gripping the handful of Tyrone's hair tighter, she shoved the head in his face. "Last chance, Officer. Give me the money or I take your head. Either one is fine with me. I get paid for my services no matter what."

The horrific agony on the head's face was too much for Darius. He wilted like a rose in winter. "In the safe in my garage…in the floor under my freezer…"

"That's better." She handed the head back to the masked man. "Get a pen and paper."

Minutes later, after having his hands duct-taped behind his back, and being dropped to his knees, Darius gave them the combination to his safe. He had almost half a million dollars in dirty money stashed there. "All right… you got your fuckin' money…just don't hurt my wife."

Cakes chuckled. "Whatever you say, Officer." She then whistled softly and two more masked men—wearing long, black rubber aprons and long black rubber gloves— emerged from the back door. "Is his bath ready?"

Darius looked around wildly. "What bath? What the hell is goin' on?"

The shorter of the two men nodded his head. "Yeah… me crackhead friend Thin Tim was right. A month ago he told me for twenty dollars he would show me something I could use. I found a couple drums of acid in the basement. Nasty stuff. Me dropped a chicken in it and poof! It was gone."

In her former home of Somalia, Africa, and in the criminal underworld, Cakes was known as the "Black Mamba; assassin extraordinaire." She nodded toward the open back door of the Lighthouse. "Take him inside."

Darius yelled with panic. "Hey! *You got your money!* Let me go! What the fuc—"

The same man that tied his hands slapped a piece of duct tape over his mouth. *Quiet*, blood clot!"

After being dragged into the same basement a lot of his victims had ended up in, Cakes ripped the tape off his mouth. "Did you have something to say, Officer?"

Even in the dim light cast by the battery-powered lantern sitting on a dusty shelf, he could tell a pair of yellow, fifty-five-gallon drums of acid were open. His urine escaped as he watched the short man drop Tyrone's head into one of the drums. Fear trumped his bravado as he yelled, "You had best to let me go; don't you know I'm a fuckin' *cop?*"

After being forced to his knees again, the Black Mamba smirked as she hoisted the razor-sharp, bloodstained blade over the terrified Darius and brought it down with amazing force, splitting his head. "You mean you *were* a cop."

Unseen, behind the dense, unkempt hedges behind the Lighthouse, Thin Tim wept in silent terror as he watched the massacre unfold. He clutched the small, glass crack-pipe so tightly in his hand it cut deeply into his palm.

Fifty-Five

"You have visitors again, Ms. Fuqua. Do you want to see them?" the Baltimore City Jail correctional officer asked Trenda for the tenth straight day.

Trenda peered between the cold steel bars. "Is it my lawyer?"

"Nope," the young red-headed C.O. replied. "It's your parents again."

"No… " She turned, walked to her bunk, flopped down and closed her eyes. "Not today." For the twelfth straight time in the past two weeks, Trenda refused to see her parents. *I'm not hardly ready for that…hell no.*

Two weeks after Darius and Tyrone "mysteriously" disappeared and missed the beginning of the trial, Trenda had been forced to remain in custody. Because of her last cross country adventure, the judge, fearing her to be a flight risk, refused to let her out on bail.

During those past two weeks, the media had had a field day. Speculation about what happened to the missing officers went from them running off as gay lovers to them being silenced by some of the green-eyed gangster—Trenda Fuqua's—criminal friends.

Per Dennis's instructions, she kept her mouth shut regarding her case. *C'mon, Denny. I gots to get up outta here before they find me swingin' from a shower rod. I'm tired of seeing my face on TV or hearin' my name on the radio every goddamn day.*

As soon as her name first hit the airwaves, her family had tried to visit her. Despite having disowned them for over a decade, they still came to support her. She could not wrap her head around why they would do that. *Fuck it. I ain't gonna waste time worryin' about that,* she thought as she stared at the bottom of the empty bunk over her head. *The only thing I need to know is how I can get out of this hell hole.*

After dinner that night, she turned on the small TV in her cell just in time to see a live broadcast of a pair of vehicles she knew *very* well in the back of a house she knew *very* well. "Oh, shit!"

She got closer to the TV and turned up the volume. A middle-aged African-American reporter spoke to the camera. "Less than an hour ago, the Baltimore P.D. received a hot tip on the $50,000 reward hotline set up by the Baltimore P.D. for information leading to the whereabouts of missing Baltimore Police Officers Darius Kain and Tyrone Dash. A neighborhood resident, known as 'Thin Tim,' found the abandoned vehicles you see behind me, that the police are surrounding with yellow crime scene tape. According to DMV records, the vehicles belong to Officer Darius Kain and Officer Tyrone Dash.

Both men, as you may know by now, have been missing for over two weeks, failing to appear at a major police corruption case here in Baltimore. This nationwide story also features the enigmatic Trenda Fuqua who sources say…"

After they showed a picture of her new mugshot, Trenda turned the TV off. "What the hell was those fools doin' at the Lighthouse?" She unzipped her orange jumpsuit, exposing the wife-beater T-shirt beneath. "They had to be up to no good. I sure hope they find those mutha-fuckas. I can't wait to testify against them."

The following day, Trenda's world turned into a *Twilight Zone* episode. A slew of reporters tried as hard as they could to get a statement from her after the drums of acid—containing evidence of human remains—were found in the Lighthouse. She had an unexpected visit from Dennis. "Wassup, Denny? I thought our next meetin' was a couple of days from now."

Instead of taking the seat across from her as he usually did, he stood behind the seat, hands in the pockets of his tan slacks. "There's no easy way to tell you this, so I have no choice but to spit it out; I am not going to be able to represent you on this case any longer."

Trenda cocked her head and furrowed her eyebrows. "Say *what?* Why not?"

He slowly paced the floor. "It's strictly business, my

friend. I have three other *paying* clients that I have to tend to. After traces of both officers' DNA on the crime scene, the Internal Affairs case is pretty much moot. I had agreed to handle your case pro bono—with the intention of recouping my fees by filing a suit—on your behalf—against the city for the pain and suffering the two rogue officers inflicted on you." He pulled a business card out of the breast pocket of his shirt and handed it to her. "This is a friend of mine, Janet Bodine. She is a very good public defender. She will make arrangements to see you in a couple of days."

Despair swallowed up her anger as she watched him prepare to leave. "So it's like that now; I bet if I was to stick my finger up your ass and suck your dick you wouldn't be actin' like this," she mumbled.

"Did you say something?" he asked while checking a text message on his BlackBerry.

"No...ain't shit left to say. I guess I'm on my own. The public defenders here in Baltimore ain't worth a damn. Thanks anyway."

He patted her on the shoulder as he prepared to leave. "You are going to be in capable hands, my friend." Just before reaching the door, he snapped his fingers and walked back to Trenda. "I forget to give you this." He reached the inside pocket of his jacket and pulled out an envelope. "Your father asked me to pass this along to you. I ran into him outside the courthouse yesterday as I was trying to maneuver past the paparazzi."

"What in the hell?" She stared at the familiar hand-writing on the letter, ignoring Dennis. *This looks like my father's handwriting!*

She hurried and tucked the letter into her panties before the guard came to take her back to her cell. Once back in her cell, her heart was beating like a hummingbird's wings. The letter visibly shook as she held it, sitting on her bunk.

After looking at the words "For our daughter" for five minutes, she finally worked up enough nerve to open it. Her breath caught in her throat as she unfolded the first sheet of paper inside. It was a high-quality LaserJet copy of an eight-by-ten photo of her parents.

It felt as if all the heat in her body flew out of her open mouth. *Oh my God!* The photo showed her father in a dark suit and matching fedora standing in front of his church and behind a woman in a wheelchair. The green-eyed, old woman, wearing a scarf over her graying red hair, seemed to be staring off into space. *Momma! Momma?*

The amount of worry she had for the woman in the picture, whom she had convinced herself she hated over the past decade, overwhelmed her. "Why is she in a *wheelchair?*"

She gently set the picture on her pillow and looked at the second sheet of paper. Her father's handwriting jumped out at her.

Praise the Lord! I can't tell you how happy we are to find that you are still alive! After all these many years, not a day went by that your mother and I didn't pray for your safety. Even though the circumstances of your return are not the best, we are nonetheless thankful to God for answering our prayers.

I hope the picture I sent you is okay. I am still trying to get used to this new age computer stuff. That picture was taken on your mother's seventy-fifth birthday last month. The church gave her a nice surprise party. I wish you could have been there. Your oldest brother, Ricky, was there; he flew out here from Washington State where he works as a bigshot for FedEx. That reminds me, you are an auntie! Ricky and his wife, Ava, just had a little girl a few months ago. And I swear, she looks just like you when you were a baby! Got those same emerald eyes, too. Well, I guess since both her grandparents and her daddy had green eyes, she was bound to luck up and get some.

Your brother Glenn is a chaplain in the Army. He is on his second tour of duty in Iraq. His wife, Octavia, has been living with us for the past year, helping me with your mother, but just moved back to their home in Tupelo, Mississippi. Glenn will be coming home for a few weeks and she needs to get their home in order.

Wow, so much to catch up on…that brings me to your mother; she suffered a stroke three years ago and was diagnosed last year with Alzheimer's. She can barely speak and is getting very forgetful. But you know what's funny? Whenever I show her your picture or say your name around her, she says your name clear as a bell! She asks me where you are every day. Sometimes a few times a day.

Trenda, we don't care about all these nasty rumors and things the press is saying about you. No matter if they are true or not, you are, and will always be, our child. Family sticks together, praise the Lord. I may have to give up my church so I can tend to your mother. She needs full-time care and we can't afford a full-time nurse right now. Anyway, just know we all love you and will be here for you, no matter what. Let me leave you with these words from our Lord:

Isaiah 41:10

Fear thou not, for I am with thee; be not dismayed, for I am thy God. I will strengthen thee; Yea, I will help thee; Yea, I will uphold thee with the right hand of my righteousness.

Amen.

As if a huge mallet had been swung and shattered the ice around her heart, Trenda, for the first time, was able to accept the love of her parents. After blaming them for abusing her for all her life, she finally understood that they were just trying to lead her down the narrow path of the righteous; not the wide, glittery, crooked road of the Damned she preferred to travel.

The letter and picture fell to the floor. She buried her face in her pillow and unleashed a typhoon of tears while replaying in her mind how badly she had fucked up her life.

Fifty-Six

After three days of tears and solitude, Trenda finally had a face-to-face meeting with her parole officer, Mrs. Kennedy. "I'm glad you're taking this news so well; anybody else about to do five years in prison wouldn't be nearly as calm as you are."

Trenda, having braided her fast-growing hair into neat cornrows, sat up straight in her chair. The images of the lives she had negatively affected, as well as ended, hung in her mind like nightmare-colored wallpaper. The only comfort she found was in the letter from her father—and the copy of the Bible she had checked out from the prison library. Even though she hadn't fully reverted back to her church roots, the comfort she found in the familiar verses and stories definitely helped her deal with her past transgressions. "Thank you."

Still shocked by how un-combative Trenda had become, Mrs. Kennedy went on. "Fortunately, it appears the alleged bounty on your head has been lifted by the alleged person or persons that allegedly wanted you dead. That means you will be placed into general population as soon as they find a cell for you. That could be in an hour or a few days."

"No problem."

"Do you still have your lawyer?"

"No. I couldn't afford him any longer."

"I guess you will need your public defender then; you could still be subpoenaed in the case involving Officers Kain and Dash. It is still being heavily investigated."

"I'll be ready if it happens."

Perplexed, Mrs. Kennedy let her reading glasses dangle from the chain around her neck, placed both her forearms on the table and leaned toward Trenda, who sat across from her. "I don't get you. What's your deal? You act as though you are going to a picnic or something." The chunky, blonde, former police officer locked eyes with Trenda. "Whatever it is, I just want you to know I'm on to your bullshit ways."

"You have every right to not trust me." Trenda looked away from Mrs. Kennedy's probing eyes. The images of how much her parents had aged over the past decade made her nauseous. *And I bet money a hell of a lot of their gray hair is my fault. Maybe this five-year stretch will help me get my shit together.* She returned her gaze to Mrs. Kennedy. "I'm ready to pay what I owe."

Fifty-Seven

L ess than a month after Trenda was shipped to the
Maryland Correctional Institution in Jessup, Maryland to serve her five-year sentence, the bidding
war for her story was turned up another notch. As world-
wide interest in what had happened with Darius, Tyrone
and Trenda's wild lifestyle reached a fever pitch, the
largest entertainment company in New York had its
sights set on getting Trenda's story. They were the best
in the business at producing hit movies, bestselling books
and reality TV shows.

"I don't care how much it cost, you go get that story!
And find the best lawyers available and get her out of jail—
the case they have against her is bullshit." Maximilian
Kirk, CEO of StarShine Entertainment, said to his number one reporter, Alexis Cannon. "Offer her a book *and*
movie deal. Let her know we mean business."

"Got it," Alexis said as she scrawled notes on her yellow
tablet before pushing her flowing blonde hair out of her
face. "But Chief, now you know every freaking paper,
magazine and talk show in the free world has tried to

get Ms. Fuqua to talk and she has refused. What makes you think she is going to give in to us?"

Reaching into the inside pocket of his $5,000 suit, he removed a checkbook, signed his name, and left the amount blank. "Money is a key that can open any door." He slid the check across his expensive desk to Alexis. "I already found out about the financial distress her parents are in. I made a $100,000 donation to her father's church to get her attention." He smirked as he removed a Cohiba cigar out of the Gondolier humidor on his desk and clipped the end off of it. "Start the bidding by telling her to fill out any seven-figure amount she wants. It's time for the world to hear her story."

ABOUT THE AUTHOR

Curtis L. Alcutt's initial effort, *Dyme Hit List*, focuses on Rio, a single African-American man who grapples with finding his soulmate after a lifetime of being a womanizer. His neighbor, Carmen, has all the qualities Rio wants….but can he commit to her?

Bullets & Ballads, his follow-up novel is an erotic, psychological drama set in the music industry. The main character, a musical genius named Apollo, is twisted into a steamy love triangle featuring Nyrobi, a gorgeous, wealthy and sexually liberated older woman and a loving, sexy and talented songstress named Tricia.

He also has an erotic short story entitled, "Not Tonight," published in Zane's *New York Times* bestselling erotic anthology, *Caramel Flava*. Curtis also co-authored the self-help book, *Your Road Map to a Book*, published by his literary foundation, WriteWay2Freedom. His heated short story, "Drastic Measures," is featured in the erotic anthology, *After Dark Delights*.

Curtis L. Alcutt's literary style is "no-holds barred" erotica combined with everyday experiences the reader is guaranteed to relate to. "I believe my story ideas come from being a shy, quiet child, always observant instead of talking," says Alcutt. "Growing up, I passed by the windows of bookstores and remember never seeing any novels with black people on the covers. I wondered what it would be like to see African-Americans instead. My love of writing song lyrics further fueled my desire to become a writer. My novel concepts were stored away for quite some time. After reading a few African-American novels I decided now is the time to write."

Curtis L. Alcutt was born and bred in Oakland California. He walked many career paths before deciding to give writing a try. "I've been a roofer, garbage man, courier, truck driver, computer network administrator and even co-owner of an auto body shop. Back in the early nineties, I had a record deal as the Rapper, "Big C." For many different reasons the deal fell through, but I never let it discourage my pursuit of self expression."

Visit his website www.curtisalcutt.com and find him on Facebook.

*Repay no one evil for evil, but give thought to do what is
honorable in the sight of all. If possible, so far as it depends
on you, live peaceably with all. Beloved, never avenge
yourselves, but leave it to the wrath of God, for it is written,
"Vengeance is mine, I will repay, says the Lord." To the
contrary, "if your enemy is hungry, feed him; if he is thirsty,
give him something to drink; for by so doing you will heap
burning coals on his head." Do not be overcome by evil,
but overcome evil with good.*

—ROMANS 12:17-21

One

"I want that green-eyed bitch dead!" Beverly Kain, the widow, yelled as she picked up the heavy crystal candy dish off of her coffee table. She then threw it into the flat-screen TV mounted on her living room wall. The image of the woman she blamed for the death of her husband blinked out after the explosion of glass and sparks erupted from the destroyed TV.

On this, the second anniversary of her husband's death, the ache in her heart ran to her head as she collapsed on her sofa. Tears of sorrow and anger ran down her face and neck, onto the collar of her pink robe. Every day since the grisly discovery of her late husband's body, she'd watched the videotaped newscast that featured a short conversation with Trenda Fuqua.

Trenda Fuqua.

The same woman alleged to have had an affair with the late Baltimore police officer Darius Kain. Nightmares of his acid-eaten, mutilated body launched her into chronic insomnia. "She ruined our lives!"

The belief that Trenda corrupted and set up her husband was undeniable in her mind. The fact that Trenda was due for an early release from prison further pissed her off. As tears smeared her mascara, she recalled the smug look on Trenda's face as she was stuffed into the patrol car after her interview.

Once her crying fit stopped, she reached into the pocket of her robe. A maniacal smile formed on her face after pulling a piece of paper out of the pocket of her robe. She then picked up the phone, blocked her number and dialed the number written on the back of her late husband's funeral program. She thought she had blocked her number but in her stressful state of mind, she put in the wrong code.

The number she called was for Mitch, a friend of Darius's that could "take care" of situations. He'd given her his number at Darius's funeral. He promised he'd look after her. His gruff voice answered. "Wassup?"

As she had done many times before, she hung up without answering. Upstairs, the muffled cries of her two-year-old son, Darius "DJ" Kain, Jr., got her attention. She hurried up the stairs, walked over to the Birchwood baby-bed, picked up the blue pacifier next to the baby's head and put it into his mouth. *You look so much like Darius…because of that red-headed tramp he didn't even get to see you.* She stroked the child's curly, dark hair. The fact that she found out she was pregnant a month after Darius's death filled her with bitterness. "I miss your daddy so much…"

"That's a lot of money," Trenda said as she examined the contract on the table. A verse she often read while incarcerated came to mind. It alluded to a majority of her past troubles:

For the love of money is the root of all kinds of evil. Some people, eager for money, have wandered from the faith and pierced themselves with many griefs.

—Timothy 6:10

She rubbed the green rosary beads in her hands and looked across the table at the tall, blonde woman. "But I can't take it. Sorry."

Alexis Cannon, top reporter for StarShine Entertainment, folded her arms on the table and focused her ice blue eyes on Trenda. The smell of new paint still lingered in the air of the recently painted conference room. The three-year-old, Cockeysville Correctional Center—or "The Cock" as some inmates dubbed it— was the most modern prison in Maryland. "Ms. Fuqua, this is one hell of an opportunity for you." She tapped the contract. "You can leave this hell-hole a very wealthy woman."

The seven-figure deal to tell her story was awful hard for Trenda to resist. But she knew in order to make a real change in her life, sacrifices had to be made. Two years ago, after the bodies of the two crooked cops that had extorted and abused her for years turned up, she had been in high demand. Along with the fact that the officers were in the middle of one of Baltimore's most high-profile corruption cases, their gruesome murders grabbed national headlines.

Tempting as it was, Trenda knew going on TV would garner her a lot of unwanted attention. After spending the last twenty-four months behind bars—and in her Bible—she had come to enjoy her anonymity. Also, she didn't want to make too many waves. Word around the The Cock was that they were going to release a few low-risk inmates due to overcrowding.

After finding out from the D.A. that she was almost on the list, Trenda went out of her way to stay out of trouble. It worked. The D.A. told her she was going to be paroled early because of her good behavior combined with the overcrowding.

Besides self-change, self-preservation was an issue also. Even though the Island Boys had withdrawn their contract on her life, she had a new set of enemies to deal with.

A few days ago, she found an unsigned envelope containing a letter, a copy of her mother's funeral program and pictures of her elderly father, brothers and their families in her mail delivery. The letter warned her to keep her mouth shut about Darius and Tyrone's "street business," if she and her family valued their good health.

Although the guard denied knowing where the envelope came from, Trenda knew she was lying. *Need to get out of here though…Daddy needs my help, especially since Momma died.* Images of her frail father played in her mind. She shook her red, shoulder-length French braids and stood up. "I gotta go. I'll get with you later."

Alexis puffed out her cheeks, exhaled, put the contract back in her alligator briefcase and closed it up. "I *will* be talking to you again."

Trenda watched the well-dressed woman exit the room. "I'm sure you will." The prison guard motioned for her to follow. She adjusted her baggy orange jumpsuit. *Two more weeks*, she thought as she was led back to her cell. *Two more weeks and I'm outta here. Hallelujah.*